A Novel

STAN HURTS

BRIAN PIETRO

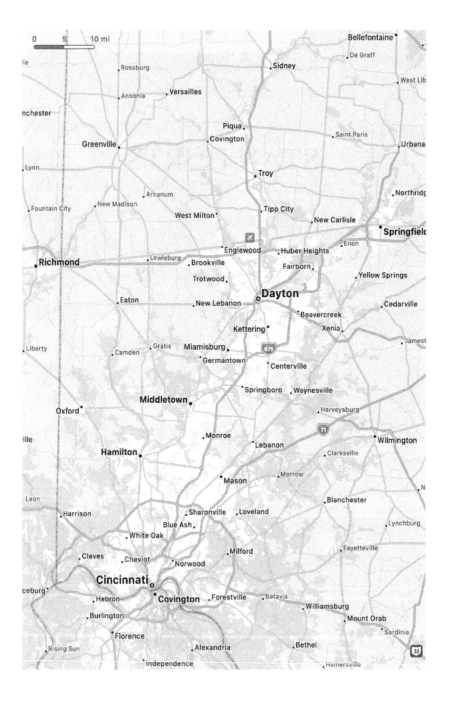

3

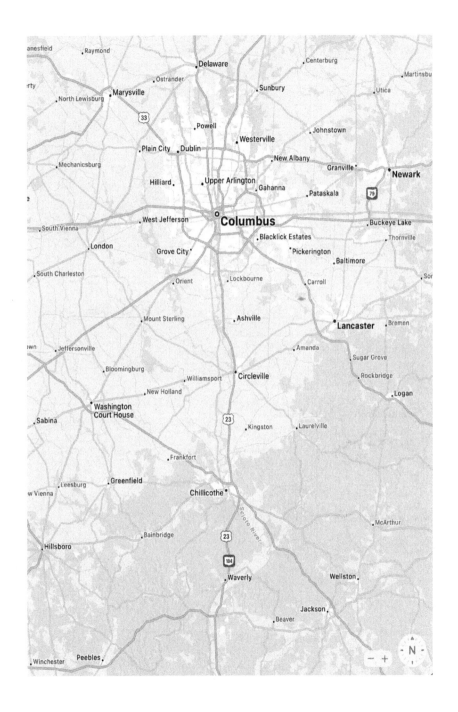

4

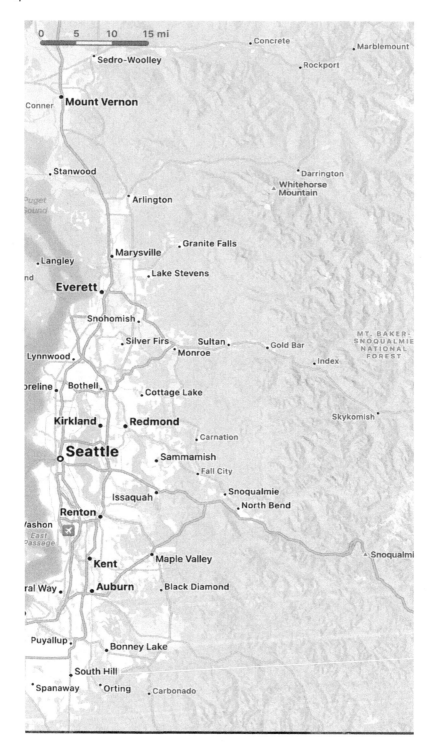

5

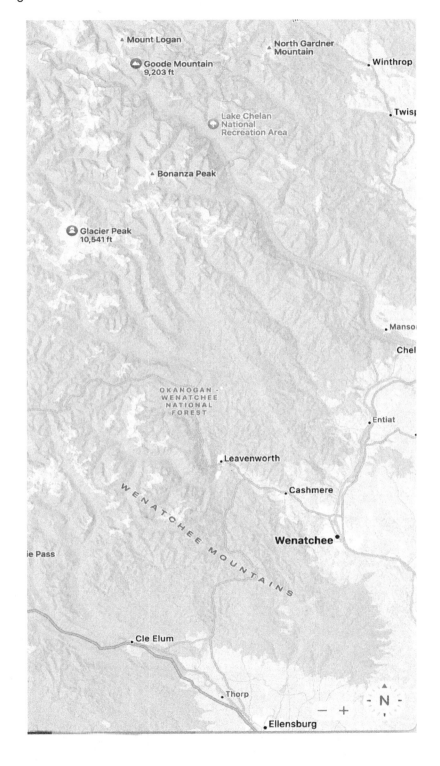

STAN HURTS

This story is based on real events and people, while at the same time, has little or nothing to do with real events or people, and as a result, could end up being confusing to some, but it should be noted that any similarities to real events or people are entirely coincidental and were not intended to resemble real events or people, however, in spite of that, there is a certain chance, albeit a small one, that some of the events contained herein will resemble rather precisely, real events or people, in which case they are factual in nature to the extent that they are, and not factual to the extent that they are not, but in either case, the author is held blameless, for he is simply recounting real events and people to the best of his ability and recollection, holding malice to no one or anything, and is in that sense, merely a reporter, a simple messenger, and as to the fictional content of the story, that's just stuff he made up.

Colin Plotnik, editor

Second Edition © 2023 ZumaWorks, Brian Pietro

The number one American killer isn't cardiovascular disease, but loneliness. People have spiritual needs, which human beings by their nature, can ill-afford to live without.

Kurt Vonnegut

There are more things in heaven and earth, Horatio, than are dreamt of in your philosophy

Hamlet

If you gotta tell people you're famous, you ain't.

Gregory Peck

Reality is an acquired taste

Matthew Perry

Note

Stan Hurts is like the guy who is walking down the sidewalk next to a tall building, and comes upon a broken piano stool, that is shattered into pieces, as if from a long fall. He stops to ponder why in the world the stool happens to be there, in the middle of the sidewalk like that, it never occurring to him, that it belongs to the piano that is hurtling straight down at a hundred miles per hour, about to smash him flat.

11

Contents

ACT I
Quisquous 15

ACT II
Many MacGuffins 203

ACT III
Bobsquatch 319

ACT IV
Ground Zero 381

ACT I

Quisquous

Chapter 1

He stood erect and motionless, staring straight ahead, small beads of sweat collecting on his forehead, dripping into his eyes. On occasion he would blink, but rarely. It was very quiet in the antiseptic room. His eyes roamed the office. Blank off-white walls, white plastic mini-blinds pulled shut over the windows, and cut-rate vinyl laminate flooring, in a medium dark wood grain pattern, well worn. It was a bitterly cold December day and he had gotten here an hour before his scheduled time, and had waited in the next room with the others, anxiously, before being called into this room.

And then the silence was broken. A tight voice belonging to a young female administrator said to him, "That's okay, you don't have to stand there in place just yet, you can relax".

He followed the suggestion and relaxed, somewhat, but his sense of terror remained, as much as he tried to quell it, to force it down into the dark, so he could present himself as a calm, in-control, and confident individual, as he had wanted to do, as he had rehearsed in the mirror the night before.

The voice belonged to Tina, a serious and weary young woman with dark medium-length hair, brown lipstick, and was joined by Rick, an already-balding young man, also serious and weary, sitting next to her. They sat in folding chairs at a folding table, recently purchased at the Walmart in Dayton. Everything in the room screamed temporary and cheap. Stacked in front of them on the table were dozens of photographs of people, mostly 8x10 color head shots but also many other types; some snagged out of a frame on the mantle, from a photo album, a clipping from a newspaper, or a production still taken during a dress rehearsal for a community play production.

The two fatigued casting assistants examined the professionally rendered 8x10 belonging to him. Tina flipped it over to glance at his resume, that he had updated and glued to the backside last night. It contained the usual assortment of truths, half-truths and untruths. She flipped it back, and she and Rick took another look at it, glancing from it to him, and back again. It appeared to be a fairly recent photo, looking to be the same person of the same age as stood before them, which is commonly not the case, but the expression on the face in the photo was entirely different than the expression of the person standing in front of them. In the photo, he had perfected the semi-smile, which is the cultivated semi-serious, earnest and confident while-looking-straight-into-the-camera while also wearing a sport coat with an open collar dress shirt facial expression, that many a young actor strives to achieve. Except he was not young.

He appeared to be about forty-five, beginning his journey into middle-age, was still in the category of the guy next door or sidekick handsome, and if not handsome, then acceptably good looking, and appropriate to play a teacher, salesman, banker, or movie theater manager, but his romantic comedy leading man days were behind him. All was not lost for he still had half of his hair, which helped matters, but combed forward so some might mistake that for a full head of hair, which only accentuated the fact he was half bald. It was dyed a blondish, or brownish, or a reddish kind of color, or it was natural, it was hard to say, and his blue eyes with a trace of green, was a nice accent. Speaking of his face, it seemed to have a permanent expression of surprise on it, mixed with depression. However, what remained was this face, which when looked at as a whole, could not hide that it had been a tough life, not a boulevard of green lights, as he had had more than his share of disappointments.

To what extent his own poor attitude contributed to that, to what extent he had given entry to negative thinking throughout his entire life, had encouraged depression, had embraced it like an old friend, had beat himself up, had focused on the negative instead of looking at the bright side, had always deferred, apologized, demurred, rationalized and always, always aimed to please, to be liked, is hard to know, but at this particular moment in time, he was not there for therapy, he was not there to explore his low self-esteem, but to audition and win the role of Nurse No. 2.

Tina leaned over to Rick, and mumbled something indecipherable, and then looked up at the hopeful, still sweating, middle-aged man, and said, "Hi, I'm Tina Alzonar, and this is Rick Gupert, thanks for coming in".

He replied, "Sure thing" which he had decided would be the right kind of polite and informal kind of a thing you would say to a casting person when they said something polite to you first. He figured that people in "the business" were usually casual and offhand, and that such a reply would be quite suitable. He had rehearsed that last night as well. But the moment he uttered it, he felt that it had been too casual, almost flippant, bordering on rude, and he immediately regretted it, and wanted to back it up with something more polite, complete, and said, "Yes, thank you, I am really looking forward to this, I hope you like it, I mean me, in the role, that I'm auditioning for, today…"

Tina and Rick stared back at him with awkward semi-smiles. The auditionee wished he could, at this particular moment, disappear, or at least start over, but it was too late, it had already begun. In his mind, which as a default was programmed to be riddled with doubt, things were already getting unstable, coming apart. As more sweat appeared, he thought to himself, "Why did I have to tag all of that on? Why couldn't I just say 'thank you' or better yet, say nothing?"

But thankfully, that moment was quickly replaced by another moment, and the moments cascaded into other moments, all set in slow motion in his mind, as if he was in a ten second delay.

Tina asked him to please stand on the mark, so they could video the audition. For a moment, he blanked, and had forgotten what a mark was, and hesitated for just a moment too long, long enough to cue Rick to say, "The blue tape on the floor, over there".

He promptly walked two steps back toward the wall opposite the table, and stood squarely where an "X" had been created using blue painter's tape. In front of him a few feet, was a video camera on a rickety tripod.

Tina said, "Yeah, that's good, and now just tell us a little bit about yourself, your background, about your acting. I see you are a member of the local stage company. Walk us into it if you could. Just look straight into the camera, give us your slate…start with your name…" and turned on the camera with her remote.

He stood motionless for one or two beats, and said, "Slate?"

"Yes, give us your name, character you are auditioning for, just look into the camera…", said Rick.

"Okay, right, got it, thanks". Stan adjusted himself, looked straight into the small video camera and said, "Stan Hurts. Nurse number two".

"Profiles please", said Tina. "Left profile, right…"

Stan faced right then left, and looked straight back at the camera again.

Tina, registering what his name was, said "Oh, I just realized you spell your name with an "s" at the end, not a "z", that's a little unusual I'm thinking". She turned to Rick and said, "That's unusual, right?".

Rick replied, "Yeah, I think so, not sure I ever saw that before", and then turning to Stan, "Is that your real name or a stage name?"

Before Stan could respond, Tina, attempting to be humorous and to relax the obvious tension in the room, inserted, "Hurts. Like something hurts, I'm in pain, ow, ouch, but I guess you've heard that one before, right?" ending with a chuckle which Rick picked up on, and chuckled along with her, enjoying the keen and witty observation she had just made.

"Yes, I have", he thought to himself, "about a thousand times, in fact, ever since kindergarten on up". He was doing all he could to keep it together, and had never imagined that his audition would include yet another reference to how he spelled his name, his given family name, modified as it was, generations ago. He painted a smile on his face, put a tight lid on himself, as he knew it was important to not call them both a couple of fucking blithering idiots, so he didn't.

He wanted this part, however small and seemingly unimportant it may have seemed to others looking in at him, examining his desires and goals, his wants and dreams. But for Stan, it was an immense fulcrum in his life, a turning point quite perhaps. It was as if his life had taken a sudden turn to the good, toward the sunlight, and had offered up to him this particular moment of golden opportunity.

Stan lived in a small midwestern town in southern Ohio. Tipp City. The name had something to do with a battle in 1811, between Native Americans and American Cavalry troops, that took place in Tippecanoe, Indiana. He had supposed it had something to do with the "Indian Wars" and no doubt was a gruesome encounter, but he was never interested in the subject enough to look it up, and know for sure, but had he, he would have discovered he had it just right.

So, here was Stan, living his entire life in this small town, population hovering around seven thousand souls, auditioning for a small role in a movie that was being shot near, and in his town. The production company had sent out an advance team of production designers, lawyers, a producer or two, the director, and various other support staff, including Tina and Rick.

Their mission was to come up with local talent that could play some minor roles in their movie. They had put up posters, talked it up in town, old school style, intentionally not posting anything on the internet as they did not want a stream of people driving there from all over as they just wanted the locals in this town to show up, as per the wishes of the director who was reportedly going "for real people", to give his film "authenticity".

For Stan, it was a monumental opportunity for him to escape Tipp City and his life in this town, fulfilling his dream to become a successful actor in Hollywood. He would of course, send for his girlfriend the moment he got settled in with a fat paycheck. He knew it was a very small role, but small as it may be, it was a pivotal moment in his life. His character would only appear briefly in two scenes, delivering two short lines in each for a total of four. But it was a part. A real part in a real movie.

He knew it was a significant intersection in his life, marking his entry into professional show business, and he could easily visualize how it would propel him into SAG-AFTRA, enable him to snag an agent or manager, to go up for other roles, bigger tastier roles, maybe get cast in a recurring role in a hit TV series, get to play a lawyer or detective, or stand eye to eye with Tom Cruise or Brad Pitt, as opposed to his twice-yearly appearances in play productions at the local community theater. It would make all the difference in the world to him. This would be the moment he would look back upon as his entry into Hollywood, and all that it promised.

Before this, his list of excuses as to why he had not ventured forth to Hollywood to pursue his dream, grew in size year after year, and all of his friends, what there were of them, would listen to him talk about his dreams, listen to him talk about acting and film history and trivia, but by this point, all of them knew it was just a bunch of talk, and Stan knew that they felt this way, and he harbored depressed feelings, suspecting they were right, and now, at this particular moment, Stan had the chance, as if by destiny, to set a new course. All he had to do was to deliver the line as expertly as he had rehearsed it the night before, over and over. That's all he had to do. He told himself that there was no pressure. No pressure at all. None. All he had to do is just deliver the line like he had rehearsed and they would tackle him, not let him out the door without signing a contract. He just knew it. He was sure of it. He told himself he was sure of it. But then he knew that if he told himself he was sure of it, then he wasn't, because if he was, he wouldn't have to reassure himself. He would just know it. He felt himself slipping into his abyss yet again, his dark whirlpool of self-doubt, and pulled himself up out of it, had too.

He had gotten past the spelling of his name, and now at Tina's request, had started to say a few disjointed sentences about his store in town, Stan's Hardware and Stuff, that he had started up about fifteen years ago in what had been a former cabinetry store, and the space had been vacant for years, and how it was now a full-service hardware store selling everything from nails to shovels, cutting keys, mixing paint, and how he had been a member of the Tipp Players theatre company for many years, doing all kinds of roles, some leading parts, some just supporting or cameos, some drama, some comedy, and that his favorite was doing the part of Martin Dysart, the psychiatrist in "Equus", one of the lead roles, which got rave reviews from both the Tipp City Chronicle and the Tippecanoe Weekly, and it was at this point that Tina put her flat palm up, signaling for him to stop talking.

"That's really interesting Stan, thank you, but now we should get on with the audition, okay?"

Stan, adrenaline pumping, nodded to the affirmative. Tina had Stan get down on his knees, still on his mark, while Rick adjusted the camera downward to frame Stan kneeling on the floor.

Tina set the scene for Stan, telling him what he already knew, that the Nurse was on his knees next to a fallen patient, in the hallway of a hospital, and that he was calling for the doctor to come right away. "Okay, great, just go ahead when you're ready, we're already rolling".

Stan said "Okay" and summoned up his years of acting experience on stage with the Players, the numerous acting workshops he had attended or created over the years, the dozens of books he had consumed about acting and the biographies of so many whose acting he admired from Bogart to Brando, the thousands of hours spent examining movies and the actor's performances, plus all the time and thought he had put in last night after he picked up his sides and went home to memorize them, analyze them, absorb them into his gut, into his very being.

The bulk of his preparation had taken place in Mandy Baxter's living room. She was a Caucasian female, married and divorced once, no kids, a Bachelor's degree from Ohio State in forest management, and his aforementioned girlfriend, who he had lived with comfortably, if not somewhat distantly, for eight years. Mandy worked at the Upper

Valley Medical Center in the neighboring town of Troy for all those years, having been unsuccessful after graduation to snag a job with State or National Parks. Apparently there had been a glut of recent graduates with the same degree at the time, and although a woman, the park services were trying to level the playing field by becoming much more diverse. The only category of applicant that was less likely to be hired were white heterosexual males.

Stan was especially encouraged that Mandy worked in a hospital, for she could supply him with invaluable details and tips, he figured. However, Mandy worked in the accounting department and had very little to do with anything actually medical, so even though she was cheerleading Stan, she didn't have a lot of personal experience to relate.

Stan was trying to be very 'method', and had gotten so granular with his preparation, that he needed to know from her what the floor smelled like in the hospital, seeing as how he would be on his knees, close to the floor, and the odor from the wax could in some way have an effect on his "inner life" with the role. Was it a medicinal odor? Lemon scented? Lavender? He felt that every small detail had the potential to trigger other things in his inner self and could however subtly, however nuanced, affect the tenor of his voice, the way he moves his head, the expression on his face, for every little detail mattered. Mandy, knowing that Stan was taking this audition quite seriously, did not dare make a sarcastic or humorous comment, even when he asked if scrubs were all cotton or a polyester blend?

So, there he was, on his knees, imagining the fallen patient. It was all about imagination and creating that inner life. He knew that the fallen patient was supposed to be an older female, but that's all the detail the script had supplied. Stan needed to make up all the rest. He went at it: she was an old woman, dressed in a pale-yellow hospital gown, with a pattern of small white daisies and orange butterflies, and was unconscious, barely breathing, her name was Isabel Plotnoy, originally from Arkansas, a black woman, and her only relative was her daughter Megan who lives in Kansas and was presently racing to the hospital to be by her mom's side. He then imagined his pale blue scrubs, itchy because they are new and a cheap poly-cotton blend. He imagined his hospital keys in his right pants pocket, one of them poking into his leg, and his cheap wristwatch with the heavily scratched face, his folded money in his left pants pocket, just enough to buy the meatloaf with green beans and mashed potatoes "Thursday Special" in the commissary two floors below. He imagined the time of day, the air temp, how many others were in the hallway, exactly how they were dressed, what they looked like, and the intense urgency of this particular moment. Key to all of this was what Nurse No. 2 had done just prior to this particular moment. This was a most critical part of his back story.

Stan determined that the Nurse had just come from a room in ICU checking in on a patient, an obese man about forty years old, suffering from various ailments but in particular, heart disease, and how the Nurse had checked the electrocardiogram heart monitor and the pulse oximetry before exiting the room, taking four steps down the hallway, toward the nurse's station, and witnessed poor Ms. Plotnoy collapsing right in front of him, dropping like a sack of potatoes.

Stan, first looked down at the unfortunate Ms. Plotnoy, then up at his imaginary off-camera listener, and screamed "Call the doctor!" with the volume and intensity of Al Pacino or Kirk Douglas, so loud that he just about blew Tina and Rick out of their chairs.

Stan looked up expectantly, hoping for unbridled praise, but instead, Tina said in a quiet measured tone, as if speaking to a mental patient, "That was real nice Stan, but let's try that again, but not so loud this time, pretend the person you are talking to is only a step or two away, is maybe another nurse, right next to you, with his back turned...camera is still rolling..."

Stan took a beat to absorb this new information, having to instantly throw out his rehearsed interpretation, and try something entirely different, on the fly. He could keep many of the details, the peripherals, for instance what he had done just prior to this scene, and the smell of the floor, how he visualized the hallway and the people in it, and the lunch he was about to have down in the commissary. But he had to trash the core of his interpretation, and the loud call down the hallway to give aid to this woman who just collapsed. He had to improvise. He knew he was good at improvisation, making audiences at the Tipp Players roll in the aisles on Improv Nite, with his antics and physical comedy. But this was not comedy. He knew that in 'straight' comedy, you're supposed to do the opposite of drama by over-reacting to little things, and under-reacting to big things. With drama, reactions should be more appropriate, but be interesting choices. Even so, good actors know how to be flexible, so he gave it another shot.

Stan looked down at the elderly but invisible Ms. Plotnoy, with a great sense of urgency and compassion. He then looked up and off-camera to the imaginary other male nurse standing near him that he would deliver the line to, and imagined that a few feet away, there was the female doctor, iPad in hand, talking to a group of other nurses, and oblivious to the deathly circumstance just steps behind her.

Then Nurse No. 2, in a most dramatic low voice, said "Call the doctor". Regrettably, Stan's volume was so low, his voice so gravelly, that the camera mic barely picked it up, as if Nurse No. 2 was about to fall asleep, or collapse next to the fallen Ms. Plotnoy.

Rick could barely conceal his impatience, and gave out a little moan. He knew they had another three dozen auditions to chew through before lunchtime, but he was very new to this, having been pulled from assisting the location manager for the shoot to help out with the casting of the locals, and he resented it, thinking it below him. And Tina, a Director's Guild hopeful, who considered herself much more seasoned, having assisted with casting two times before, once for a music video and another time for a low budget TV pilot, and felt she was quite good at pulling good auditions out of people, and equally good at diplomacy, being able to navigate the delicate and explosive egos of actors. She said to Stan, "That was a very interesting interpretation, thank you, but I do believe you need to speak loud enough to have someone hear you. Why not try saying the line more simply, not as dramatically, how's that for an idea? Can you do that for us?"

Her condescending tone was not lost on Stan, and he knew that he had to conform to what they were looking for, which would win him the part, and once cast, he could then take creative license and give depth to the performance. He further knew that he had impressed them with his emotional range but that what they obviously wanted him to do is underplay the line, to throw it off, make it "real". Stan, knew that he had three more lines after this and wanted desperately to be able to do them. But he also knew what Tina was talking about.

He knew that the adjustment from stage to film acting was huge, and that he must bring it down a few notches from the first take, but not too far down as with the second take, so that the camera, poised so close and intimate, would believe him, accept him, root for him, and most importantly, be able to hear him. His years of being on stage, even though a very small one with a house that had only sixty-five seats, had in a certain way, ruined him for the much more intimate and naturalistic style of acting, that movies and TV required. He said to himself, "Think small".

Again, Stan looked down at the poor Isabel, out cold, and raised his head to an off-camera nurse, and said in just the right volume, "Get doctor". He tried again, knowing he muffed the line, but stayed in character, did not break, and said, "The doctor, he needs to be here", and realizing he was running wildly off script, perhaps true to the moment, but he had to deliver the line as written, so he went at it again, and said "Go…get someone, the…doctor" sounding as if he was very unsure of the line he had memorized and repeated last night over three dozen times. It could have been four dozen, he wasn't sure, as he had fallen asleep with the script on top of his face. But now, his mind was seizing up, making him go up, go blank, as he prepared to go at it again.

Tina mercifully interjected "Hey, that's really good Stan, I know where you were going with that, really good stuff, I mean it, creative things happening, love it".

Stan knew that he was finished, that there was no redemption possible, that those additional three lines would never be spoken by him in this audition, that all of the work he had invested in creating his imaginary Nurse World was crashing to an end, and that Tina was trying to be nice, let him down easy in her own snarky little way. Rick was just being a brat. His failure hadn't been Tina or Rick's fault, for they were just doing their jobs, filtering through the first batch of people so that the actual casting director could make the final decisions. He knew that.

He also knew that he had failed in the most stupendous way imaginable. He knew that the line was a good line, easy to memorize, easy to say. He knew that the mountain of preparation he had thrown at it was beyond over the top, and that it had choked him, and that his judgment, his common sense, was nowhere to be found. He mumbled a "Thank you for their time", tried to put on a solid happy face, and shuffled out of the plain room into the lobby, loaded with other expectant auditionees, some seated, some leaning against a wall, some of them fellow actors from the Players, and some from various walks of life in town, all of them looking at him, trying to read his face, trying to determine if he nailed it or they still had a chance. He walked through the room straight for the door, trying to hold it all together, walked out into the hallway that was in the rear of the equally plain office building, inhabited by various plain lawyers and accountants, pushed open the glass door to the outside, and squinting into the sun, flopped into his nondescript old metallic bronze Toyota Corolla with oxidized paint on the hood and roof, fired up the tired engine, his head packed full, and headed toward his hardware store, barely able to think.

Somehow, Stan had managed to hit a new low. He was not destined to be in "Hospital Wives" after all. The entire dream had exploded in a sudden blinding enormous flash of light. His life had become so completely nondescript and unimportant, he just wanted to curl up someplace under a rock, and disappear.

Chapter 2

Stan knew there would be questions for him once he got back to the store. He had made such a big deal about it, to anyone and everyone, and yet had done what he could to conceal his excitement about the prospect of getting cast, but it was obvious he was amped up, and finally and at last, was beginning his journey toward a solid and successful acting career. How could it not be? He had prepared his whole life for this it seemed.

He pulled up in front of the store, turned off the engine, gripped the steering wheel and said to himself loudly, "What a fucking idiot! I know what a mark is, I'm not a Goddamn kid, for Chrissakes, I know what a damn mark is! What's the matter with me!? And a slate! Fucking stupid idiot!" He fought back tears of complete frustration, knowing that by now, if anyone was inside the store, they had seen him pull up and were speculating as to why he hadn't gotten out of the Corolla by now. Why did he drive to the store anyway? Maybe he should have driven down some lonely dirt road, screamed at the top of his lungs, beaten the hood with his fist, thrown rocks, jumped up and down, stomping the anger and disgust and self-loathing clean out of him. But no, he drove to the store.

Stan dragged himself out of the car, resisted slamming the door, and walked as if he was happy, downright perky, for he could feel eyes on him, or thought he could, and he was not about to reveal his incredibly dark black bottomless state of depression to anyone, he was not going to show his cards. He walked up the wooden steps to the front deck of the store, feeling like he was under water, but still putting on the act, looked about and saw no one, which was a definite relief. The usual assortment of beach chairs, river tubes, towels, and a barrel full of economy umbrellas was there, in full defiance of winter, as always.

Summoning his courage and with a deep inhale, he walked into the store and was greeted by…no one. The place was empty. The music that he insisted be played all the time had been turned off. He felt that some nice, not obtrusive, music should fill the air for the customers, to create an ambiance. He favored Scott Joplin, Mozart, and melodic folk songs that were flavored with just a little fun, and of course, blue grass. There was a stack of CDs next to the portable stereo as the concept of blue tooth had not visited the store as yet.

But all was silent except for the faint sound of a broom being whisked along the cement floor in the back of the store. He walked down the "Paint and

Sundries" aisle to the back, and there was Dave Clendon, who he had coached in little league many years ago, a younger guy, around thirty, tall, dark haired, big mustache, burly, and Stan's quasi business partner, his most loyal friend, his wing man, guy Friday, one man cheering squad, sweeping the floor with a push broom. Tears welled up in Stan's eyes, so grateful to see his friend, and so grateful no one else was around.

Dave, barely glancing up from his chore, said, "So, how'd it go?"

Dave knew that the odds were against Stan, because there were at least five other people in town who he knew for a fact were going for that same role. There were many roles being offered, and many locals lining up to give it a try. Dave, even though uninformed about the ways of movie making, casting, acting, and show business in general, knew enough just from talk around the store, that the reason the movie was going to have locals in it was because they wanted real people, not actors, and even though the big net they cast included the local theatre company, what they most definitely did not want was any "acting". Dave knew Stan very well, and knew how he could be. He had been to every one of his plays, whether he had wanted to go or not. He had seen Stan always make the larger choice over the smaller. He knew that with this audition, Stan would probably go overboard, make a big deal about it, invest way too much energy into preparation, go in, all tensed up, and blow it. It wasn't a slam against Stan, for he loved Stan, but he also knew how he was, had always been.

The back aisle of the store, that housed the tall stuff like PVC pipe, guttering, ladders, didn't need sweeping but Dave figured it might be the safest place to be when Stan got back from what was almost certainly going to be a devastating encounter with reality for his longtime friend and former Baseball coach.

Dave had turned off the music because if he heard "Nine Pound Hammer" one more time, he'd lose his mind. He had nothing but admiration for Tony Rice and his wonderfully expert guitar playing, and singing, and his very talented band, but oh my God, enough was enough. Besides which, he felt that upbeat music might be just a bit too painfully ironic as Stan returned from his experience, and wanted there to be a neutrality to the place. Ordinarily, an absence of customers in a store is not a good thing, but this afternoon, it was a blessing. Humiliation doesn't like too many witnesses.

"It didn't go so hot. I don't think I was right for the role. I think they wanted somebody younger, and I got a feeling, somebody shorter", said Stan.

Dave, before he could stop himself, said "Shorter than five-ten?" and then realizing his slip, and wanting to help provide a soft landing for his friend, said, "Yeah, sure, that's probably it. They'll probably cast Ned in the part, right?"

They both got a good laugh out of that one, for Ned was the polar opposite of Stan physically and temperamentally. Ned was quite tall, very thin, dark haired, and most importantly, always upbeat, was always gushing with something kind and positive to say, just the kind of person most people can't stand to be around. There's only so much sunshine that a person can spread around before becoming annoying, and that was Ned.

"He'd make a perfect nurse" said Stan, laughing along with Dave.

Then there was that moment of silence.

Dave, stopped his sweeping, and gave his friend a good long hard look, straight in the eye. "Hey, not getting the part is not the end of the world, you know? You probably made a real good impression".

Stan, trying to keep the flow of that kind of thinking alive, said, "Yeah, maybe I didn't hit a bull's eye but there's a good chance they'll remember me for some other part maybe, or those casting people will remember me when they cast something else". But it was an act, Kabuki Theatre in the PVC aisle.

Dave knew what had probably happened, and Stan knew that Dave knew, and it wasn't really necessary to review it, to explore the why's and what's of it, but there was a fresh new layer of darkness over Stan that Dave noticed, even if Stan didn't.

Then a voice rang out from the front of the store. "Anybody home?"

Dave and Stan, thankful for the intermission, glanced up to see an older guy, maybe in his late sixties, standing in the front doorway. He held a new looking cowboy hat in his left hand, had on a slick new pair of black cowboy boots, a fancy western style snap button shirt embroidered with yellow swirls and curls, and his right hand was shoved into the front pocket of his new and creased Levi's. His clean-shaven big smile complimented his slicked down Brylcreemed hair, trimmed above the ear, and dyed jet black.

Dave greeted him and walked up to the front of the store, as Stan took up the rear. As the two approached the stranger, they observed him observing them, and the store. There was not a whole lot to examine, as Stan's store was a very standard issue hardware store, and only earned the name "stuff" because he carried a small assortment of non-hardware goods such as seasonally, a good supply of inflatables and other items suitable for sun bathing and tubing alongside and in the Great Miami River, not more than ten minutes out of town. Beyond that, the place was predictable and lackluster, offering up the usual end cap displays of spray paint, masking tape, and hand tools. The prices were as low as Stan could make them but he couldn't even begin to compete with the larger chain stores in nearby Dayton. His was a store of convenience, carrying predictable merchandise presented in a predictable and non-imaginative way. It was an interesting kind of psychology, for Stan could go deep into detail and inventive thinking when it came to his acting, but when it had to do with the store, he seemed to be void of ideas that were not straight down the middle. The store was, in a word, boring. And to add injury to insult, the merchandise selection was often chosen by a sales rep, and was a generic standard mix from the distributor's catalog of suggested items, no doubt created by algorithm. Also, the inventory levels were anemic. One shopping visit from a carpenter could wipe him out of sixteen penny sinkers or two-inch deck screws. There were empty gaps on the shelves, displaying nothing but air, and Dave did the best he could to keep pace with the dust and cobwebs on the empty peg hooks.

The visitor introduced himself. "Howdy pards, the name is Holsteen, Max Holsteen, like the cow but not spelled the same way".

Max was accustomed to a polite chuckle after his customary one-liner, but Dave and Stan simply stood and looked at him, not knowing quite what to think.

Max began to walk around the front of the store, and when he pulled his right hand out of his pocket, they couldn't help but notice that his right arm was atrophied from some kind of injury, presumably in the far past, hard to tell, maybe a war injury, and he was able to move it, but from the elbow down, it was fairly stiff. His misshapen hand worked well however.

Noticing them giving more than a glance at his arm, he stopped and volunteered to them much more than they wanted to know: When he was a teenager, fifteen years old to be exact, working on the family farm in Montana, he had a horrible accident with their old John Deere tractor. It rolled over his right arm and hand, after he had hopped out to move a log out of the path, and had forgotten to set the brake. The Deere kept rolling and ended up in a culvert. He had to walk, in twenty-five degree temperature, with ice on the ground, a light rain starting, all the way back to the ranch house, about a mile, with his arm mangled and bleeding, in excruciating pain, cold as hell because his jacket had been ripped off of him. It took another forty-five minutes in the family pick up, over a horribly bumpy road, to get onto the main highway and into town for the doctor to patch him up. Not one of his better days. It took five surgeries at their community hospital to set his arm as good as possible, and to this day, he gets shooting pains. It set his parents back many thousands of dollars and caused a lot of deprivation in their lives, up to and including cancelling their plans to have another child, hopefully a daughter. "Damn near lost the whole farm to the bank", he said. He couldn't run a farm, doing a lot of the work himself, what with his arm that way, so he sold it after his parents died, and went into various business ventures. He wished he still had the farm, still misses it.

About the last thing Stan could have imagined was having a complete stranger walk into the place and deliver a vastly sadder and more life changing story than anything that had ever happened to him. Stan, in a rare moment of clarity, was able to stand back and look at himself. Here he was, crying over a blown audition and this guy walking around for life with a ruined arm. It was humbling, to say the least.

Max went on to explain that he was visiting his brother who worked not far away, in Vandalia, at the airport, and was on a self-guided tour of all the small towns near there, including theirs, to check out all the small hardware and general stores. He had visited Huber Heights, Fairborn, New Carlisle, West Milton, and now Tipp City. He was planning on visiting Troy and maybe Piqua next, but he figured the hardware stores in Piqua might be too big, might be franchise or chain stores, or too "vanilla", and he was after local, family-owned places, like this one, Stan's Hardware and Stuff.

Stan and Dave stood silent and totally engrossed as Max shuffled back and forth, laying out his story, not being able to take their eyes off his hobbled right arm that he waved about, using it to punctuate the high points in his tale. Max kept referring to his arm as his "gimp arm" which made both members of his audience cringe, being unsure if that term was supposed to evoke a laugh or be a cue for them to nod empathetically.

Digging in, Max stated that the purpose for his visit, was to carefully examine each and every store, to get a "feel" for them, beyond simply checking on what kind and brands of inventory they carried. He explained he was trying to capture the "vibe" of the stores he was visiting.

The word "vibe" coming out of this weathered old cowboy face, with his Roy Rogers wardrobe and with such a distinct Montana accent, was a little unsettling, out of place, but he seemed to be quite sincere, and liked their store well enough they supposed, but from his manner, it was obvious he didn't see anything about it that was exceptional, or even very interesting.

Max explained, while leaning against a post and fiddling with a pair of Channelock pliers, that the reason for his tour was to help him create a hardware or general store back home, in Ventura, California. To both Stan and Dave, this last reveal seemed so out there, so much at odds with this guy's overall look, his style, and his vibe, it didn't make sense. There was something incomplete about this guy, or something he was hiding.

The threesome spent the next twenty minutes walking around the store, with Dave pointing out various details about the products, or why he chose to put one thing there, and the other thing somewhere else. Stan would add background color by giving details about a distributor, the latest model of a weed trimmer, or comparing types of house paints, and the comparative rate of sales between the various categories of products, from paint to electrical. It was not the most riveting of conversations, strictly for the devoted, but Max seemed satisfied with all the information, purchased a bag of stale potato chips that were on a rack near the register, and slapped down a twenty, saying to them, "Thanks boys, sure do appreciate it", and left.

With the memory of the audition from hell shoved away for the time being, Stan was able to refocus on matters at hand, taking an inventory of PVC fittings, while Dave busied himself up front, doing routine dusting and neatening. A few customers wandered in, some with a direct intent on buying a garden hose or can of paint thinner, while others floated around, window shopping for a tube of caulk or a new bow rake. As tumultuous and potentially traumatic as the day had begun, Stan felt comforted, settling in to the routine of a typical day at the store, which was a good calming medicine for him. But back here on the ground, in reality, he knew that his store, nearly deserted on most days was about to go extinct if he didn't do something about it. Somewhere in the back recesses of his mind, he sensed that something significant was about to be put into motion.

Chapter 3

The word "home" can mean different things. To Stan, the word was more of a physical location than a feeling of being "home" or having "homeliness". For one thing, as mentioned, where he lived was not his house, but belonged solely to his longtime girlfriend, Mandy. During one of their many discussions that revolved around the topics of permanence, intent, and steadfastness, she had made it abundantly clear to him that she had no intention of going a step further with him until he was able to "give himself up" to their relationship, and go "all in". Phrases such as these would turn Stan's blood cold, as it all pertained to the notion of commitment, which was something Stan had a very difficult time with. It should be apparent by now, that Stan was not just a complicated guy, but seriously screwed up, due in part by his well-meaning but unskillful father, and the fact that his mom had died when he was young. If there had been love openly expressed in his childhood home, maybe Stan would have grown up straighter and taller. If Stan had been given, or had somehow discovered or created, a certain kind of circuitry in his mind, something that would have enabled him to have more self-confidence, that would have solved it. His was a glass totally empty, approach to living. Had it been otherwise, things may have dominoed, and allowed him to lead an emotionally balanced life. But it was not to be. He understood commitment in the abstract, knew intellectually what it meant, could have defined it in a spelling bee, but he had never embraced it while embracing Mandy.

Mandy was a very attractive woman, a "catch" as Dave would say, and was constantly being sought after by many in the hospital. She'd receive many unsolicited little gifts of chocolates, flowers, and cards from various fellow employees and even the occasional patient or doctor. Most of these advances were polite, lightly romantic, rarely vulgar, but to the one, she rejected them for her heart belonged, however illogically, to Stan. She was simply goofy for him, and loved all of his idiosyncrasies, could not help herself. They had been together for years. And that had become a problem, an issue, a big impassable thing standing between them. She was deeply conflicted because push had finally come to shove and her clock was ticking. Often, a casual remark would escalate to a fierce battle of the wills between them, an off-hand joke would be interpreted as a veiled insult or challenge, and then off they would go, yelling, pounding fists on tables, slamming doors, stomping feet, crying, accusing, defending, wiping away tears, hugging, holding, needing, loving. What a mess.

But this cycle was growing old and brittle, and no longer serviced them. Each time they entered the arena to do battle, they each knew the other's position, the other's style of war, their moves, tactics, tricks, their reverse psychology and their reverse-reverse psychology. There were no more surprises, and even their make-up sex had lost its pizzazz. The tank was near empty, and each knew that there had to be a tectonic shift in their relationship, or else. The problem was, not surprisingly, that Mandy was the more mature, evolved, open, in-touch-with-her-feelings person in the relationship, while Stan was the master of avoidance, always uncomfortable in his own skin, unable or unwilling to open up, or lavish Mandy with love, barely able to even indicate love, and certainly emotionally crippled when it came around to the topic of marriage and children. Looking at it from the outside, it was all so pathetic. Here was Mandy, this beautiful and adorable young woman, on the outer cusp of where young starts to meet middle age, being stretched thin by this needy, selfish, and unavailable guy who had delusions of grandeur about his acting, put only the lowest possible amount of time and energy into running his store, and annoyed everyone with his narrative about his future life, his future dreams, his future ambitions. Everything was about him and his future, about him avoiding the here and now. Mandy, tears rolling down her cheeks, would stand in the middle of the living room, and plead with him to wake up, make a choice, to *do* something. He would counter with tales of woe about his childhood, and then she would go apeshit on him, accusing him of leaning on that worn out excuse as a way of deflecting her. She would continually threaten to leave him, or rather, make him leave, as it was her house, not his, or even theirs. This comment would of course make him explode, accusing her of various manipulative, emasculating, and sinister things, for she had of course plotted all along to use him, and then eventually throw him out. The whole thing was ridiculous and had devolved into being ever more ridiculous. A team of therapists would probably be incapable of rescuing their relationship, deeming it unsalvageable. But they hung on, for love was the glue, in spite of it all.

Mandy was a terrific fix-it person around the house, while Stan was a fantastic cook, bringing to full circle their gender reversal roles. They were both however, terrible at housekeeping. They didn't have a lot of extra money to spread around, that was a clear fact, but they did recognize their mutual shortcoming and had hired a maid to come in once a week and perform basic necessary chores, so as to allow the small wood-framed house to be relatively clean and livable. They had run their course on housekeepers, from the daughters of neighbors, to daughters of friends at work, to individuals advertising in the local papers, and the epic struggle to find the right housekeeper could inspire a book. They had finally found a wonderful woman who had posted a "Maid for hire" note on the local market's community bulletin board. Her name was Zelda, and she visited on Saturdays. Mandy was usually home then, and often times, Stan would go in late to the store, if at all. Zelda was from a warm and loving Guatemalan family, most of whom were still living in their home country. She was virtually perfect in every way. Her hourly rate was not low, and in fact, was the most expensive of any they had ever hired, or considered hiring, but that was okay, for Zelda had managed to seamlessly blend into their life, helping to be a calming and reasonable soft membrane between their two hard edged defiant selves. There was something soothing about her presence in their home, and they came to realize that her housekeeping skills were perhaps the smallest reason she was of great value. She had an infectious positive attitude that couldn't help but puncture Stan's cloud of pessimism, however temporarily, and contributed mightily to Mandy's ability to temper herself, to look upon Stan in a balanced way, to take in the whole landscape, and to realize in a calm way, that however the relationship finally turned out, she was a person of value, and destined to be a mother. Zelda is quite likely the reason that Stan and Mandy had stayed together for this long.

Stan knew he had to make a change in himself. He had always known this intellectually, but now, the fortress he had erected to protect himself emotionally, had become tired, and the old lies he would tell himself were just that, tired and old, and had become much less effective. Back then, he fell back on a series of excuses, delaying tactics, just about anything he could summon to halt the advance of his inner truth. That avoidance technique wasn't working nearly as well these days. He had run out of excuses to fall back on.

It would not take a wizard to determine that one of his big attractions to the Players was that he was given an opportunity to be someone else for a few weeks of rehearsal, and for a month's worth of weekends in performance, for a total of twelve shows. The shows would run Friday and Saturday nights, and Sunday afternoons. Whether the show was a hit, or a bomb, they would run the full scheduled course of performances. Considered a hit would be an average attendance in the thirties or forties. A bomb would have audiences of ten or less. Return visits were a sure sign of success. The Chronicle and Weekly were usually kind and generous in their assessments, offering up their sports columnist and assistant to the editor respectively, as reviewers. The reviews in the Chronicle would be printed on the Thursday following the first weekend of performance, while the Weekly printed theirs the Wednesday after, one day prior, which pitted the two papers into a fierce competition, the advantage going to the Chronicle, that could and did make last minute changes after reading the Weekly's review. The shows were always at least marginally well done, with one glaring exception.

A few years back, Bruce Dentent, the director of the Players, mounted a production of the venerable hit comedy, "Barefoot in the Park", usually a big crowd pleaser. It starred two talented local women, playing the young and spirited romantic couple (portrayed in the 1967 movie version by Jane Fonda and Robert Redford) but Dentent's version had one in a wheelchair and the other blind. It can only be assumed that Dentent was trying to be quite modern and ultra-diverse with this interpretation of the iconic 1963 Neil Simon Broadway hit, but the local audience was made so self-conscious by the difficult physical restraints put upon the couple, living on the top floor of a New York City brownstone with no elevator and lots of physical comedy, that the scenes and punch-lines were flat and uncomfortable, and the overall effect, rather macabre. Both papers had managed to massage out of the production, kind things to say, one even going so far as to compliment the choice of the wallpaper on the set, and how it had defined the psychological tone of the show.

But that was the thing. Both papers had always been in a race to see which could be the more insightful while complimentary. Sometimes they would lose their readers in a fog of pompous adjectives and references freshly looked up on Google, but generally, they would attempt to top the other with the more glowing report as witnessed from the second row, center, in the small theater. For those readers who cared at all, the reviews would be consumed hungrily and could greatly influence attendance. Every effort was made to treat the reviewers with due respect and courtesy, to offer them free refreshments, a preferred parking spot, a batch of free passes to the next production for their families, and gift certificates to the local Chuck E. Cheese.

As for Stan, he had appeared in numerous productions over the years, too many to list here in full, but in addition to his appearance as Dysart in "Equus", he also polished off three Tennessee Williams' plays, two Arthur Miller's, two Harold Pinter's, two August Wilson's, and one each of Edward Albee, Thornton Wilder, Eugene O'Neill, Noel Coward and Moss Hart. It was a rather sophisticated group of choices made by Dentent, for a community theater. Ordinarily, Stan played a leading role but as often, did a solid job in smaller roles. He prided himself on foreign accents but most ended up sounding like either Cary Grant or Gabby Hayes. But regardless, the one thing that was true, was that Stan was very well-liked as a local play actor, and box office would usually do well on opening weekend if people knew he had a large role. The guy up on stage was a different person than the one found in the store, but he was the same individual.

Acting savants, and even the more casual observer, would agree that an actor's preparation could be both complex or simple, and with explanations as to how an actor does not in fact actually become someone else, unless he is psychotic, and some actors are, but that the actor adapts and adopts into their heart and mind, many of the behaviors, mannerisms, beliefs, reactions, and choices of the character, as written down in the script, but also blends into the recipe quite a bit of themselves (for that is impossible to avoid) creating a unique presentation to the audience.

Another actor approaching the same role could do things differently, in terms of applied technique and preparation, but would likely deliver a presentation roughly the same were it not for the existence of the actor themselves, the X factor, that would drench the performance in their unique and inescapable personality traits, mannerisms, reactions, facial expressions, "takes", voice, and so forth. Same role, with some-times very different results. The actor can use a variety of tools from their tool bag to achieve the goal of becoming a hybrid of the character and themselves. The most famous involves working what is termed, from the inside out, called The Method, that can take the actor on a very deep and meaningful multilayered journey using "sense memory". It can become very detailed, all toward the end goal of delivering the actor into the waiting arms of the character, and psychologically removed from the real person that they themselves are. They will stay in character all day sometimes, to preserve the delicate bubble they have created around themselves. It can be tricky business, with some actors succumbing to various forms of psychosis, self-adulation, and delusion. The technique was developed originally by the famous Russian acting teacher Konstantin Stanislavsky. Sometimes the results are spectacular.

Some actors may choose what is termed working from the outside in, known as the Chekhov Method. It was named after the actor and coach, Michael Chekhov, not to be confused with his famous playwright uncle, Anton Chekhov. The Chekhov Method uses various physical techniques, called psychological gestures, to help the actors arrive where they need to be, and often very quickly. Most actors, young and old, green or experienced, adopt some aspects of both The Method, and the Chekhov Method, whether they know they're doing it or not. There have been many spinoffs to these two basic schools of thought, with locally famous acting coach's names grandly attached, having offered their interpretations for consumption by young hopefuls in acting workshops, everywhere. The use of pure method has faded over the years, and has become but one tool in the bag, not the only tool, for most actors. The acting mantra, regardless of technique, is that it is about reacting, not acting. It is about listening, not talking.

To know this about basic acting technique and how an actor approaches a role is not too dis-similar from knowing how Stan approaches life. He acts and talks more than he reacts or listens. Stan has lived as if he was a narrator speaking in third person about his own life, often detached from his real self, as if a character in one of the plays he had appeared in. While Stan had enjoyed absorbing all of this acting technique information over the years, he saw on the horizon, an industry-wide acting cataclysm coming in the form of chatbots and holograms, replacing writers and actors, and he hoped he could get in on the action before the existing medium vanished.

The blend of all this education and these traits are his backstory, and help us to understand this earnest and confused person, Stan Hurts, from Tipp City, Ohio, age forty-five, single, childless, average height and weight, never married, owner and operator of the Stan's Hardware and Stuff store, located on the east side of town, near the intersection of North Tippecanoe Drive and Main Street, which was an okay location, surrounded by various other businesses including an auto parts store, a pharmacy, two hair salons, a pizza place, the Dairy Queen, the fire and police departments, and the Hong Kong Chinese Restaurant, which was surprisingly good overall but the orange chicken tasted like it was from frozen.

Stan's mind had many escape routes, dark alleyways, secret passages and rooms without windows or doors. His persona was a veneer he showed the world and under that he had become hollowed out, corroded by years of self-loathing, clandestine relationships with the many aspects of his personality and mood swings, all blanketed by his fantastical hopes and dreams.

Stan also hosted nightmares almost every night. The usual assortment of desperate and spooky plot lines would develop, usually involving Stan being chased to the edge of a waterfall, or a cliff's edge, or toward the gaping mouth of a giant sea monster, lurking around the very next corner. Stan would wake up with a scream, usually waking Mandy, and then lay awake for an hour or two, as the images faded, the raw fear subsiding. In these nightmares, he would never turn around to see what was chasing him, but he knew it would be an unthinkably horrible monster of some kind, something he didn't want to see, so he just kept running. It would never catch him either, but vanish at the last second, as his toes were gripping onto a ledge, a split second from falling or being consumed.

This is one reason why Stan would often be slightly hunched over, hands shoved in his pockets, only looking someone in the eye for effect or out of necessity. When he would park his faded Corolla in the lot next to the store, he would usually be holding his canvas satchel, stuffed full of purchase orders, inventory lists, print-outs of possible future items to introduce to the store which he rarely if ever introduced, and also often times, a half-eaten tuna sandwich on sourdough.

It was on one of these typical days, as winter was taking an exit and things were starting to turn green, that he arrived at his store, parking not in a prime parking slot, but away a couple of rows so the customers could have the prime, that he slouched his way up the stairs, past the usual displays on the deck that Dave usually put out when he opened, and made his way inside, plopping the satchel down on the register counter. With any luck, there would be a customer or two inside about to purchase, and hopefully something more than a bag of small screws or a can of spray paint. Stan didn't really care too much for the big-ticket items, for the profit margin was paper thin, and all the sale of a circular saw would do for him is reimburse him for having bought it, with a very small return. It was a loss leader. The profit, what there was of it, came from the mid-level items, such as multiple gallons of paint, and the sundries to go with, or long handled garden tools, or from his eight-foot-long wall of Stanley hand tools, which was perhaps his most popular section in the whole place.

The "Stuff" part of the store consisted chiefly of the river stuff, the heavy-duty t-shirts, flannel shirts, and sweatshirts. The fun stuff for the river was more of an attractant, so the customer would not be tempted to go to the local pharmacy or the large and pristine Chuck's DIY Center on the other side of town to pick up similar items. But after all was said and done, after all was purchased, merchandised carefully on a shelf, and sold, his store was not booming. It never had. Stan agonized over this many times, and tried finding solutions by changing the style of the sign on the building, bulk-stacking different types of items up front, putting various things on "sale" to spur purchases, but in the end, the number of people who frequented the store was finite, and if they needed something, they bought it, and if they didn't need it, they didn't. It wasn't so much the quality of his customer base, but the quantity.

More and more people were traveling the extra miles to Chuck's, the town's only expanded home center style store, located on the outskirts of town on the west side. To Stan's surprise and concern, it had opened less than a year after Stan's did and had had an immediate negative impact. At Chuck's there was a considerably larger selection of goods, often times at lower prices. Chuck's, was part of a co-op buying chain, and Stan's was totally independent. In spite of slightly higher prices and less selection, many people in the immediate area had an affection for Stan's, but that affection, like Stan's home life, was wearing thin. It was becoming increasingly difficult for those loyal to Stan's to remain loyal, as his inventory levels dwindled along with the selection. It was a Catch-22 dilemma. The declining sales led to declining stock which led to declining sales, which led to less ability to buy more goods which led to declining sales, and so forth. As the sales went down, the amount of money Stan could extract from the store as his profit, had slowly become meager.

He did not however, penalize Dave for this, but kept Dave on at his current salary, and gave him a small raise each and every year. Dave was all too aware of the store's trouble and although glad to have the job, to be Stan's partner of sorts, to help his friend weather the storm, he became increasingly self-conscious about the whole scenario, as he could be a drag on the operation. Nothing could have been further from the truth of course, as Dave was a very personable guy, and often times, people would walk past Stan to get to Dave for his homespun humor, his good looks, his knowledge of tools, paint, and at times, his overall attitude about life. Stan was seen as a black hole, into which, a good mood could be swallowed whole.

At the other end of the long counter that had the register, were a few stools, set up to give a little country feel to the place. A lot of regulars would show up, coffee mug in hand, take a seat and hang out for quite a while, enjoying the fresh brewed coffee, pitching a buck or two into the donation jar. Also, he had Dave as a people-buffer, which allowed him to not have too much one on one with people, but just all he could tolerate, and yet gave him a chance to catch up on the local gossip, hear what somebody's son or daughter accomplished in high school or what college they were bound for. On occasion a joke was told that was actually funny. Stan discouraged political talk, as he knew it could sour the whole thing, and in fact, had a sign tacked up at the front door that read, "Leave Your Politics Outside".

He had a host of regulars that included Bob Kaminsky, who was probably the most colorful of the bunch. He was a large and grizzled, old-looking outdoorsman, and a near-hermit. It was hard to determine his age, but he had to be north of sixty. He had a full white beard and a weathered face, with large gnarled hands. His usual attire always included a flannel, and either jeans or overalls. The interesting accent was his footwear, which were a pair of Earth Shoes, no doubt snagged off of Ebay. He would often come in not long after opening, and sit sometimes for hours, before shuffling off to do his chainsaw wood carving out of a big stump of wood, transforming it into a bear or deer, and set up shop with his old flatbed truck full of carvings, just steps outside of city limits on West Main Street, otherwise known as State Route 571. He had become a bit of a local legend, and did fairly well with his carvings, most usually with travelers, not being shy about asking for a top price. He deserved it, for his bears actually looked like bears, instead of large porcupines.

There was one day when Bob was at the counter, sitting on his usual stool, as Stan worked behind the counter, re-arranging the Buck Knife display.

Bob gave Stan a "pssst". With a jerk of his head, Bob motioned for Stan to come closer, all discreet-like.

Stan, tolerant of this old guy who lived on the fringes of Tipp society, put aside his busy work and edged close to Bob.

Bob, with a quick glance to his right and left, held up a small Ziplock baggie, that appeared to contain some mud. Bob gave it a little jiggle and in a hushed voice said, "Looky here what I got. Squatch scat".

"Excuse me?" said Stan.

"This here's squatch scat my friend" still holding up the small plastic bag of mud, "Found it myself, not more than a two weeks ago".

Stan, holding onto a straight face, leaned in and took a good long look at the mud, and looked up at Bob saying, "Looks like mud, Bob".

"Mud my ass" said Bob, jerking the sample bag back, and sticking it into his jacket pocket.

"I'm sorry, but it does", said Stan.

Bob snapped back, "What the hell do you know, smart guy? This here's the real thing, collected it myself up near my trailer I keep over in the mountains. Beautiful place, but you believe me, the place is crawlin' with those ape men". Bob was visibly offended, looked down and the counter to contain himself, took a few moments to decide his next move, and then made it. He abruptly got up off his stool, and walked out of the store with a big snort.

Stan stood nonplussed, and then to said to himself, "What do you do with a guy like that?".

Walter Kenny and Allen Giraldi were the other two oddball regulars. Walter spent lots of time at the counter, while Allen usually flew in and out of the place, rarely having the time to settle in, have a coffee.

Allen was a local landscaper designer by title, but most of his work came from weed clearing, tree trimming, stump grinding, and using his wood chipper. Bob's primary source of tree stumps came from him. Allen would usually come in around mid-morning and was always in a hurry. It seemed he was always in crisis mode, having to do an emergency job involving a fallen tree, a collapsed fence, part of a washed-out bridge, or meeting a weed clearance deadline edict handed out to a homeowner by the fire department. His boots were always covered in mud, even in the driest of months. His undershirt and long sleeve flannels were invariably covered in sweat, mud, and assorted fragments of leaves and twigs. Always unshaven. Always sweaty. Thin as a rail. Dark haired. But pleasant, always pleasant. He had a full-time girlfriend that eventually he would marry, everyone speculated, but perhaps the most interesting element to his personality is that four years ago, he was the second-place Ohio statewide chess champion. One of those guys that can see five moves ahead, anticipate what the opponent is about to do, and if need be, change course in a split second to counter an unanticipated move against him. He could walk down a line of ten players with ten chessboards, make moves on each after just a few seconds of study, and beat every one of them, almost every time. Otherwise, he came across as just a regular, blue-collar guy. This is why Stan always kept a chess board on the far end of the counter, just past the stools, so that anyone, but especially Allen, could fly in, make a move on the way in, allowing time for Stan or whomever, to make their move, and then Allen, supplies in hand, would go to the register end of the counter, dump it all in a pile to be rung up, walk briskly to the chess board and after one or two beats, make his move, then pay for the goods, always with cash, and take off. This would happen two, three times a week, and with such regularity of timing, that it often created a small crowd of people, especially kids in the summer, waiting for him to make his entrance. Sometimes bets were laid. Unlike Bob, he was a good, regular and loyal customer, but had a ton of quirky habits, said bizarre little sentences as if he had early onset

Tourette, talked to himself in the aisles loudly, and when pulling out his wallet to pay, would blow air loudly through his pursed lips, in what was not a whistle or a hum, just the sound of air being jetted out, and finally, would burst into laughter as if having heard a very funny joke.

And then there was Walter. Oh my, where to start? Walter was short in stature, but wide, and most of it, muscle. He had a thick neck, stubby nose, a slight speech impediment, and was tormented. He had done four uneventful tours on nuclear subs (two years on the USS Alaska and six on the USS Wyoming) working his way up to Combat Systems Officer, came back home, couldn't tolerate civilian life, became restless, got a hot tip from a former Navy buddy, joined up with an off-the-books American military envoy team, aka mercenary team, for the U.S. Army going to various off-the-books places throughout Asia, performing mostly reconnaissance missions, or at times, guerilla warfare assistance to the locals, as they fought forces opposed the U.S. or its allies. It paid extremely well.

At times, it could be a horror show for Walter, prompting visits to psychologists. He was discharged with disability benefits after his final incident, which was harrowing.

He had a lovely and enduring wife, who didn't understand the first thing about PTSD, nor wanted to, so they had grown apart. She just wanted everything to go back to normal, how it used to be, and pretend her husband had never gone away on his undisclosed missions, and witnessed what he had witnessed, or done what he had done. His wife encouraged him to achieve being normal by behaving normally, to go out and get a normal job, so he could get back into the flow of normal regular life. It was not to be. Walter failed at any type of job he took, and quit not long after being hired. Even the simple and low paying ones he could not sustain. "Too much pressure" he would say. Sometimes when something, or someone, is broken, it can't be fixed. Sometimes there is no such thing as "normal".

He would sit at the counter and talk to Stan about his times aboard a nuclear sub, Ohio Class, armed to the teeth with Trident nuclear-tipped missiles. Often times, they would park underwater next to North Korea, in a modern day "fail safe", barely within international waters. Every two or three months, they would be relieved of their post by another sub, and on it went. It was an open secret that they would be there. North Korea knew it, and the U.S. knew that they knew it, and pretty much every government anywhere with an army, knew it. But the public, by and large, did not know it, so the saber rattling between politicians and their officials, broadcast on national TV and reported in papers, was always disturbing to the general public, with families in Homer, Alaska, looking to the skies, fearful of seeing North Korean missiles flying overhead on their way to Seattle. The Trident's were state of the art, and nastier than anything ever cooked up by any military in history. Two dozen or more of them to each sub, and each had eleven "independently targetable reentry vehicles" contained in the tip, each armed with a thermo-nuclear warhead, all of which would deploy a few thousand feet off the ground, fanning out to various targets with alarming accuracy, which meant if things ever "went sideways", as Walter phrased it, virtually "every developed square inch of that contrary nation would be vaporized within about twenty-five minutes, by roughly two-hundred and fifty hydrogen bombs. The people too". The grim reality of his purpose on the sub as the CSO, weighed on him greatly.

After Walter had returned home from his two-year stint as an "advisor", he took to walking for miles around town, going from one side of the town to the other, from South County Road to the west, to South Third Street to the east, from Arapaho Trail and Comanche Lane to the north, to Maple Hill Cemetery to the south. Lots of walking and thinking. He had discovered the store on one of his treks, and the stools within. He quickly became a regular visitor, finding the place to be warm and non-confrontational. He usually visited three times a week, toward the end of the day. He would sit forlornly, and if Dave or Stan were anywhere within earshot, and there were no others close by, he would talk mournfully about his life.

To the most part, Stan heard horrendous combat tales from Walter's mercenary days that occurred after his "submariner days", one after another, and the U.S. government he worked for was not always the hero in the story, usually was, but most certainly not always. These were not told to Stan as if he thought himself some kind of a hero, or a brave guy. Instead, all the stories were full of shame and regret. He did not see himself as someone who had done good, but who had added to "the troubles".

On one of his off-the-book envoy assignments, actually his last assignment, the one that got him discharged, they were aboard a U.S. Navy ship, underway to an undisclosed location off of the coastal town of Mueang Trap, Thailand, there to lend "comfort and aid" to nearby insurgents fighting across the nearby border in Cambodia. This information was not volunteered to Stan by Walter, but pulled out of him after a series of heart to hearts at the counter over a period of weeks.

The tragic part of the story, the event that was the root cause of his PTSD, was that while aboard the Navy ship, before their mission had even truly begun, a helicopter came in to land on the helipad, in rough seas, and one of the young soldiers under Walter's command was standing close to the helipad, and not sheltered behind a protective bulkhead as required. They all had headphones and helmets on, and Walter tried to yell at him to move back, but his voice was drowned out by the deafening sound of the surf, wind, and chopper blades. Even with his headphones on, the young recruit could not hear Walter yelling at him to get back. In a flash, the chopper was caught in a huge gust of wind and water, lurched violently to the side, landed on the helipad with a ferocious jolt, then slid off the pad into the water, the blades snapping off and breaking apart, the pieces flying wildly in every direction, hitting some of the ship's rigging and vent caps, slicing and dicing them into high velocity shrapnel, which struck the young soldier in five places, killing him instantly. The crew of the chopper all survived, miraculously, but all Walter could do was kneel down by the fallen soldier, blood streaming everywhere, and weep. He felt it was all his fault, and that he should have anticipated, taken much better precautions.

Stan listened to this story late one afternoon, with the store empty, and thought to himself "if only I had heard this weeks ago, before my audition. I could've used it". For obvious reasons, Stan did not share that thought with the crestfallen Walter, as it would show him to be shallow and selfish. Instead, Stan did the best imitation of an empathetic friend he could, and listened to this and all the myriad stories Walter had pent-up inside of him. Apparently, no therapist Walter had ever gone to was of any help. He was labeled as "resistant to therapy" and shoved in the corner by the Veteran Administration's bureauracy. Walter came to the store's counter on a regular basis, and while Stan was not the most com-passionate-acting guy in Tipp City, Walter could sense he had a well spring of compassion bottled up inside.

So, there you go, it wasn't that Stan was a complete narcissist or shallow, but that he was so mixed up and closed off himself. It was difficult if not impossible for him to comprehend another's distress or tragedy, and Walter had put him to the test. Stan had feelings, deep powerful ones, locked down deep, screaming to get out. By the time they squirmed their way to the surface, through the labyrinth that made up Stan's mind, they produced a quiet and repressed guy. That aside, these talks did them both some good, as their patient-therapist friendship grew roots.

Chapter 4

Stan liked the arrangement he had established, with Dave coming in early to open up the store allowing him to arrive later, usually between nine and ten in the mornings. Sometimes on Saturdays, in the off-season, Stan would come in late, just to close things up. They were closed on Sundays, and on other days would on occasion spell the other by having one take off extra early while the other finished off the day. This was one of the benefits of it not being busy most of the time. In the summer months, they'd open up on Sunday as well, and bring in a part-timer to help fill in the schedule. Gary Sanderson was just such a person. He was an older guy, around sixty-eight, very affable and helpful with customers, of average height, a large belly, mostly bald, and notably always wore a crisply ironed long sleeve dress shirt, creased slacks and had a fresh shave. This stood in stark contrast to how Stan and Dave often looked, both usually with stubble, wrinkled shirts, and unkempt hair.

Gary had a sense of authority about him, having had a long career as a senior pharmaceutical salesman, working for a very large name-brand company, with a small support staff under him at the home office in Cincy (Cincinnati), and traveling to a number of surrounding states, checking in on the larger chain store clients. His salesman chops were second to none. He and his wife Lorraine decided to move to small town life after his retirement a few years earlier, and they settled on Tipp at the suggestion of a friend.

But Gary was the restless type, didn't know much of anything outside of peddling legal drugs, and didn't especially like doing activities such as golf or bowling, didn't like joining clubs such as the Moose or Kiwanis, didn't have the temperament to volunteer to help the poor, lost dogs, or the community garden, and didn't know enough about Baseball, soccer, or swimming to help out at the high school, so for him, finding a nice little part time job was ideal. The fact he hardly knew anything about what the store carried, mattered little, for his warm personality made all the difference, and brought some much-needed sunshine into the drab store.

As mentioned, his sales skills were adroit, often greeting a customer who entered looking for a "cheap can of paint", and finished the session with the customer purchasing two cans of expensive paint, plus a primer, brushes, rollers, roller pan, rags, and masking tape (the expensive kind). And it wasn't just "salesmanship", it was good advice and help he always offered. It didn't take Gary long to learn the ropes, for product knowledge is simple stuff, but what cannot be learned is personality, and Gary had oodles of it.

So, put another way, Gary educated and helped customers, guided them to the correct choice, that was best for them, that would make their chore easier, make their life just that much better, and if by chance it also resulted in a big sale, terrific. Gary became the go-to guy in the store, to such an extent, that his employment there mushroomed to year-round, but still on a part time basis. Whatever extra payroll had to be handed to him, he more than made up for with his participation. Often times, a new customer would assume Gary was the owner, simply by the way he looked and carried himself. And that was fine with Stan and Dave, figuring that once in a while if an infrequent but dissatisfied customer came in hot, Gary would be on the receiving end and quell the person's wrath, often turning it into an additional sale.

Gary had been with the store for about a year, and in that year, Stan had reflected on his life more and more, but in some odd way, the introduction of Gary to the place had helped calm his nerves. The Zelda-Gary combo he called it. He also had Dave, and knew that Dave was a rock, and a loyal friend, but they rarely socialized. Dave had his own life to live, rarely spoke of his personal life, and didn't blend it with work. Gary on the other hand, was far more open, often times inviting Stan and Mandy over for a Sunday early supper, especially in the cooler or cold months when the store was closed.

It had helped to calm down Stan's jangled nerves and dark thoughts, and help him and Mandy to feel like they were a couple, enjoying the company of another couple. Lorraine, a prim and proper woman in her late fifties, would politely inquire about their future plans, such as which church they were going to choose for their marriage, how many kids they wanted, and which cook books were Mandy's favorites? It could get oppressive, but even so, she became their mutual surrogate mother, somewhat filling the void left by their mother's both having passed years ago. But it went only so far, as Lorraine could easily sense a tension between the two, and would not press too hard for answers to her questions about their future. What was not said by the couple spoke volumes.

All of the camaraderie with Gary and Lorraine was icing. It was a nice addition to Stan's life, and made things at home a touch better, gave him and Mandy a chance to talk about themselves as a couple to others, which helped to define their goals, but invariably their responses were at odds, with Mandy expressing intentions to have a real home, and Stan expressing intentions to figure what in the hell life was all about. Mandy was planted firmly in the here and now, and Stan was all about what's going happen next, as if he was just a passenger in someone else's life.

Once in a while Stan would take a very circuitous way to the store in the morning, driving down streets unfamiliar, stopping to gaze at a house or street full of houses, or drift over to Chuck's and park discreetly, to see how many of his customers he could recognize going in. Some mornings he would drive a ways out of town, not far, only three or four miles, and pull over, stop the engine and simply look out through the windshield if it was cold or wet, and in the summer, he'd roll down the windows and let the breeze flow thru, what there was of it. It could be so humid.

He would just sit, staring off into the distance, looking at the flatness of the land, the seemingly endless rows of crops, the occasional distant farmhouse or old barn. Sometimes he could hear the drone of a distant tractor working over some land, tilling the soil or creating nice straight furrows for the next planting. There was lots of corn, tomatoes, squash, and cu-cumber to put in. Small family-owned farms were of course on the chopping block, and most had thrown in with others and formed co-ops or had simply joined (or been taken over by) large "Big Ag" corporate interests headquartered far away in another state, or even in another country.

Things had certainly changed from the original days of family run farms and ranches, just inside the duration of Stan's lifetime up until now. Once in a while, Stan would come across a lone farmhouse, looking like an Andrew Wyeth painting, all by its self, small but stately in its own way. Sometimes there was activity in the front yard or porch, in which case Stan would drive on, not wanting to be accused of peeping or stalking, but other times, most times, there was no activity and he would park across the road and take it all in.

He would imagine what it would have been like to have grown up as somebody else, or leastways, in a completely different environment at home. He would imagine a well-tailored and funny dad that knew how to stay home on Saturday nights, not make up phony baloney excuses as to why he's coming home so late or not until Sunday morning. Somebody who actually wanted to be with him, and do things. And a mom who was not in so much pain, and constantly griping about her lousy lot in life, it never occurring to her that part of her life included Stan, and maybe how lucky she was to have such a fine young boy as her son? Nope. That never happened, unless she got a bit too tipsy on a Limoncello gin cocktail, in which case the compliments to Stan would flow, followed by numerous pats on the head, followed by speeches that were all about "what if" and "one day" and "if things were different" and so forth. Then, after it became too much like an Edward Albee play, the deus ex machina would appear in the form of a distracting phone call, a mailman, or a fire engine wailing by, which would prompt the usual ending with her in tears, and exiting to the bedroom, slamming the door, cueing the curtain to fall. Utterly delightful it was for the young boy. And then, when he was eight, she died of kidney failure.

These types of memories followed him around everywhere. He couldn't seem to escape them, as they had attached themselves to him like leeches. He always believed that if he looked at his life in retrospect enough times, from enough different angles, examined every detail, every trauma, he would discover the secret door, leading to happiness. It was a hopeful but uninstructed thought, for he always went on these explorations without professional assistance, so he was without guidance, direction, and rudderless.

On one such a Saturday morning, with the weather still undecided between winter and early spring, he found himself parked on the side of the road, across from a farm house, one of his regular stops, reviewing his past, and enjoying a slight cooling breeze.

It was out in the country, about four miles from the center of town. The road was a secondary, not traveled all that much, as there were shorter routes between points A and B to be had. He had parked on the dirt shoulder, under the shade of a big Weeping Willow. He stared across the road to a quaint little farmhouse, yellow with white decorative scrolled trim at the roof edge, set back from the road about two hundred feet, two story, very traditional in every way. It was surrounded by acres of flat farm land, with the next closest structure being an old barn, half a mile away.

It sat there, all by itself. There was no one home, and in fact, it didn't appear that anyone had been living there for quite some time, but it looked like someone visited it from time to time, to keep up appearances. The front porch looked as if it was getting swept of leaves and dust on a regular basis. The flowers in the window box seemed well maintained. The house itself, although fairly old, was kept up, with no peeling paint or loose roof shingles. But in spite of this attention, it seemed deserted. He had never seen anyone there. The front yard, and in fact the entire yard all around the house was devoid of any kind of landscaping except for a well-maintained lawn, fresh and green.

But that was it. It was the most minimalist house and yard he could think of. But it had one other feature worth mentioning, a tell of sorts. The entire yard, about half an acre in size, and square, was surrounded by an overly tall chain link fence, about eight feet tall, and on top of that, razor wire. This was a feature not commonly found on farmhouse fencing anywhere he knew of, and usually reserved for detention centers and rental yards housing expensive farming equipment. Stan knew why this was, and always wondered how many others knew. Maybe everyone? He never brought it up in conversation, nor did anyone bring it up to him. It was Harold Pinter's weasel in the liquor cabinet.

Stan could see in his side view mirror, three boys approaching in the distance. He figured they were headed to the nearby creek, more like a wide dirt culvert, to try their luck catching some fish, judging by their fishing poles and boots. Two boys had big floppy hats on, and the third, a Cincinnati Reds ball cap. They were talking animatedly and when they came up beside Stan's Corolla they jumped back with a start, not having realized the car was occupied.

Stan said "Hi guys" pleasantly.

The boy with the ball cap said "Hi" back, and then they stood looking at Stan, as if they all had the same question for him.

Stan broke the silence by saying, "So, looks like you guys are headed down to the crick?" and offered, "Might be a little late in the morning to catch anything".

One of the boys spoke up, "We don't care, it's just fun to go down, throw our lines in, or find some frogs".

Stan, almost wistfully, said, "Yeah, good froggin' down there for sure".

"We don't do nothing to hurt 'em, just pick 'em up, put 'em in the water".

"Oh yeah, I figured that", said Stan.

More silence.

One of the other boys said, "So why you parked here mister?".

Stan, a little defensively, said, "Just hangin' out before work, I like the looks of this farmhouse".

All the boys turned and took a look at the place, just to be sure of what he was talking about, then turned back to him.

The same boy said, "We heard this place is a fake. That they keep missiles down there, below it".

Stan gave a little smile and said, "That's right. They're called silos. I heard they have five of them, out there in the field behind the place, all disguised".

The boy's eyes grew large with astonishment.

"Yep, that's right. Air Force guys show up here in costume, dressed like farmers" said Stan, with a sly smile on his face, "and go in and then there's an elevator, takes them down about four stories, into their command center. Somebody's there all the time".

All the boys were frozen in rapt attention. Then, one of them broke and let out a big laugh, and was joined by the other two, and then by Stan. The boys took off, giggling and talking excitedly about Stan's joke.

Stan stared at the farmhouse, the deserted but well-kept farmhouse, thinking to himself that sometimes you tell people the truth, and they just don't believe it. Which gave him an idea. Stan cranked up the engine, hung a U, and headed for the store.

Chapter 5

The Corolla slid into a front primary parking slot, and Stan swung open the door and got out with an uncharacteristic bounce to his step. He went up the stairs, two at a time, went inside, hurriedly greeted a couple who were debating on which garden rake to purchase, whisked by them and located Dave in aisle two, stocking boxes garden fertilizers.

"Hey Dave" said Stan with a new kind of assurance to his voice.

Dave noticed that, put the box on the shelf, and looked at Stan quizzically, "Hey Stan, what's up?"

"Some exciting news" said Stan, continuing "and you are gonna love it, I mean *love* it".

The hair on Dave's neck began to stand up.

Stan pulled Dave deeper into the aisle, to be sure there was no one listening.

"Okay, I don't have all the details hammered out yet, but this is the gist of it…" and then grabbed Dave's elbow and ushered him over deeper to a far corner of the store, in the back aisle next to the ladders.

Dave hoped this would be something really big, really good, like Stan he was getting married, or he had just won a cruise around the world.

Stan in a low voice, giddy with excitement, laid out a new plan, which was "highly confidential, and top secret stuff". On occasion Stan would have to stop, take a few breaths, buying himself some time to figure out the next detail.

"Okay, what we're gonna do is take advantage of people's natural curiosity. You know, like how some people are curious about things here around town, like when something is odd, or new, different. You know? So, I noticed how when Chuck's opened up, all kinds of people went there, curious, wanted to check it out, because it was, well, it was new, right? Same thing with me when I opened up, remember? People came streaming in from all over town. They were amped up, and bought stuff just so they could. You remember that, right?"

Dave, trying to track what he was saying, and noticing the beads of sweat forming on Stan's forehead, watching his crazed smile, hearing the tremble in his voice, was very hesitant to do anything but agree. "Yes, I remember that...".

"Okay, okay, then this here is what I can do about that. I'm gonna open up again". Stan, believing he had given a thorough explanation to his new fantastic idea, stood, expectant, waiting for Dave to give out a yelp, a high five maybe, something, anything.

Dave was motionless, with a fixed look on his face, a mix of wonder and concern for his friend. He gave a quick glance around to be sure they weren't being overheard, then in a gentle and reassuring tone of voice, said, "But Stan, you know, we're already open. You know that, right?"

Stan nodded, "Well sure, I know that".

"I'm glad to hear you say it".

Stan continued. His reasoning was that a newly opened store in a small town such as this, always gathers interest and curiosity, which brings in lots of lookers, many of them buying things. If the store is right, those curious once, will come back again and again. Stan was at least self-aware enough to know that Stan's was a utility store, not sexy or fun, just a plain ordinary store. Holsteen, the old fancy cowboy guy, had made him realize that. Stan wasn't too sure how to replace the ordinary with sexy, but he was going to try, but first, he had to attract people.

Stan got close to Dave, looking up in his face, with the intensity of a tent revival preacher, "If people like the place, the service, the merchandise, you know, all that crap, then the store has a chance of building a customer base, right?

Dave, alarmed, said, "Uh huh".

"I earn their loyalty, and from that core of people, perhaps two or three-hundred strong, they will spread the word. But get this..." Stan's expression became manic, "What if it wasn't exactly a new store, but a new *owner*? Stan took a step back, nodding and smiling, so he could take in Dave's reaction of wonderment.

Dave stood looking at Stan, with no wonderment.

Stan brought it up a notch, in a very loud whisper. "What if word gets out that "Stan's" has sold the lease to someone, and that that *someone* was going to probably make changes, upend things, maybe turn the place into something else entirely, disturb the natural established order? People don't like change. What about that?"

"Well, uh, it's an interesting idea, but how are you planning on doing that? Do you actually have somebody who wants the lease?"

Stan, realizing his friend was acting a little dense, said with multiple shakes of his head, "No, no, no, *no*. You don't get it. People will behave predictably. When they hear about the big change, they'll swarm in, I'll jack up prices on key items and then put them on sale. Get it? Then they'll start talking to me about how much they're gonna miss me, and want to know what they can do to help, you know, lend support somehow to the old store, or give me a bunch of advice for the new owner, what he should carry...ya see?"

"Uh huh, okay, go on..." Dave said, troubled.

"You don't get it, I can tell. Once people are all fired up, talking about the store at Kroger's, Dollar General, Circle K, and Big Mike's Gas 'n Go, and churches, temples, and synagogues, whatever, in town or maybe other towns, it will go viral. Donchya see? People will flock in, want to know all about the new owner and the new plans, pick up a sale item, and talk it up to everybody!"

Dave, his eyes wide, "Uh huh".

"Now this is the sweet spot...Once I have sensed the wave is over, I will let it be known that the new owner has pulled out of the deal, but I will graciously thank everyone who had come in and shown an interest, and that I will be adopting many of the new fresh ideas that were offered. It can't fail".

"Well, it could, but -" said Dave, before being cut off.

"I will have gotten a ton of free advertising by word of mouth, will have had a good shot at earning loyalty from old *and* new customers alike, and in the end, I will appear to be the gracious hero, saving the community hardware store, and earning new respect. People hardly ever believe the truth even when you lay it in their lap. But a good lie, a tasty one like this? Wow. It's inventive marketing, right?".

Dave, sensing that Stan had come to the end of his presentation, started to breathe again, and had taken note that not once had Stan used the words "we" or "us".

Dave said, "Yeah, very interesting plan Stan, very interesting. Let me think it over, but yeah, really interesting". Dave could not escape the corner fast enough.

As Dave was retreating, Stan said, "Hey, and fill Gary in, okay?"

Stan barely slept that night, and when he came into the store the next morning, he was amped up by his new plan. He couldn't relax, could only keep thinking of all the details of how he would launch his scheme. Even Mandy, somewhat hesitant about the ethics involved, was behind him, so happy to see him energized for a change, focused, on the way to somewhere. He had presented it to her as a "small promotional gimmick", leaving out many details.

There was a small back room in the store, with a shelf unit against one wall to house the sparse amount of back stock they held, and un-used displays scattered about, with "Return to Vendor" items stacked up in the corner, and an old desk, covered in brochures and catalogs. It took Stan about five minutes to clean house, and establish the beachhead for his secret plan. The night before he had drawn up sketches and made lists at home. He grabbed them from his satchel, laid them out on the table or tacked them to the wall. It was a war room, and it was time to put everything into action.

Meanwhile, Dave and Gary stood on the other side of the closed door, listening to all the activity, and to Stan who was talking animatedly to himself.

"He's turning into somebody else" stated Dave, with sadness. As for Gary, he had seen this kind of breakdown before in his former corporate world, when the pressure of deadlines and sales goals became too much for someone.

Stan, swore them both to complete silence, and rarely consulted with them after this. Theirs was to watch over the store, act "normal" and just go along with the plan, silently. They were to deflect any and all questions from outsiders, and refer them to Stan.

The first thing Stan did was order a vinyl banner for the outside of the store. It arrived six days later. It was eighteen feet long, three feet tall, with bold red lettering, and not inexpensive, but Stan figured, it was a very important investment. He and Dave got on ladders and attached it across the face of the building. They took a few steps back to take it all in.

"NEW OWNERSHIP COMING SOON"

It was not meant to be subtle, but to stop people in their tracks. He was correct. Once the sign went up, it didn't take long for people to take notice.

The first time Stan heard directly about it, was when he went across the street to the small local convenience market to grab a couple of things. Carl Lethrow, the tall and severe looking owner of Lethrow Auto Sales a block away, was behind him in line and tugged at his sleeve and said, "Heard about your banner. You gettin' out huh? Found a new sucker?" and chortled wickedly, his boozy breath enveloping Stan. This was not the response he was hoping for, but he was steadfast.

After this shaky start, he had encounters of the more positive kind on the short walk back to the store. One person commented from his car that was stopped at the light, another on the sidewalk, and yet another in the crosswalk. Stan fielded questions in as vague a way as he could, but soon realized that for all of his planning, he had skipped over a key element: he had not created a back story for his imaginary new buyer, as his acting had taught him to do. It was an oversight, a rather large one, but nothing he could not improvise his way out of, he being so good at that.

And it was fortunate that Stan was good at this, for the moment he got back to the store, with a ready-made sandwich and soda in hand, Mrs. Drummer, the pinch-faced retired high school English teacher and occasional customer, cornered Stan next to the paint can shaker.

"So, what's this fella's name, the new owner?"

Stan's backstory was not quite up to speed, and he came up with "Mike Scalopini, and his lovely wife, Judy" off the top of his head.

"Who the hell is that? How do you spell that?" said Drummer.

Stan spelled the name out for her slowly, as if he was still one of her students, and gave Drummer the story about the new owner, about his plans, about his past, about his wife, making it up as he went along. Stan finished up saying, "He's the new owner now, a very nice fellow, Italian guy I think, and his wife, well, you'll just love her" reassured Stan.

Drummer was anything but satisfied and drilled him for another two minutes before letting him up for air. As she walked away, she said for all to hear, "A greaseball huh?" Doesn't that beat all?"

The back story Stan had dreamt up on the fly was that Mike Scalopini and his wife, had always wanted to own a little store in a small town, and they were going to move from Brooklyn to Tipp City in another month or two, and start making changes. The name "Scalopini" was the best thing Stan could come up with. He had mis-remembered it from a take-out menu a few weeks ago. The Italian dish is actually spelled with two "L's" in the middle, not one, as in Chicken Scallopini, or Veal Scallopini. Unbeknownst to Stan, Scalopini with one "L" is the name of a type of mole, but it is doubtful anyone will ever bother looking that up. In any event, Stan got over the first hurdle and was on his way.

Two days later, the announcement in the Chronicle appeared on page three.

It was not the most expertly written notice, and Stan could only afford a very small one, but he figured it would get the point across, and he was correct in that assessment. The whole thing blew up. People streamed into the store, wanting to know all about the new owner Mike, and his wife Judy. Stan kept improvising. One time at Dayton Airport he had noticed a display of crocheted farm animals, just as an art installation, so he figured, why not? To one inquisitor he said, "She crochets farm animals. They'll

> STAN'S HARDWARE AND STUFF is closing. A new owner is taking over the space, and will be making some big changes. Stan Hurts, owner and proprietor, is sad to be leaving but knows that the place will be in good hands. Come on in for some good deals!

be selling them here. She'll do some on request if you like. I hear she'll even do the baby Jesus in a Manger scene, but you gotta give her a couple of months".

Improvised words flew out of Stan's mouth faster than he could retrieve them. There were many contradictions. Many people were fascinated by the concept of a guy from Brooklyn, an Italian guy no less, that wanted to uproot himself and move himself and his wife to some little ho-dunk town like Tipp, in the Midwest, and open a store. For some it made for a charming story, but for others, it didn't hold water. Stan had to do something about the leaks.

With Dave and Gary helping the sudden upsurge of customers, scrambling to stock the shelves, and to ring merchandise up before going to the next customer, there was not a lot of time for talk, or for thought, it seemed. Stan was pretty much on his own, flailing around, trying to make stuff up, and not mess up, in the process.

Tony Lanaro, owner of the Fresh Look Hair Salon a few blocks away, and of Italian descent himself, was most curious about Scalopini, and questioned Stan at length one afternoon, perhaps being the only person who had noticed the peculiar spelling, and also highly suspicious of a fellow Italian who had a peculiar spelling. For him, it spelled trouble. He wanted to know "what kind of changes this Scalopini guy had in mind", and Stan explained that he thought he would keep some of the hardware but also wanted to bring in a line of tires, and maybe over in the corner, a fresh bakery. Stan's reasoning was that the more ridiculous the answers, the less likely people will question him further. Stan was mostly correct in that guess, except for one very notable exception, the over-fed and sweaty landlord.

Stan had never factored Neil Riptick into his equation. To him, Riptick was a non-threat, a small speck, that he could easily handle if and when the absentee landlord ever got wind of the scheme. Chances were better, Stan reasoned, that Riptick might hear about it after the fact, so no harm, no foul. But there was a storm brewing, as Mr. Riptick was at that very moment, sitting in his office on the second floor of a mixed-use commercial building on East Main Street that he owned, in Bexley, Ohio, a town just to the east of Columbus, reading a message he had received from his cloying nephew Ransom, who happens to live in Tipp City. The transcript stated, "Please tell uncle Neil that it looks like Hurts is up to something again, cus he has a banner on the store saying something about a new owner or something. It's a big banner. Oh, and see you later sometime, Ransom, and come over for dinner".

"I wrote it down exactly like he said it Mr. Riptick" said Alice Newton, who was Neil's "Outer Office Executive Assistant" and sole employee.

The call had come in from Ransom at the close of business the day before, after Neil had already left.

Neil, annoyed that among Alice's many skills was not the ability to write a properly written message. She would always give him exact transcripts of what the caller had said, instead of a simple message that quickly summarized. But he couldn't blame her. He had discovered her years ago when he had been dragged into court by a disgruntled tenant, and she was a fledgling court stenographer. He lost the case, but won her over, with promises of more prestige, money, and status. He had predictably, lusted for her the moment he saw her but she rebuffed his advances from the start, always had. He had attempted to gain her sexual gifts many times in the beginning, but the last attempt was when he walked up suggestively close to her while she was sitting at her desk.

With her winning smile and bright clear eyes, she looked up at him and said sweetly, "You best keep that thing zippered up, or I'll get myself a good attorney over in Columbus, I know lots of 'em, and sue the living shit out of you, Mr. Riptick".

Her fame and fortune never did arrive as a result of being hired by Neil, although she did well by him. She was a good-natured person, not abrasive or ill-tempered like Neil. She was the perfect counterpoint for him, smoothing over numerous legitimate complaints from tenants over the years. Even after he married, he never got over being rejected by her with his clumsy and crude last advance. But he knew her to be of value to the business, knew his many shortcomings, and their business relationship matured into something of worth. They both knew that at the end of the day, she was the actual boss, as evidenced by her unusually high salary.

Riptick rubbed the notepad paper between his thumb and forefinger, back and forth, as if he could get from that a reading, like a clairvoyant. Of course, he wasn't a clairvoyant, in fact, pretty much the opposite of one.

Stan had buffaloed Neil many a time over the course of their relationship, pushing the envelope countless times, and Neil had always succumbed to

Stan's ability to dance around with words and assurances. All kinds of issues had arisen in the past, such as painting the face of the hardware building something other than plain white, with Neil finally agreeing to painting it a pleasant blue-grey shade. Neil paid for the labor, and went so far as to buy the paint from Stan, at retail. The color turned out to be bright turquoise, and Stan expressed total exasperation with the painters for making such a stupid "mistake". There were other things in the history books as well: Expanding the size of the deck in front of the store. Allowing there to be merchandise displayed on that deck. Stan selling ice cream confections from a Good Humor freezer in the store, over the objections of another other tenant two doors down, Lloyd's Ice Cream Shoppe. Allowing Stan to paint the windows with caricatures of Tipp City council members with hammers, garden rakes, paint brushes in hand, as if working (the general consensus around town was that the members of the city council were a bunch of lazy do-nothings, never worked at anything, so there was an edge to the cartoonish parody). He allowed Stan to invent names of holidays as part of his promo campaigns to stir interest in the store. There was "Kumquat Harvest Day", "Adopt a Penguin Day", "Free Ice Cream Next Door Day", and "Tell the Landlord to Lower My Rent Day". That last one had an especially hard bite to it as Stan was habitually late with rent, always pointing to his low sales and lack of support from the landlord.

This particular issue stuck in Riptick's throat, as he knew he had been "less than transparent" with Stan from the get go. "Completely dishonest" is how Stan described it.

In the beginning, before Stan signed the lease, Riptick had promised Stan a variety of things, in order to help him promote the new store. Those promises included sponsoring a "Grand Opening Day", with a collection of jumpy-jumps for the kids, pony rides, giant helium balloons, hot dog and pizza vendors, and a spate of ads in the local papers. All paid for by Riptick. This is what induced Stan to choose this available space to lease, instead of a better one in the busier west part of town. Location, location, location, right? This location wasn't bad, but wasn't great.

The problem was, after Stan signed the lease, moved in, purchased many pallets-worth of merchandise in anticipation of grand opening day, it became apparent that Riptick had no intention of backing up any of his promises, all of them verbal, not a damn one of them on paper. When Stan was finally able to track down Riptick in person and confront him, Riptick acted surprised, and hurt, that Stan would ever suspect him of being anything other than totally honest and above board. When Stan reminded him of all the promises, Neil said that they had been just "spitballing, coming up with possible ideas, and they were not promises at all" and then added, "when we were talking, we were just talking, not *talking*". What could Stan say to that?

Aside from the ridiculousness of Riptick's claim, the result was that when Stan opened his store, people heard about it through the grapevine, and trickled in, but the initial opening was very flat, and that flatness never left, never created the base the store needed, and Stan took it as being his fault, because he knew he was a lousy businessman, that he didn't have the killer instinct.

Most likely, Riptick had acquiesced on Stan's building facelift color and out-of-the-box marketing ideas because he knew he had totally bamboozled the wannabe actor, and someplace in his fossilized heart, he knew he owed him something. But this news about a new owner, that was going too far.

Riptick managed many properties, some his, some belonging to others, and he was a busy guy. A lot of his time was spent developing new clients, so he could manage their commercial rentals in the greater Columbus area. He was a regular at local IHops and Applebee's, always on the prowl for a business owner in need of some expert advice and management services. He also managed a number of his own properties, spread far and wide, some as far afield as Toledo to the north and Circleville to the south. Stan's little hardware store was a satellite and a nuisance, barely worth the time it took to manage him. In fact, Riptick dreaded the fifteenth of each month for he knew that the odds of getting a rent payment from Stan was slim, which would necessitate him to pick up the phone and attempt to get Stan on the line, a few days later, which almost never happened as Dave (and then later, Dave and Gary) would field the calls, promising to leave a message, which went nowhere, which then required Neil to drive to Tipp City.

About eighty miles and an hour and a half later, Neil would roll up in front of the store, intentionally showing up at odd hours to catch Stan off guard, which over time, worked less and less well.

In the end, sometimes after multiple attempts, Neil would walk out grasping the rent check. But since he was in Tipp, he would feel obliged to visit his brother Jim Earl, who lived not a mile away. Those visits, if timed poorly, would include an invite to lunch at the local greasy burger stand, which Neil invariably paid for, or an invite to supper with Jim Earl's wife Nance, and their doughy teenage and not very bright son, Ransom, who had to be one of the least appealing people Neil had ever met. After departing their house after a nearly inedible homemade meal, always slathered in salt and paprika, he would have to stop at the nearest mini-mart and down a hand-full of Tums with a milk chaser, to help neutralize the experience.

Nance was a big fan of paprika because of her knowledge that it had first been introduced to the "old world" *from* North America, and then had spread to other regions of the world. She liked all things native American, except for actual Native Americans. Why everyone else had to be subjected to the peppery and patriotic spice was a wonder. "Maybe, just maybe one day, that kid can learn to eat with his mouth closed, let the food stay inside his mouth" Neil would bitterly tell himself on the drive home, downing a second hand full of Tums. He subjected himself to this occasional torture because he had made his mom a promise, may she rest in peace, that he would always look after his younger and "not as talented" brother, through thick and thin. Neil may have been a louse in any number of other ways, but he knew how to keep a promise to mama.

It should also be said that Neil Riptick, while greedy, wasn't a dumb person, just someone who always overestimated his intelligence, and to make matters worse, was devoid of normal, socially accepted good manners. "Ebenezer" was his given nick-name around the store.

Riptick knew he would have to trudge over to Tipp City yet again, and pay a visit to the hardware store, but he was in no hurry to do it. In fact, he reasoned, if he let Stan have enough rope, he might hang himself by violating the terms of the lease twice (being over sixty days late with the full rent, and subleasing) and that might allow him to sleep better, knowing he had evicted his biggest headache.

Stan knew that not being able to pay the rent was no joke, however. And he knew that he had to do something to turn the business around, and slapping a new color on the building, or dressing up the front deck with more merchandise, or inventing a new holiday in order to promote the place, were no longer the viable ideas they once were. He had to do something much bigger, on a grand scale, something theatrical. This is what had led Stan to decide upon the new owner promotion.

His promotional stunt had worked, and worked surprisingly well. Stan would read the temperature in town, going from place to place, in particular, Billy's Diner, to hear what people were saying. He had gotten a lot of initial buzz as hoped, which had translated to some very good days at the register, but things were starting to go flat again. Stan found himself in a tough spot, for he had enjoyed the invention of a pending new owner, but there were still people nagging him everywhere about who Scalopini was, when he was going to arrive and take over, and what was he going to do with the place? Stan, in very round terms, had fielded those questions, but had been so sloppy that people were beginning to notice the contradictions, and compare notes. In order to draw more customers in, he needed to extinguish the growing skepticism. Instinctively, Stan knew that he had to expand on the scheme, and make it even bigger, more outlandish, in order to get it going again.

Later that day, sitting on the cozy living room couch back at Mandy's, he was channel surfing and came upon "Judge Judy". She was in the middle of raking the owner of a dry cleaners over the coals for not being more present at his business, not being more in-person, more hands-on, with his crew, which led to whatever in the hell the complaint against him was about. That part wasn't important, but what struck Stan between the eyes was the "in-person" part of it.

He knew he had an idea, a gem of an idea, but he couldn't quite reach out and touch it. He walked into the kitchen to micro himself a bowl of Campbell's, glancing at the clock, wondering when Mandy would get home from her new-found sculpting class. It seemed she was spending more and more time away, perhaps on a self-improvement binge, or perhaps as a way to avoid direct contact with him, he speculated to himself. The soup was hot and he sat back down on the couch but alas, the TV judge had been re-placed by a "King of Queens" re-run. He didn't care, for he had other things rolling around in his head. He slowly spooned his lentil soup but could not take his mind off the in-person thing. And then it came to him.

Chapter 6

Mike Scalopini was coming to town! Stan had made a phone call from home, drawn up another announcement, trotted it over to the Chronicle, and returned to the store to share his brainstorm with Dave and Gary. Although the store had quieted down in the last couple of weeks, it was still considerably busier than what had become the norm before the entrance of the Scalopini's.

Bob and Allen were inside, with Allen setting up the chessboard for a new game, having beaten Bob in about three moves. Bob was hunched over the counter, reading a dog-eared book, no doubt having something to do with Bigfoot. It was too early for Walter to have arrived. There were other people there as well, milling about, examining the "Sale Table" for a good deal on a tool box or fertilizer pellets.

Stan located Dave and pulled him aside, next to the end cap display of tape measures. He motioned for Gary to peel himself away from Henry Larkspur, as he was demonstrating the many wondrous advantages of a cordless drill.

Gary excused himself, irritated that Stan had likely ruined the sale. Henry was a very difficult fish to catch, and he would hang onto a power tool, always a corded power tool, until the pot metal casing had cracked, the paint had faded off, the cord was split open in various places and patched with any random type of available tape, and with sparks flying out of the motor, followed by a spurt of blue smoke. This to Henry was still an adequate piece of equipment, properly broken in, not to be carelessly tossed out in favor of "some (racist Asian pejorative deleted) piece of plastic crap". Gary, had a way with customers hard to please or convince, which is why he was so exasperated when he joined the huddle.

Stan said, "Sorry Gary, didn't mean to mess up the sale, but I have got some big news for you guys, and I mean, *big*".

By now, even Gary, patient to a fault, had reached his melting point with Stan when it came to his far-fetched ideas. Dave had a much longer history with Stan, was more tolerant, or perhaps simply better at sticking his head in the sand. Even so, both of the loyal compatriot's stood and listened to Stan's hushed voice as he laid out his latest big idea.

During the huddle, Dave had to excuse himself from the strategy meeting to ring a customer up, or Gary to cut a house key, but they would immediately rejoin and catch up on the particulars. Once Stan was done outlining the plan, they broke and went in their respective directions. Gary went to track down Henry, who had now drifted over to the display of drill bits, and Dave to help Anita Sanders with choosing which beach chair to buy. Stan went to the small back room, and nervously paced up and down in the confines, going over his plan a dozen times, like a prisoner in a cell having hatched the perfect escape plan.

Two days later, the sloppy Chronicle announcement appeared. It was positioned on the

---

MEET AND GREET Mike Scalopini! The new owner of Stan's Hardware and Stuff. He will be at the store this Saturday the 14th, from Noon to 4:00. Come and meet him, have some free snacks, bring the kids, have some fun. Lots of sale items! Everyone welcome!

same page three, but up higher and more prominently, thanks to a little help from Sally Lewters, the advertising coordinator at the paper, and also Stan's friend.

Harriet Trowner, a large and tough woman with a raspy smoker's voice, was the owner and chief editor of the paper, and would always give Stan a squinty and not too friendly stare when he walked in, as if she didn't trust Stan, or like him overly well either, so special favors did not come forth. Sally on the other hand, loved to accidentally give Stan preference. To be clear, theirs was purely friendship, no romance even implied. Mandy had always been suspicious of the friendship even so, not entirely believing that there was nothing going on, or perhaps would go on if Stan were given half a chance. Not likely that chance would ever materialize, even if both Stan and Sally had wanted it. Sally was married to Comstock Lewters, the head tow truck driver over at Tipp Towing. Comstock was built like a large tree; tall, round, strong with thick bark, and in general, massive. You could put him in a hairy costume and convince Bob he was a Bigfoot, no problem. Maybe even without a costume. He was known for being very slow to anger, but the imagination soars thinking about what he might be capable of, had there ever been some funny business going on between Sally and Stan.

Stan figured that he had been at a crossroads, to either fold up and abandon his scheme somehow, or to escalate it to new heights, leaving no doubt that it was a for real thing. The entire purpose of the scheme was to garner interest, enjoy short-term sales, and then when it fell through because the new owner backed out of the deal, people would be left with an overwhelming sense of relief that their friendly community hardware store would still be around, and Stan would receive some respect, and long-term sales. It all seemed so simple. But the plan didn't go far enough to work.

That's where Scalopini came in. Stan had it all wired. He had called one of his delivery drivers, the one that delivers plumbing and electrical parts to him (the store's slowest-moving category). His name was Ray Delworst, a dark-haired, dark-eyed, middle-aged guy, who could easily pass for Italian-American. Stan asked him to sit in as Scalopini, as a "joke", and in return Stan would give him a nice big bag of assorted t-shirts and sweatshirts for his family. But it all had to be very hush-hush. Ray, once convinced it would be a harmless prank, agreed to the plan.

Ray was rarely if ever, seen by the general public, or by customers in the store, for when he did show up for the infrequent delivery, it was always at the back double doors to the store. Ray was essentially a total unknown in town, and would not be recognized, especially if he were clean-shaven, dressed nicely, not in his usual worn and torn dark blue Dickies ensemble.

Through the course of the last few weeks, Stan had had an unfamiliar feeling of contentment. We won't go so far as to say "light-heartedness" for that was something that rarely, if ever, was visited upon Stan, but it was the lack of depression that Stan began to notice. It was a foreign sensation, to not have a forty-pound weight on his shoulders, or to sleep through the night free of disturbing chase and hide nightmares. Mandy took notice as well, and when coming home with dried clay on her hands from class, could not but help see how Stan seemed more buoyant.

His sense of ease did not motivate him to discuss anything with her about the store or certainly about "the plan", so in that respect, she was in the dark. It's because she had been the one to say she didn't want to know any details about his next "hair brain scheme" so he figured she was sincere in that request, and told her little if anything.

Over the past number of nights, Stan would sit himself at the kitchen table with Mandy's laptop and type away deep into the night. Hours and hours were consumed. Anyone could have easily seen that he was a man possessed, on a mission, so Mandy steered clear.

Most of Mandy's days were spent out of town at work, so she was not exposed to small town gossip or rumors to the most part. Not that she had not heard some, for she had, here and there, little disjointed tidbits, that she would forget about shortly after hearing.

But then one day, she had been doing some shopping in the historic district of town, where there was a very specific kind of thing she wanted from a specific store there, near the intersection of Main and Second Streets: a selection of beautiful clay modeling tools from the old fashioned five and dime store, that had a small section devoted to arts and crafts. The arts and crafts store that used to be on the west side had closed down, and now this small quaint little place was the only store in town she knew of that caried sculpting supplies.

Once carefully selected and purchased, she took her tools in a small paper sack, and headed back toward where she had parked. She slowed and halted to watch a small parade of Ku Klux Klansmen march up Second Street, stop at Main, turn around and march back. It took about fifteen minutes, and Mandy stood watching from the sidewalk, stunned by how out of place an event like this seemed, in this day and age, in her very own town. She had known they were a presence in the area, had heard about their secret gatherings, but even though their cross-burning days were gone, had been outlawed, they still seemed so much a thing from the past, and intimidating.

The police were there, escorting the small parade of about twenty, presumably men, all hooded-up. They hadn't bothered to dispatch one of their newer Interceptors but opted to dust off their old blue and white Ford Crown Vic for the event. They had a boom box playing some military-sounding music and carried a couple of banners with slogans about God and America and purity. They had no doubt applied for, and received, a permit, which is why the cop car was there, light bar flashing, leading the way, keeping the peace. Very few people stood and watched like Mandy had, not wanting to be associated with the small event, or have it suggested they were in favor of it. They instead hustled into a store or made a beeline down the sidewalk and turned the corner. Mandy figured, with a black population approaching zero, and the majority of the white folks in town not the most progressive, they could get away with this. It was while Mandy was standing, transfixed by this bizarre little parade, that Virginia Stoppor, an old schoolmate acquaintance from high school days, slid up next to her and watched silently with her for a few beats.

"I think these people have lost their friggin' minds", said Virginia.

Mandy turned, recognizing her old schoolmate and gave out a little squeal, as they hugged and laughed a bit, but not too loudly, for the parade members might get the impression they were being laughed at.

The two women stood for a few more moments, taking in the weird and disturbing review. They had some small talk, caught up on things, and as Virginia parted, she looked back and said, "See you Saturday".

"What?" said Mandy.

"Saturday. You know, over at the store".

Still puzzled, Mandy took a step toward her and said, "The store? What's happening?".

Virginia, surprised how such a big event could have slipped Mandy's mind, said with a laugh, "You know, that Scalopini guy, the guy who's buying the store, he's gonna be there. Don't tell me you forgot?".

Virginia went on to describe the details as stated in the announcement in the paper, and all the other many things she had heard around town about the new owner. As all of those words were coming out of Virginia's mouth, Mandy's head was filling up and at a certain point, she could no longer hear, as if she had gone deaf, and checked out. When Virginia's mouth stopped moving, Mandy knew that she had stopped talking, and said a perfunctory "Bye, see you later" and headed home.

To say that Stan was greeted with warm and open arms upon arriving home that early evening would be somewhat inaccurate. What followed for him was a hair-raising interrogation, that centered around the topic of "How fucking crazy are you?"

Mandy railed at him for over two grueling hours, expressing her dissatisfaction with his sense of right and wrong, his I.Q. level, his sense of decency, his utter lack of anything resembling common sense. It was a large, all-inclusive, and in-depth critique, delivered at a very high decibel level, highlighting Stan's many former mis-steps, lost opportunities, and his inability or unwillingness to make even the smallest correct decision. She probably went overboard, it is fair to say, but her inner rage had finally reached the surface. Wisely, Stan did not offer up any argument or resistance to the drubbing he took, but sat listening, actually making eye contact throughout, knowing he had crossed a significant line.

When at last, Mandy had exhausted herself, Stan stood up, walked a few steps toward her, but not too close, and humbly and sincerely said, "I'm sorry I let you down".

Mandy, all too used to Stan's impressive array of defense mechanisms, was caught up short with his simple admission. She broke out in an explosion of tears, trying to explain herself through her sobbing.

Stan stayed put, saying over and over, "Yes, I know, I know".

When Mandy could finally catch her breath and talk intelligibly, she stated, in a calm voice, "Maybe this crazy idea of yours is supposed to increase business, like your other ideas, I dunno, but maybe you've gone too far this time Stan. I'm worried about you".

These words, perhaps more than any others, hurt Stan deeply, for he realized he had finally managed to shake Mandy's belief in him. He knew that their relationship could probably endure most anything, but if she no longer believed in him as a person, there wasn't much left. He could only nod sadly at her last comment. She headed to the bedroom, and he went to his usual place on the couch, picked up the remote, and withdrew into the millions of pixels on the flat screen,

Stan knew he had to do a quiet tactical retreat when it came to combat with Mandy. He knew that once the meet and greet was over, and the rest of the plan played out, she would come around, and realize that her boyfriend was something of a marketing genius. But for now, he had to walk around the house as if avoiding land mines. She was usually up and gone for work by seven, and her exit was announced by the door slamming, not a word out of her. Knowing the coast was clear, he got ready for work and took off as well.

With one day to go before the meet and greet, Stan spent most of the day before double-checking his inventory, anticipating an upsurge in sales in certain categories. He also prepped the area in the store where Mike Scalopini would sit and greet the guests. He cleared off a table that was on the opposite side of the store from the register counter. It would house the snacks and cans of soda. He dusted, polished and arranged the entire vignette, pulling a tall chair over into position, and covering it with a horse blanket and a soft cushion, and draping the nearby window with a shear red curtain borrowed from Mandy's linen closet, as if awaiting a dignitary from a distant exotic land.

Dave and Gary gave him wide berth, exchanging glances with one another.

The next morning was the fateful day, and there was some light rain, but Stan seemed oblivious to that as he stepped out of his car and made it inside the store, laden with a large box full of snacks and cans of soda. "They're two more in the car, if you could go get them, please…?" he said to Dave.

Gary's shift wouldn't begin until eleven, and only three customers were in the store, all seeming to know what they wanted and not needing any help.

Bob was seated at his usual place, writing notes to himself.

Allen entered in a bigger rush that usual, grabbed two spade shovels, and flew out, slapping cash on the register counter, and belting out "Keep the change!" as he hurried out. He hadn't even paused long enough to make a chess move.

Dave came up the stairs with the two additional boxes, and plopped them down on the counter. There were packs of party snacks, covering the gamut from sliced cheeses, chopped veggies, cold cuts, crackers, cookies, dips, chips, diet and regular sodas.

The big surprise came out of the Printing Palace box that Stan carried in from the trunk of his car. He had picked it up first thing. He bustled over to the table, pushed aside some of the snacks Dave had already arranged so neatly, and started pulling small paperback books out of the box, stacking them in three piles. There must've been a hundred of them. Stan was very hyper, mumbling inaudibly to himself. He stood back, took in the whole scene, and rubbed his hands together approvingly. He looked back at Dave with a feverish grin, saying, "Yes, this is it. We did it!" and then scurried over near the register.

Dave, thinking about the "we", and trying to look as nonchalant as he could, slipped over to the table and picked up one of the books. It had an amateurishly drawn illustration of a farmhouse and barn, with a little fence out front, and a couple of horses. There was a skyline in the background of a large city, was it New York?

The title and author were the surprise: "In the Middle of It, My Life and Times Up Until Now" by

Mike Scalopini. "This is getting to be way too creepy", thought Dave, knowing that Stan was no doubt the author and artist. Dave flipped open the book to check out the first few pages, and it looked like a regular and normal book, with a chapter listing, an "about the author" page, and then the chapters, fifteen of them, page count of 231 pages, but of course, there was nothing regular or normal about this. Dave slowly put the book back on the stack and pivoted his head slowly toward Stan, who was still over at the counter, busily arranging and neatening, until perfectly positioned, the business card holder and spare change dish next to the register. Dave stared at his friend, but did not want to make any sudden moves or talk loudly, as if he had come upon a large Brown Bear in the woods. Stan seemed content, whistling while he worked, but Dave's eyes were growing very large, and scared.

Dave's concentration was momentarily interrupted by Bob, standing in front of him.

"You guys carry any electronic type stuff, radio stuff?"

Dave, tilting his head so he could keep a steady eye on Stan, mumbled by rote, "No, we don't, just regular household electric goods, but maybe you should try going over to ABC Electronics Equipment, they'll probably have all that kind of stuff", finally looking at Bob.

Bob with a "Hrumph" shuffled toward the door, and then loudly to no one in particular, "You guys oughta carry basic electronic stuff, not all this other shit" and away he went. Stan had vanished.

Perhaps he was in the back, or on the deck? Dave wasn't sure. He walked over to behind the counter, rang some folks up, and after they left, the store became very still and quiet. It was just Dave and the store and the table over in the corner, heaped with snacks and books, and the ceremonial chair. It was almost eleven in the morning, and the time was nearing.

Gary showed up, hung his cardigan on a hook, and immediately noticed the table and chair set up. Dave motioned to him, and they huddled behind the barrel of brooms over in the corner, as a blind,

"You're, tellin' me, *what?*" said Gary, his eyes growing wide.

"I'm telling you Stan has lost it, he's snapped", replied Dave. He continued, "Go look if you don't believe me, it's a damn book, written by the fake guy, Scalopini".

Gary, still having a hard time accepting this, walked over to the table, snatched a book off the stack, and thumbed thru it quickly, glancing up every few seconds, scouting for Stan. After a minute he stopped, carefully placed the book back on top of the stack, and dashed back over to Dave, still hiding behind the brooms. In a loud whisper he said to Dave, "Oh my Lord, you're right, he's gone haywire. What do we do?"

Dave said, "Well, I've been thinking about this for a while, and we gotta be careful, because I think Stan is real delicate right now, sort of on the edge or something…here's an idea, what if we intercept Ray out in the parking lot, tell him to go home, maybe give him some cash or something".

Gary said, "Could work I suppose, but I hate to think what Stan would do if he found out, and he *would* find out", and added for emphasis, "Stan, he'd go apeshit".

Dave considered this for a moment and agreed, "Yeah, you're right, this boat has already sailed I guess".

Gary and Dave fell into a long silence, both examining what their options were.

Dave broke the silence, having reached a conclusion, "We are totally screwed, there's nothing we can do at this point, we should've stopped him a week ago".

Gary could only nod in agreement.

Dave said, "Okay, this is what we'll do, we let this whole thing blow over, act like there's not a thing in the world wrong, and once it's all done, we'll clean up, and then go over to Stan, and just tell him he's gotta stop, he's gotta come clean, tell everybody it was just a big joke, and maybe most folks will be okay with that?"

Gary, nervous and not overly convinced, said, "Yeah, okay I guess, I don't think they're any good choices left, so yeah, we'll just do that and then maybe we can talk him down, go get him drunk or something, ha!"

"Okay then, that's our plan", said Dave.

"Not much of a plan but it's all we got", said Gary. "Besides which, I'll bet hardly anybody even shows up".

And there was a good chance of that, for the light rain earlier in the morning had now become a hard rain, which meant that no matter how many free snacks are put out, and no matter what the level of curiosity is, rain always frustrates attendance.

A few minutes later, Stan walked up the stairs to the store with Ray, both of them getting drenched by a cloudburst. Apparently, Stan had been in his Corolla with Ray, and had explained what the set up was, what to say, what not to say, and so forth. He further briefed him on the book, detailing a few things Stan had put in it for Ray to know about himself as Mike Scalopini. Things such as, where he was born, about school and work, his wife and her crocheting, and that he had big plans for the store renovation, and was undecided about which way to take it, "maybe tires, maybe clothing, maybe specialty canned and bottled jams and jellies, he just wasn't too sure".

The stage was set: Ray as Mike, sat in the chair, dressed in slacks and a white dress shirt Stan had bought him for the occasion. He also got him a tie but at the last minute decided it was a little too dressy, and Ray took it off. It was noon. Not a soul in sight other than the four men, all waiting for the curious to appear. The rain had lightened up. Then it was five after noon. Still as a graveyard. And then it began. Just a trickle at first, and then a flood. A wide assortment of Tipp City regulars started coming in.

Some were familiar faces to Stan and the boys, while others were total strangers. But come they did. In pairs, as families of four, solo, some dressed up, others fresh from work, and with the surge came a shaft of sunlight through the storm clouds, as if on cue. The rain had stopped and been replaced by a beautiful spring afternoon, with the temperature in the low seventies. Ideal. When it came to direct questions about his wife or Brooklyn, "Mike" would make a wisecrack or pretend he hadn't heard the question, and keep talking about his plans for the store. More than one person in line had noticed that, and thought it odd.

For Dave and Gary, the success of the event was not a good thing. For Stan, it was the perfect event.

For the following four hours and forty-seven minutes (they ran over due to the large response) Ray sat in his chair, signed his book, fielded questions expertly about the store's future, and reiterated over and over, how unlikely it would be for him to continue it as a hardware store. "*Very* unlikely".

Stan couldn't have been more pleased with Ray's performance and when it was all over, and the snacks had been entirely consumed, the stack of books (retailing at $9.99) had dwindled to only fourteen (eighty-six sold at 9.99 = $839.16 minus the cost of printing brought the experience to a net profit of $293.06). Stan immediately realized that he could have charged $14.99 and done considerably better, but that was okay, for the main goal of planting the seed in the minds of the public had been accomplished, better than he had expected.

Stan had asked Dave and Gary to keep count of how many folks had come in, but they had been too busy cowering behind the counter to keep track. They just knew it was a lot. Stan didn't keep count either, as he had been too busy glad-handing and talking remorsefully about how badly he felt that their local hardware store was most likely going to go away, and that he was going to make a change in his life, doing something else, he wasn't too sure what, but something, and he hoped people would be able to adjust to shopping at Chuck's even though it was far less personable and the customer service was mediocre.

Meanwhile, during all of this, Mike Scalopini carried on, a small pile of Extra peppermint foil gum wrappers growing on the floor next to him. Everyone seemed to have bought the show, perhaps some more than others, but seeing the real guy in person made all the difference, even for those on the fence.

The lone exception to this was crafty old Bob, dressed in his usual flannel and jeans, leaning up against the Coca-Cola machine in the corner. He was out of most people's line of sight and had kept a steady eye on the proceedings. It's not that he knew about the trick, or recognized Ray, or knew anything about anything, but he sensed something was just not right. Once in a while he'd glance over at Dave and Gary, and see how they were doing their best to stay clear of the action. Something was up, something was definitely up, he just couldn't figure out what.

Noticeably absent from the festivities was Mandy. Around one o'clock she had driven up and parked, looking through her windshield at the commotion inside. She had very mixed feelings about the entire affair. On the one hand she wanted to support Stan in his latest marketing gimmick, no matter how outlandish, but on the other, she thought it was maybe too outlandish, too deceitful, and she was tired, just plain tired of it all. She discreetly approached the store, and looked in a side window. She saw Scalopini, just as Virginia had said, saw the table of refreshments and a line of people waiting to talk to the "new owner" and have their books signed, some wanting selfies, and saw Stan nearby, arms folded, with a beaming smile. She couldn't talk herself into going inside, and left, feeling a strange new sense of separation from her longtime boyfriend. Once home, she managed to temporarily overcome her sadness, with a nice hot soak in a bubble bath and a glass of Pinot Blanc. Make that, three glasses.

Chapter 7

It didn't take long for Harriet Trowner over at the Chronicle, to get wind of the turnout over at Stan's. She had only one field reporter, the young and enthusiastic Mateo Escalante, working part time at the paper while enrolled at Edison State Community College in Piqua, about thirteen miles away, taking general required courses to get his A.A., with an eye toward a journalism major. His schooling took up a lot of his time but he felt fortunate to have gotten hired onto the paper, so he could venture out to cover various local events. The timing worked out so he could take his camera and notepad to the Klan march of last week, and there, spotted Mandy across the street, but by the time he was able to cross, she had gone. He had wanted a juicy quote.

Unfortunately, his schedule did not allow for him to attend the Scalopini meet and greet, as he was obliged to help his uncle set up and run a yard sale. A few of their yard-sailors had come from the event over at Stan's and had told Mateo about it, but second-hand news would not qualify for an article. He knew, to be the best cub reporter he could be, he would need to show some resourcefulness and get himself over to the store as soon as he could, before the story went cold.

Stan had gotten home that Saturday night late, to a dark house, Mandy already asleep, no dinner left out for him as was the norm, so he figured he best not disturb her. He watched "Dr. Phil" at a very low volume while polishing off a bag of chips with salsa, then bunked out on the couch.

Arriving at the store the next morning to open up, he made his way up the stairs, and waiting for him was the always eager Mateo. "Good morning, Mr. Hurts".

"Stan, just Stan, thanks Mateo", he replied as he unlocked the door and went in, Mateo close behind.

Stan flicked on some lights, and did a once-over of the place, noticing abandoned paper plates, cups, and napkins tucked away on various shelves and displays. He had told Dave and Gary to go on home and that he would clean up. He hadn't cleaned up as nearly as well as he had thought, and as he walked around, a small waste basket in hand, he bought some time, wondering what the purpose of Mateo's visit was. Could he know that Scalopini was fake?

Mateo followed him around like a puppy, at first silently and then asking him all about the event, about Mr. Scalopini, and seeking details about when exactly Stan was going to close up the store, and when exactly Mr. Scaloplini was planning on opening his? During this, Mateo had picked up the book and was thumbing through it, noticing the abundance of typos, misspellings and many other errors on every page. Obviously, Mateo thought, Scalopini was not overly-educated, or had a terrible editor.

Stan, relieved that his cover was not blown, had all the routine answers down pat, and delivered them to Mateo one after another. Mateo thanked him for his time and exited, leaving Stan with an uneasy feeling.

Turns out, editor-in-chief Trowner had decided about two weeks prior, to start doing featured articles about current newsworthy trends in town, and in the general region. She wanted to highlight "change" in the weekly paper. She felt that her reading public ought to be better informed as to what was headed their way, whether it be a new shopping center being approved, a significant shake-up at city hall, or something to do with an issue that would affect real estate values, perhaps an issue concerning polluters or another farm being consumed by outsiders. She wanted her paper to transcend stories about Beefsteak tomatoes or fertilizers, or what some third grader had painted. She wanted her paper to be more of a verb than a noun. She felt it had become too static and routine, concentrating on the drab and obvious for far too long, and wanted to jazz it up. She also knew that in so doing, it might attract new readership and increased sales of ad space, which had been on the decline these last couple of years. In this respect, both Stan's and the Chronicle were on parallel tracks.

Trowner had decided, upon reading Mateo's rough draft about the demise of Stan's, and the introduction of a whole new type of store, that it had the potential to tentacle out and affect many people, perhaps positively, perhaps negatively. She decided this was the perfect candidate for her first article, ripe with potential for speculation, and for exploiting fear of the unknown, her two specialties. She instructed Mateo to go back and dig some more, get some insider info, something that would arch eyebrows, especially as there seemed to be an air of mystery surrounding it. If she needed to embellish a little, that was fine with her.

So again, Mateo ventured out to pay Stan a visit, at his very first opportunity, which would be after Psychology 101 the next day, which ended at 2:00, putting Mateo on the doorstep of Stan's at 2:27, pen, pad, and camera in hand.

Stan was not overly thrilled to see Mateo again. He didn't want to offer up any more details or behind the scenes revelations to the young journalist, mostly because he hadn't made any further details up. As hard as Mateo tried to bend the conversation to what the new owner was up to, Stan tried equally hard to redirect, and talk about the loss to the community and how sorry he was. Mateo, summoning up his courage and interview tactics, could smell a good story, and began to get more aggressive with Stan, pushing him to reveal the *real* reason he was leaving, the *real* reason he wouldn't talk about what Scalopini was up to. The more Stan insisted there was nothing beyond face value going on, the more Mateo was convinced there was.

Mateo at last eased off, thanking Stan for the time and left. Mateo knew he was sitting on a live bomb, and couldn't wait to get back to Harriet and tell her about it. There was "something very fishy about this Scalopini guy", Mateo thought. "After all", he said to Trowner, "it is an *Italian* name, and you know what that could mean...". As if slapped in the face, Trowner instantly knew what that could mean.

By the time Mateo polished off his fifth draft, with Harriet lurking over his shoulder in the "Press Room", which was also Harriet's office, Sally's office, the lunch room, and storage room, the article had grown in size, giving a comprehensive profile of Stan Hurts and his store, plus a generous amount of ink given to speculation, much of it spurious, about Mike Scalopini and his farm animal-crocheting wife, Judy. It was obvious to anyone who knew the whole truth, which was limited to Stan, Dave and Gary, that Harriet had over-reached in a very big way, and by doing so, she was continuing to parallel Stan, using fiction to promote.

The article achieved its primary goal, to attract readers to the paper. The story went big. For the first time in years, the paper had to do a second printing and re-stock paper racks all over town. Their online presence was amateurish and not user-friendly, as Harriet had never embraced or properly funded the whole idea of an electronic newspaper, but in spite of that, many gobbled up the news that way as well. People all over town could be seen with their noses in their laptops and cell phones. Trowner had put a spin on the story, implying that Scalopini might have ties to the underworld. It didn't take much for the pace to pick up after that.

With the Chronicle's unexpected boost, Stan's gambit was turning into a runaway hit, as more and more people came into the store. But there was a hitch that was not part of the plan. Trowner had lit a fire. People came in, not to mourn the imminent death of the hardware store, but to inquire with Stan as to why he had gone into a deal with such a questionable and sketchy character as this "Scalopini guy, if that even was his real name?" as one customer put it. The perceived inconvenience of losing Stan's, was eclipsed by the general public's sense of peril of over losing Stan's. Their very welfare and safety seemed at stake.

"To hell with the nails and paint, what type of person are you unleashing on us, Stan?" was the composite outcry.

"Don't you care about us?"

"What's the matter with you?"

"Are you crazy?"

Perhaps the most impassioned protest came from Anita Sanders. While flinging her recently purchased beach chair into the store, in front of a group of wide-eyed customers, she screamed "This guy's some kind of a mobster, isn't he? He's going to end up destroying our town, you just watch! This is just the beginning! Thanks Stan, thanks for nothing" and stormed away, not even asking for a refund for the red, yellow, green, and blue cabana-striped three-position extra-wide beach chair with wooden arms, padded headrest, cup holder, back-pack straps, made with Sunbrella marine-grade fabric. It was a very nice one, and not cheap.

Frozen in this moment, Stan came to the realization that maybe, just maybe, things were not turning out quite as he had planned, and perhaps his runaway hit had turned into a runaway train.

Next came the Weekly with a reporter to do a small follow-up, and then the big guns, in the form of the Dayton Dispatch, sent a senior field reporter to Stan's, accompanied by a photographer. Both papers were now in a race with the Chronicle to the bottom. In particular, the reporter from the Dispatch was exceptionally rude, while allowing unauthorized photos of everything in sight, all the while pushing Stan about the "truth".

Stan pushed back, saying that Scalopini was a good guy, wasn't up to anything under-handed or dangerous, that he was a good solid citizen, "and wouldn't you rather talk about the loss of the hardware store?"

"No" was the simple answer given.

Stan knew that a monster had been created, or was about to be created once the Dispatch article hit in a few days. This was not part of the plan. True enough, Stan had created the seed of it, but thanks to Harriet, it had metastasized into something un-recognizable.

After the Dayton Dispatch people left is when Dave and Gary saw their opening. Stan seemed down in the dumps, maybe beaten, and they wanted to take this moment, when he was weak and demoralized, to talk him out of pursuing his scheme a moment longer, to get him to confess to the community about making up this ridiculous and now out of control promotion, his "joke".

Stan was incensed, and felt they had betrayed him, were no longer his loyal friends. Explosively he yelled, "You both should get out and not come back!".

They were shocked, never having seen their usually soft-spoken and depressed store owner lash out like that.

Dave had reached his breaking point weeks ago, but held on out of a deep sense of loyalty, but now, his friend was so far gone, so committed to this insane idea to such a degree, he wanted out, was embarrassed and wanted no part of it, did not want anyone to associate him with this scheme.

Gary was not nearly the committed friend to Stan that Dave was, but in an old-fashioned kind of a way, felt a sense of duty to Stan and to the store, as if it were a ship, and Stan the Captain. Well, Stan was not much of a Captain and this ship was breaking up on the rocks as far as Gary could tell, so whatever loyalty the two may have had for Stan or the store, was now evaporated, and both took their exit, heading directly to Das Lunas Mexican Bar and Grill to share two pitchers of margaritas. It seemed that many of the people in Stan's orbit were wrapping up their days' drinking.

Stan stood alone in the store, with none of the regulars seated at the counter. It was almost closing time, so he folded up early, carrying the merchandise in from the deck, ringing out the register, turning off the heat, checking that the back freight doors were locked, hitting the lights, and about a dozen other little things as part of the closing routine.

All of this gave him some time to reflect on the state of things, from him and Mandy, to him and Dave, and to where he was now. During Mandy's lambasting, she had called him "unseemly", which he figured was bad since it started with "un". He confirmed that later when he looked it up: "Not fit or decent". That about summed it up.

People who knew him well, knew the whole thing to be a hoax, and disapproved of him fiercely. Those who didn't know him nearly as well, seemed excited and curious about the change about to happen, while others had grown suspicious, thanks to Trowner and her colleagues. He was enjoying some celebrity but was paying a big price for it. The plan had started out pretty good he thought, but it became too unwieldy thanks to all the press, and it had taken on a life of its own, and now everything in his life seemed in ruins. This is not the sort of thing a person prone to depression, needs. But Stan was not ordinarily the type to blame self-made problems on others, and this was no exception. He knew he had screwed up, had done a lot to undermine his closest relationships, and it all circled back to one thing: failure. If he could only devise a way to turn this whole ridiculous thing around so he could not fail, but succeed in creating what he had set out to do. He desired to reap the benefit of the community's love and support. He paced back and forth in the empty dark store, up and down the aisles, talking to himself and the cans of turpentine, paint brushes, and the garden hoses, for he knew he could find a way to turn this mess around.

Exhausted and beaten down after two hours of brow beating himself, with no good ideas being hatched, he went out the door, locked up, went to his car and headed home. Again, he came home to a dark house, no dinner left out, the cold war had evidently gone into full swing. The chips and salsa having been depleted, he turned to a bowl of mixed nuts and a couple of beers. He settled on some "Monk" reruns to end his day, and fell asleep, a bowl of nuts upended on his chest, half a bottle of beer perched sideways at his side, and drifted off to a cheery night of scary figures chasing him down a dark trail in the forest, instead of a dark alleyway, for a change of pace.

A few more days followed, fairly uneventful, save the fact Stan was working the store alone which was counter-balanced by many fewer visitors. Things were going into a lull, with the Chronicle, and copycat Weekly articles, fading in people's memories but the Dayton Dispatch article about to break. "Who knows? Maybe they'll decide that there's not enough there-there, and not do the article, and Stan will be spared the effects of further yellow journalism?" he thought out loud to himself, in third person. He was doing a lot of that lately.

"What was worse?", Stan thought, "for the Scalopini narrative to keep living or to tell everyone the truth?" It seemed that the obvious choice was to keep the Scalopini story alive, for the truth would surely destroy him and do the opposite of setting him free.

Stan soon got his answer. The Dayton Dispatch published their article about Stan, his store, Scalopini, and the projected future of all. The article's headline was subtle:

MAFIA COMING TO TIPP CITY?

The paper had to print an additional eight thousand copies. Their online site crashed twice.

Stan thought, "At least it's not on the front page". It was proclaimed the "story of the year" by some, and "worthy of a Pulitzer" by the Dayton mayor. And there were photos. The photographer had shot so many of Stan, that many had caught him in mid-sentence, or making a split-second grimace or dour expression. The paper chose the least flattering ones.

As for the public reaction, complete mayhem was unleashed upon the quaint little neighborhood hardware store, with people clamoring for more details. There were many more visitors than buyers, practically all of them total strangers to him, as if Stan's was a new destination, an unexplored "mystery spot".

Stan had now been shoved into the sidelines of his story, with the now infamous Mike Scalopini taking center stage. Any attempt by Stan to come clean would now only raise more suspicion and ridicule, as it had become too late for the truth. Initially, the story spread to other cities, other states, but then faded, as many news outlets tried searching for Scalopini throughout Ohio, New York, and Illinois, but could not locate him, or find any record of his name. But it all made sense, as Lanaro put it while applying some dye to a customer's hair, "This guy is a mob guy, maybe a capo, so what, he's gonna use, his real name?"

When Stan went home at night, he was no longer greeted by a dark house. Mandy would be up, at her computer or chatting on the phone. She'd point at a pan on the stove indicating his dinner. She was no longer overtly mad at him, just passively mad at him. At least it was an improvement. He would try to engage her in talk and she would politely have just remembered there was "something she had to do" in the next room. She didn't raise her voice, didn't question him, was not sarcastic or biting, but instead treated him like he was some distant cousin visiting, one that she didn't particularly like, but felt obliged to be polite toward. It made Stan, a person with an uneasy personality and delicate self-esteem, all the more uneasy and brittle.

Then, two days later, he awoke exhausted. He hadn't had his usual parade of nightmares or could even remember getting up in the night to visit the bathroom. He was spent. He simply couldn't bear another day of being riddled with questions at the store, being indirectly accused of aiding and abetting a criminal, and all the while, experiencing record-low sales. He figured, "I will go fishing". He crafted a crude hand written sign on cardboard and taped it to the inside of the glass front door of the store. "Gone Fishing", simple as that. And fishing he went.

The moment he was behind the wheel of his trusty Corolla, he felt a great sense of freedom. He moved down the road, buzzed past the yellow missile house, hung a right and headed to his favorite fishing spot along Honey Creek. The Corolla didn't like the bumps in the dirt road but before long, he found himself all alone by the creek, surrounded by Sycamores. He heard the burbling water over the rocks as he opened up the trunk to grab his gear, not used in over two years. A rush of boyish excitement washed over him, leaving all the nastiness and darkness behind. He managed his way over some small round rocks, down a dusty trail and to the creek's edge. Nobody in sight. Heaven. He expertly tied a venerable Ducktail Jig lure on his line, as if he had been doing it every day. A bare single hook with Velveeta often did the trick, but for a change, he thought he'd try the lure as well, to make things more interesting. He threw his line in the water, moved over to a comfortable-looking rock, sat down and waited, watching his bobber. The fly fishing was better upstream, with wide and slow moments in the creek's flow, but it was a much longer drive and he was so anxious to be out in it. This spot would do just fine for today, doing a little simple stream fishing. And then there was tomorrow! Who knows how long he'd keep the store closed up? Maybe days? Maybe for a week, or more! He could do anything he wanted, for he was now free. If only that could remain the case, it would indeed be wonderful, he thought.

When the day was nearly over, the dusk thinking of coming on, his belly demanding some food, Stan packed up his gear, having caught and released no less than eight good-sized Rainbow Trout. He had thought he had hooked a Steelhead for a moment, but then realized it was just another Rainbow. That was okay, it was all about the strategy of the hunt, not the catch.

He drove back down the dirt road, the sky turning orange, and stopped at the Dairy Queen for a double cheeseburger, fries and a chocolate malt. He felt like he was twenty, with the entire universe of the future spread out before him. He knew of course he wasn't, and it wasn't, but he so enjoyed the feeling of not being oppressed, depressed, leaned on, pushed around, and underwater. He had had such a good day, he decided that absolutely, he would do it again tomorrow. Maybe he'd discover a whole new fishing whole up Honey Creek or some other creek altogether? He chomped on his last French fry, dabbed in a mix of ketchup and mustard, politely cleaned up his table, and went home.

Mandy's behavior was the same as it had been lately, but he could tell she knew something was different about him. For a change, he did not try to engage her in any conversation, but instead, complimented her on her hair, which he never used to do. She took the compliment guardedly, figuring he was about to say something stupid, but he didn't.

The creek turned out to be his salvation, however temporarily. He would return there for many days straight. It was perfect for him, with the breeze through the trees, the hours spent looking into the dark blue flowing water, and only the rare sighting of another fisherman. It was for him the perfect therapy. He saw deer drinking in a pool downstream a few feet, unaware of Stan sitting on a rock in the shade. He watched birds flitting about, and a family of Raccoons having a drink. One afternoon he even got to see some River Otters playing in a small waterfall. This all made for exquisite days, and peaceful nights.

On the horizon, the twists and turns of happenstance, of coincidence, or what some call destiny, were waiting in the wings for Stan, as his storyline does not end here.

On day number ten, Stan decided to venture to the store and see what's what. He pulled up, went up the stairs, and saw a small pile of papers and cards, deposited in front of the door. His "Gone Fishing" sign was still taped to the inside of the glass door. He opened the door, carrying the papers, and with his boot, shoved aside the small pile of mail on the floor that had collected below the mail slot. He locked the door behind him and went to the back room, reading an assortment of messages, hand written by an assortment of his customer base, many unhinged, all gravitating in content around the same two general themes: "Dump Scalopini", and "Go fuck yourself!"

He had been hoping his days off fishing might allow for a cooling down period, and a turnaround in the attitude of his retail constituents. Maybe he'd end up the hero after all? He needed to turn all that anger around, turn it into energy, use it to his advantage. That part of it he knew, but as to how to reach that goal, he was lost.

There came a rap on the glass front door. It was an insistent tap tap tap tap tap. Louder and louder. "Who in the hell could that be?" thought Stan as he strode to the front. A delivery? Mandy? Dave or Gary? Somebody with a flat tire? Someone in distress? He came pretty close with that last guess. It was none other than Neil Riptick, staring at him with his beady eyes through the glass. "Oh yeah, the rent", Stan thought to himself.

"It completely slipped my mind", he said to Riptick, unlocking the door and allowing the obviously stressed-out landlord to enter. He added, "Hey, I'm sorry about the late rent, really, but believe it or not, I have it, all of it. I know it's six days late, well, two months and six days, but really, I'll just cut you a check right now".

Riptick stood rigidly, staring at Stan. After an uncomfortable silence he said, "You think I drove all this way to just collect a rent check? Is that what I am to you, an errand boy?"

"Well, no, no, I didn't mean that, I just meant..." said Stan apologetically.

Riptick shot back, "Yeah, yeah, I know - I'm not here for just that, Hurts, I'm here about something else. You know what I am talking about, right?"

Stan thought to himself for a moment, fidgeting with some of the notes he had been reading, and then, bam, the obvious hit him. "You mean the Scalopini thing?"

Derisively, Riptick said, "Yes, the Italian guy thing. What kind of bullshit are you trying to pull Hurts? You must think I'm the biggest idiot you ever met?" Riptick's volume rose, veins on his forehead bulging. "You think for one lousy second, I'm going to let you lease this place out to somebody else? You know, or *should* know, that in your lease, on page five, paragraph two, it specifically states you cannot sublease without my written permission. You are aware of that little tiny small unimportant detail?"

Stan, mumbled, "Maybe I did, I don't really remember, could be, if you say so, must be true..."

"Are you fucking nuts, trying to get away with this? And I don't give a flying fuck if this guy is a mob guy or not, I eat those bastards up for lunch. Mob guy, my ass"

Those were a lot of questions, and a lot of statements, and Stan mentally sorted through them one by one. At last, he had his wits and replied, "I'm not. No. No. And No."

"What're you, some kind of a comedian?" blared Riptick.

"Well, no, I wasn't trying to be funny, it's just that I..."

Riptick laid into him again, his blood pressure maxing out, "It's just that I, it's just that I...save the bullshit, and tell me you haven't actually been stupid enough to make a deal with this Scalpino, Scelapenni"

"Scalopini" said Stan, delicately correcting him.

Riptick continued, "Scalo-who gives a shit? Well, what is it? I'm gonna have to sue the shit out of you, kick your ass out, or what?"

"No, no, not necessary, really, I can fix it, really" said Stan, not knowing what in the hell to say next. He "knew he had to throw water on this situation and fast. Just when things were drifting back in his direction, Riptick has to come unglued and blow it up again, what is Stan going to do?"

Stan had been so used to being by himself up at the creek, that he had gotten used to talking quietly to himself, sometimes in third person, muttering his way through thoughts. Without realizing, he had thought aloud, much to Riptick's astonishment. It actually made Riptick stop talking, and just stare at Stan, mouth agape.

After a couple of beats, Riptick managed to say, "Oh Jesus, Hurts, you've gone all looney, haven't you?"

Stan, not sure if he had gotten that call right or not, lamely said, "No, I don't think so...".

Riptick reached into his coat's inner pocket, and pulled out an envelope, addressed to Stan. "It's your lucky day asshole" said Riptick. Waving the envelope in front of Stan, he went on, "This here is an evict notice, for you" and handed the envelope over to Stan. He continued, "You have a choice my friend. You can either get the hell out of here in thirty days, for violating the terms of the lease, or you can pay an increase in rent with a new lease, a *big* increase, or you can go to hell".

Stan considered the options and then said, "What about the fourth option?"

"What fourth option?" said Riptick nastily.

"Well, seems to me I haven't violated the lease by leasing to somebody else, because it hasn't happened yet, and I didn't sign anything with Scalopini, not yet, it's all verbal, so I haven't really violated anything, right?"

Riptick, taken aback, said, "...Go on..."

"If I tell Scalopini the deal is off, then I haven't broken my lease, and if I hand you the rent check right now, all of it, I'm good on that too, is how I see it, right?"

Riptick, who had rehearsed his insults, threats, and his ultimatum the whole way there, stared at Stan, wanting to kill him with a laser beam coming out of his eyes. After a long hard stare, Riptick said in a low voice, "You step out of line one more time, just one more time, and you are history". And then, looking around, added, "This dumb little store, who are you kidding anyway?" And with that, Riptick turned and walked out the door into the morning light, got in his Lincoln, and took off.

Stan looked at him do his tactical retreat, and said out loud, "I gotta hand it to him, that was a pretty good exit".

Stan opened up the doors to the place, carried out the deck displays, greeted Bob as he took his stool, and greeted the smattering of customers, mostly workers needing to pick up some additional supplies for their jobs, and began to think through his situation. What it all boiled down to was this: Riptick had to be convinced that the Scalopini deal was off. The customers in the area had to be convinced that the deal was off. But due to all the press he had received, so much of it false and distorted, it wouldn't be nearly good enough for him to simply state that Scalopini had pulled out, or that he had decided to cancel the deal with him. Nobody would believe him at this point. He had done too good a job faking people out.

Stan had to come up with another angle, something much more dramatic. He needed a way to get rid of Scalopini that did not make Stan look like the bad guy, for it would leave permanent scars, and lingering doubts about Stan's honesty and integrity, that would hurt, not help, his business. His self-esteem couldn't get any lower, so whatever insults were hurled at him next, didn't matter, that was a non-issue. But the important thing is he had to fix the Scalopini situation. Somehow, he knew, Scalopini had to go away, and not on an airplane, or go back to Brooklyn, but go away permanently, slamming the door shut on all future speculation. Stan realized that there was only one way to get rid of the mobster that was about to take over the town. He had to be whacked.

Chapter 8

Stan had never murdered anyone, or had ever plotted to do so. The fact that the intended victim did not exist, further complicated matters. Fortunately, killing an imaginary person was not a crime, so he didn't have to find ways to evade the police after the deed was done, but seeing as how many were convinced Scalopini was real, the evidence that he was dead had to be real, without that evidence pointing to Stan. If he only wanted to kill off Scalopini in his mind, he could, with the flick of a switch, but this was different. Stan had to kill him off in such a way that it was believable to both Riptick and his audience of customers. He couldn't just one day say, "Oh, by the way, Mike had a massive coronary, dropped dead at his favorite mafioso restaurant" and that would be that. Not only had the three papers turned Scalopini into the Tipp City Godfather, but Stan's vague but plausible descriptions of Scalopini beforehand to many dozens, and then with people meeting him at the store, some buying his book, had cemented everyone's impression that this guy was an actual real person, with a sweet wife who crocheted. Of course, they believed it. What kind of a sick person would make all of this up?

Stan had done a convincing job, and now he had another to do, and it had to be done right. It had to sound and appear irrefutable. Stan had been operating alone in an echo chamber these past few weeks, with no one he could turn to for advice, or to play devil's advocate, let alone help him with the murder, but that was okay, he was used to it.

Many days went by, and Stan had come up with an assortment of ways Scalopini could have died from an accident in the store, such as the entire wall of house paint, hundreds of cans, falling over on top of him, killing him instantly. It was a weak idea from the beginning. Dramatic yes, practical no. Not only would Stan have to sacrifice many gallons of paint, with lids popped open, paint spread all over the floor, but it would necessarily involve a call to the fire department, and the police, to examine the scene, do forensics if they deemed it so, and of course, to take away the crushed body of the deceased.

Stan's mind was in such turmoil that he couldn't at first see that the play-out of the "killed by paint cans" scenario would not work, but he thought this idea through anyway, to be sure he was not overlooking something. Stan had thought of many other similar ideas, but they all required at the end, a crushed, mangled, burnt, or torn-apart body. But as he was a solo thinker, and the thinking not being very clear, he had to drag himself through this and the other five "accidents" either in the store, or the parking lot. He had even thought about having it happen in a nearby field, felled by an aggressive steer. But again, the damn body. At last, Stan concluded that any scenario that involved an accident, that then led to a medical emergency, would lead to the discovery that Scalopini was fictitious, and worse, that Stan was a liar.

And then the obvious finally came to him. What if Scalopini died, but died with no witnesses, and died in such a way that his body was not recoverable? Stan thought of exotic and impractical ideas, like having him fall out of a private Cessna while leaning out of the door too far to snap a scenic shot. But what of the plane? The pilot? Stan went through a variety of these kinds of ideas as well, involving buses, taxi cabs, garbage trucks, and motorcycles, even an escaped lion from the nearby Safari Junction, but realized the death could not come as a result of another party having to be involved, such as a driver, or a pilot, or a zookeeper, or Scalopini's caddie while on the golf course in a lightning storm. It could not involve another person, whether a witness or a murderer, it had to be a solo accident. Clean. And then he remembered his days by Honey Creek.

The creek had many personalities. In most spots, the creek is fairly shallow, not overly wide, but in other spots, it grows to thirty feet across, about six feet deep, and sometimes with swift currents in the middle. When he had been doing his fishing, he had thought about taking up kayaking. He had been daydreaming about lazy afternoons paddling along with the current, taking in the scenery. After all, he sold the things in the store. He had at any given time, about four of them, presently in bright orange, lime, yellow and white. He had one double in stock, and three singles. He sold all the accessories too: paddles, backrests, floatable coolers, sunglasses, sun hats, and gloves. Just about anything a kayaker would want. But it was unlikely anyone would attempt kayaking Honey, for while it did have sections of being wider, deeper, and swifter, to the most part it was a medium-sized creek, not suitable for kayaking for more than a thousand feet at any given point. But then there was the Great Miami River, that runs near to Honey Creek, on the same side of town. In fact, the Honey was a tributary of the Miami. Lots of people do kayaking along the Miami, which is why he carried all those goods. Why not set it up so Scalopini went out to the river, launched himself in a kayak, was a total novice, and apparently drowned and vanished? Maybe by the time this was discovered, his kayak would have drifted for miles downriver, and had not been reported as being found? He thought it totally plausible. The Miami starts at the Indian Lake Reservoir, all the way up at Russel's Point, about fifty miles northeast of Tipp City, and flows southward about thirty miles all the way down to Lawrenceburg, Indiana. About eighty miles in all, before joining forces with the Ohio River and continuing on. Eighty miles is a lot of miles, and there are a thousand places a kayak, drifting aimlessly down the river, could get caught up in a large eddy, disguised by boulders or overhanging trees, or could get wedged underwater by a fallen tree trunk, or grabbed by some resourceful teenagers who had a lucky day down by the river, hauled it home, stuck it in their barn or garage, and neglected to report it. In other words, it would be easy, and maybe likely, that the kayak would vanish, especially if it had been given a head start by having been launched in the late part of the day, and being allowed to drift for hours overnight.

What about the unfortunate novice kayaker? Human bodies are much harder to have disappear. They can show up at the most unfortunate of times and places, and instantly gather swarms of emergency personnel and onlookers, which often leads to the media showing up, and the police, which then leads to the murderer being found if easily solvable, which this would be, which then leads to the perpetrator serving lots of jail time or worse, and well deserved. But this is in the real world, as in "reality", as in there being an actual body to recover from the river.

"What if there is no body in the first place? It must be plausible that no body was found" Stan muttered to himself, feeling that he was on the verge of coming up with a sensational and foolproof idea.

As luck would have it, the Miami River is home to a wide variety of fish, wild birds, and animals. There's Bass, Saugeye, the Crappie, Catfish, Rock Bass, Small Mouth Bass, and the Northern Pike. There are many types of birds as well, from the varieties of Warblers (Chestnut Sided, Yellow Throated, Blue Winged, Cerulean) and so many others, including the Bobwhite, Woodcock, Chickadee and of course, the Northern Cardinal, the state bird. Lots of animals too, from the North American Raccoon, Virginia Opossum, the occasional American Red Fox or Northeastern Coyote, Whitetail Deer, and Northern River Otter. A wide spectrum of nature's abundance on display.

Nestled among all those names is the Northern Pike, often overlooked because there are many fish that make for better eating, and this one is difficult to catch.

The Pike has earned a reputation for being at the top of the food chain in the waters of the Miami. It is a voracious eater, a carnivore, and goes after just about anything imaginable, from small to large. Especially if already dead or dying.

If a Pike, or let's say a school of Pike, were to encounter a dead body in the river, perhaps stuck on a log, they would make short work of it. They could dispatch a mafia kingpin in about a day, with the scraps washing away or falling to the bottom, and vanishing. So, there it was, Stan's new plan: No body, no crime.

But there was one more thing to figure out: If the kayak was recovered, and everyone believed that Scalopini was a real person, including the police, they would as a matter of routine investigation, trace his disappearance back to where he purchased the kayak. If it were recovered, and it would be advantageous to Stan if it were, it would establish evidence of his disappearance, and of his very existence, and it would by all appearances be a new kayak (since it had just come brand new out of Stan's inventory) and not beat up and well-used, which would imply a recent purchase, somewhere. Although only officially seen in public once, at the meet and greet, there was no other evidence that Scalopini existed or owned a kayak. So, to be thorough, the police would want to do an investigation linking the kayak to Scalopini. If they could not come up with a recent and recorded purchase by him of a kayak anywhere near, that might drive their curiosity to look wider, to look deeper, and at some point, conclude that there never had been such a person, which again, would point to Stan being a liar. "So, kayak found, yes, Scalopini found, no" was Stan's plan.

If on the other hand, there was an assertion that he had purchased the kayak someplace, such as at Stan's, then the police would no doubt stop right there, look no further, and be satisfied with having connected the dots? Not likely. They would want to talk to the person who had sold the kayak to him, whether at Stan's or Chuck's, or Walmart in Dayton. This would undoubtedly lead to no evidence, or conflicting evidence, as the police interrogated the alleged cashier multiple times over, looking for inconsistencies. The only way that could work is if it had been Stan who sold him the kayak. Stan could probably do a convincing performance, but could he do it three or seven or fourteen times over, never contradicting himself about what day it had been, what time, the weather, how Scalopini was dressed, and a hundred other details? Not likely. Also, they would want to track down the store's copy of the receipt, trace back the form of payment.

There is no receipt because Scalopini never bought a kayak because Scalopini doesn't exist. Furthermore, all the store's daily register tapes have dates on them, so Stan couldn't ring it up now for a purchase made a week ago.

There would be many places the story could fall apart under scrutiny, and again, it would point to Stan being a liar.

What if no one sold it to him? This question led Stan to the one and only logical choice in this tangled storyline: Scalopini stole the kayak.

The Tipp City Police Department was small, well financed relative to their size, had good people working there, "serving and protecting", had a lot of modern equipment, including newer Ford Interceptors, and smart-looking uniforms. However, what they did not have is an abundance of staff. Unless an unsolved crime had some type of special importance to the department, or to the town as a whole, chances were good it would not stay in their focus very long, as they had so much low hanging fruit to pursue. The case would stay "alive" in their files, but if they hit a dead end, they usually let it stay there. A vested business partner, a son, daughter, or spouse could trigger a closer look, or of course, a widow could.

"Oh shit, I forgot about his wife Judy!" Stan suddenly realized, speaking his thoughts loudly to an empty store. "What am I going to do with her?".

Stan thought his whole plan had been scuttled, but then he realized it didn't take much to convince the town's folk of a "truth". He would simply remind everyone that she had never come to Tipp in the first place, that he had never met her, spoken to her, never seen one of her crocheted animals in person or otherwise, had never even seen a photo of her, and that she had stayed back in Brooklyn, while Mike did all the foot work, and that Stan had heard through the grapevine that she had decided to take a boat tour of Norwegian fjords, or some other damn place, to help heal her tragic loss. She was never in Tipp, and therefore had never been seen by anyone, never photographed, never spoken to, so there was very little to go on in the first place. It seemed air tight to Stan.

Stan had never seen the purpose of installing a burglar alarm at the store, or hiring a service to patrol. It had always seemed an unnecessary expense. He was required by Riptick to carry very basic insurance, but that was mostly about slip and fall claims, and the insurance company did not require that he carry any coverage for theft or damage to his merchandise. However, as part of the lease agreement, Stan had to include damage to the property as part of the policy, which Stan always thought to be unfair, for after all, it wasn't his property, but the landlord's. In any case, George Polanski, one of five lawyers in town, had patiently explained to Stan that the landlord was not in violation of the law by requiring this, that the landlord was taking advantage of Stan, but that practically all landlords take advantage of their tenants, "so join the club". The point was, he didn't have coverage for theft, which is why he did not file a claim, and thus, no paper trail.

Stan needed to document where Scalopini had acquired his kayak, and he figured, if he could at the same time defame the alleged mobster, as a small-time low-class thief, that would make Stan seem better, by comparison. Stan would be a victim, not a perp. The notion of Scalopini busting into his store, would be typical criminal behavior, consistent with the bent-nose image that had been made of him. It had credibility.

Stan decided he would break into his store, and leave behind some kind of evidence that Scalopini had been the thief. Stan had to sacrifice a kayak to do so, but it was well worth the wholesale cost in order to put an end to Scalopini, and this roiling nightmare he had created.

Early the following morning, around three, Stan parked remotely and walked over to his store, dressed all in black, wearing work gloves. He carried with him a large framing hammer which he used to shatter one of the large display windows in the front. He walked in as if the burglar, grabbed the white single kayak, and a paddle, intentionally knocking over some merchandise in the process, dropped a piece of evidence on the floor, and left the way he came in.

He then drove, with the kayak tied to his roof, all the way out of town using dark streets, and parked next to the Miami. He untied the kayak from the roof of his car, and carried it to the river's edge. He took the same hammer and smashed a gaping hole in the bow, as if it had violently struck a rock, and threw it into the current. He carefully rubbed out his footprints, and messed up his tire tracks, jumped back in his car and took off, undetected.

Later that morning, as expected, he was roused awake by a call about his place being broken into. The call came from Harry Johnson, the proprietor of Tipp Bait and Tackle.

"Stan, this is Harry. You best get over here to your place. I was getting myself a couple of donuts over at Paul's and noticed your place had been broken into, looks like". This was said breathlessly by Harry, with a great sense of urgency.

Stan, shocked at the news, thanked Harry, and proceeded to do what a store owner would do in such a situation. He jumped in his car, still in his pajamas with a heavy jacket, and rushed to the scene of the crime.

Sure enough, it looked like some jackass had smashed Stan's front window and helped himself (presumably one guy, not a woman, not a bunch of guys) to a kayak, the son of a bitch. It was then that Stan suddenly realized, he had failed to leave the evidence in an obvious enough place, so he nudged it into the center of an aisle with the toe of his boot.

Stan called the police, and was rehearsing "outrage and shock" as a patrol car showed up, light bar on, no siren. The lone officer was Gladys Williams, a woman of generous proportion and of African-American persuasion, known around town as "Happy Gladys" because she was usually in an upbeat mood.

At this early hour she was not overly happy, but quite business like, as she carefully walked the crime scene, taking copious notes along the way. She had a barrage of questions for Stan of course, all of which he answered expertly. Smashed window break-ins were not all that common in town, so she wanted to capture every morsel of evidence she could. Stan was distraught, shocked, and dismayed that anyone would have done such a thing, and said, as he had rehearsed, "Why did they go after the kayak, walking past the expensive power tools, and Buck Knives?"

Gladys noticed a discarded pack of gum on the floor, it was the Extra brand, peppermint flavor.

"This yours?" she inquired of Stan.

"Nope, not mine" he said.

She picked it up with her latex-gloved hand, and stuck it in a baggie. All the while, she surveyed Stan as he continued naming various expensive items that the burglar did not take. She thought that his over the top behavior, and his well-groomed, and stiffly presented words, were probably due to shock, and nothing else, but she also knew he was an amateur actor, and maybe he was acting, but poorly.

It's true, that Stan, for all of his acting studies, had never learned the simple advice given by Spencer Tracy, as paraphrased: "The best actors are the ones who don't get caught at it".

Stan thought to himself he had pulled off a very believable performance and had not fallen into the trap of overplaying, as with his disastrous "Get the doctor" audition. He thought he had played it just right, not too much, not too little.

Gladys was not as convinced, for she had seen people in distress and shock before, and was giving Stan the benefit of doubt, as this was what Stan was probably and legitimately going through. She was also experienced with people lying to her, and she had gotten pretty good at detecting that. There were all kinds of tells, from body language, the tone of voice, facial expressions, choice of words, distractions, deflections, mis-directions, and it was especially helpful if she already knew the person, which was often the case in a small town, and knew their behavior in a normal everyday situation. She could tell that Stan was possibly outright lying, or lying by omission. There was just *something* about his behavior that did not ring true. This was by no means proof of anything, just Gladys's instincts raising red flags.

She didn't want to tip Stan off that she had any suspicions of him at all, but did ask him generic questions such as to who he thought the burglar could have been, or if there was someone who had a beef with him, or if a recent customer had shown an interest in the white kayak, and so forth. She then folded up her notebook, expressing how sorry she was that he had been broken into, and left.

Stan, having accomplished his award-worthy performance, started to clean up the mess left behind by the burglar. He muttered to himself, "She saw it! She saw it, picked it up, stuck it in her little evidence bag! This is fantastic!"

Turns out, the next day, about twenty miles south, in the town of Moraine, two young brothers had pulled a kayak out of the Miami River in the late afternoon, and then realized it was of no worth since it had a big hole in the bow, and told their dad about it, who then called the cops, since it appeared there had been an accident or maybe foul play? The Moraine police came out, looked at the kayak, felt that a hole this large probably could not have been made by it hitting a rock, but it was inconclusive, put out a bulletin which was picked up by the police in Tipp City, with the info being pitched over to Gladys, since she had just responded to a break-in involving a kayak, just the day before.

By then, Gladys had turned the case over to Detective Victor Hernandez.

Hernandez had spent most of his detective years in Chicago, and had come to Tipp about ten years ago, and was now very close to retirement. He also had a serious drinking problem that he concealed as best he could, but it was an open secret. When he had first arrived, he was instantly liked by everyone, known for his pleasant manner, kindness, generosity, strong work ethic, and ability to listen well. The Chief became aware of his drinking problem over time, not immediately, as Hernandez was an accomplished drinker, skilled at masking. Since he was a Detective, and not on active patrol in one of their blue and white Interceptors, the Chief concluded he would keep a very close eye on him, not have him work on overly difficult cases, and in fact, work only the easiest, but otherwise let him slide. At the time, he reasoned that Hernandez was an otherwise valuable addition to the force, and so long as his drinking was kept in check, he would be of use.

The years had gone by without major incident, and at this juncture, the Chief felt that since the Detective was so close to the end of an otherwise noteworthy career, and a pension, at this point only months away, he didn't want to screw him over. But his drinking had become worse and was now apparent to even the most casual observer.

His drinking had come on, no doubt, as self-medication for being on the front lines in Chicago, and having witnessed some the worst things a person can do to another. The Chief had effectively put Hernandez out to pasture these past few years, and the Detective knew that, but Hernandez had his dignity, and was doing his due diligence while reading through Officer Williams' report. Something seemed off to him.

The kayak report was one of dozens of reports stacked on the Detective's desk deserving his attention, but as the break-in had been so recent, it was fresh on his mind when the news from Moraine came in. The occasional side window or back door break-in is not headline news and normally the Detective would have given it about as much attention as the other low grade unsolved cases or complaints he was assigned to look into, including a petty shoplifting of two bottles of Gatorade, a public urination claim being filed against someone, an excessive dog barking complaint by someone who lived half a mile away from the alleged offending dog, a car vandalism, and a missing Gray Parrot.

Ordinarily this report would be thrown in with the others, no more important than the Gatorade or parrot, but there was something about the incident, that was off-center to the Detective. Perhaps it was the theft of a kayak, of all things? Or that it had occurred at Stan's, a store widely known around town to be in the eye of a hurricane? Or maybe how dramatically obvious the break-in had been? There was, after all, a wooden back receiving door to the place that could be opened fairly easy with a crowbar and muscle, so why the front window? Gladys had already handed him the baggie with the gum wrapper in it.

There was something "sexy about the kayak case" as the Detective put it. He wanted to jump on it as it offered him a little more intrigue than the usual bullshit stuff he was being delegated. It had an element of mystery, now that the stolen kayak had been located and identified as Stan's. Also, he wanted to grab the file before the Chief pulled him off of it, sensing it could well be about a missing person, or foul play, potentially. The Gatorade heist could wait.

He visited Stan two days later, as part of his full-round of inquiries, gathering more details. Stan, anticipating a visit from someone like that, had rehearsed a variety of plausible sounding answers.

The Detective arrived at the store in the afternoon, pulling up in a plain wrap Crown Vic, and getting out of the car wearily, unsteadily. He was of average height, overweight to the degree most men are at age fifty-nine, had a regulation cop mustache and a handsome full head of salt and pepper hair, brushed back, that framed an unquestionably Hispanic face, somewhat bloated and red from the booze, that had seen a tremendous amount of grief and horror. His attire consisted of tan slacks and a brown sport coat, accented with a very loud orange paisley tie. His badge was on his belt next to his concealed Glock. He walked up the steps carefully, but he always walked carefully, always on the lookout for the unexpected clue, but also because he was usually inebriated by this time of the day, his drinking habit having become noticeably worse these last few months. Stan could not help but notice he was sloshed, but was not going to be judgmental, but open-hearted, toward the dear Detective that had the power to cuff him and haul him off for murder, if he so chose.

The Detective was tight-lipped during the interview in the store with Stan, but did reveal to him, that they had concluded Mike Scalopini had been seen chewing that same exact type of gum at Stan's meet and greet, but it was not in the budget to do a DNA analysis of the found wrapper, at the present time. Hernandez also shared that he had spoken to three different and unrelated people who stated they saw Scapolini with that kind of gum. This put an obvious and direct possible connection between the stolen kayak and Scalopini.

The Detective seemed to accept all of Stan's answers at face value, but then again, the detective had skills. Hernandez knew something was squirrelly, as had Officer Williams. Hernandez, pacing about the store like a Bloodhound, said, "It is beginning to look like he broke into the store, stole the kayak, and evidently perished in an accident involving the kayak, although all of this is highly circumstantial, far from fact. No actual proof links the break-in to him, as there is no evidence beyond the empty pack of gum. As for the damaged kayak, if in fact he did steal it, it is an open question whether he actually perished in the river, plus there is no motive yet discovered, not to mention, no body or evidence thereof". Detective Hernandez said the last part grimly, as if investigating a gruesome gangland shooting, with dead bodies strewn all over the store. His past refused to stay in the past.

For Stan, this was perfect. It was too tangled, and ultimately full of nothing, with no substantial clues, and with no record of Scalopini even being in existence under that name. It all was very foggy. The case was a dead end for the department, and that's all Stan ever wanted: to be rid of Scalopini without any strings, without anyone coming back on Stan to somehow hold him responsible. Folks would be relieved that the town was cleansed of such an obviously unappealing and horrible person. Any fallout from this conclusion would benefit Stan. It was a triumphant win for Stan. Stan could now be the hero.

Perhaps it was a touch of astral influence that had come into play next, much to Stan's advantage? As Detective Hernandez was making his way back to the police station, his car got into an argument with a lamp post that had been placed inconveniently on the corner of West Main Street and Bowman Avenue. The Crown Vic was up on the curb, the grill indented around the shape of the lamp post, steam flowing from the smashed radiator, and the Detective pacing back and forth, caught in the most awkward of awkward situations. Unfortunately, there had been many witnesses to the event and the Chief had no choice but to react, else his neck would be on the line.

As per usual, there were a slew of postings on the Chief's bulletin board announcing openings in other towns, in other departments, for those who might in some way qualify for a transfer, a lateral promotion or a real one. As it so happened, there was a posting for an entry-level Detective at the Oskaloosa Police Department, in Iowa. The Chief had but only two choices he could offer Hernandez. One being dismissal and forfeiture of his pension, and the other, to arrange for his transfer to Oskaloosa and take the lowly position, and live out the remainder of his career safely behind a desk, probably being assigned even more lowly and humiliating cases than in Tipp. The Chief had no choice, nor did Hernandez. At the end of the following week, with a whimper, the Detective turned in his Glock and badge, said a few "goodbyes", and went home to pack and move west on the next Greyhound.

Detective Hernandez's sudden departure more or less squelched any further official investigation by the department, of the missing Scalopini, but it had no effect on the papers, who were about to print the articles about the kayak and the missing Italian, with their libelous and maligning tails hidden firmly behind them, but print them they did. It wasn't on the front pages, and they didn't send reporters to interview Stan. They only printed a short article on the back-most page of their papers, stating that Mike Scalopini was presumed dead by kayak, due to circumstantial evidence. Enough people would see those articles, and enough gossip would spread, to slowly get out the word.

As Stan sat at the counter, with Walter to keep him company, he read over the short articles, again and again, chuckling to himself, and thinking, "It will only take Riptick a few days to realize that Scalopini is now part of the past, and for the locals to realize that I'm going to stick around, and I'm not a liar or villain. This is such a great narrative that has been created! Fate has intervened and cut a clear path for me to retain my store, and better yet, it's become a story about redemption. I'll be seen as a man who has made a bad decision, in having offered the space to Scalopini without a proper background check, but thanks to a force of nature, or by coincidence, or Godly intervention, with clear eyes, I have been given the opportunity to have a second chance, which with great humility, I will take. I will become more sympathetic in the eyes of his public, less distant to them, they will like me, for I'm only human, like the rest of them…"

"Ain't no proof of anything. Maybe he offed himself?" said Walter, being the voice of experience about things murderous or deadly.

Stan, caught off guard by Walter's comment, realized he had again been thinking out loud, with Walter hearing it all. "Offed himself? Like killed?"

"Yeah, like killed, as in suicide". replied Walter.

Stan sat in stunned silence, realizing that Walter had hit the proverbial nail on the head. Stan had thought he was out of the woods, but he now realized, that this simple statement from Walter revealed a major flaw in the plan. Stan had to get it across to the police that Scalopini had killed himself, for some desperate and sad reason, and he had chosen to do it by drowning, and to stage it so it looked like an accident. This would close the case. If not, they might look for a possible murderer for months, or years, the dark cloud of suspicion forever hanging over Stan's head. Stan pushed himself away from the counter and had some serious thinking to do, and fast.

He couldn't call up Hernandez and say "Oh, by the way, I just remembered that Mike said he was depressed and might kill himself". Obviously, that would not fly. It had to be physical evidence. Then it came to Stan: "A note. A suicide, note!" That was it. The only sample of his handwriting was in the books Ray had pre-signed on meet and greet day. Stan could practice the handwriting and then author a note. Perfect.

Stan went to the back room with a copy of a signed book, and started practicing, using the same type of pen that Ray had used. After a few practice runs, Stan wrote a note on a ripped out page, of one of the books, as he thought it would be more dramatic that way. It said: "Life disgusts me. I hate everything. I have enemies everywhere. They're looking for me. What do I know about running a store? I don't know what kind of a store I would even have? Women's shoes? Jamba Juice? It's time to leave. I'm going to steal a kayak and go down the river. With any luck I will drown, or at least end up somewhere else. MS."

Stan figured that a note that wasn't an outright suicide note, for that could be too obvious, that suggested suicide, desperation, and escape, would do the trick. Leave it to the police to figure out whether the hole was the result of smashing into a rock, or a hammer smashing into the kayak just before some silk suits from Brooklyn wiped him out. It would be proof that Scalopini stole the kayak, and was entertaining suicide, and at the very least, trying to escape or elude some mafia types? Let Hernandez and the police draw their own conclusions, reasoned Stan.

Stan thought the note was perfect, and that the handwriting was very convincing. He crumpled up the note, rubbed it on the floor as if it had been there for a while, and stuck it partially under the foot of an end cap shelf display, near the kayaks. He walked away. He went to the front of the store near the register and turned to Walter. "Hey Walt, would you mind getting me a bag of number eight size brass wood screws, Phillips? I need to fix this shelf, keeps coming loose." as he wiggled a shelf next to the register.

Walter said, "Sure thing" and walked over to the section of wall that displayed all of the bagged screws, which just so happened to be next to the end cap shelf unit with the note stuck under the foot. Walter, having grabbed the small bag, happened to notice the note, leaned down to pick it up, and the corner tore off, as it was still under the shelf foot. He walked over to Stan, while glancing at it, and said, "Hey Stan, you might want to take a look at this...".

Stan, puzzled, took the note and read it, became very alarmed, then read it again but this time out loud, so Walter could hear.

"Wow, talk about a coincidence?" said Walter.

Yes, it was indeed an amazing coincidence, Walter having just mentioned the possibility that Scalopini had "offed" himself. Stan thought it best to close up shop early and get this note over to the detective, because surely, it looked like important evidence.

Stan walked up to the Detective's desk delicately, having heard rumors of the car accident, and was alarmed but pleased that he was packing a cardboard box, and cleaning out his desk. He handed him the Scalopini note. "Why do you think it was on the floor, under that shelf unit?" asked Hernandez.

It seemed a loaded question to Stan, so he treaded very carefully, "I was thinking the same thing, but maybe he wrote it after he broke in, and in all the mess he made stealing the kayak, knocking things over, he lost track of it, it ended being kicked aside, stuck under the foot?" said Stan.

Again, it seemed to Stan that no apparent alarm bells were going off in the Detective's head, and the answer was more or less what the Detective had been thinking as well, as he said. "Thank you, Mr. Hurts, I'll look into this if I can, and you take care now".

"Oh yes, I will, thanks" said Stan, and walked out of the station house jubilantly, knowing he had plugged the last hole in his story, and that Hernandez was on his way out.

It being a scandalous event, and the papers not being inclined to shy away from such gratuitous stories, were quick to get wind of this latest find, thanks to Stan making casual mention of it to a dozen or more customers. A day after that, Hernandez was swarmed by the curious at Billy's Diner, wanting to know every sordid detail, but he was having a last cup of coffee, about to head to the bus station, and could only state that "It is an on-going investigation, no comment". The reporters from the Dispatch that had shown up were aggressive, stopping people in the streets, and willing to connect the dots even when there were no dots. The Weekly followed suit. Mateo characteristically, took a lighter touch, but it was anybody's guess what Trowner would generate using his notes once he got back to the Chronicle's office.

The papers issued their latest publications, and gave the mafia-kayak story space on page two and three, respectively. The reaction was large and immediate. Just when Stan's customer base had grown bored with the story, here came fresh information to ignite more flames. Again, a flurry of customers appeared in the store to see what else they could learn, or to embellish and gossip about? Stan was delighted he could count on human nature. Dave and Gary even came in to say hello, to see how Stan was holding up, but kept their mouths buttoned up to everyone else in the world. Mandy had gone out of town to visit her sister, and wouldn't be back for another couple of weeks.

But the key and important thing was that Stan had finally managed to orchestrate an exit for his unharnessed plan, and it appeared he had landed on the winning side of the whole imbroglio. People came in with smiles, glad to hear of the demise of the "horrible mobster", glad to see Stan, appreciative that he had listened to his customers and was beginning to lay in new suggested merchandise. It warmed their hearts to know Stan was going to stick around, and that he would begin to change the look of the store, based on numerous suggestions from his buying audience. Stan was being absorbed into the tribe.

The only unaddressed issue was Stan himself. In the past, Stan had dabbled with therapy but it never seemed to click just right. He wanted self-discovery, wanted change, but when it came right down to it, he was afraid of it, and resisted with all his might. He figured that the discovery of hidden demons would be worse than the ones he already knew. Or maybe he was just lazy, finding it easier to avoid than explore? He had been handed some self-help books but again, nothing clicked. He was depressed, so constant it was, that he felt it a normal state of mind, nothing out of the ordinary. When something good happened, such as this latest turn of events, he felt buoyed, but it was only temporary. It wouldn't take too long for him to sink back to his normal mode. His was a makeshift life, where there is always hope for something better to come around the corner, but hope is not a strategy, and Stan's life by and large had not been given proper care and feeding.

Stan knew it was up to him to get better, to be better, but his philosophy told him that he knew that some people are nuts and no matter what they do about it, no matter what kind of self-improvement methods they employ, or books they read, or pills they swallow, they will always be nuts. Maybe he was one of those, he feared? Maybe it was about acceptance, not change? Stan didn't feel that his constant state of depression was a disability, just a personality trait and concluded that he had to learn to live with. Everyone else, looking at him from the outside, figured that he needed some kind of help, or else his life would dissolve. People lately had come in and said things to him such as, "Hey Stan, when you get to feeling better, why you might just want to take off for the week and go to Cincy, see a Bengals game?".

But there was a disconnect. His new-found supporters weren't literally talking about him taking in a game, but talking about throwing the shackles off. He didn't get it. "Why would I want to go to Cincinnati", Stan thought to himself, "I don't even like football".

Over the next couple of weeks, he had many well-intentioned food-bearing visitors: Mrs. Loady brought him carrot cake. Mr. Dowd brought in some fudge brownies with walnuts. Ashlee and Trinity Glabbers, age eleven twins, brought in some homemade donuts and cheesecake. Apparently, everyone had agreed the best way to thank Stan, and help his mental state, was through his stomach. He had lost some weight, and the treats were welcome.

Chapter 9

The past had happened in a blur and now Stan was on a whole new and higher level. Over the following weeks, he brought in a wild assortment of new merchandise. Business was on a definite uptick and appeared to be staying that way, especially when word got out that a fresh pallet of something new had been delivered. Stan had simply taken from all the suggestions he had received, and put them into action. Gone were the days of his ego always determining what he would carry in the store, and not, or lazily letting some sales rep make the call. This was the new Stan, open to suggestion, ready to move into action.

Stan needed his guys back, and did a sincere Mea Culpa to both Dave and Gary, visiting their respective homes, hat in hand, literally. Both Dave and Gary reacted similarly. They both felt that Stan had gone way too far out on a limb, had been deceitful, selfish, gotten them mixed up in a scheme they disapproved of, and in a word, that Stan had behaved "stupidly". There was complete agreement on all points. Stan pleaded with both men to please come back to the store, for things would be different, and that there was "no need to lie anymore", that he "never would again", and that by some wonderful twist of fate, he "had escaped the claws of his wretched deception". It was very colorful language, and both men let loose of their resistance, shook hands with Stan, and agreed to come back.

The moment Dave and Gary showed up, they had lots of work to do. There sat three full pallets, with more on the way, all shrink-wrapped, ready to take apart. There were not only a wide variety of new types of merchandise, but they also had to rearrange the shelving in the store and bring in more tables to accommodate all the new categories.

Up until now, Stan's had been all about traditional small-town hardware goods. But now, there was an explosion of variety: From photo frames to candles, wind chimes and kid's books, Pendleton blankets and cowboy hats, a much wider selection of t-shirts and sweatshirts, bird feeders and whirligigs, and then outside on the deck were many more varieties of beach chairs and water toys, beach towels, inflatables, and front porch fountains made from sawed-off whiskey barrels. He even had a full line of kayaks, in every imaginable color. Stan had spent very liberally but the reaction from his customer base was more than obvious, he had hit a home run. He even brightened up the place with a new counter, new stools, and bought an old upright piano so that the people who could play, would play. The whole store had taken on a new life, bringing in a much wider swath of local citizens. Some of the old-timers complained there was too much space given over to the "fun stuff" but they were in a minority. The register ring-outs at the end of each day told the story.

At the other end of town, Chuck's had succumbed to over-reach, had ballooned its inventory far in excess of common sense, had brought in all sorts of expensive hardware and outdoor items, such as sit-on-top mowers, gas-powered augers, various sizes of flat hauling trailers, ready to assemble gazebos and storage sheds, and even started a pickup truck rental yard, which made no sense at all, as practically every family and business in town owned at least one pickup. The long and short of it is that Chuck's imploded and had to close its doors. How much of that had to do with Stan's resurgence is hard to gauge, but one thing was for sure, Stan and Stan's had been given a second chance.

The season changed, the weather turned its usual turn, mornings were colder, the days shorter, leaves were moving from green to yellow, and the high sales of summer went away, as river tubing was not fun in overcast fifty-degree weather and icy water. But all of that was to be expected, and Stan still had his base of hardware goods to fall back on.

Bob, who had been gone most of the summer, came back in every few days, intense as ever, covered in wood chips from another carving, and took up his usual position, admiring the new look of the store but complained that the coffee was still awful. Allen was still rushing about, traipsing in with his muddy boots, playing a move on the chessboard and scooting out, seemingly obvious to the changes. And Walter, dear Walter, was still seated in place, but on a new stool with a new counter, immersed in himself. But even he showed some signs of improvement. He would sit sometimes for hours, sipping on a Delaware Punch, a daring step up from his usual Coca Cola, and would sketch pictures of animals.

Driving rains, and then snow, inhibited sales, and sometimes, even entry into the store, but it was all expected, and planned for. As for Mandy and Stan? Things had warmed up considerably, and the two were actually starting to talk about something more permanent, which Stan took constant needling about from Dave and Gary. Stan's Corolla had finally been driven its last mile, and he gave it to an enthusiastic neighbor's teenager, to tinker with. Stan had already spoken to Carl Lethrow over at his car lot, and negotiated the purchase of a very clean 1998 Chevy Z71 Silverado extended cab pickup, in white.

Stan would venture out to the mud or snow encased Honey Creek on days that were not raining, and find the four-wheel-drive truck very useful, and fun. All in all, the darkest days of Stan, starting nearly eight months before, had been replaced by an entirely new set of milestones. Stan's melancholy, his constant companion, had not gone away, but it certainly had some new competition. Stan could now see a reason to get up in the morning, to set goals, was able to see ahead, and perhaps more importantly, to want to see ahead. It was a whole new perspective for him. At times he felt awkward with these new feelings, such as going to a cafe' with Mandy on a Sunday afternoon, and actually enjoying it, not nervous, but being in the moment, not wanting to be somewhere else. He knew it was a good change, a healthy change. He would laugh at himself sometimes, thinking back how his ridiculous scheme had by some circuitous chance, delivered him to this happier and much better place in life, not the least of which was Mandy, who loved him dearly, and behaved like she actually liked him, and liked being around him. But there are seasons to everything.

Many allusions are made about the cycles of the weather, of the seasons being like the cycles of a person's life. You've heard it before, Fall, Winter, Spring, and Summer. There's some truth to the comparison. Let's take Stan as an example: Stan had come through decades of dark grey gloom, perhaps generated by the circumstances of his childhood, and perhaps due to genetics, but probably both. But whatever the root causes, he had now emerged a man, in his mid-forties, who had finally broken through to the other side, had "gotten it", and the sunshine was coming on, and he could see and feel what it looked like, felt like, to be "normal and well-adjusted". He had, in a very unlikely way, snuck through the back door, so to speak, and beaten his demons. It wasn't, he reasoned, something as simple or superficial as the store doing better, making more money, but that something inside of him had fundamentally changed. His old fears and haunts were now pushed away, into the far background, or perhaps had even been eliminated altogether.

But sometimes things that were thought to have been vanquished, haven't been. And they can linger, live on undetected, not thought of or considered, and don't actually go away, but only seem as if they've gone away, and in fact have become worse, such as a bacterial infection that quietly worsens, or pulled weeds that will stubbornly sprout yet again in greater abundance, or a dead person that turns up alive.

Time had ticked by and winter was considering a retreat as indicated by signs of an early spring, and Stan was busy in the store doing an inventory of Pendleton blankets, undecided as to whether he should bring in a few more, or let it be. But something else was brewing a few miles away:

Ray Delworst, the longtime employee of Blankenship Plumbing and Electrical Supplies, and former Mike Scalopini impersonator, was on the job, pushing a hand truck loaded with plastic crates up the sidewalk. He was making a routine delivery of toilet valves, under-sink repair parts, faucets, and water lines to McPherson"s Hardware, in New Carlisle, a mere ten mile, fifteen minute drive eastward from Tipp City, on Highway 571.

New Carlisle was one of many small satellite towns in the orbit of Dayton, but like most of those towns, they were their own self-contained universes. It was different from Tipp City in certain detailed ways, but to the most part, the same. There was very little need or desire for anyone living in Tipp, to travel to New Carlisle. If you needed the services of a "big town" doctor, or a larger car dealership, a big box store, or a movie house with a bigger screen and nicer seats, you'd make the drive to Dayton if you were motivated enough. Dayton was only about fifteen miles away, about twenty minutes southward on Interstate 70. But New Carlisle? What Tipp citizen would have a reason to go there? We can think of one: Anita Sanders.

Anita had made quite a show of herself those many months back, flinging her expensive new beach chair onto the floor of Stan's Hardware and marching out very self-righteously. At the time she was considered a folk hero by many, for making such a public denunciation of the former Stan, and his condoning of a mafioso. But that was then. The sentiment about Stan and his store had shifted considerably, after the evidence pointing to Scalopini's suicide became public, and with Stan becoming warmly regarded, what with all the new neighborhood-friendly merchandise packed into the reinvented store.

For months, Anita had intended to go to Stan's and apologize about throwing the beach chair, and for bad-mouthing him around town, but something always seemed to come up and interrupt her plans. Truth is, her pride kept her away. She had taken such a forceful and public stance that it was a hard come down. She had also gained quite a few supporters back then, who would listen to her rants about Stan, and praise her. There had even been a small movement started to throw her in as a candidate for mayor, but that fizzled.

To be fair, a person acting ridiculously, often finds it quite difficult to come to terms with their pride, and admit that they have been the fool. And the more ridiculous they have been, the harder it is to face it. 'Pride' is what some call the "kidney stone of vanity". Pride is powerful, and can convince someone they were right all along, and they hold onto that belief, no matter what anyone says. The word that fits this is, "obdurate". Even though public opinion had since time shifted against that person's opinion, even though that opinion was likely incorrect in the first place, even though the opinion had been based on "alternate facts", they hold on and refuse to let go. To admit that they were wrong all along, is a very hard hurdle for some to get over.

Anita was one of those types. She had gone too deep and now she was stuck there. After all, prior to the Scalopini scandal, she had earned respect in town, having served on the board of the Boys and Girls Club, been the president of the parent-teacher group at the elementary school, and volunteered for a variety of organizations around town: there was the Friendship Club, dedicated to helping out seniors, the Kids Will Be Kids campaign, dedicated to raising money for new schoolyard play equipment, and then fundraising for Shadow Needs Help, a campaign to raise money to refurbish the bronze statue of Union Army Colonel Daniel Rouser's horse, located in the town's historic district.

She was an active and high profile, do-gooder. Knowing this about herself, probably gave her some air under her wings, which propelled her, gave her license, allowing her to feel justified in making such a grand gesture that afternoon in the store with the multi-position, multi-colored cabana striped chair.

At the time, many were triumphant in their position, energized, and proud to be associated with her, but now, those same people did not want to be associated with her. She had lost quite a bit of her credibility over the recent months, with many diverting their eyes when she approached on the sidewalk. Even at church, she was not greeted as warmly.

That last part may seem ironic, being a church, a place that is supposed to, among other things, represent love and forgiveness? The thing is, churchgoers are social, and tend to appreciate and welcome people who are like themselves in belief, who walk the talk, who have humility before the Lord, not stubbornly hold onto pride and vanity.

The icy reception at her church had cut Anita deep, and she was in a quandary, for she had been consumed by her own quicksand. She had, by her actions, embarrassed all that she represented, all the organizations that she was a member of, and all the people who belonged to those groups. Her past accomplishments, topped off by the now infamous "beach chair throw", all took back seat to the rebirth of Stan's. People love winners when they're winning.

Unlike Stan, she had not come to the community indicating a willingness to change, to appear humble or repentant. She seemed to have not learned her lesson about admitting your own, all-too-human, weaknesses.

This is where it thickens. Anita visited her mother about once a month, usually bringing some kind of a gift, whether it be fresh cut flowers or a box of See's. Her mother and her would discuss Anita's many past accomplishments in Tipp, and about how well she had been doing these past five years, since her husband Paul had keeled over and died at the Thanksgiving dinner table, his face planted in a half-eaten plate of turkey, mashed potatoes, green beans and a side of homemade cranberry sauce. Everyone in attendance had scrambled to his rescue, trying the Heimlich, CPR, calling 911, but Paul was dead before his face hit the gravy.

The graveside service for Paul had been quite gut-wrenching as he had left the mortal coil so very young, without a trace of warning. There had been a large group in attendance, including Stan. The cemetery that day seemed to get everything wrong, from confusion over the time of the service that had been scheduled a week before, to the location of the burial plot, and even the mortuary's hearse being challenged entry at the front gate of the cemetery. Anita had contacted a pastor from an alternate church on the other side of town, since the pastor at hers was "unavailable".

The humorless Reverend Dooley presided, reading two psalms that seemed especially scary. Anita had always struck Stan as the fire and brimstone type, and it was apparent the service was much more about Anita than Paul. The service was over quickly, which was okay with everyone, as a stiff cold wind had erupted and was blowing off hats, and knocking over the flowers. Stan and five other men carried Paul's casket to its location a few feet away, and slowly, a wench with straps, lowered it into the ground, to the sobs of Anita. Luckily, they had no children to be traumatized by Paul's sudden exit, and unluckily, they had no children.

If Paul had been the type of man to visit the doctor on a regular basis, and the doctor had given him a physical, he would have discovered absolutely nothing wrong with him. His heart simply gave out one early evening, due to an aortic dissection, while he was saying something about fishing and enjoying his traditional Thanksgiving meal at home with his loving wife and two cousins and an aunt who had driven in from Columbus. It was the definition of tragic.

On these visits to New Carlisle, Anita's mother would empathize deeply with her daughter, trying to mention various good memories about Paul, and her relationship with Paul, always going for the silver lining. What she carefully avoided bringing up was her daughter's recent fall from grace in Tipp, which was still a hot topic of gossip around town. The other unmentionable was anything about Stan. It triggered her daughter, and was the start of disagreements, old haunting memories, bitter arguments and usually followed by Anita making an abrupt exit.

Stan had been Paul's friend, perhaps his closest, and the other way around as well. Stan missed his buddy. They had known one another since high school, long before either had met their loves. Paul had married Anita many years ago, after only eight months of dating, but they knew it was right, and were meant to be together. Paul had gone on many fishing trips with Stan over the years, and a constant source of comedy was Paul asking Stan when he would finally find someone and get married, and once he had found Mandy, when they would finally get married?

For Stan, Paul was someone he admired for his quiet and self-assured ways. He wasn't a depressive type like Stan. He was outward-looking, thoughtful, considerate, not wanting to push his opinions onto others, or try to impress people by being the smartest guy in the room. What made that last quality so meaningful was that Paul may have been the smartest guy, having worked his way up to be the Head of Development and Engineering at a Dayton-based tech company, specializing in creating cyber risk management systems for customers all around the world. Paul could "see" software, as if his mind painted a picture of it before him, and he could describe how one aspect linked to another, how they worked together to "out-think" a security threat. He could talk about the complexities endlessly, in a blur of tech-talk, and all Stan could do was try to hang on for the ride. It was far beyond Stan's grasp, not just intellectually, which it was, but in terms of their personal philosophies about life in general. Stan, unlike Paul, was more terrestrial, and not at all a dreamer, an imaginer, a person who was comfortable chasing or creating theories, or things not physically there right in front of him; a true product of the Midwest. But when Paul died unexpectedly on that November evening, Stan's dear friendship was vaporized in an instant, and was never replaced.

Before that, Anita had liked Stan well enough, he supposed, but they had never really clicked entirely, and when Paul had passed, Anita took on an almost combative attitude with Stan, which for quite a while puzzled him, for he had always been a loyal friend to her husband, and had always treated her with the utmost respect. At times in the past, they had shared a few laughs together over dinner, or at a picnic, so it was puzzling. It wasn't until much later that Stan figured out that Anita had an attitude about him because he was the survivor, because he had not died like her husband, and he supposed that in her traumatized mind, she thought, why couldn't it have been him and not Paul? She resented him for it. So much blood under the bridge, so much history, so many lives intertwined, sometimes quite by accident or happenstance, and sometimes as if by fate, all of it, like lives without coincidence.

So, there he was, Ray Delworst, dressed in his usual dark blue Dickies, looking as Italian as ever, pushing the hand truck up the sidewalk and into the front door of McPherson's.

And there was Anita, having just parked her Dodge Caravan in front of McPherson's, because she needed to pop in quickly and buy a bottle of B-12 vitamin for her mother's newly planted Petunia's. Her mother had bought the flowers at the local nursery, Johnny's Garden, just days before, and had her gardener put them in, but had forgotten all about the B-12.

That's where Anita figured she could be of help, by stopping at the hardware store, and where she had stopped frozen in her tracks on the sidewalk, staring ahead, as the infamous mafia kingpin, Mike Scalopini, disguised as a blue-collar delivery man, approached her, pushing his hand truck. She could not forget his handsome but menacing good looks, his lanky body, and that half-wicked smile of his, at the meet and greet, the same smile he had just then flashed at her, as he hung a right into the store with his stack of crates. She was panicked, didn't know what to do, who to call or alert, that this horrible person was far from dead, but alive and well, and disguised as he was.

Evidently, he had not recognized her, which was understandable, as he had met a flurry of people on that day at Stan's, nearly a year ago. She had even bought one of his books, and had him sign it. But he couldn't possibly have remembered her? Or could he have? Her blood ran cold as she realized she was possibly in mortal danger, had been "made", like in that DeNiro movie she saw years ago with her cousin Denise at the Dayton Multiplex.

Anita stood, not knowing whether to flee or stay. She could flee, and that's what most people would have done, but Anita wasn't "most people". She put on her best game face, and walked into the store, three-quarters sure that Scalopini had not recognized her. She was very rattled, and faked looking at a display of Windex, near the store's front counter.

A red-haired man, about thirty, appeared and asked her if he could help? She had been here before and recognized him as Nick, the grandson of the original McPherson.

She muttered to him out of the side of her mouth, "That delivery man, what's his name?"

"You mean Ray?" was the reply.

"Ray?" she repeated.

"Yeah, why, what's up?" said Nick.

Anita abruptly pulled on Nick's sleeve and escorted him a few feet down an aisle. "That man, Ray, how long have you known him?"

Nick, a very friendly and agreeable type of fellow, began to get a little nervous. "Ray? Hell, I've known him since I was about fifteen, when I first started working here. What's it to you?"

"How old are you?"

"Twenty-nine. What's this all about?"

"Fourteen years? Seriously? And he's always been called 'Ray'?"

Nick pulled away from Anita, suspecting her of being on something, or just a nut, "Yeah, he's always been called Ray, cuz that's his name lady". With that, Nick walked out of the aisle, annoyed.

Anita rushed up to him, catching him, pulled on his sleeve again. "His name was never Scalopini? *Mike* Scalopini?"

Nick gave her a long stare, the gears in his head going around, and he erupted, "Oh yeah! That's right! The Italian guy!", letting out a big laugh, "Yeah, I remember that now, he told me all about it, what a hoot!".

Anita, quickly angered, said with a clenched mouth, "Hoot? What is that supposed to mean?"

Nick, with a shrug said, "You know, a joke, something funny. A hoot. He told me all about it, were you there?"

"So, you mean Scalopini, that whole thing with him over in Tipp, that *whole* thing, it was some type of *joke*, is that what you are saying?"

Nick, now spooked by the interrogation, said, "Yeah, that's what I am saying. Why don't you ask him yourself?"

Right on cue, Ray came from the stock room with an empty hand truck and headed for the front door for another load. Nick turned to him and said, "Hey, Ray, one of your fans is here to say hello".

Nick turned around to follow Ray's puzzled expression, for the mysterious woman had already vanished out the door, leaving Nick and Ray wondering.

Anita figured, either Nick was misinformed and Ray actually is Scalopini, in which case Anita's cover would be blown, putting her and Nick in mortal danger, or, the whole Scalopini thing was a "joke" like Nick said, and once revealed, Nick would get the jump on her, joke with Ray about it, who in turn would tell Stan or others, which would deny Anita justice. She would still be considered the kook. She had to think this through, and fleeing the scene was the best choice available.

Anita called her mom with apologies, that something had come up, and she would visit soon. Anita tried to keep her cool, tried to concentrate on her driving, all the way back to Tipp. But where should she go? The police station? The Chronicle? Maybe she should just go home and think this out, not make a rash decision, borne of panic?

But clear rational thinking had not always been Anita's best attribute. As popular as she had become, pre-beach chair incident, she was known to have a short fuse, and sometimes make less than cautious decisions, on the fly. When Anita knew she was right, she was *right*. And in this case, she knew there was only one thing to do, and that was to clear her name of all the defamation she had suffered these last long months. She had to protect herself. "To hell with Stan", she thought, "and that fake dago. To hell with them both".

She knew one thing for sure, that by telling the police, she would be scrutinized and they would keep it quiet while they investigated, if they even bothered to. Plus, if Scalopini actually was who everyone had said he was, he could easily track her down. If she told the Chronicle, they would likely blast the news all over town, giving her a protective veil of publicity that Scalopini would not dare puncture, and at the same time, liberating Anita of all the condemnations and ugly rumors that had been hurled her way for having insulted the now-beloved Stan.

Stan was now the golden boy, and she the goat. She clenched her jaw, pressed down on the gas pedal of her 2017 family van, the car Paul had bought for them in anticipation of having a family, and had these last five years, kept her connected to her late husband.

Carl Lethrow had on more than one occasion, driven by her home slowly, after her husband had passed, and always behind the wheel of a used sedan he had just acquired, trying to entice her with it, something he felt was more appropriate for a widow to drive, and besides which, the resale value on his lot for a van such as hers was through the roof. She had been afraid he was making a move on her, trying to seduce her with the charms of a Nissan Sentra or Ford Taurus, and she remained oddly titillated, but unavailable, to his drive-by advances. What she didn't know, was that all he was interested in was the van.

These thoughts and others tumbled through her mind, and she was seething at the thought of Stan continuing to get the upper hand. She could not wait to exact her revenge. Where to go? The choice was blatantly obvious. She didn't know all the details as to how deep Stan's deception had gone, but as far as Anita was concerned, it was every woman for herself.

All of this thinking was accomplished in the short fourteen-minute drive, traveling just over the speed limit, before reaching Tipp. She pulled into the parking lot of the Chronicle and marched inside, presenting herself to the front desk. Sally put down her turkey and Swiss on rye, and asked her what she could do for her?

Anita broke down in a torrent of tears, causing Trowner to leap from her desk and go to Anita's side, sensing a frontpage article.

"Oh, my dear, what can we do for you?" said Trowner. So much of what Anita had to say made no sense, but that was not something that necessarily bothered Trowner when weighing the pros and cons of an article. The big leap had always been that Scalopini had been a hoodlum. There had been a ton of hearsay created and stoked by the Chronicle, but hard evidence was lacking. It was true that he had disappeared under very suspicious circumstances, but this latest twist in the story was a bombshell. It was a tangled mess of speculation mixed with deceit, but speculation about deceit was what the Chronicle was all about, and that was what made this latest iteration of the ongoing story click. For Trowner, it was a no-brainer: print it.

Trowner at first, thought she should dispatch Mateo to McPherson's, but then thought the better of it. "What if Scalopini really is a mobster", she thought, and she had been instinctively onto something, and he truly was a dangerous individual? She's going to put Mateo in harm's way? Even that was too far a reach for her, so she decided to just run with the breaking news as supplied to her by her anonymous source.

Many expressions have been coined to describe what came next for Stan, to describe what had landed on his head. A "pallet of bricks" is a common one. A meteor the size of Denver was closer to an accurate description. Sometimes bad news comes in layers, gently at first and then more forcefully, more pronounced. Not in this case.

The newest weekly edition of the Chronicle hit the stands the following morning, containing the usual assortment of small-town news, print ads promoting stores, services, and the standard selection of classified's, with the obituaries and crossword puzzle planted in the inside back cover. What was remarkably different this time was, of course, the mention of Scalopini having been found. There was nothing subtle about it. It was a headline banner, stretching clear across the top of the front page that read:

SCALOPINI STORY IS A FAKE.

At first blush, this could have made the paper look like a fake, since they had helped to invent and promote the lie, but as people's memories are short, it helped to fit the last missing piece of the puzzle into place. People all across town gasped at the headline. Gas station attendants stopped attending, barbers stopped barbering, Officer Williams stopped drinking a cup of coffee at Billy's, and Stan stopped breathing.

"Man, oh man, are they ever going to come at you" Walter said to Stan with a chuckle.

Stan leaned on the store counter, clenching the paper in both hands, staring in horrified disbelief at the headline. He was usually pretty good at thinking himself out of jams, but no great ideas were coming forth. His brain was locked up.

"I sure wouldn't want to be you right now" said Walter, walking toward the door, "I better get going before the shells start to drop" and with that, he exited out the front door, leaving Stan alone, rigid as a statue.

The locals started showing up at the store the very next morning. They weren't there for sale items. They wanted Stan's head on a stick. They gathered outside on the deck like a swarm of bees that had been jostled awake from their hive by an intruder. The swarm was a group of mostly women, about a dozen. Stan stood at the ready, behind the counter, while Dave stood guard by the door should somebody try to get physical, and while Gary crouched behind a display of Betty Boop beach towels.

They marched in, blowing past the hapless Dave. They advanced on Stan and started peppering him with accusations, skipping past questions as to the truthfulness of the article, for most everyone knew the article was based in truth, or something close to it. They wanted Stan to recant. They also knew Trowner and her paper well enough to know she was fond of embellishment, but she had never, or almost never, just plain made something up. They laid into him, screaming profanities like oil riggers.

Stan was too dumbstruck to mount a defense, so just took it, and took it. Dave got a few fingers wagged in his face, but while guilty as an accessory to a hoax, the brainchild was Stan, and the lion's share of venom was delivered to him, as it should have been.

After the group had vented their wrath, they all left as one, gathering again on the deck, and then parted in their respective cars, many carpooling. These people were organized, and this was just the prologue.

A few hours later, just after lunch, another group showed up, comprised of all men. They too did not look especially happy, and once they had gathered as a mob on the deck, they streamed into the place. It was like they were going to stage a smash and grab, but the only thing this group wanted to smash and grab was Stan, who had by now sunken into despair, sitting behind the register on the floor, knees up, and muttering to himself, while they assailed him with the most horrible accusations and threats. Once in a while, Stan would look up and try to answer a question, but it was pointless.

Before the two groups had shown up, Gary and Dave had tried to give counsel to Stan.

Gary had found Stan by himself near the key cutting machine, and had tried to console him, telling him sweet nothings about how it was all going to be okay, but of course, Stan was not having it.

Dave, whose bedside manner needed some work, found Stan staring out the window, just minutes before the first group had barged in, and said he thought the outcome would be initially "devastating, and could possibly come out okay, eventually, maybe".

The pack of men that comprised the second group, had no intention of smoothing things over, or coming to an understanding. They wanted Stan to go extinct, to vanish, to simply and completely go away, and leave them and their fair town alone. Memorable quotes included:

"You think we are idiots?! Morons?!"

"What? We too stupid to know how to drive to New Carlisle or Dayton to pick up a garden hoe or can of paint thinner?"

"What in the hell makes you think you are better than us?"

"Do you know my wife is at home right how, crying her eyes out, feeling like a damn fool thanks to you?"

"You are a complete fucking low life, why don't you drop dead, do us all a favor?"

"You better watch your back, you fuckin' piece of shit".

It went on and on with the words screamed and spat at Stan, and it went on for over an hour.

They finally left, managing to accidentally on purpose knock over three displays, only breaking fifteen items, so on balance, that was pretty good, could've been far worse.

As they walked out the door in the late afternoon, Stan glanced up, and outside on the deck, stood Mateo, his pad and camera in hand. He had a somewhat terrified look on his face, and was afraid to come in. Stan went to the door, and waved him in, assuring him he would not be harmed.

Mateo's assignment had been to wait out the anticipated angry mobs and then go in, get a fresh reaction from Stan. The reaction was certainly "fresh" but far from printable, as Stan roamed the store, flailing his arms, saying every curse word known, and some unknown. He cursed about the landlord, wholesale prices, how the town betrayed him in favor of Chuck's, and how people were such hypocrites, "as if they had never told a little lie in their lives".

Dave and Gary could only stand and watch their boss and friend, disintegrate. Mateo took a single photo of Stan, who strangely, decided to pose next to the sunglass spinner display with an odd smile fixed on his face, as if he knew this shot would be of historical importance one day. Mateo thanked Stan for his "time and transparency" and left.

Dave took a look out the window to see if there was a third wave of marauders about to descend, but no, it seemed quiet in the parking lot. Dave looked at Stan, and not unkindly said, "Hey, pal, what are you going to do about this?"

Stan, having fielded about two hundred such questions already, but not expressed nearly as politely, looked up at Dave and said quietly, "I don't have the slightest fucking idea".

The day at the store came to an end without further drama, and Stan drove home. He parked next to Mandy's car in the driveway and hauled himself out of his truck. It was almost dark, but in the light that was still lingering from the sunset, he looked over and could see there were objects scattered about on the front lawn. He walked around to the front to get a better look, past the picket fence and gate, and realized they were cardboard boxes full of stuff, *his* stuff, some having spilled their contents out on the lawn, as if thrown with great velocity.

The boxes contained all of his clothes, shoes, jackets, and his other possessions such as books, CD's, plaques given to him by the Players, old programs from plays he was in, a frying pan and wok that he had apparently, at some forgotten time in the distant past, contributed to the kitchen, and a box of his favorite cereal, which Mandy couldn't stand, Crunchy Raisin Bran. His life's personal possessions, except for his Z71 and the clothes on his back, were on grand display. Then the sprinklers went on, just in case it wasn't perfect enough. He darted around in the spray, picking up his soggy belongings, and threw them in the bed of his truck.

Of course, he did the obligatory knocking on the door, and then pounding, and then yelling, pleading, begging, but there was no response from inside. The door that was never locked, was locked, so forced entry was his only other option, which he opted to not do, not wanting to tempt Mandy and spend the night in jail. He had bunked down in the store's back room before, so no big deal.

He and Mandy had had their skirmishes in the past, but this was a totally new variant, a new level of horrible. He was so defeated, out of answers, out of moves, unable to come up with a clever angle, a way to equivocate his way out of this tight space, the only move he had left was to curl up on the small couch in the back room. He pulled a Pendleton over him, and closed his eyes. He didn't sleep much, as those old demons started skipping their way back into the front of his mind, having a party.

The morning arrived, crawling. Stan awoke, having finally gone to sleep around four, with his internal clock telling him it was six, time to get up. He quietly opened the door just a crack to see if Dave or Gary by chance had arrived extra early, to give him grief, but they hadn't shown up yet. He cracked the door open a bit more to see if there were any angry villagers with pitchforks waiting for him outside, but no one was there. Things were already looking up. He slipped his over-shirt on, slid into his boots, and moved into the store quietly, carefully, hoping that this new day would bring him fresh insight, showing him the pathway out of these dark woods. But nope, no insights, no clever ideas exploding in his head. Just a dull throb, as if hung over.

He didn't want to prop himself up as a target in the store for a second day, so he made his way to his truck and headed for the diner, knowing some fresh brewed coffee and a buttermilk stack might put a positive spin on his latest failure.

Arriving at Billy's he took his usual place at the counter and waited for Lou Anne to appear, as she always had every weekday morning for years, and talk him up with some morning chatter, a weather report, a positive assessment of his looks. He only got one part of that right: Lou Anne was there. She walked over to his spot, plopped down a ten-ounce mug and poured it full with coffee, not leaving room for milk, which she always had. She said not a word to him, barely even glanced at him. He finally spoke up and said "Hey, Lou Anne, how's it going?"

She froze in her steps, turned to him and approached him, putting her elbows on the counter, leaning in to him real close, and said in a low voice, "Far as I am concerned, you're just another customer I gotta serve, that's it. You have pushed it too far this time buddy, too damn far. You are on top of my shit list" and rose up to leave, and then as an afterthought, returned to Stan, who by now was stupefied. She leaned in again, adding, "And if you go and try to complain to my boss, she won't even believe it. Comin' from you, it's just the kinda thing you'd do, making shit up". And with that, she slowly raised herself up straight, keeping a steady eye on Stan as if he was a venomous snake, and walked away.

All he could do was bury himself in the menu, hoping there had been no witnesses. After a few beats, he grabbed the courage to take a peek to his right, and there were no less than a dozen of Tipp's fine citizens, all giving him the death stare.

Stan decided to skip the pancakes, over-paid for the coffee, and fled to the sidewalk. He was afraid to make eye contact with anyone. He made it to the safety of his truck, revved the engine, and decided to do a drive-by of Mandy's place, just to check things out. When he arrived, he pulled up at the curb, and saw that her car was gone as he had expected, but it seemed she had found a few other things belonging to him out in the garage, which she had deposited on the lawn with the same sense of abandon as the first batch.

He hopped out and loaded up his power tools, hand tools, a couple of sleeping bags, an old tent and other assorted camping items, a couple of fishing poles, his tackle box and the creel Paul had given him countless years ago. The tent was perhaps the most symbolic and significant.

He got back behind the wheel, and started to remember: it was in that very tent that Mandy and he had first made love, while camping at Brookville Lake, about seventy-five miles, and an hour and a half away, in neighboring Indiana. He was caught in a memory, and took his hand away from the ignition. He just couldn't drive away. Faraway thoughts invaded his mind as he looked out through the passenger window. He remembered the smell of the water that weekend, years ago, and the feel of the warm breeze that had come up in the late afternoon, the beautiful alpenglow on the mountains at sunset, the campfire, and the horrible tasting RTU stew he had bought, and then in the morning, he could still hear the birds, it had to be hundreds of birds, all chirping and singing away, greeting the new day. It was like a bird orchestra, "a symphony", he had said to Mandy that morning, and then they laughed, and made love again, it had all been so magical, so perfect. It was about as perfect a memory as he ever had. He took a long stare at the house, trying to imprint it in his mind, and all the good times that had happened there. Then he turned the key, pulled away, and that was that.

To state the obvious, this chapter in his life was not doing his depression any good. All he could see is the downward dark spiral, materializing in front of him. It was his hostile and unwelcome acquaintance, come to visit.

He knew that eventually Dave or Gary would show up and open the store, handle everything. He figured that if he pulled off the road and just sat there, he could think this whole thing through. He sat for an hour, thinking that some revelation would strike, but no such luck. He fired up the Chevy and decided to try his luck at Kroger's. "Maybe", he thought to himself, "I can get lost in the market, do a little shopping for the micro and mini-fridge at the store, and slip out without making waves?"

It didn't take too long for someone to discover him. It was in aisle five, as he was reaching into a cooler for a bottle of orange juice. Worst of all, it was a little kid, couldn't have been more than eight years old, wearing the usual blue jeans, t-shirt and ball cap garb, about fifteen feet away.

"Hey mommy, look, it's that bad guy from the hardware store".

The kid's mommy didn't look over, for she had already spotted Stan and had decided to ignore him, but now her cover was blown. She said, "Yes Tom, I know." and pushed her shopping cart away, her kid craning his neck backwards to get a parting glimpse of the bad guy.

It was this way all over town, and as the mid-morning turned into the late morning, and then that into the early afternoon, it became a sick game for Stan, trying to find a single person who did not seem to despise him. He did find many who hadn't a clue who he was, had never shopped his store, had paid little or no attention to the "scandal", but those people didn't count in Stan's mental scorebook. All he wanted to do is find one person, just one, who he knew, who knew the store, and who did not seem to hate him.

After casually dropping into seven more establishments, he found not a one. It had been an ocean-full of blank looks or scowls, and it was unbearable, so he sought refuge back at the store in the late afternoon. When he arrived, there were no customers inside, only Dave seated at the counter, reading Car and Driver. "I just *knew* you'd remember where the store was", he said to Stan sarcastically.

"I don't think I will be able to take it if you hate me too", said Stan.

Dave, realizing he hadn't picked the right time for sarcasm, put down the magazine and said simply, "Hey man, I'm here for you, but I gotta tell you, you are in a world of hurt. Not one customer today, zippo. And this I don't have to tell you is busy Friday, so something is up, something is definitely up".

Stan looked at Dave, taking all this in, shrugged his shoulders and lugged his grocery sack to the back room. He started to empty the bag onto the table and into the fridge, and when he looked up, he saw Dave consuming the doorway with his large frame. Stan had never fully appreciated how large in fact, Dave was. He was huge. Or maybe Stan had gotten smaller?

Dave had something on his mind. "Hey boss, I've been doing some thinking and well, I was offered a job at Costco, in Centerville, and I'm thinking I better snag it, you know, before it's gone, and things here are headed down, pretty fast, you know…and Marlo, she's really been on my case…?"

Stan thought, "Marlo? Marlo Guttenburg? Marlo's on his case?" Dave's girlfriend was perhaps the one person in town who would not despise him, the *one* person who might defend him when everyone else had walked away. She had always seemed to "get" him. This was very bad news.

Stan, already staggering from so many body blows, could only say, "They offered you a job? How'd they manage that, all the way up here?"

Dave replied sheepishly, "It's only a thirty-minute drive and they, they looked at my application, wanted me to start right then and there, but well, I said I should talk to you first…".

"Yeah, that's a good move Dave, employers like it when you show respect for the last one…" said Stan distantly, already detaching himself from his old friend and partner, not being sure if he was glad for Dave, or furious at himself.

Stan took a step toward Dave, gave him a level look, and continued, "We been through a lot, you and me, and this whole mess is something I did, I don't have any excuses, and I'm sorry I got you and Gary all tangled up".

Dave, with a sudden and embarrassing urge to cry, turned away from the doorway, retreating to the front of the store, saying over his shoulder, "Yeah Stan, I get it - we'll talk". Dave picked his jacket up off a stool, and walked out the door, far more sad than angry, so that was that.

Gary and Stan did not have a similar talk, for Gary simply stopped coming in, didn't even bother to pick up his last paycheck. Stan was worn down to a stub, too low down to protest, or to even call him. So, that was also that.

The ensuing days offered the same hostile menu to Stan, as he tried to conduct himself as if all was normal, and that this episode of darkness surrounding him, and by extension, his store, his livelihood, would pass relatively soon. That became his daily mantra to himself as he turned the key in the lock of the front door, hit the lights, looked at the sheet of plywood covering one of the front windows where Scalopini had broken in, and called the glass repair shop yet again.

Once in a great while, a customer would happen in, aim toward an aisle and come back holding some type of hardware item, pay for it silently, and leave. It was rare that any of his "general" merchandise moved at all. The display of stuffed animals on a table became such regulars, never being exported under the arm of a parent, that he began to give them names.

His need to re-stock various goods across the breadth of the store came to a standstill. All of this was punctuated by Allen, who had blown in one day with his muddy boots, whisked over to the long-handle tool section, grabbed a spade shovel, went to the chess board and noticed no one had countered him yet, went to the register where Stan stood and then, he paused a moment, looked around him, turned back to Stan and said, "Hey, where is everybody?"

It was true, Stan was now the sole owner and operator of the Tipp City Hardware and Stuff Museum, and things were looking increasingly bleak. The number of ring-ups a day could be counted on one hand and the day's totals a fraction of what was needed to keep the place open. Stan, during his better days, his hero days, that had lasted for a good long stretch of months, had wisely tucked away "buffer cash" for a rainy day, and he had been dipping into that fund on a regular basis, just to pay basics like utilities, outstanding invoices, and had put aside some in an envelope to cover the cost of the window replacement insurance deductible, should they decide to ever show up.

It had been three long weeks of retail deprivation, and deprivation of his soul, and he knew that one or both of those things were going to go bust unless he did something to actively jump-start them. He hadn't bothered attempting to contact Mandy, seeing it as futile. He hadn't heard a peep out of Riptick, as this month's rent had been paid promptly, with only enough left in the can to barely cover the next month, but after that? If this boycott continued, he'd be out of all conceivable luck. The drought had to end, somehow.

Sometimes he'd close up shop and take a drive, in an attempt to clear his head, or conjure up friendly angels. "Hospital Wives" had wrapped up shooting months ago, and he would drive down streets and could remember the small army of crew members and the fleet of trucks that would gather, sometimes blocking off a street, or taking over a grocery market, or a city park, with tents and tables set up for the cast and crew to eat, with hot meals created in the lunch truck, others gathered in small groups by their respective trucks, talking about whatever those guys and girls talk about, but always on the ready to be called into action, to bring a certain shirt to the set, or a side table, a cable or a fake tree on a wood base. He was spellbound by it all, and the amount of equipment and people it took to set up a single shot.

What it would have been like as Nurse No. 2, with the crew all huddled around him, getting ready for his big scene? He imagined what it would have been like to be one of the actors, assigned a small room in a trailer, his name on the door written on a piece of white tape, his wardrobe of light blue scrubs inside, waiting for him. A mini-fridge stocked with sodas and water. A bag of Goldfish crackers on a small shelf, a small padded bench in front of a table and mirror to check on his hair and makeup, or go over his lines, and then a knock on the door, with a production assistant saying, "They need you on the set in five minutes Mr. Hurts", and then him opening the door, looking down at the young person, and saying modestly, "Hey, just call me Stan" because he was a genuine and humble person, someone the entire set would grow fond of, who they would get to know and admire, in the short span of the two days he would be with them, but the director would have been so impressed with his work, that he would have insisted on expanding the role of Nurse No. 2 to something much larger, perhaps two or three weeks of work, and give the nurse an actual name, like Randall or Edmund?

He also knew something about life on the set, that he longed for, ached for, and that he would not get the chance to experience: having a family, however temporarily. He knew that on most sets there developed a close bond between all working on the show, with the crew and cast becoming intertwined, sometimes developing close personal ties, meals, movies at the local movie house, sharing secrets, hopes and dreams, fears, and on occasion, bodily fluids. And just as quickly, once the show had wrapped, those relationships, with rare exception, vanished as surely as Paul had, and would be recreated again and again on different sets with a whole new group of people, once strangers. Stan knew it was a flash, just an impression of something close and personal, a simulation of a deep bond, on a job that was all about simulation, but it didn't matter, Stan had wanted to have some of that.

As he continued to drive, some of the tailings of the shoot were still to be seen. They had built a set of a train depot in a city-owned field, and laid down some train tracks. No train was needed, just the appearance of an old country depot. Maybe it was some kind of a flashback scene? The city fathers were so fond of it, that they asked the movie company to not tear it down when the left, and if they could keep it? It stood there now, by itself in the field, tall weeds having their way all around it. No one on the city council had been able to secure a majority vote on their particular pet idea, as to the use of the structure, that was fully three-dimensional, not just a fake flat front with exposed studs and support timbers in back, but an actual room inside with plywood flooring, real windows, and a decent roof. The council had debated a co-op flower and fruit stand, but no consensus. They considered it for the centerpiece of a newly conceived chili cook-off day, but that idea went nowhere. It did however serve as a symbol of the council's inability to govern, and would likely sit there un-used for years, and slowly fall apart. Stan drove down Plum Street and slowed down in front of the house they had used as the exterior of the main character's house.

What had supposedly taken place inside of there he could only imagine, and whatever it had been, it had taken place on Stage 3 of the Cincinnati Stages, a rental facility for visiting production companies located an easy seventy miles away, where they had built the interior set of the house.

He then drove by the exterior location for the little league ball field, Kyle Park, where much of the city's actual little league took place, where he had first met Dave in his Mets uniform. To top off his excursion, he drove into the historic district, officially called the Old Tippecanoe City Restoration and Architectural District, but of course, everybody just called it "Old Town".

It was there that the oldest hospital in town was located, Tipp General Memorial Hospital, and it served as the exterior for the lead character's place of employment. It was in those halls, actually a hallway set on Stage 4 of the Cincinnati Stages, that Nurse No. 2 would have had his first scene, having come upon a fallen patient and calling out for help. He said to himself in the privacy of the cab, "If only I had done that line better at the audition, if only I had not prepared so damn much, and had come in looser, more confident, with more sleep, then I could have shown them what I'm really about, could have easily gone over and hit my mark without hesitation".

But then, as he slowed the truck down to a stop, staring up at the hospital, it came to him that maybe he had shown them what he was all about, and there wasn't much there, just a bunch of hot air and meat. The blare of a diesel truck horn behind him snapped him out of his daydreaming, and he took off, glad to be driving away from those memories.

He drove around town all that week, doing a lot of daydreaming, remembering, doing a lot of shoulda-woulda-coulda: his high school days, his first job, first girlfriend, first fight, first time drunk, first car, first dog, first play production, his childhood home's location, now a Jiffy Lube, the Presbyterian church he would attend from time to time as a child, his dad and mom, his first day of the hardware store. And what of his beliefs, his dreams, his notions of what destiny and God was all about? Where did all those things go?

The anger he had for himself had become less sharp, subsumed by self-loathing. There was not a moment in that week, when he believed, he was going to get a break, that the town was going to remove its boot off his neck.

He'd go back to the store, and look about the well-stocked but deserted aisles. The phone never rang.

There was a part of him that was impressed with the thoroughness of the banishment he was being dealt. There wasn't of course, literally, an organized plot against him, with clandestine meetings over at the Lion's Club, he had not become that paranoid. But it seemed all too apparent there had been a sudden and sharp, overly-dramatic and communal decision to disgorge him, to declare him and his store persona non grata. It was a show of force. It was shock opera.

And then, one morning, rolling off his too-small couch in the back room, his back stiff and aching from too many nights spent there, his bare feet complaining against the cold cement floor, he had finally had enough, and decided to make a move, to make a change. First, he needed a better place to stay.

He rolled over in his head a list of people he knew in town who might be willing to offer him some shelter until he got on his feet. Perhaps people he knew to have a spare bedroom in their large house, or a vacant little guest house on the property. "Really, anything would do", he would say to them, after tracking them down either at home or at their store or business, or by chance, seeing them at the local market. But all of those possible candidates, each and every one of them, gave their regrets. Some with a sympathetic grasp on his hand or shoulder, others not as sympathetic, wanting perhaps to grasp him around the neck instead. He had played out his hand and come up pathetically short.

It was finally dawning on Stan that there was nothing temporary about his being placed in exile. He realized that he just didn't need a new place to sleep, but perhaps an altogether new town to live in. It was at this moment he remembered Bob, good ol' Bob.

He remembered that quite some time ago, Bob had offered to have him come visit him at his permanent camping site in the Northwest. This was long before all the dust-up and troubles. Maybe the offer was still good? Bob would venture there, sometimes for a month at a time, sometimes all spring or summer long, and sometimes into the fall. Rarely in the dead of winter. It was his faraway getaway, where he apparently liked to gather mud in baggies. But that was then, and maybe Bob, like all the others, had changed his tune? But Stan didn't think so, for all along the way, Bob had silently watched the store's drama unfold, never taking a side publicly, never speaking a word, and yet remained steadfast, always coming to the store when in town, and always giving Stan the feeling that he too understood what it felt like to be an outcast, and that in some, yet to be defined way, were mates.

Bob had led a hermit-like life for quite some time, traveling the many miles to his campsite and doing who knows what, but his invitation had seemed sincere, and he had made it quite clear that the invite was solid gold, good for anytime, and Stan could show up unannounced, whenever he felt like it. Stan had learned from experience that when Bob had not come around for a week or two, he was no doubt out of town, at his spot just outside of Index, Washington. According to Bob, it was a lovely site amongst the trees, next to a flowing stream, at the foot of a mountain range. Bob told him the trees, mostly Redwoods and various others, were thick as grass there, and the air crisp and clean, full of the scents of the forest. Great fishing, a nice little town, good people. It sounded wonderful.

Stan figured the only way to make this happen, was to make it happen suddenly. Stan started to assemble a plan that would help propel him out of town, but it was complicated. If anybody got wind of his plans, he was sure that one of his many detractors would find a way to mess it up for him. His brain started to cook, the gears moving, and the old Stan started to appear. He felt energized for the first time in weeks, for now he knew where he was headed. Well, he actually didn't know exactly where because he had no idea where this small dot of a town in Washington was. A quick search revealed that it was outside of Seattle about eighty miles, tucked into a deep beautiful forest, just as Bob had said. It was not close. It would be a long drive, covering nearly twenty-four hundred miles, and take him two or three days to get there. But that was okay, for what Stan needed now was a complete change, something dramatic and positive. This was it.

Stan gave the Chronicle a call and asked for Mateo. He arranged for the young reporter to show up at the store, end of day. Mateo complied, not sure why he had been summoned, but all too glad to be in on a possible scoop. When Mateo arrived, Stan ushered him in, offered him a soft drink, and laid out his plan.

There were myriad details, but the gist of it was that Stan was going to go away for a while, and he had decided to liquidate the entire store's inventory, at a deep discount.

The good news was that practically all of the product sitting on the shelves was paid for, so anything over cost would be a win. If he had to dip below cost, as with the power tools, he would. He knew it would come out okay in the end, and sell off most of the goods above cost. "It will all come out even in the end" became Stan's inner-dialogue.

He wanted Mateo, who was in Stan's estimation about the only person left in town who he could trust, and who was able and available, to conduct sales on the next four consecutive Saturdays. The first Saturday would be an across-the-board discount of twenty percent, followed the next Saturday with thirty, and so on. By the time they had reached fifty percent on the fourth Saturday, Mateo would be authorized to wheel and deal, get whatever he could for anything, up to and including all the shelves, fixtures, furniture, the old piano, you name it. Mateo would deposit the proceeds into Stan's account at the local Wells Fargo, and later on they would settle up, giving Mateo a ten percent cut of all sales. Not a bad deal, seeing as how after it was all said and done, the sales would amount to around a hundred thousand bucks, possibly more.

It was important that the fourth and last Saturday be in fact the last day of the sale, so that they would not move into the following month, when rent was due. Stan said he would deal with Riptick, and negotiate some kind of a graceful or otherwise, exit. Besides which, Riptick would do summersaults upon finding out that Stan was out of his life. Stan would publish an ad in the paper to get things going. Otherwise, this was all to be top secret. After this entire plan had been executed, Stan would give Mateo an exclusive interview about anything he wanted to know, including about his trip to Washington to see Bob.

Mateo was more than enthusiastic, slavishly thanking Stan. Stan gave him a pep talk, about how to not get conned or bullied into selling something too cheaply, that Mateo had to be able to read the customer, figure out if the person was on the level or not, willing to pay according to the rules, or just going for the cheap. First and foremost, he cautioned, "stick to the rules no matter what". Twenty percent off meant just that. A customer who wanted preferential treatment, more of a discount? Fine, they should come back next week, and it'll be thirty percent off. Stan, as remorseful and ashamed as he was, had no apology to make, no love lost for his one-time customers. They had locked arms and essentially ran him out of town, so they were not to get any kind of special treatment.

The elephant in the room, was the question as to whether the boycott would impact the Saturday sale days. Would anybody show up? That was unknowable. But regardless, Stan was outward bound, and however temporary his visit to Index might turn out to be, he wanted to come back to Tipp, if he came back at all, with a fresh slate. He gave Mateo "break the glass" instructions so if the sale was a flop, he had instructions for Mateo to call Nick over at McPherson's Hardware in New Carlisle, appreciating the irony, and give him a ridiculously low offer for whatever remained, the one proviso

---

BLOWOUT SATRDAYS at STAN'S

20-30-40-50% OFF

THAT'S RIGHT, STAN'S IS GONG OUT OF BUSINESS (FOR REAL THIS TIME) AND EVERYTHIG IS PRICED TO GO!

---

being, he had to take it all, and pick it up before the end of the month. He gave all of these instructions to Mateo, and more, with the assumption that he would be away from contact, which might be out of necessity due to the remote location he would be in, or out of choice, not wanting to have anything to do with the scuttling of the store.

Why Stan had to pay an extra twenty percent to the paper for bold face, Sally had to explain to him three times over, and Stan never did get it, but he knew, splurging would or might, pay off. Turns out, there is no policy at the paper for bold font but when Stan walked in the door, Trowner could smell desperation. Sally was only following orders and felt bad about it for weeks. Stan felt especially taken advantage of since they had typeset his ad with two typos, making him appear to be an idiot, not an impression he needed to underscore.

In any case, there it was. Yet another plan that could not fail. Except this time, it hinged more on human nature and its close partner, greed. Stan felt this plan had a better chance of success for that reason, confident that the townspeople he used to call customers, some even friends, were capable of putting aside their deepest convictions against him for a discount on a circular saw or a can of spray paint.

They did not let him down. The first Saturday created an acceptable response, and Stan, binoculars in hand, parked undetected behind a stand of trees on the far end of the parking lot. He could see the occasional customer coming and going, and always going with something in a bag or box. He didn't expect the first Saturday to be gangbusters, but felt it would seed the following three, communicating to the neighborhood that the sale was legitimate. Besides which, there was an unspoken conspiratorial belief in the air, that the more they bought, the closer they were to ridding themselves of despicable Stan. Buying something there was for the collective good.

Stan stuck around to witness the second Saturday and the flow of merchandise exiting the store was fairly constant, and apparently, Mateo was handling it well, giving rise to Stan's hope that this would all work out well.

The set-up and punch style of Stan's life up until now had been an unbroken cycle, but now it appeared he had devised a way to "shake things up", to "break the rules", and "chart a whole new course" for himself. These were catch phrases he would repeat to himself over and over. Before the third Saturday rolled around, Stan was at Sickies Garage Burgers in Bismarck, North Dakota, enjoying a double cheeseburger with chili fries and a chocolate milk shake. For Stan, it was a gourmet celebration meal. He had actually managed to blast out of town, leaving his enormous mess behind him. What he would do once in Index was an unknown, but hanging out in the forest with eccentric Bob had to be better than anything back in Tipp.

ACT II

Many MacGuffins

Chapter 10

Stan's truck behaved without a hiccup, got reasonably good mileage on the open highway, and made for a comfortable place to sleep curled up in the extended cab's back seat. He would pull into a welcoming parking lot, always on the lookout for a Walmart or similar, and it timed out pretty well. He went through a thunderstorm, discovering his passenger-side wiper was of no use, and had to stop and pick up a replacement at a Pep Boys. Pretty dull stuff, isn't it? But that was the whole point of it for Stan. At last, peace and calm lay before him, with no angry stares, no retail desperation, no enemies or furious girlfriends, and no out-of-control wild schemes.

He thought seriously about stopping at the animal shelter in Missoula, but then thought the better of it, not wanting to subject a dog to his new experimental life. "Better wait, see where I settle down next, *then* a nice dog", he said to himself.

He also gave lots of thought to turning southward on Highway 395, just beyond Spokane, perhaps checking out the acting scene in L.A., but he knew that was a loser idea, at least, for now. "Maybe, once I can get my bearings by visiting Bob for a week or two, I can consider that, count up my proceeds from the sale, head that way, pick up a dog along the way?" It sounded like a fairly good plan to him.

But what lay before him was the long drive along Interstate 80. He had just passed through Billings, leaving behind Interstate 84, and was driving with determination. The long hours invited thoughts to seep in.

He got to thinking about when he was a kid, and how he'd sometimes get in trouble at school or home when one of his plans had gone astray, or worked well. He remembered one time when he had snuck into the elementary school's cafeteria kitchen with a friend, and put blue food coloring in the mashed potatoes. The school's volunteer parent lunch server thought it was an authorized "school prank" and served the dubious looking spuds, but when the principal heard of it, it was memorable. He caught hell for that one. And then there was the time he put a glob of fresh wet clay containing lots of air bubbles into the school's kiln. The result, was it blowing up, with hardened clay shrapnel destroying everyone else's pottery. Ruining everyone else's pottery was not the intent, as this had only been designed as a distraction so he could rifle through his teacher's desk to steal her obnoxious whistle she would always blow to quiet the classroom down. He got suspended for that one. He had done many stunts like this, most not as bad, but he had gained a reputation at a young age, for pulling pranks, and devising schemes. His dad, Sean, would get a phone call from the school, requiring him to leave work and have a sit down with the vice principal. He would always say to himself, "Oh Lord, looks like Stanley has done another cockamamy thing".

When Stan's mom had passed so sadly, Sean got an "A" for effort in parenting, but he was simply no good at it, in spite of how sincerely he tried. In the past, when Ginny had been around, he had been offhand and careless as a dad, and had not been a model husband, staying out all night sometimes, obviously fooling around, acting like an irresponsible teenager.

For Sean in his new role as a single parent, being blunt had always been better than using finesse. Expressing something harshly was always chosen over expressing something lovingly. He was simply overwhelmed by parenthood, out of his depth and wanted quick solutions to complex problems. He had stopped drinking however. He had worked various jobs over the years, but when Stan's mom passed, he had a good situation going as a franchise owner-operator of a medium-sized and successful tire shop, for the last three years. It was a part of a small regional chain of tire stores, randomly sprinkled throughout Iowa, Indiana, Illinois, and Ohio. Milton Stubbs, a native Midwesterner and owner of the chain, acquired small mom and pop's whenever he heard of one that was about to go under, and the owner's desperate to escape from under the weight. Stubbs would come along and snap up the place. He'd shut it down for a month or two to give it a facelift, find a buyer for the franchise, have that person indoctrinate the old employees about the way to do things, or hire new recruits if that failed, sticking his "Milty's Tires" illuminated box sign on the building,

Stubbs had a formula, that by all indications worked well, with all the shops turning a profit. He would come into town periodically, Sean having lunch with him every three or four months, always at Billy's Diner.

After their first such meeting, Sean said to Stan over dinner that night, "Milton seems an okay sort, a black guy, did I already mention that? But funny thing, he never seemed to be *here*, though, you know, like *present*, like he'd always be thinkin' about something else, sorta weird in that way, but he has a lot to think about I'm sure, an okay guy though, I think we'll get along fine."

Sean was no slouch, and worked long hours to meet all the sales goals, always striving for the best Yelp reviews. He did okay, money-wise, and they were comfortable at home. Stan didn't see his dad a whole lot, and became a latchkey kid once he was old enough to fend for himself. It wasn't an entirely bad upbringing. No gangs or rats in the alleyway's, food on the table, new clothes, video games. In many ways his upbringing was wholesome compared to many, but it lacked the key ingredients that only the presence of nurturing parents could have provided.

His dad was now in his seventies, had given himself a decent retirement package, and was living comfortably in a highly manicured retirement village that featured a man-made lake with ducks, and a fearsome HOA, just outside of Dayton. Stan would visit him from time to time, but they weren't close, never had been, even when Stan had been a kid. Sean just didn't know how to have fun, never had. Maybe that's why Stan's imagination raced with schemes, as an escape, a defense, or maybe it was an expression of his submerged rage? Stan didn't know the answers and had no particular curiosity to go exploring those dark hallways. In fact, Stan was not curious about a lot of things. He was a pragmatic kind of a guy, always trying to put one foot in front of another, not look back too much, unless of course, he looked back.

He knew a few things about his family tree from what his dad had told him over the years. For example. he knew that "Hurts" was a derivative of "Hurtsman", a name of English origin going back multiple generations. He had been named after his great grandfather, Stanley Hurts (1879-1958) who had come from Maryland in his thirties to settle in southern Ohio. The move was inspired by job opportunities in the steel industry, and by wanting to escape the developing and widespread prejudice against immigrants in Maryland in general, and certain nationalities in particular, such as Italian, Irish and German. Most people at that time assumed that he was of German derivation since the name Hurtsman sounded like a German name to many. Even worse for the young man, some thought it to be a Jewish-German name, which did not help him trying to make his way in the very white world of Maryland in 1910.

To avoid any possible future confusion or conflict, he decided to shorten the name, and allow it to be homogenized, and flow into the stream of all the other new Americans with their foreshortened names, coming from all over the globe. New town, new name, new life.

He applied and had been hired by the Otis Steel Company in Cleveland, situated on the shores of Lake Erie, working his way up from being a purchase order expediter to Vice President in charge of Purchasing and Importation of raw materials. But what greeted him there from his first day to his last, was just another iteration of that same xenophobia, this time aimed not at him, but at the Polish immigrants, or descendants of immigrants, who were the primary work force of the mills at the time. Never let it be said that grandfather Hurts was a not true American, patriotic as any, and felt no connection to his ancient English roots, but each and every time he saw the effects of bigotry, it cut him deep and made him question his new-found patriotism.

Of course, during the last chapters of grandfather Hurts' life, World War II had turned an acetylene torch onto that German and Italian, and in some quarters Jewish, prejudice. The only thing that spared him being a pariah was the alteration, years before, of the family name. After the end of the war, the company was consumed by a larger concern, the Jones and Laughlin Steel Company, that shuttered the Otis factories along the lake's waterfront, which was good timing as Stanley had retired just the year

Stanley Hurtsman b. 1879 d.1958
m. Priscilla Brodski b. 1885 d. 1961
Child: Charles Hurts. b. 1911 d.1986
m. Eileen Newbury b. 1912 d. 1992
Child: Carla Hurts b. 1949 age 73
Child: Linda Hurts b. 1950 age 72
Child: Sean Hurts b. 1951 age 71
m. Virginia Johnstone b. 1958 d. 1986
Child: Stan Hurts b. 1978 age 45

before. Even though not a factory worker, and not exposed directly to the numerous environmental hazards found on the steel plant's floor, he had been exposed indirectly, and suffered failing respiratory health, due to breathing in silica dust and exposure to high levels of carbon monoxide, but in spite of that, lived for a good long time.

As for family, he had been married once, to a lovely Polish girl, Priscilla Brodski, he had met at a picnic. They had an only child, Charles (Stan's grandfather), who had remained living in the Cleveland area, and while still in the Army, had met Stan's grandmother, Eileen Newbury, at a Canteen on a crowded Saturday night, when the unknown comic team of Abbott and Costello had come into town to entertain the commissioned and non-commissioned soldiers.

Charles had two daughters, and a son, in quick succession. The two daughters, Carla and Linda, led good but non-extraordinary lives, were married, divorced or widowed, worked, all the usual things. Stan had rarely seen his two aunts, for both had moved away soon after Stan was born. Carla to Phoenix and Linda to Toronto.

Then Stan's parents, Sean and Ginny, had him, a healthy baby boy delivered on the exact predicted day, and now here he was with his store, childless and aimless, the non-extraordinary legacy of his family intact, driving to the great unknown Northwest to find himself, or was it to lose himself?

Chapter 11

He got to the Wenatchee Mountains, finding himself in rugged mountainous terrain. He gained in elevation, driving on the 90, to the 281, to the 28, and to the 2. All the same contiguous road but with different numbers every few miles. He was surrounded by what seemed an ocean of pine forests, as far as the horizon in all directions. He drove in amazement, having never realized how incredibly vast those forests were. He got out once at a view point, to take in the expanse and was in disbelief. At home he had seen corn fields that seemed to go on forever, but nothing like this. The trees went on for miles and miles, like infinity. Out there, "a person could really get lost", he said to himself, which was a good thing. Even though there were small towns and hamlets hidden away up remote country roads, the vast majority of the landscape was unconquered by human development, and quite possibly in the higher regions, had never been explored by modern people, but probably by Native Americans, he figured. Yes, there were logger roads snaking through, but for scale, they were like a narrow string laying on an immense front lawn, for all the impact they had.

The afternoon was growing late, and he wanted to press on so he could arrive to Bob's campsite before dark. Bob had ciphered written directions on a paper bag at the store, and Stan had kept it secure in the backroom desk, for all that time. He now referred to it, and got a kick out of Bob's instructions that substituted the names of roads with descriptions of landmarks. Instead of writing "turn right on Index Galena Road", he would put "right on road one-hundred feet after 3 giant pine trees on left, nxt to big boulders". This also included little drawings of trees, boulders, rivers, bridges and such. It was frame-worthy, and gave Stan reason to make a few wrong turns, but Stan's good general sense of direction put him back on course, and about an hour before dark, with the sun having slipped behind the mountains, Stan hung a right and headed down the road to Index.

The town was quaint, small and lovely. It was nestled near a river, the North Fork Skykomish River, and surrounded by dense forest. He nosed his truck into town over an old metal trestle bridge and parked, looking around at its utter quaintness, smallness and loveliness. Whether it was actually inside of the borders of the Mount Baker-Snoqualmie National Forest, or just outside of it, he wasn't sure, but the vast majority of the territory seemed untamed. Stan didn't have time to linger there in town, and wanted to get up to Bob's trailer before it got much darker. He turned and headed out, making a left on a secondary road, as indicated by Bob's scratching's.

The road went from asphalt to gravel to dirt, was fairly bumpy, narrow in places, and Stan figured he'd eventually come to the site. Stan read the paper bag instructions that stated, "Take the L fork after big tree". Well, there were many forks along this solitary road, no doubt taking you to various homes tucked away in the woods, and as for big trees, there were only a few thousand of them, so his landmarks left something to be desired. In spite of that, Stan spotted a road shooting off to the left and on a hunch, followed it as it traveled across a shallow stream and into the woods.

Stan felt he was on the correct road, came to another fork, hung a right, and came to a campsite he could see through the trees, next to the creek. There was a trailer that fit Bob's description of a "long ass Airstream", which this one was; a thirty-foot Panamerica, that had seen much better days. He pulled up, turned off the engine, and saw Bob come from behind the trailer and taking some dry clothes off the line. Bob turned, didn't at first recognize Stan or his truck, stiffened up, but then just as quickly, saw that it was his old Tipp City store-owner friend, and gave a big wave and broad smile. Bob seemed a little leaner, and his beard a little longer, than the last time Stan saw him, how long ago had it been? Three months?

Stan climbed out from behind the wheel, his back aching and legs stiff, returning the wave. "I hope this is okay, barging in like this…", said Stan.

"Barging in? Hell, this ain't barging, this is visiting!" Said Bob, walking toward Stan, arms outstretched. He gave Stan a big bear hug, and said, "You comin' to stay a while I hope?"

And Stan, relieved by the warm greeting said, "Well, yeah, if that's okay, don't want to get in your way".

Bob gave Stan a big grin, saying, "Get in my way? What're you, nuts? Stay as long as you want!" And with that animated and warm greeting, Stan and Bob grabbed Stan's tent and sleeping bag, and set up his site, about twenty feet from the Airstream.

Let's set the scene: The site was in a clearing off the dirt road about a hundred feet, next to Excelsior Creek. The site was squarish in shape, about sixty feet across, sheltered on three sides by a dense mixed stand of Redwood, Spruce, Paper Birch, Doug Fir and Black Cottonwood. The creek was one of many tributaries that flowed into the Skycomish. At this point, it was wide, about twenty feet or more in width, but shallow. It flowed at a moderate pace, had plentiful small to medium-sized rounded moss-covered rocks in it, and on occasion, deep pools that Stan figured most certainly housed some big trout. It had a wide sandy bank leading to it on the camp side, but on the far side, was crowded by a dense growth of mostly Spruce and Black Cottonwood. Most other parts of the creek were not as accommodating, with dense trees or bushes, and rocks, crowding both sides. There was the occasional sand bar in the middle of the creek, some with fallen trees laying across. Long strands of light green moss, hung eerily from many of the trees, and there were ferns everywhere.

The campsite itself was now comprised of Stan's old Kelty tent on the left, about ten feet from the wood line, and on the right, about twenty feet over, Bob's vintage trailer. It was one of the larger ones Airstream had ever made, but now sat well-weathered, sporting flat tires and a very oxidized aluminum shell. Stan noticed that the door to the trailer seemed much newer, and sturdier. It appeared Bob had fashioned some bars across all the windows, as well.

Bob's 1965 very faded light blue Volkswagen Beetle was parked nearby, but it seemed modified, with the rear engine hatch removed allowing for an obviously larger aftermarket engine conversion. There was a rock-lined fire pit with a cooking grate just steps from the trailer, with a lone folding chair, the laundry line, an "outdoor shower" bag hung from a nearby tree, and near that, a heavy-duty wood picnic table with attached benches, the kind the National Park system puts in, but this one, old and worn, was no doubt salvaged from elsewhere. The site was flat, and clear of rocks, thanks to Bob. It was dusty, but contained a large percentage of Loess, (a sediment that collected from windblown glaciers from long ago. It is very fine in texture, almost like powder, and commonly found in the Northwest).

That last part, about the Loess, was the first of dozens of natural science factoids, that Bob would impart, over the course of Stan's visit. For all of his uneducated, grumpy, and hermit-like persona, it seemed Bob had educated himself rather well on topics mostly having to do with nature. He seemed blissfully unaware of the outside world, which suited Stan just fine.

Because the site was in a hollow, with mountains on either side, direct sunlight came later in the morning, not at dawn, and retreated early, leaving open shade and a steep temperature drop for a few hours before becoming dark. It was cool there this time of year, early spring, but not uncomfortably so, especially as compared to Ohio. Once the tent was set up, and various other belongings put inside, the two friends sat by the open fire.

Bob was in his dilapidated webbed patio chair, and Stan in his "Anita", a new multi-color, multi-stripe, cabana beach chair, one of a handful of things he had salvaged from the store before departure. He had actually brought two matching one's, but Bob declined the gift, preferring his, with its loose and dangling webbing. They spent an hour talking about the turbulent events concerning the store and Stan's departure, about the forest, the people in Index, the weather, details about Dave, Gary, Allen, and Walter. Bob knew that when the conversation had turned to

Mandy, he had hit a nerve, so the Mandy topic was cut short.

They sat and stared at the flames for a long while, enjoying some of Bob's cheap Chianti in metal camp cups, and enjoyed the peace. Suddenly, Bob bolted up from his chair and went into the trailer, returning with another bottle.

"Time to reload that cup?" He said to Stan.

"Me? Oh no, I'm all done in, please go ahead…"

Without missing a beat, Bob topped off his cup and took it in one swallow, followed by another and another, like somebody in a speed drinking contest. Stan had heard the rumors about Bob's bingeing ways, but this was the first time he was an eyewitness to it. Bob drained the bottle in about ten minutes, while becoming increasingly more talkative, which then became boisterous. Bob, pretty well hammered, stood up unsteadily, and started pacing back and forth, muttering to himself. Stan couldn't make out what he was saying, but Bob was obviously agitated, working something over in his mind, disturbed. After Stan watched this go on for about five minutes, Bob just as suddenly, sat back down in his chair, staring at the fire silently, brooding.

Stan, wanting to tread lightly, said, "Hey Bob, I was thinking I'd go off to my tent now, I'm pretty bushed".

Bob, looking up from his gaze at the campfire, said, "Yeah, you go on, that's good…" Then his expression changed, turning steely. His words were slurring,

"You know, they saw 'em, Daniel and Davy, they both saw 'em".

"Daniel, Davy?"

"Daniel BOONE, Davy CROCKETT!" roared Bob.

Stan was beginning to realize that Bob was not a happy drunk. "Really? I didn't know that". And then after a moment, "Saw what?"

"Yup, they both did. Not at the same time, different times, different places, one in Texas it was and the other in Kentucky it was or Tennessee, but not important, that part, but they damn well saw them a squatch, 'hairy ape men' they called them, you know that?" It was a rhetorical question as before Stan could reply, Bob continued, "Yeah, they sure did, they wrote on it, they weren't no bears either, those pioneer frontiersman guys, brave shit they did...so nobody call me nuts, I ain't fuckin' nuts". With that, Bob stumbled to his feet and made his way to the trailer, slamming the door behind him.

"Now what have I gotten myself into?" thought Stan. He sat thinking how best to react. He was worried this might be something he does a lot. He could hear Bob slamming around in the trailer and then it became quiet, with Bob presumably finding his bed and passing out. Stan realized that if this was going to be a regular thing with Bob, he would have to leave, but he was no stranger to this behavior, having been well-schooled by his mom.

Stan was nodding off, and it was time to crawl into his sleeping bag. He put out the fire, and laid down in his tent, turned on his new store-salvaged battery powered LED Coleman lantern, and opened his book. He didn't want to think about Bob's drinking or Daniel or Davy. He wanted to preserve this feeling of the peace in the woods that he felt when he first arrived, and his having been able to triumph over his troubles back home by orchestrating the perfect escape. He picked up a book that he had brought with him, "Islands in the Stream" by Hemingway, and went to the page he had dog-eared.

He loved this book, had read it once before, but not for a long time, and began reading: "In the night, Thomas Hudson would wake and hear the boys asleep and breathing quietly, and in the moonlight, he could see them all and see Roger sleeping too. He slept well now and almost without stirring".

Stan read a few pages, put the book down, his eyes heavy, and could hear the sounds of the creek, the occasional sounds of small critters, Opossums and possibly Mountain Beavers, scurrying about, and the night birds, the Common Pauraque and the Northern Saw-Whet Owl. Bob had educated him earlier around the campfire about them. "Bob sure knows his stuff", Stan thought, drifting off, his pain and stress becoming lighter, shedding off of him.

A narrow streak of bright sunlight hit Stan's tent, and he awoke, feeling like a new man. He sat up, rubbed his face awake, not having had a single creepy nightmare, but had the sudden need to take a leak. He dashed out the tent flap in his boxers and t-shirt, found the nearest tree to hide behind, and let loose. He realized, that for the first time in memory, he had slept through a whole night, had not awakened once, hadn't gotten up once needing to pee or otherwise. Maybe it had been the long drive, or the Chianti by the fire, or the dawn of a whole new attitude, but whatever the cause, he felt great, better than he had in a long time.

He stepped out from behind the tree, and realized it was cold. He stepped into a shaft of warming sunlight and looked about. On topic, he wondered about the toilet situation and noticed a pale green Andy Gump stationed near the opening of the site, near the road. He then noticed how quiet it was over at Bob's, saw his Beetle still parked in the same spot, and figured he was sleeping in. With the way he drank last night, it was no surprise.

His eyes then caught something up high, a reflection of something, and glancing up he noticed an aluminum pole, very oxidized, about two inches in diameter, but quite tall. It was attached to the backside of the trailer, and shot up into the air at least thirty feet. On top of it was bolted an old-fashioned TV antenna, the type found on roofs of houses across America in the fifties and sixties, before cable. "How about that?" thought Stan. "He's probably got a TV in there, nice", and gave it no more thought.

Stan went back into his tent and unpacked some jeans and a flannel shirt from his duffle bag, slipped on his boots, and emerged looking like a genuine camper. The stream's beautiful sound was a constant, and all of his nocturnal critters and bird friends were tucked in for the day. They had been replaced by

Western Gray Squirrels, of which there were many, and the birdsongs of the Spotted Towhee and Red-breasted Nuthatch, among others. Bob was a wealth of information.

Speaking of which, it seemed very quiet over at Bob's trailer, so Stan walked over and gave the front door a little knock. No response. He knocked again, just a little louder. Again, no response. He sure as hell wasn't going to start pounding on the door, for Bob surely had his routine, which might include not getting up until later in the morning, whether hung over or not.

It was now just after nine, and the sunlight was starting to fill the campsite pad. Stan was yearning for some coffee, some breakfast, but figured he'd just wait for Bob to stir and then they'd come up with something. Also, when it came time to shop for food, Stan had brought some cash with him, a good amount, for he did not want to be sponging off of Bob, but contribute generously. After all, if Stan didn't have Bob in his life, he'd be in a very hard way, living alone in some generic motel in a generic friendless town, so he wanted to be sure he was the perfect guest.

Stan found a nice flat rock to sit on, bathed in sunlight, and retrieved his book from his duffle: It became ten o'clock which became eleven, and still, no Bob. Stan was beginning to get concerned, and quite hungry. He grabbed two protein bars from the front seat of his truck. Could it be that Stan's arrival, the wine, the excitement of his appearance, caused Bob to have a heart attack of some kind? It was a morbid thought, and Stan admonished himself for it, but Stan had a wide streak of morbid in him, and was growing increasingly disquieted. It was now well after eleven, pushing noon, and still no Bob. Stan got up stiffly from the rock, and walked over to the trailer, this time determined to wake Bob. If he was wrong, and it turned out Bob usually slept until noon, then he'd owe him a big apology, but he had to be sure.

Just as he reached the trailer, who should appear from down a trail next to the trailer, but Bob?

"Hey partner, sorry I'm a little late, got caught up" said Bob with a big smile.

Stan stood back and said hello in return, immediately wondering where Bob had been. It was really none of Stan's business, of course, but Stan had gotten up with the first light of the day hitting the site, more than three hours ago, which meant Bob had been up that trail going to who knows where, before that. And Bob looked fresh and bright, no trace of the night before. No fishing rod either. Just didn't seem to make sense, but hey, what exactly was normal when talking about Bob? Stan decided the best thing to do was not make any kind of comment at all, just go with the flow.

Bob had a large knapsack, which he slid off one of his shoulders. He reached into his pants and pulled out a key, opening the door. During this action, Bob said to Stan, "Sorry, force of habit, I'll keep it unlocked from now on when you're in camp. Time for a little breakfast, don't you think? Or is that lunch?"

Stan agreed, quickly adding "And, just so you know, I'm not coming here empty handed, I intend to pick up some groceries later".

Bob gave out a little laugh and swung open the door, walked up the metal steps, saying over his shoulder, "Come on in Stan, welcome to ground zero".

Bob walked into his trailer, followed by Stan, and set his knapsack down on the Formica-top table that served as his everything-table. It was heaped with books, boxes and bags of various nutritious powders, grains, cereals, nuts, dried fruit, plus flashlights and batteries, bottles of vitamin supplements, and a very hard to miss Smith and Wesson 44 magnum long barrel, laying on its side in and amongst the health foods. Its barrel was a polished stainless steel, with a black rubber grip. It looked new, and if not new, then kept in very good condition. Next to it, a box of shells.

Bob was busy fussing around, unpacking his knapsack onto the kitchenette counter, while Stan surveyed the table's contents. Obviously, Bob ate lots of "natural" type foods, which was not what Stan would have thought about Bob. He figured he was strictly the hamburger, bacon, and pork rinds type.

As for the hand gun, it made sense, for out here, isolated as he was, most any kind of a person could just saunter up, announced, with less than friendly ideas in mind. Visualizing Bob wielding an impressive "Dirty Harry" revolver was difficult though. Bob had always struck Stan as being a somewhat grumpy, and unfocused type of older person, incapable of hard aggression, an aged hippie perhaps, and certainly not someone who would own a gun, let alone such a formidable one. It just didn't fit. But last night's tutorial about native small mammals and birds came as a surprise, and now this morning, there were more surprises.

Stan took his gaze off the gun and watched Bob unpack his knapsack of what appeared to be a bag of dry plaster, some cheap paint brushes, a putty knife, binoculars, an empty plastic bowl, two apples, three Snickers bars, a smaller hand gun of some type, but more modern looking and black, and other assorted items. Stan was trying to connect the dots. He looked back at the items laid out on the table, trying to do so, but he suddenly realized how the trailer was decorated.

All around him, on virtually every available wall surface, were taped hand-wrought graphs, with red, blue, black and green Sharpie lines going up and down next to listed months, air temperatures, weather conditions, the cycle of the Moon, and various other things Stan could not decipher. There were topographical maps, not only of their location, but many others throughout the state, plus Oregon and California. The maps had circles drawn on them, some with tiny hand-written comments next to the circles, written in red or blue pencil. On the far wall he had photos that looked cut from magazines and newspapers. Stan's eyesight wouldn't let him make out what the photos or articles were. Over in one corner was a bulletin board, and push-pinned into it were Bob's collection of Ziplock-bagged mud samples.

Bob was done emptying the knapsack, and turned to Stan cheerfully, and said, "Hungry?"

Stan, politely breaking his stare of Bob's walls said, "Yeah, sure, sounds great".

As Bob opened the small fridge, taking out a carton of oat milk, a plastic container of organic blueberries, yogurt, eggs and turkey bacon, Stan continued to scan the interior of the trailer.

Past Bob, in what looked like would normally be the bedroom space, there was a table and desk chair, with what appeared to be a small bed against a side wall. He couldn't make out much in detail, and didn't want to get busted examining the place, but from what he could see, it looked like a ham radio set up, a rather nice one at that. Receivers, radios, a headset, and all kinds of gear with dials, switches and buttons. Stan had no knowledge or experience with any of this type hardware, but it looked professional. No TV set in sight.

By now, Bob had finished preparing two bowls of organic granola topped with yogurt and blueberries, and had fried up a mess of eggs with bacon. Stan was famished. Bob cleared off some space on the table, and they both slid into the half round booth surrounding it, on opposite sides. Bob had quietly moved the 44 off the table to the vinyl tufted bench seat next to him, and Stan obliged by pretending to not notice the move.

They ate in silence for a few moments and Stan attempted some lame humor by commenting on all the graphs and lists taped to the wall. "You have very interesting wall paper", delivered with a smile.

Bob looked up from his cereal bowl, having consumed the eggs and bacon like a bear, and said, "Not wall paper".

Stan, hungry but eating much more slowly, said, "Yeah, this is good. Yogurt on cereal, who would have thought?"

Bob, with a smile said, "Yup. Been eating granola for years with all kinds of toppings, sometimes breakfast *and* dinner".

Stan, still intent on making light conversation, replied, "Good stuff. I'm more used to McBreakfast", with a self-conscious laugh at the end.

Bob looked at him, and in a suddenly serious tone, said, "That shit'll kill you pal".

Stan was bursting with curiosity, and finally said, "So, Bob, looks like you're into ham radio stuff, I never knew".

Bob, with a slight nod to his side in the direction of his equipment, said, "Yeah, I dabble".

Stan, realizing that might be as deep as Bob is willing to go on the topic, took furtive looks around, at the photos and clippings, more carefully this time. Stan had first noticed how bad his farsightedness had gotten on the long drive here, not being around familiar landmarks, but now, even in the confines of the trailer, with good lighting, he was finding it impossible to glean any details from so far away.

Again, he tried to fire up a conversation by indicating all the graphs and maps, saying "Looks like you've got yourself a hobby".

Bob, sat across the table, assessing his friend and visitor, as if measuring what he should say. After a few beats, Bob pulled his hulky frame up from the table, grabbing his bowl and depositing it into the sink, and said in a friendly manner, "So, you want to see something?".

Stan, still working on his bowl of cereal, his eggs and bacon half-eaten, said, "Sure". Stan was beginning to get a feeling, and it was a sensation he had had many times before, when about to stumble upon a realization he had made a terrible mistake.

"C'mon on over here, you'll get a kick out of this", said Bob.

Stan stood up from the table, and made the few steps over next to Bob, who was standing next to the wall where the baggies had been push-pinned into the board.

Now that Stan was standing closer, he could see there were a dozen or more baggies, all with globs of mud or dried dirt clods in them, and all labeled with a Sharpie: "8/30/17 upper creek" was written on one. On another, "4/5/19 near waterfall". Bob had apparently bagged and labeled many samples of dirt. There was "4/16/22 cottonwood grove" and "5/17/18 top of mountain" and "7/20/22 at big boulders". It went on like that, all over the bulletin board. Bob had been going deep, studying and cataloging soil samples, to what end, Stan had no idea, but obviously, Bob was being quite thorough. Bob pulled out one of the pins, and delicately presented a bag full of dirt clods to Stan. "See that?" said Bob.

"Yeah, sure do", said Stan, becoming nervous from Bob's intensity.

"You know what you're lookin' at? We talked about this before, you remember?" said Bob.

Stan, feeling intimidated, and attempting some humor to lighten the moment, said, "It's not a clump of dirt, some dried up mud, I'm guessing?"

"Well, you'd be right on that one my friend", said Bob. With a smile, Bob continued, "This here's squatch scat, just like I said before".

Stan, fully realizing that Bob was dead level serious, that Bob had no sense of humor about this, and was not pulling his leg, wanted to beam himself up out of the trailer that instant, to go somewhere safe, populated by many people, maybe a big mall, where he could blend into the crowd and disappear.

Bob, with the intense look of a fanatic, and holding the bag up, shook it a bit, and said, "It won't hurt you, it won't bite" and let loose a burst of laughter.

Startled by the eruption of loud laugher, Stan said, hesitatingly, "Sasquatch excrement? That's what you are saying this is?"

"That's what I'm saying", said Bob.

"I just thought your collection was dirt, you know, like you were kidding around", which was an obvious lie, and then, "I thought they might be soil samples, you know…". Bob was studying him closely.

Stan, now suddenly realizing he was dealing with someone quite likely unhinged, someone large, armed with an enormous revolver, and a second gun, a binge drinker, prone to sudden mood swings, and alone with him in a very isolated forest campsite, decided to stay calm, and not reveal the mounting fear rising up inside of him. Bob was displaying his "Bob the nut case" personality, as often seen back at the store, which Stan was now realizing was likely to be the only version of Bob there was. Stan had wanted always to see him as a somewhat eccentric old guy, with a few odd, but charming, harmless beliefs, who loved the camping life, to justify his traveling all this way to seek refuge.

Stan took a step sideways, positioning the baggie further from his face,

Bob, mollified somewhat by Stan's seeming innocence, pinning the bag back on the board, his feelings hurt, his back turned to Stan, and said quietly, "Soil samples my ass, this ain't dirt Stan, these here are samples of actual scat, I collected. And these here are just some what I got. There's tons more in those drawers" pointing to a cabinet in the radio room.

Stan, took a deep breath, did not want to say the wrong thing, and drew upon his acting experience, wanting to not appear condescending, but interested, and curious. "Okay, you're telling me you have gone around, out there in the woods, and collected clumps, samples, of Bigfoot excrement, is that what you are telling me?".

Bob gave Stan a stern look and said, "Don't call them 'Bigfoot', Stan, just makes you sound ignorant".

"Oh, okay, all right, Sasquatch then, that's fine, so that's what you are saying Bob, is that all these bags here have poop in them, from a Sasquatch?".

Bob, trying to stay composed, replied, "First off, we don't call it 'poop', you sound like a child. We study it, it's called scatology, and it's a science, Stan".

"All right, got it, sorry - it just caught me off guard, you know, all these bags of, scat, hanging on your wall, not what I was expecting, you know?" And then after a beat, "We?"

"Yeah, they's a whole bunch of us Stan, all over, thousands of us, where you been pal?"

Not wanting this conversation to become confrontational, Stan said in a calm voice, "Thousands? Really? And where would they be?"

"All over", said Bob. "They's all over the place, most every damn state. Bunches here, other nearby places. Researchers, scientists, investigators. All over. Don't you ever watch the news?"

"Well yeah, but it's usually about a war someplace or a car pursuit or somebody shooting up a bunch of people, but I must've missed the Sasquatch news". That last part he regretted, thinking that Bob might feel it snarky.

"You gotta look for it a Stan, put some effort in, it won't just be sittin' there each night on the TV, is that what you think?"

"No, no, I was just saying I hadn't kept up with all this information you know, like you do, that's all".

With that, Bob realized he had probably shocked his friend, had bungled the presentation and his attempt to introduce Stan to the world of Sasquatch. "I'm sorry Stan, I didn't mean to shake you up none".

"No, no, I'm fine, really" said Stan, glad that they had apparently gotten over that hump, and that it didn't seem Bob was going to shoot him.

Bob surveyed his friend, and detecting no insincerity, said to Stan, "Listen, I know this whole thing must be new to you, but that don't mean it's not for real". Bob motioned for Stan to follow him into the radio bedroom.

Stan followed Bob in, getting a much better look at the space. The walls were covered with more photos, more articles, and now Stan was close enough to be able to read the headlines, make out the photos. There were clippings, some faded and yellowish, others appearing whiter and newer, with headlines reading: "Sasquatch Reported Near Mt. Hood", "Bigfoot Visits Rainier Campground", "Sasquatch Seen Swimming Near Vancouver Island", "Footprints Found at Crater Lake", "Area X Revealed", and most notably, "Sasquatch Encounter near Index". There were a dozen more like those. Stan's first thought was "Trowner would have a field day up here". Bob stood and observed Stan, allowing him to soak it all in. There were various color photos, most were blurry, some showing a Sasquatch (or perhaps a guy with a dark hoody on), some with circles drawn in red around a spot allegedly showing where the Sasquatch was in the frame (it could have been a tree stump or a bush). It was hard to objectively say. Whatever the actual subjects of the photos were, it was immediately apparent that no one had managed to get the Sasquatch to sit down for a studio session, so a well-lit shot could be taken, that was in focus.

Stan, having absorbed most of the photos and clippings of headlines, looked at Bob and said, "So, you are really into this thing, I can tell" which was the understatement of the century. Stan added, "This Sasquatch, you think he's around here, is that it?"

Bob, as if showing a new piano student where middle C was, patiently said, "Stan, it ain't just one. There's a whole bunch, a big extended family I reckon, and they live up there, way up in the woods" motioning toward the mountain range.

"A family? Wow, that really is something..." replied Stan, convinced that Bob truly believed this.

Bob had already figured Stan to be the quintessential Sasquatch skeptic, as a result of the way he had reacted to him in the past at the store. Being a true believer, Bob was used to rejection and derision, which is why he usually kept his beliefs to himself. Bob had also overheard Stan's gloomy narrative of life, which colored everything that he saw and felt. He knew that Stan was a good person, but was someone that had shut himself off to the possibilities of life, and needed direction. For Bob, Stan was ripe for conversion, to see the truth.

Stan, sensing this, was hopeful the conversation was over, and he could escape to the comfort of the outdoors, go to his tent, take a walk, most anything would have done. Instead, Bob motioned for Stan to step a little closer to his drawer cabinet. Stan, realizing he was still in the magnetic pull of the unhinged gun owner, obeyed, and took a couple of steps toward the cabinet, where Bob stood, proudly. Bob gingerly opened a drawer, revealing the contents: plaster casts of foot prints.

Bob, not being able to contain his enthusiasm, started pointing to the various castings, that were housed in the many drawers. He'd pull one out, and hold it like it was a precious cut gem or fine chocolate, presenting it to Stan, but not allowing Stan to hold it, it was too soon. Each one had a tissue wrapper around it, and a piece of masking tape with writing, identifying where it had been cast, and when. They had been cast in various weather conditions, in dirt or mud or sand, or in the Loess, which is incidentally, the "perfect kind of dirt for a good clean print", Bob pointed out to him.

"Hardpan is what you don't want", said Bob. "It is made of clay, it's hard, almost impervious, like nature's cement, impossible to get a decent cast from that, unless it just rained, but even then, can't see any detail, ridge lines, that kinda stuff", he added.

Stan could see that some did show detail, while others were sloppy and vague. The toes were defined, and Stan noted to himself, that the big toes were unusually large, not to mention the casts themselves, being fifteen inches long or longer, and eight or more inches wide. There were also a batch of much smaller castings, made by "their kids" Bob said. They did indeed appear to be from many different "individuals", as Bob referred to them as. There was such variety, that Stan knew that whomever the makers of the prints were, these prints were not made from a fake stiff wooden foot, there was simply too much detail to most of them, they looked too lifelike, and there was too much difference between them.

Bob had separated the castings that he thought had been made by the same individual, and even Stan could see the similarities. Stan hadn't yet touched upon the ham radio equipment that dominated the room, but figured, it had to somehow be tied into Bob's obsession.

This entire thing was overwhelming, and Stan needed some fresh air. Before Bob had a chance to motion him toward another exhibit, Stan said quickly, "hey, Bob, I need to stretch my legs for a bit, okay?"

Bob, seeming a little dejected, said, "Okay bud, I gotta go through my notes anyway, to get ready".

Stan did not want to know what Bob was getting ready for, as it would likely draw him into more presentations of undeniable evidence accompanied by wild unfounded claims. It was a sad come down for Stan, for just as he was beginning to adapt to this new environment, after just one night and a morning, and warming to his eccentric and harmless companion, he had to admit to himself, this whole thing was a huge mis-step. He had to get the hell out of there.

Stan opened the door and walked down the metal steps into the fresh mountain air, not sure what he wanted to do next, or where to go. Impulsively, it occurred to him that now might be a good time to flee, while Bob was busy inside doing his notes, not suspecting a thing. It wouldn't take long at all, he figured. Break down the tent, throw it and his duffle bag, lantern, into the truck, grab the cabana-striped chair, and off he would go. It would take about four minutes, max. It could be done. But should he? This was the question. Bob had an extremely outlandish hobby, had guns handy, they were alone in the forest, about four miles from town. and he obviously had a drinking problem that had the potential to turn violent. But Stan was desperate for a rationale for staying.

"I'm going to fly out of here because Bob has a fixation on Bigfoot?" he thought. "Because he drinks too much once in a while? What if he was fixated on collecting pine cones and cataloging them? Or samples of tree bark, or rocks, or leaves?" Just because his Bigfoot hobby was bizarre, Stan reasoned, didn't mean he couldn't live with him. "We don't have to agree on *everything*. We had a terrific time around the fire last night, before Bob went on his binge" he thought, and Bob was "more than capable of conducting himself in a normal and coherent way most of the time, and he possessed so much knowledge about the forest and animals".

Stan walked down to the stream, looking at the deep charcoal blue hue of the water, and needed to find his rationale. He talked to himself. "Live and let live, that's what I'll do. And the guns? Okay, he's got guns. So what? I might have one too if I lived here.

You never know what or who might intrude, and these days, you can't be too careful". He walked a few feet in the wet sand, and then back again, gathering his thoughts, and continued speaking to himself. "All I have to do is get along with Bob, listen to him, maybe gain a little knowledge about nature, excluding the Bigfoot nonsense, not get in his way and not challenge him, and definitely not display any skepticism about his hobby, and all will be fine. He's not a violent guy".

So that was it. He would stick around for a few more days, tops, unless Bob went to a higher level of crazy with his drinking. It would give him time to sort things out, come up with a plan. Maybe he actually would go to L.A. and see what the acting scene was all about? He'd never forgive himself if he took a pass. The chances were a million in one, "but hey, maybe I will stumble upon the right audition, and I will be on my way, it's a long shot, but it's not gonna happen if I don't try" he encouraged himself.

But what was the ham radio set up all about? It was far too sophisticated to be just for fun, there had to be more to it. And that antenna! He debated with himself as to whether he should go back to the trailer, and ask Bob about the radio equipment, but he thought the better of it, and instead, figured he'd walk down the road and check out the little town of Index.

It wasn't a short walk, but he needed some time to think things through, so the four leisurely miles went fairly fast, with only two vehicles passing him in ninety minutes, a Jeep and a pickup. They were both headed away from town, in the direction of the campsite. Both cars were older, and covered in dust, so he deduced they must be locals. Both drivers gave him a good long look as they sped by, raising clouds of dust. But not unfriendly looks. He arrived at Fifth Street, which took him over the beautiful old steel bridge, spanning the river, and then into town. There wasn't a lot to it, as he had noticed before, but now he was looking more closely and on foot. There was a bar and grill, fire station, post office, a combination laundromat and yoga studio, a boarding house that looked quite old, but very well kept up. Some late model cars, clean ones, were parked neatly out in front belonging to travelers, he figured.

The one store, located on a small side street, that immediately attracted him was the Index General Store. Every establishment, it should be noted, was called the "Index" something or other, never with a person's name or some other designation other than the name of their very small town.

He walked inside the general store to the sound of a small bell on the door. Nobody was around. He scanned the place, which was surprisingly large in square footage. It had the usual small-town-in-the-woods feel with a creaky wooden plank floor, old neon beer signs over the reefer stocked mostly with Bud, Pabst, and Coors, and a wonderful assortment of merchandise, just not much of it. In the back were a couple of wheelbarrows and a stack of trash cans, some stock tanks, and rolls of livestock wire. There was a small but complete grocery on the one side, and then on the other side, tools, propane canisters, flannel shirts, and a whole section devoted to trout fishing. He was instantly jealous of this charming little place, probably barely making a profit, wishing that it was his. He walked down the aisle labeled "Angling", and he thought to himself, "Huh...angling". That's what his dad had always called it. That word and "cockamamy" were two "dad words" that stuck out in his memory.

He got a sudden rush of missing his dad, remembering the days spent fishing with him along the Miami or the Honey. It was one of the few times he could remember when his dad was focused on him, giving him the impression, he wanted to be near his son, doing something fun. Stan didn't want to become too wistful, standing there in the aisle, for he knew himself well enough to know that soon, wistful would morph into melancholy, and that is one thing he intended to avoid now that he was here.

He walked up and down a couple of more aisles, surveying the paper towels, jars of peanut butter, and cans of soup, and the sad-looking fresh produce section. He figured, he may as well grab some fresh fishing supplies, and went back to the "Angling" section, grabbed a new lure, some four-pound test fluorocarbon line, and a jar of Balls O' Fire salmon eggs. Half way to the front counter, he thought better of it, and went back to trade the four-pound for six-pound, as the creek looked like it could house some big ones.

By then the storekeeper had shown up, carrying a broom and dust pan. He looked to be about sixty, was thin with a weathered face, as if he used to be a cowboy or ranch hand, but now his health or age had made him decide to become a retailer. He didn't seem sad or angry about it, just resigned to his fate, making the rounds sweeping up. He looked up at Stan, did a quick nod, and headed toward the register. Stan put his goods down on the counter and smiled, thinking about the role reversal. "Anythin' else?" said the storekeeper.

"No, no, that'll do, thanks". After a beat, Stan added, "nice place you got here," and with a smile, "name's Stan"

The retailer gave Stan a quick look, checking for sarcasm, found none, and said dryly, "Thanks. Name's Jack". He had a classic antique cash register, that made up for its inefficiency by being so very beautiful. It was a National, and must've been from the early 1900's, with artisan tooling on the wooden body, and the brass register drawer, with beautifully rendered trim designed with vines and leaves made of brass. and with brass keys. It was a show piece. It took the storekeeper a long while to manually ring in each individual item. And then he had to calculate the sales tax, using a pad and pencil. This gave Stan an opportunity to look past the storekeeper's head, to the wall behind. There were all kinds of things to look at, from a large "Trout Life" wall calendar, to a cluster of snap-shots of people holding fresh-caught fish, and an assortment of taxidermy Rainbows and Browns.

Included in the charming mountain store hodgepodge, was something that caught Stan's eye. He leaned forward ever so slightly. What was in the color photo he was looking at? It was a blow up, an 8x10, and it appeared to be of a large brown or black bear, standing on its hind legs, next to a Black Cottonwood, looking in the direction of the photographer, who seemed to be about twenty-five yards away. Someone had circled the subject of the photo using a ball point pen, and then, an arrow pointing to it. The image looked blurry to Stan, and it was hard to make out. He kept looking at it, hoping his eyes would come into focus, but no luck.

The storekeeper finished his task, and said, "That'll be twenty dollars, eight-one cents".

As Stan fumbled for his wallet, he asked, "So, what's the photo of? I can't quite make it out, looks blurry, my eyesight, you know…".

The storekeeper took the twenty and single from Stan, entered the amount on the register, and then hit the "amount tendered" key, with the drawer springing open, accompanied by a little internal bell sounding off. It was quite a production. The storekeeper handed Stan his nineteen cents, and indicating the photo on the wall over his head, said, "Well that's because the photo *is* blurry. Ain't your eyes, not altogether least-ways".

Stan took the change in the flat of his palm, and stuck it in his pocket absent-mindedly, transfixed by the blurry photo. "So, what is it anyway, a bear, right?".

The storekeeper gave Stan a look, and chuckled, "No, that ain't no bear".

"Oh, right", said Stan. "Not a bear. Okay". He didn't want to appear too much the out-of-towner, the tourist stopping by on his way to a resort with stupid questions, but he had to hear the answer he knew he was going to get, and asked, "What is it?"

The storekeeper had no time for this, had lots of chores to do before closing, so he moved from behind the counter, headed to his rounds. With his back to Stan, walking away, he said, "We call him Tripleby'".

Stan, still looking up at the photo, then to Jack, quickly replied, "Tripleby?"

The storekeeper, continuing to move away, said, "Big, bad and brown". With that, he hung a right and went down an aisle, out of sight.

Stan stood looking after him, and then looked back at the photo, squinting. "Who's kidding who around here" he said quietly to himself. Then it hit him. "Tripleby. Triple B."

His other visits around town were not nearly as eventful, Bigfoot-wise, as he strolled around the hamlet, which was only three blocks long by four blocks wide, mostly made up of small wood-framed houses, most of them well kept, but some looking a little ragged. The fire station was the volunteer type, so no one was there. The post office consisted of a locked room with P. O. boxes, and a metal mail deposit box outside. The bar and grill was where it was happening.

Stan went inside and found about ten people there, seated at either the counter or in booths, most seemed like locals, judging by their dress, but it was hard to be sure. The bar was in an adjoining room on the opposite side, packed with customers, mostly locals, their voices and laughter spilling into the dining half of the place. There was a magazine rack and a shelf with post-cards, maps, camping knives, and the usual assortment of souvenir items.

When he walked in, some had given him a cursory glance, and returned to their coffee, pie, Salisbury steak, or meatloaf. Stan slid into a small booth, opened up the tattered menu, and scanned the choices, many of which had been taped over or crossed out with a pen. In spite of that, he found a tuna melt that sounded pretty good, with fries.

The usual but brief banter came from the waitress, and the food was delivered fast and hot. He chowed down, thinking of Bob's critique of his eating habits. Their big lunch seemed hours ago. A different waitress showed up, asked him how his meal was, that the other waitress's shift had ended, that her name was Hailey, and ended up having a long talk with Stan at his table, with almost everyone having cleared out during this in-between lunch and dinner time slot. The bar was still hopping.

They didn't talk about anything personal, mostly about fishing, the trees, the Snohomish tribe, hunters and hunting, what the most popular maple syrup was in the restaurant (Mrs. Butterworth's) as opposed to the best in the house (Anderson's), where most people did their "serious" shopping (Monroe), and of course, what her estimate was on how many people in town believed that Tripleby was for real (two-thirds).

Stan walked back up the road to the campsite. He had been gone over four hours. He was enjoying the solitude, the dense forest all around him as he walked, the day getting later, the shade starting to take over the valley. When he arrived, Bob's old Beetle was parked in the same place, and his truck was just as he had left it. The door to the trailer was swung open.

Stan walked to the trailer, not calling out, but instead, walked quietly up the stairs, and inside. He was unsure what kind of a mood he would find Bob in, and wanted the advantage of surprise. The moment he walked in, he heard Bob talking to someone and saw that he was in the back room, at his ham radio table, his back to Stan, headphones on, with a mic positioned near his face. He was turning dials and flicking switches like a mad scientist. Stan couldn't make out what he was saying, so he moved in a little closer.

Bob's hands moved off the dials and he said, in his gravelly voice into the mic, "Yes, I've had a similar experience once, up near Hogarty Creek, 'bout four summers ago".

Then he paused and listened.

After a long while, Bob spoke up again, "That sounds like you got outta there just in time Ellis, just in time. Let me ask you, what you think he was trying to do, just scare the living shit out of you, or somethin' maybe worse?".

Again, there was a long silence, much longer this time, with the person on the other side apparently responding.

This back and forth went on for quite a few minutes, with Bob responding again, "Yeah, that's a lonely road all right, even in the daytime, but hell, at night, not gonna find me out there. You figured they were walking you out, paralleling you til you got outta the area?"

Again, Bob listened, and finally the conversation had drawn to a close, with Bob thanking the person for his "terrifying account" and cautioned him "to be careful out there". Bob waited a moment then said, "Be sure to tune in this Friday, I got a good one for you, about two guys who were hiking Cape Flattery about a year ago, and how they damn near didn't get out alive, from the sounds of it. 'Til then, this is Bigfoot Bob signing off", and Bob hit a switch, turning off the receiver, and another switch for the router. Bob took off his headphone, checked his tape deck, and turned that off as well. He swiveled around in his chair to discover Stan, leaning in the doorway. He was exuberant, with a beaming smile. "Hey Stan! Where you been partner? You hear any? Oh, guess not, had the speaker turned off, but it was pretty good. That guy was pretty damn shook up, let me tell you".

Chapter 12

Seconds later, with Stan trying to hide his astonishment, Bob let out a little chuckle, shook his head, took a kerchief from his pocket and wiped his forehead of sweat. "You my friend are in one of the *hottest* hot spots in the Northwest. That guy, Ellis, he was tellin' me 'bout his encounter just up here a ways, near Whitehorse Mountain, and man oh man, was he ever rattled, I mean scared fuckin' shitless, I am tellin' you".

Stan didn't know what to say, where to start, and finally said, "So, you been doing this a long time, these calls?"

Bob, looking at Stan quizzically, sensing his friend was a little confused, maybe even a little scared, talked to Stan in a calm voice, and for the next few minutes gave him a grand tour of his set up, showing him all the equipment, what it does, how his TV antenna, perched high above the trailer, adapted to pick up a Wi-Fi signal, takes that signal through his router, how he can accept live phone calls from cell phones, and how he can playback recordings or past recorded calls, to his listening audience.

"Yes, been doin' this for six years now, call myself 'Bigfoot Bob', I guess you heard that, got over three-thousand listeners, new folks calling in every week". And then he added with a chuckle, "I hate that name,

'Bigfoot', very disrespectful, but it sells the popcorn, you know?"

All Stan could do was absorb all of this, while wondering if Bob had any memory of last night, or if he had simply blacked out. Stan was trying to be very non-judgmental about Bob's mental health, tried to suppress thoughts of how unhinged he had become, and how potentially dangerous he was to himself, and perhaps others. It also occurred to him that Bob was not just doing this to spread his dogma, but that he enjoyed being a celebrity, an authority about something, and seeing as how no one could disprove anything he was saying, he was protected, in a bubble.

Stan took the tutorial, and was genuinely interested in what sober Bob was teaching him, and wanted to show he respected him. Bob spoke of the calls he had received, filled with rich details about encounters. There had been sounds heard in the forest, foot prints, suspicious arrangements of tree branches, rocks and pine cones sailing through the air, the sounds of foot falls, and on rare occasion, an actual sighting.

It was a delicate balance, for Stan had no investment in the whole Bigfoot thing, but was invested in his friend, as screwed up as he was. He also was aware that there were two sides to Bob, and he wanted the nice side to stick around, not go dark. Stan thought about the dirt clod scat samples, pinned up in the other room and stored in the radio-bedroom in drawers. He thought about all those plaster casts in other drawers. He thought about the photo in the general store. It was as if the entire community was suffering from some kind of mass delusion, or perhaps they all knew very well, in the back of the collective mind's, that this whole thing was rubbish, but it was something they could agree on, something they could merrily focus on, talk about, not something as polarizing as politics or religion, something that would tie the isolated forest community together, and also, that it might bring them the occasional paying visitor.

Stan had no knowledge that Index was a "hot spot" or not, but his guess was that it must be considered as such, why else would Bob have chosen this place over so many others?

As Bob continued demonstrating his equipment, like a kid with a new toy, Stan thought that if Bob in fact had three-thousand listeners, or even half that many, obviously this shared belief gave comfort and an explanation to a large collection of impressionable people, who would see a bear out in the woods and think to themselves, what an odd-looking bear it was? And all those spooky sounds? Screams and hoots and whoops coming from deep inside the woods couldn't possibly be a known animal, right? The wood knocks couldn't possibly be a dry limb falling from a tree, or a normal and documented animal knocking into something, or the sound of footsteps in dry leaves is never a deer? Or a bear or elk, never stands to reach for some wild fruit or berries? Stan could sit down and write a hundred examples of normal everyday causes, up to and including, misinterpreted tracks, or partial tracks that didn't look like a bear track, but in fact, were. It was so easy to believe in something this unorthodox, for no one could entirely dispute you as there was no negative evidence disproving Bigfoot. The believer was safe in their cocoon, and some had found Bob, to help validate their misguided beliefs.

Stan knew he was a considered by Bob to be a skeptic, but Stan thought of it more as simply being realistic and objective. All this "evidence" that Bob had collected, all the testimonials from his callers about their "encounters" wasn't so much about Stan being a skeptic, but about a mass hysteria enveloping all of these crazy ass Bigfoot groupies, all shook up about the scary wild world we live in, and looking for answers to their questions, their fears, looking to explain the "unexplainable" even though it was very explainable. Deflecting, and characterizing someone like Stan as close-minded or a cynic, served the irrational believers well. It was important to smear someone like Stan, a person holding perfectly reasonable doubts about an undiscovered population of ape-men roaming the entire country. No doubt, primitive people, many thousands of years ago, living in caves, did much the same, when confronted with thunder-storms and earthquakes, assigning those events to something supernatural, with others seeking more realistic explanations.

Stan thought it ironic that the fundamental reason he had to leave Tipp was because people don't like being taken for suckers. And now here he was, buried in the forest, having watched Bigfoot Bob and his callers take one another for suckers. Stan knew he had some mental health issues, but all of *this* insanity? He wasn't nearly as far gone as Bigfoot Bob. This gave Stan all the more reason to plan his exit to Hollywood, and maybe sooner than later.

Stan had knowingly escaped the turmoil and sadness of Tipp City, and was not trying to sugar coat it, to call his "escape" by some other softer and kinder word. He knew that troubles will follow you, and that you cannot simply change location, and that all those troubles will obediently stay back. He knew that those troubles were contained inside of his head and not floating around in space. He further knew, that no one gets to go through life unscathed, and that carrying the baggage of pain and tough memories, was all part of the human condition. This is basic fundamental stuff, and he was aware of that. He had once played a character in a play that was fraught with pain and indecision, so he knew it to be true. But he was not about to permanently typecast himself as a moody and gloomy. This monkey wrench was a problem for Stan's Grand Plan. It required that he make a revised plan. Stan needed to find a completely new environment, which might then springboard him to a whole new outlook, but he had not calculated Bob being so nuts. He couldn't allow this unplanned wrinkle to ruin his overall original plan to forge a new life. He was a pragmatist and knew it, and would handle this crisis in a pragmatic way, and improvise.

Stan was all too aware that someone with less self-awareness, "someone who liked to entertain fantasies, might be prey to all this Bigfoot ridiculousness", he thought to himself, but not him. And he was right about that. Stan simply did not have that kind of a personality, that kind of viewpoint of the world around him. He believed in real-life practical things, good or bad, and did not indulge in fantastical beliefs as a way to explain away life's tough realities. Stan was not a "rainbow bridge" kind of a guy. Not to say he didn't hold the door open, for he did. He knew he had deeper beliefs, perhaps even spiritual beliefs, and was sure that one day he would find them. As for Bob and his beliefs, if it made Bob happy or fulfilled to invest so heavily in this belief of an ape-man stomping around in the woods, then fine, let him have at it. Stan being a guest at his campsite did not mean he had to throw in with Bob and adopt his beliefs. But Stan had to be careful, so as to not be perceived as challenging Bob, countering him in any way. It might become volatile, even dangerous for Stan, for he remembered seeing the Smith and Wesson, and had watched Bob let loose on a Chianti-fueled rant. Besides which, it simply wouldn't be polite to challenge his host's beliefs, no matter how zany.

For the next three days, Stan politely declined to go on "walkabouts" with Bob, in search of new evidence. Stan would invent all kinds of reasons to not join him: feeling a little nauseous, wanting to walk into town, wanted to check on an oil leak from his truck, wanted to start writing a book, needed to figure out his future financial plans, and so forth. Stan may have lacked certain valuable emotional traits, may have dismissed self-analysis in favor of "real-time self-awareness", whatever in the hell that meant, but he had a good imagination.

Bob would consistently head out about eight in the morning, and return at about three in the afternoon. Bob came back empty-handed on two days, except for more baggies of dirt clods, but then on the third day, came back with a freshly-made foot print cast.

"This one here I found 'bout two miles up, just off the trail, musta passed it on my way up, or else maybe it was made after I already passed, hard to say" said Bob excitedly. "This one is a big boy" he added. Bob took the plaster cast from his knapsack gingerly, and laid it on the picnic table.

"It is a big one for sure" Stan said supportively. Any one of a number of people in the small town could be at their kitchen sink right now, rinsing off their fake latex foot, he thought to himself.

It wasn't a matter of Bob having low intelligence, or being gullible, but it was about this whole "belief" thing, this kind of circuitry in some people's brains that allowed, or required, their belief to override reason, facts, and common sense. "Some people need to believe" thought Stan.

Anyway, there he stood, looking at Bob as he carefully brushed off the contaminating bits of dirt and leaf, from his latest casting. It looked like a big human foot to Stan, with nothing extraordinary about it, except for the enormous sixteen-inch length. Stan thought it was either a very bad case of dysmorphia with one of the locals, or more likely, a local with a wicked sense of humor.

"Just off the trail" said Bob, while brushing off the debris with a stubby paint brush before taking it inside to the safety of a drawer.

"Unusual, to be so close to the main trail, that's different", he said to Stan, holding the cast up in the strong light of his desk lamp. He showed Stan a couple of features, and Stan, being the good guest, paid rapt attention.

Bob, pointing to a crease in the print with a pencil, said, "See here? A non-human primate has dermal ridges running laterally along here, and here, see? In humans, those ridges also run perpendicular, but none here at all, and then see here, at the base of the hallucial metatarsal? These ridges are flowing lengthwise, along the side of the foot. You don't find that on a human foot, no sir". A ten-year old kid who knew nothing of anatomy or anthropology would have been mightily impressed, and Stan, listening to this tech-talk, more or less fell into that same category. Who was he to disagree?

It occurred to Stan that his keen abilities at recognizing bullshit was due to his keen ability to create it, and it might be put to good use, giving him a hobby while visiting Index. He needed an activity. Two or three hours of fishing was a nice daily routine for Stan, but he would love to burn up one or two more hours discreetly debunking Bob's nonsense.

Stan thought that while Bob went off in the woods looking for evidence, Stan could, while appearing to be a clueless visitor, do some snooping around in town, and maybe even find the Bigfoot culprit. Perhaps he'd come upon a carelessly unlocked garage door, and inside a work bench with molds and a big tub of liquid latex? He'd have to be careful of course, not wanting to shake up a nest of Bigfoot zealots, or a lone hoaxer with a gun, but it could be fun to see if he could discover the source, even if he told no one about it. But first, Stan needed some first-hand experience, so on the fourth day, he told Bob he'd go with him on one of his walkabouts.

They set out at about eight, with the air cool and the sun just beginning to splash some light down into the hollow. At first, it was not a tough hike, only gaining altitude gradually, but then it became steeper about a mile up. Bob stopped and pointed out where he had found the print the day before. It was about twenty feet off the trail, downward, near the creek, in small patch of soft sand. They went down and took a look at it, weaving their way through a stand of saplings. It was pretty much the same as yesterday, Bob commented, only now a little more crumbled, not as fresh, what being in moist sand, and with the damp air from last night. There was only the one print, sitting squarely in the sand patch, with a carpet of leaves and branches on the one side of the track, and the creek itself on the other. They looked around for a few minutes, in search of a second print, but no success. Bob called it, and they walked up the gentle slope to the trail and continued on.

Bob had in mind a location he thought to be potentially ripe. Bob was always in the lead, with Stan behind him about ten feet. Bob would talk almost non-stop, going on at length, disgorging his bountiful knowledge onto his student: "People can't just dismiss all this shit. To say all this evidence is fake is to dismiss the cultural heritage of the earliest inhabitants of this land. It's disrespectful. All the Northwest aboriginals knew about this hairy wild man, hell, dozens of tribes have wood carved masks, people just think they made this shit up?" Bob did not have the eloquence of a university professor or anthropologist, but he had memorized the key words and passages pretty well. Stan walked silently behind Bob, with the occasional "Uh huh" or "Yeah", just to let his host know he was being attentive. Stan noticed, that on this hike, Bob had brought his canon.

They had gone in about three miles, and took a break, sitting on some rocks, drinking some water, eating protein bars. It was obvious that Bob was in his element. He no doubt saw himself as some kind of a Crockett or Boone, an adventurer, a trailblazer, and perhaps someone who would attain a certain measure of fame by being the first person to take a clear, close, and non-blurry video of "the ape man". Bob always had his cell phone at the ready, hanging from a bright orange silicone lanyard around his neck, and had rehearsed picking it up, hitting the video record button, and holding the camera steady, with a wide-angle horizontal frame. And then with his two fingers, zooming in on a distant object. He could perform this in about three seconds flat. Not bad.

Bob, talking over his shoulder to Stan, would explain that the big reason no one had captured a good video image before was due to a number of factors, including an inferior quality smartphone camera or lens, a low battery charge, poor lighting such as a strong backlight, or a sharp contrast between bright sunlight and dark shaded forest (where the Sasquatch invariably was), the inability to properly focus the shot, and then of course, fear. Bob said that fear was probably the biggest reason.

"Most people, even those thinking they are fully prepared to encounter the big guy are not ready at all. They talk themselves into that impression of their ability, but when the moment is actually upon them, they'll freeze or run off like little scared rabbits. This is why a three-second video response is so critical". Bob went on to explain, "The big guy doesn't hang around for portraits. He knows what a camera looks like, knows what a gun looks like, so he usually jets off, outta sight, gone". Most people, he said, "Were too damn busy pissing in their pants, fumbling with their cameras, to come even close to getting a shot, a good one anyways. The trick is" he said, "is to stay calm, move your arms smoothly, not be in a rush, to be efficient, and move the camera up smoothly, turn it on, then check the autofocus, then zoom in, check the focus again, and do this within three seconds or else he's just gonna be gone and you'll be takin' a dandy shot of where he was but ain't no more". This earned a big laugh out of Bob with Stan doing all he could to laugh along.

The remainder of the day consisted of Bob examining broken branches along what seemed dear trails, collecting scat samples that looked all the world like they were from deer, not an omnivore, and photographing the smallest of clues, all while recording narration into his cell phone:

"This appears to be a freshly broken branch, about forty-four inches off the ground, within the last twenty-four hours judging by the freshness of the break. The branch break is much higher than a deer or a bear native to this region could make. It is broken in the direction of the stream bed, but we're not close to that here, about two hundred feet up in elevation from there, and a good thousand feet away laterally. No evidence of footprints, but the ground is quite hard and covered in leaves and small branches, so they would be very difficult to detect anyways".

On and on like this, trying to sound as much like an authority as he could manage, like he was some kind of a primatologist out of a university. Sometimes Bob would hand Stan a baggie with dirt clods or broken branches inside, or a hair sample, which looked suspiciously like it was from a deer, or the stuffing of somebody's torn puffy jacket, the hair-like strands having been blown perhaps for miles, until floating down onto a branch, ready to be bagged and tagged by Bigfoot Bob. Bob would impart more scientific mumbo jumbo on him, such as discussing the evolution of primitive tool use by ancient members of the genus Homo that used simple stone tools as far back as 2.5 million years ago, and one to two million years ago, their sophisticated use of tools, and returning to well-established home base camps, and the use of controlled fire.

"None of these things have been observed with our big friend", said Bob. "He could be a hominid, but he split off from our tree a long ass time ago, but they is smart" he concluded.

They continued their ascent up the trail, rarely traveled at this point, suffering from lack of use, erosion, and deferred maintenance. They were in the dense forest above Index, perhaps in the Baker-Sno National Forest, perhaps not, as nothing was posted. No one maintained anything, and visitors this deep into the woods were quite rare.

The area was once owned, inhabited, and controlled by the Skykomish tribe. In more recent times, unincorporated Index became a hub of the logging and lumber business. Gold was discovered not too far away, in the late 1800's, which helped to bolster the town's population. Shortly thereafter, rail lines were put down next to town, and used by the Great Northern Railway, primarily as an aid to the logging companies, which explained the large steel trestle bridge that spanned the Skykomish. Presently, the biggest attraction to the town is plentiful trout fishing nearby, and a five-hundred-foot tall, granite wall just north of town good for "dirt bags looking for a large slab". And, oh yes, Bigfoot. The population hits its peak in 1907, with one-thousand citizens, but had since time steadily dwindled to its current one-hundred and fifty. Bob was an encyclopedia.

Bob and Stan reached a clearing. It was a grassy field, mostly marsh, that was no doubt created by deep snow pack suffocating out the trees, with the constantly moist soil rotting out the tree roots. It was about two-hundred feet in diameter, circular in shape, and surrounded by a dense tree line. Bob motioned for Stan to walk slowly, and make no noise. They stood off the trail, just inside the tree line, and observed the stillness. Bob ushered Stan to a large flat rock, perfect for sitting upon. Bob pulled a lunch for them from his knapsack, and spread it on a kerchief atop the rock. They enjoyed some bread, cheese, apples, water and Hershey bars. They spoke little because that's how Bob wanted it. They were there to observe, and if lucky, to see or hear "Mister Big". Bob had deduced that this kind of a meadow was the perfect place for a squatch to hang out in, or around, as it was full of tasty plant life which attracted deer. As they ate, bird songs could be heard, and the occasional argument between squirrels. There was very little breeze, so the sound of it through the pines, was barely audible.

Bob quietly recounted to Stan, a caller who told him of an incident that occurred in a setting much like this. The caller was a few miles in, near where he lived, and heard a loud roar-scream coming from not too far away. He was instantly frozen with fear, knowing this was not the sound of anything he had ever heard or hunted. He felt queasy, felt the vibrations of the sound in his chest, and fell ill, disoriented, but managed to stumble away. Whatever it had been, paralleled him down the trail, inside of the tree line about fifty feet away, and every time he stopped, it stopped. If he stopped too long, he'd get a small rock thrown at him. This went on for two or three miles, until the man had reached the main road and his truck. He never saw what had made the sound, but it was a sound he would never forget.

Stan thought that this should win first place for the Scary Story Around the Campfire contest, if there was one. And Bob told it in such a convincing way too. Bob grew quiet, and slowly ate his food, looking into the distance. Out of the corner of Stan's eye, he caught a movement of something that seemed large, on the opposite side from them, on the right, about sixty yards away. He slowly reached for Bob's arm and pulled on his sleeve. Bob looked up at him and Stan motioned with his chin, to look over in the direction of the movement, which was now definitely the movement of something large and dark, and from what Stan could tell, standing on two feet. Bob slowly turned his head, saw the large silhouette, while smoothly going for his cell phone that was harnessed in his lanyard. Bob lifted the phone to his face, turned it on, and with two fingers, zoomed in on the dark creature, and started filming. Bob's shoulders were tense, but then relaxed. He put down the phone.

"Black bear. Ursus americanus. Common name Olympic Black Bear, common throughout the Pacific Northwest. Population of about twenty-thousand in

Washington. Lots of them around here. By 'lots' I mean there's probably ten or fifteen in this whole range of five-hundred square miles" he added, with a broad wave of his hand. That broad wave startled the bear and he took off, disappearing into the woods. Bob gave Stan a look and said, "Thought you had yourself one, didn't ya? Go on, admit it".

Sheepishly, Stan said "Well, yeah, maybe, it made me think for a second". And it had.

Bob gave Stan a big grin, and tousled his hair like he was a kid.

"That boy there, he looked to be about four-hundred pounds, not overly large, maybe a female, maybe a juvenile. They can get upwards of five-hundred or more, but hell, even a big one looks tiny next to a big adult male squatch. I mean, really small".

Stan regarded Bob a moment, then said, "So, you've never seen one, in person, have you?".

Bob with a small shrug said, "No, can't say I have, but that is not necessary in order to know those fuckers are out there".

"How come he was standing?" Said Stan.

Bob, packing up the knapsack, and hopping off the rock, said, "He was probably checkin' us out, wanted to get a better look. Besides which, he, or she, looks more intimidating that way. You were a little intimidated, right?" with a laugh.

Stan thought back to seeing that photo of Tripleby.

Bob had an urge to go deeper into the woods but he hadn't brought any camping gear, and didn't want to push it too hard on his "city friend", so they made the marshy meadow their furthest point in, and headed back toward the campsite. The usual three o'clock return became a five o'clock return, because Bob's solo routine had been altered, but that was fine by Bob, for he liked having company on his walkabout, it was a nice change, even if it was with a skeptic.

Dusk was fully on when they arrived and Bob went in his trailer immediately, shedding his knapsack and grabbing a six-pack, which he brought out with him, and placed on the picnic table. He and Stan grabbed some small logs from the firewood stack, and quickly built a fire, settling into their chairs, with a can in hand. Supper could wait. It was a clear night, no clouds, and getting very cool. Bob downed his first brew in two long gulps, and popped another one open. Stan was well behind his pace, and worried about Bob's. About thirty minutes into it, and Bob on his fifth, Stan suggested making some dinner, to which Bob replied grandiosely, "Go for it, buddy!"

As Bob continued to knock back beers, Stan retreated into the trailer, popped open a can of green beans, pulled some mushrooms out of the fridge, threw in a variety of whatever he could find to add to the mix, heated it up in a big frying pan, made some rice, and called it dinner. Actually, it was pretty good, Stan thought, but by the time he could deliver a plate to Bob, it was too late. Bob had sunken into one of his hammered funks, and only stared at the dish Stan had prepared.

The Mandy-thoughts had invaded Stan while making his frying pan meal. Each time he saw or did anything that even remotely reminded him of her, or of them together, it sucked him back into memories. He had made many frying pan dinners for them. But unlike a rom-com, theirs was not entirely a "meet cute" beginning, but simpler, more under the radar, slower to come on. Stan was here in the mountains to apply medicine to his wounds, not dredge up old painful memories, so he concentrated on the hot fire, ate his meal, and zoned out.

By the time Stan was done eating, Bob had picked at his, taking maybe two bites, it was totally black outside, with the creek gurgling away, and some of the night birds flying around, beginning to sing. Bob was also flying. "I can hear shit other people can't, you know" slurred Bob from his chair.

"How's that?" asked Stan.

Bob had gone a few nights without getting looped, but now, he was going deep into it again, with the exaggerated emphasis of a cliche' drunk, and said again, "I can hear shit you can't".

"Oh, all right, that's pretty interesting" said Stan, trying to placate his troubled friend. It quieted down for a few moments, and then Bob leapt up from his chair and began to pace back and forth in front of the fire, like he had done before. He cast a huge shadow on the nearby trees as he went back and forth, talking loudly, angrily, and punctuating the air with his arms and fists. It appeared Stan was not going to be able to gracefully slide away to his tent, to skip the show, and was in for a ride.

Over the next hour, Bob ranted on, spilling his guts about his quest to find "the squatch" and expressed his contempt for non-believers, for the government, for the National Park system and all of its employees, for game wardens and cops, for "they were all in on it, the fucker's". What it all boiled down to was that Bob was furious that not one official, after six long hard years of being on the air, with all his research, with thousands of listeners, and call-ins weekly, had ever paid him a visit. Not one came to ask him about his evidence, where he found it, or any other pertinent detail.

Bob, turning to Stan, suddenly very conspiratorial, said, "It's because the fuckers already know everything I know, probably more than I know. Those fuckers already know everything about it, who the fuck are they kidding, not me those fuckers, not me, they are in on the whole thing already, that's why they never come around to ask me shit because they already know all the shit" as he nearly fell, stumbling over the rocks around the fire.

The way Bob saw it, the big money concerns, from lumber companies, to ski resorts, to enormous chain stores selling sporting goods, to the National Park Service and State Parks, all wanted to utilize the vast forests of America, or to make giant profits from promoting them, or continue employing thousands, to keep the whole system up and running. They encourage people to go out in the forests and camp, or hike, or ski, or cut timber, or go to some resort, and they did not want the truth to come out, for if it did, the feds would clamp down on everything, would "destroy all those industries over fucking night" if it came out to the public. And, according to Bob, certain unidentified feds knew it, were helping to blanket over the whole thing, for the good of all concerned. "Hell, fuck me, the fucking Russians have already put Sasquatch on their endangered species list, you think the EPA wouldn't do the same fucking thing if it all came out in the open? You think for one fucking second the feds, the Congress, CNN, are gonna let Mr. and Mrs. middle America, with their little fucking kids, drive into a park, in their fucking little electric SUV, let them fucking walk around, let'm camp, get killed, for fuck's sake?" Well!!?" said a wild-eyed Bob.

Stan could only sit and agree, wholeheartedly. "Shit, this guy's gone off the rails" Stan thought to himself, being very careful that he didn't say that out loud. Later, Stan would look that little factoid up, about the Russians, and sure enough, they had put the Sasquatch on their list, much to his amazement.

Stan listened to his friend rail on, and thought how unrequited far-out theories often cause some of the crackpot faithful to devolve into reclusive and angry paranoids, and it appeared Bob was not an exception to that, poor guy.

Bob finally ran out of gas, stumbled into his trailer, and collapsed onto his single bed in the radio-bedroom. Stan closed the trailer door, put out the fire, looked around in the dark, smiled at the bird calls, and the scampering of some squirrels or Opossums, crawled into his tent, and laid down to "Islands".

The next morning, Stan got up about eight to discover that Bob had apparently taken off, presumeably on one of his walkabouts, which considering his condition from last night, was fairly remarkable, but apparently normal for Bob.

Stan enjoyed the morning light spilling out over the mountain ridge, sat at the picnic table with a cup of coffee for a while, soaking in the warmth, enjoying the sound of the stream. He began to think about Bob and his drunken rants, and felt sorry for the old guy. He was now beginning to realize that this was a pattern of his, but the threat of it getting worse or becoming violent, was unlikely. Bob had plateaued, and was evidently comfortable with it. Stan was satisfied with his conclusion and took another sip.

Stan's plan to find the imposter, the culprit, to go around town and somehow discover whose garage or tool shed contained the latex foot seemed a less brilliant idea than before. The more he thought about it, the more he realized what a stupid idea it indeed was. With a town so small, everybody had already spotted him, or been told about him, over at the bar and grill, or general store. Most probably knew he was at Bob's campsite, but what about Bob? Not a single person had visited him there. In a community rich with fellow enthusiasts, you'd think at least a few would have paid their respects, shared evidence, hung around and told tall tales? Bob was radioactive, but why? The only person to visit, but not on a social call, was Jack's kid from the general store, delivering groceries once a week in his old Datsun pickup. He was certain people talked behind Bob's back, and even the smallest amount of curiosity expressed by Stan to a local about Bigfoot tracks, would be met with extreme suspicion, especially since he was linked with Bob?

Even though Bob had made this his secondary, if not his primary home, maybe he was not good enough for the locals? Maybe Bob was considered an outsider, an outcast, just as with Tipp? His dogged belief in Bigfoot would make him a welcome addition, one would think? But maybe not. It could have been something as simple as human politics at play. Perhaps the owners of the more upscale bed and breakfast wanted to dissuade the kook image of their town being a Bigfoot epicenter? Maybe their clientele, or the more upscale ones, the upper crust from Seattle they were trying to attract, were above such nonsense? Perhaps, the B&B was in hand-to-hand combat with all the local Airbnb's that had cropped up in the recent years? What with their grand looking hotel, such a centerpiece of the town, perhaps being the retail anchor of the town, they have a lot of sway, a lot of pressure they can apply? Maybe if the owners of the general store or bar and grill were to be known as friends of Bob, and therefore were encouraging of the Bigfoot myth, their businesses might get some resistance next time they had a Health Department inspection, or a visit from the Agriculture Department for weights and measures, or the State Liquor and

Cannibis inspector came by? Maybe in a place this small you had better go along to get along? This was of course all speculation on Stan's part, but he was a bit of an expert on how a community can apply downward pressure on a business if they disapprove.

Also, people who genuinely believe they've had an encounter with one of these things, are not usually given to talking about it. In fact, even in a town such as this, with maybe two-thirds of the people being believers, as Hailey had guessed, nobody likes being thought of as an eccentric, or stupid, or laughed at, or being considered an attention-getter. If some of the fellow citizens of Index also believed in what you believed, then that was fine, and you might talk about it in the privacy of somebody's house, or while leaning against your pickup, outside the general store, but it would be discreet. For the other one-third segment, the very thought that a grown person would entertain such thoughts, the stuff of a kid's nightmare, was beyond ridiculous. The credibility of that person would be thrown into considerable doubt, and they would be forever tagged.

And what of the believers? What was their actual story? How many had seen, as had Stan, a black bear standing on its hind legs, waving its arms, maybe roaring at them? What small percentage of them could actually claim having seen one, and not seen a bear? Maybe none of them. But, when the seed of fear has been planted in your head, when some goofy preconceived idea has been introduced, and even if a complete skeptic and non-believer, you find yourself up high in the woods, by yourself, and you see what could be a Bigfoot peering at you from behind a distant tree, you are probably going to get out of there as fast as your feet will carry you, believing you may have just had an encounter. If on the other hand, you look at the distant dark creature looking back at you, and know it to probably be a Black Bear, or wanting to clarify if it is or is not, it is not likely you will advance on it, to get a better look. Black Bears do not have the same unpleasant reputation with people as do Brown Bears, but nevertheless, if you're up in the high country, alone, you are in their living room, and advancing on one could get you into some deep trouble. They do eat meat, and their sense of smell is figured to be up to three-thousand times better than a human's. They can run upwards of thirty-five miles an hour, and the fastest person on Earth runs at twenty-seven. So, good luck with that if you decided to hang around and get a better look.

In the end, fear can be a big player in all of this, whether fear of some mysterious dangerous creature lurking in the high country, or perhaps peering at you through a bedroom window at night, or into your tent? Even the biggest skeptic may have a small part of their mind reserved for the fear factor. "It's primal, it's all about our monkey-brains" said Stan to himself.

What it amounted to, Stan realized, is that the whole subject in town was no doubt a locked vault, and nobody but nobody was going to reveal a thing to Stan, and in fact, might intentionally throw him off track, just to keep him away from the truth, or to just have some fun with the tourist.

But then, something else occurred to Stan, which had the deep awful resonating ring of truth to it. What if the maker of the fake feet, was none other than Bob himself?

It made sense, didn't it? Bob told him how he would sometimes exaggerate a story that had been told to him, and then tell it on the air. He was not above faking people out if it enhanced his image, entertained his listenership, Stan figured. And Bob inflated his own stories as well. Everyone was under the distinct impression he had seen a Bigfoot, because that's what he would say on air. Why not literally, take the next step and do fake foot prints? What's to stop him? Bob always went alone up there, and on rare occasion, rare enough to be believable, would come down the trail with a plaster cast. What else was hidden in his knapsack, Stan wondered? Was there room in there for a sixteen-inch-long latex foot, perhaps? Maybe this is why Bob seemed radioactive? Stan had no point of comparison, but perhaps other enthusiasts, ones that had credibility among other "researchers", saw Bob as a naked imposter, which only helped to make the entire subject look phony.

Stan figured he was on to something. Also, there was a rusty small metal storage shed behind the trailer, the kind people have for storing gardening tools and such. It was locked securely with a big chain and padlock. It is not inconceivable that inside of it was Bob's latex foot workshop, replete with all the necessary supplies and molds? It might be worth investigating if he could somehow get the key.

Even though Stan figured he might be onto something, he realized that if he started going into town playing Columbo, the end result could be having Bob exposed as the faker. Bob was a lot of things, not all of them noble and upstanding, but at his core, he was a good person, who had generously offered Stan sanctuary, when no one else would. So, Stan was now going to turn on him, likely expose him for his hoax? Stan knew something about pranks and hoaxes after all, and if indeed Bob was the source of the tracks, then fine, who gives a damn, what does it matter, who is it really hurting? Stan knew he was right about this. Knew enough about how people in a small town can be tribal, knew how they would come at Bob like people had come at Stan. He decided to be the friend to Bob that he had always thought himself to be, and dropped the whole thing, and that if Bob had a secret, it was safe with him.

Having run all of this through his head, he needed a break, so he grabbed his gear from the truck and walked down to the stream to do a little "angling" to clear his head, concentrate on something outside of himself, and he was doing no harm, for it was all catch and release. He walked downstream about a hundred yards, pushing past overhanging branches, maneuvering over rocks and boulders along the side of the creek, and found a terrific deep pond just past a small waterfall, got his bait on a hook, dropped in a line, and wham, caught a Rainbow in about five seconds. He hauled him up, a big one, took the hook out of the fleshy lip, and eased him back into the water. The part of fishing that Stan liked the most was the waiting, was the lack of action, so this pool, as perfect as it obviously was, did not offer Stan the serenity he was looking for, so he moved on, to a wide and deep part of the stream, and cast his line in there, knowing the chances of catching a fish in the swifter water was less likely. He called that one right, sat back against a big rock, and settled in, staring at his red and white bobber move with the current. Next thing he knew, he woke up, having drifted off against the rock, with his line and bobber all tangled up in some branch overhang on the other side of the stream. Stan got up, took off his boots, rolled up his pants, and made his way to the other side. The stream was about three feet deep in the center and the rocks all rounded, and slippery. The water was freezing. He got to his line in the branches, cut it loose, and returned to his sleepy place. And then, he remembered. This is close to how he had met Mandy.

Years ago, he had been fishing along the Honey, had seen her downstream a few yards with a group of friends. He couldn't tell if one of the guys was a boyfriend, or a boyfriend to one of the other ladies. There were three women and two guys, so it was anybody's guess. Stan saw Mandy from a distance, but knew she was special. Nothing romantically precious happened, such as his retrieving her caught line in a tree branch, or grabbing her hat from the current, and then being locked in a gaze with her, as he handed her the bobber or hat back. Nothing even close, and in fact, the group was just hanging out by the stream, not fishing. Mandy glanced over at him a couple of times, even gave a little wave to him, and pantomimed to him if they were being too loud for his fishing? He smiled and shook his head "no", and gave a wave back.

It wasn't until he had met Mandy, that Stan had come up from the watery depths where he usually resided. Until then, he was living in a very dark place, many fathoms below, to torture the analogy some more. From the moment he had met her, he could feel years of crap shedding off of him, and felt lighter, less depressed, so there was for him this immediate connection. For her, he may have triggered her maternal instincts, and the need to take care of this man-child. Anyway, over the next two weeks, they bumped into one another three more times. They would exchange nods and move on.

They had probably already seen one another around town, maybe for months, or even years, but it wasn't until that moment at the creek, that a switch had been thrown and now they were on one another's radar. At the third meeting, or fourth, if we're counting the creek, Stan built up the courage to approach her, at the dry cleaners, and start up the obvious conversation about having seen her at the creek, and other places, and all the predictable self-conscious small talk. She seemed to tolerate all this preliminary talk, but seemed intent on getting further along, getting past the tedium of the first dance steps.

She knew what he knew, even if he was too big a coward to admit it. They liked one another from the first second, and that was it. After this, they were inseparable, with Stan moving out of his depressing hovel of an apartment to her house, a quaint little wood frame place on the outskirts of town with a picket fence in need of some fresh paint.

Stan snapped out of his daydream, tried to shake it off, for what followed next in the storyline was not nearly as wonderful a memory, for it involved his shortcomings. As he walked back upstream toward the campsite, he had a revelation and not an altogether good one, but he had opened himself up emotionally, and had apparently made the big mistake of feeling his feelings. He hated that.

He realized that his break up with Mandy wasn't about all his nonsense with the Scalopini hoax, or any other nonsense he had cooked up over the years, but it was about one inescapable fact: Mandy no longer loved him. Maybe at one time she truly did, but currently, in real time, she did not, and that is not the kind of thing you can get back. She had Stan-fatigue, for Stan was an exhausting kind of a person to be around, because it was always about him.

Stan believed that it is some type of magic, beyond the pheromones, that the X-factor of love exists at all, and once it has been betrayed by neglect, or by repeated stupid acts, which seemed to be Stan's special ability, then it dry rots, it is a goner, not able to be resuscitated.

He found himself standing by a tree, near the stream, caught up and lost in his thoughts.

"Yo, Stan, you in a trance of somethin'" said Bob, standing a few feet away, puzzled by Stan's odd demeanor. Bob had splashed his way in the water toward Stan, and sure enough, Stan hadn't heard a thing.

Stan looked up, grateful to have been rescued from his self-analysis, and said, "No, I'm fine, just doing some thinking, you know…".

Bob, not wanting to pry, or being forced to listen to his friend's rudderless self-involved thoughts, thrust a plaster cast toward Stan with outstretched arms, and a broad smile, saying, "Hey man, look what I got. Another fucking print. Another one! Second one in a week, what the fuck?"

Stan looked at Bob, now convinced that his amazing discovery was just another stupid hoax. It occurred to him how very similar he and Bob were in some ways, and how their respective nonsense was like acid on a relationship. He knew he couldn't be around Bob much longer, for the secret had been blown, and for him to continue to hang around Bob, would mean he was part of the whole shebang, just like Mandy would have been if she had stayed.

Chapter 13

The next three days were spent much like the past few days. Stan would lull his time away, plotting his exit. It would be very soon, as Stan figured it, any day now.

Bob's routine was consistent. He would depart in the morning, return in the mid-afternoon, often with various bagged samples, but not another plaster cast. Bob was surgical with his deception, not pouring it on too thick, but just enough to lure the believer or wannabe, into his web.

Stan would try to discover a new fishing hole, upstream, or down, even though the spot right in front of the campsite was the perfect one. It struck him as odd that Bob had never shown much interest in fishing, being in such a prime location for it. In fact, Bob seemed oblivious to the whole endeavor, often clomping around in the stream within earshot of Stan while he was fishing, rinsing something off or grabbing a pail of water, and scaring away all the fish within a hundred feet. Sometimes he could even see Stan, just a few feet away, see him with his line in the water, and was clueless. Or maybe he thought it was funny?

Stan put in more time reading of "Islands", trying to not read too fast, not wanting it to end, and spend some quality time napping in a hammock he had discovered rolled up behind the trailer. After rigging it between two trees, it became Stan's favorite place to be, often drinking a can or two, before taking a nap. Pure indulgence.

One morning Stan drove into town and bought three bags worth of groceries for them, plus two twelve-packs. He knew they wouldn't last long with Bob, but he wanted to pitch in and contribute to the cause, leave Bob with a favorable memory of him, as he knew departure time was nearing.

For Stan, this had been the best kind of therapy, even with the likes of Bob as his camping partner. He was sad to know it was ending soon, but also knew he wasn't cut out for the camping life, or the isolation that being a Bigfoot "researcher" required, even if he did believe.

The "Bigfoot Bob" podcast would air twice a week, sometimes in the early evening, sometimes in the afternoons, and Bob would take hours to get prepped for the show. This left five days in Bob's schedule for evidence hunting and his raging beer-driven rants. It was a schedule he kept to with fair precision.

When showtime arrived, Bob would sit down to the mic, take calls, offer his perspective, commiserate with people who were still rattled by their encounter, some of them having allegedly occurred nearly twenty years ago. People were generally embarrassed to talk about it, but had built up the nerve to go public, feeling that Bob's podcast was a safe place for them. On his podcast, there was no shame, no need to apologize, no judgment or embarrassment, only acceptance and understanding. Bob would delicately pull their confessional stories out of them. In a way, Bob had taken on some of the qualities of a pastor. People would confide the most amazing and personal things, some of them completely irrelevant to the topic. Others callers were bolder, supposedly having had an encounter a very recent week or two ago, and wanted to declare it, shout it to the world. Bob especially liked the callers who lived in the state, for they were near his ground zero, but often times, calls came in from all over; from Tennessee, Texas, upstate New York, Pennsylvania and yes, even Ohio.

Stan would sit discreetly, and listen to the show, often two hours long or longer, depending. His ears perked up with the Ohio callers, one in particular who claimed to have had a terrifying encounter with two of the ape-men in the Salt Fork region, lapping over into the state park there, which was to the east of Columbus, not far from Tipp. It was very remote, densely wooded, and had labyrinths of caves. Stan was familiar with the region, having gone there a few times over the years, and the caller's description of the terrain was accurate, but the largest animal Stan had ever seen there was a very fat Beaver.

A recurring theory was that these hairy creatures lived in the caves located there, and for that matter, in cave systems all over, numbering in the thousands across the North American continent. Of course, the caller never saw the big guys, just heard them growling, screaming, and paralleling them as they bustled their way out of the woods. All of these stories shared a very familiar plot line, many of the details quite similar, to such an extent that it all sounded rehearsed. People do ridiculous things in order to be momentarily "famous".

After one show, as they sat around the campfire, Stan trying to be as delicate and non-confrontational as possible, had to know something about the way Bob's mind worked, and timed it when Bob was pre-hammered.

"So, Bob, when I asked you if you have yourself ever seen one, you said no? For real?"

Bob, not the least bit offended, said, "Yeah, that's the truth of it".

"So why do you say you have on your show?"

Bob fell silent, reached for his first beer, and leveled a look at Stan. He took a long swig and looked at Stan some more. "This is the way I see it. I know he's out there, sometimes I can feel eyes on me. I see the prints, the scat, the hair, hear all the stories, so I know what it is I know. My people want to believe, and it's my job to help them along with that. So yeah, I embellish some, take it a step farther than the absolute truth. I swear, sometimes when I been out there, if I had turned around a split-second sooner, taken another couple steps around that bend in the trail, I woulda seen him, I know it, I been that close".

Stan knew when to shut up, and held up a can, and said, "Cheers".

Stan wanted to press him some more, about his latex foot theory, but Stan wisely didn't bring that up, for it could only be a lose-lose situation for him.

If it turned out Bob was in fact the maker of the fake feet, and was the hoaxer making the impressions up the trails, by the streams, then Bob would be stripped of his pride, would fear being exposed, fearful and threatened that it would destroy whatever credibility he had, and that would not go well.

On the other hand, if Bob wasn't the hoaxer, then Bob could erupt with indignation at the very thought that Stan had no belief whatsoever in his world, in his podcast, in Sasquatch, or in Bob, for that matter. That wouldn't go well either.

Best to clam up, Stan thought, leave my theories to myself. Bob was still giving Stan a hard long look, and opening another can said, "I think you need to come with me tomorrow, let's take a different trail". Stan could hardly refuse, having treated Bob's campsite for two weeks as his own personal hillbilly resort, so he said, "Sounds good to me".

The following morning, there was a cold wind, and lots of cloud cover. Bob, standing on the steps of his trailer, surveyed the sky and said to Stan, "This'll blow over. She's just irritated right now, got some cold air pushing her, but it'll die down in an hour or two". Having imparted his meteorological skills onto Stan, Bob instructed him to help him lug stuff to his Beetle. Apparently, they were going on a road trip. Once the knapsacks, bags of casting plaster, two twelve-packs of beer, a five-gallon Jerry Can for gas, two loaves of organic whole wheat bread with jars of peanut butter and preserves, sleeping bags, tent, and various other supplies had been crammed into his sad looking little car, Bob said, "This is just in case we wanna stay a day or two. Okay, let's mount up!".

Stan slid into the passenger side, with the entire back seat packed full of all the supplies. Bob squeezed himself behind the wheel, slammed his door shut, wiggled the stick, and turned the key. The engine tried to fire up but quit, and after the third try, it fired up with a roar. Bob said, "It's been a while since I stretched her legs".

This was not Stan's first time in an old Beetle. When he was twenty, his girlfriend Lisa May Jergens had a '72 Beetle, and while some of the cosmetics were different, it was essentially the same car as what Bob had, except for one notable difference: Bob's engine sounded like it belonged in a Mustang. Bob looked over at Stan with a grin and said, "Sounds nice, don't she?".

Yeah, Stan thought, she sure does. "What's in her anyway?".

With pride, Bob said, "A four-cylinder, 2.3 liter Ford Pinto engine. I converted the whole thing myself years ago. New cooling system, new wiring, new tranny, nasty muffler, and best thing yet, she's a 4x4".

The Beetle sat up higher than normal, and the tires seemed a little large for an assembly line model, but the exterior paint was so shabby and worn, it distracted from those details. Bob threw it into reverse with a lurch, pulled the wheel to the left, and they took off, going across the shallow section of the Skycomish that Stan had come across, and then left, further up Galena Index Road. The Beetle was a tough little thing, made lots of noise, but it had authority. Stan held on to whatever he could, as they bumped along the main road.

After about what Stan figured to be ten miles, Bob slowed down, scanning the woods for a place to park, maybe set up camp. "Oh yeah, there she is" said Bob, yanking the wheel hard to the left, and the Beetle taking the potholes and rocks with ease. They came to a wide part in the river, and Bob threw her into four-wheel drive. They forded the stream without a care, the tires churning through the water, scaring the hell out of all the fish, and probably any other living creature within two miles. They went up a small embankment into a clearing, and parked in a swirl of dust. Bob got out, stretched, looked about, and in a hearty voice said, "Come on out Stan, this is where we need to be! We're out in it!".

Stan hoisted himself out of the cramped cab, looked at Bob who was surveying the area, and also stretched, "Where are we?".

Bob, his frontiersman circuitry all fired up, said while gesturing, "Over thataway is Howard Creek and then just a click over is Lost Creek, but we're not going over there, we're headed over thisaway, to upper Salmon Creek. It'll take us in deep. Nobody, and I mean nobody, goes up in there nowadays. Not even hunters. Just too much damn work. I've always wanted to come up here, just never got around to it".

Stan thought to himself, "Oh great, just what I wanted, a strenuous hike through a dense forest", but he held his tongue, wanted to give Bob as much latitude as possible, for in just a day or two, unbeknownst to Bob, he would be gone, headed south, hoping to land a job as the zany neighbor in a new sitcom pilot, or maybe peddling laundry detergent in a commercial. The possibilities were limitless.

Bob and Stan dragged all the gear out of the car, pitched the tent, gathered rocks and dead wood for a fire later on, and kept all the food items locked up inside the Beetle, should a wandering bear discover their site. With knapsacks fully loaded, and on their backs, they set out, headed toward Salmon, cutting their own trail as they threaded through the trees.

"It sure is beautiful" said Stan, stopping a moment to catch his breath.

"Oh yeah man, this is the spot, and the fish in there? This is the place to catch some *big* ones", said Bob.

They found the stream, and stayed close to it, as the ascent became gradually steeper. They would stop once in a while to catch their breath, take a swig of water, and when that ran out, would dip their brightly-colored metal bottles into the icy water to refill. They were so high up, so far from any kind of contaminants like a cabin or a pasture, that the water was clean, pure and tasted wonderful, having traveled over granite slabs, high up in the mountains. But for all the appreciation of nature, Stan knew that Bob was on a mission, and they were not working this hard just so they could look at pretty birds or a nice stream.

They had hiked about four miles, but they were tough and slow miles, not enjoying the benefits of a cut trail, but instead, moving between trees, over dead wood, rocks, pushing through branches, so the two were pretty well wiped out when they reached a clearing, a huge clearing, similar in appearance to the marshy one they had visited before, this one perhaps carved out by a glacier long ago.

Stan sensed they were getting close to where Bob had wanted to go. Bob stood motionless, listening to the wind through the tops of the trees, to bird calls, the stream rushing by, but now it was a few hundred yards away, below them. They had veered away from the water about half a mile back due to huge granite outcroppings near the water. Stan slid his knapsack off his aching back, and leaned up against a rock. Bob wandered out into the clearing and looked about, bent down to get a hand full of dirt, and tumbled it around in his hand for a moment, considering it, letting some fall through his fingers. He brushed his hand off on his jeans and said, "Okay Stan, this is the spot. I think this'll do just fine".

"Whatever you say Bob" was Stan's reply.

Bob slid his knapsack off as well, unpacked some of the contents onto a rock, grabbed some slices of bread and started slathering peanut butter and strawberry preserves onto the slices with his large hunting knife, handing Stan the first sandwich. He then pulled out two apples, and quartered each, handing Stan his.

Next came out the obligatory Hershey bars and slabs of cheddar cheese. Bob did this in a methodical way, not at all rushed, but precise like a surgeon. All this while he spoke, not looking at Stan.

"I know you think of me as some kinda uneducated nut, Stan, and that's okay, I get it. I mean, I get it because it's true. I *am* uneducated, and I do come across as nuts. Guilty on both counts, but none of that means I'm makin' shit up, you know, I mean, not entirely?"

Stan was taken aback by the sudden and uncharacteristic transparency Bob was exhibiting. He sat silently, hoping Bob would reveal more, for maybe this was leading up to a confession about the latex feet? What Stan didn't know is that Bob was coming unglued.

Finished with constructing lunch, Bob stared off into the distance, the wind heard through the tall trees, the birds singing and chirping, the water down below pouring over rocks into deep pools. After a few moments, Bob started talking, and it slowly developed into one of his rants:

"People don't know about biomechanics, how the foot works, how it works with the ankle, the leg, it all works together and whether we're talkin' a human, a gorilla, a squatch, the tracks they leave are different, the feet, they're different, they all evolved different, adapting to their needs, their environments. The foot of a mountain gorilla is altogether different than a lowland gorilla's foot. You know that, Stan? You remember, I was talkin' about how I can hear stuff you can't? It's true. I can. Most people can hear down to about twenty megahertz, that's twenty million hertz, it's a frequency Stan, just like my radio is a frequency, ya know? I can hear a low hum most folks can't. The big guy, they say he can make sounds lower than that, lower than twenty megahertz, sounds you can't hear, but you can *feel* them. It's called infrasound, Stan. I'm not stupid. Other animals have it, use it, to communicate, or to confuse or depress their prey. Tigers, they have it. Giraffes. They think gorillas have it. Why not our guy out there, maybe he has it...?"

And with that, Bob started to tear up, actually started to cry, and Stan didn't know what to make of it, or what to do. Here was this bigger than life, grizzly-looking outdoorsman friend of his, out in the middle of nowhere, tears rolling down his sunburnt cheeks, choking down a PB&J, and crying.

"What in the hell am I supposed to do?" thought Stan. An awkward moment passed. Then a few more, with Bob turning away, trying to conceal his emotions, to suck it up.

Finally, Stan said the only thing that he could think to say, that he ought to say. "I'm sorry Bob, really. I'm sorry".

Bob, still turned away, said, "Yeah, thanks...I'm just so God damn sideways by all this, so fuckin' pissed off that people think I'm crazy-nuts. I ain't. I know what I know". He then went silent, still looking away, rubbing his eyes dry.

For Stan, beyond the immediate anxious situation out here alone with unstable Bob in the wilderness, his trusty 44 no doubt tucked away in his knapsack, he realized that he had on his hands, some kind of a "emotionally unstable" person, or genuine nut job, or call it what you will. In spite of Bob's self-assessment stating otherwise, it seemed there could be no other conclusion. Stan thought silently to himself: Bob was part of a collaborative insanity. He was in search of a touchstone. He was deeply committed to comparing what he thought to be apples to apples. He would read up and compare "studies" of human foot prints to alleged squatch prints. He would hear on other podcasts, stories of hair samples brought in for DNA analysis, with most of them being from bears, elk, horses, deer, humans, and once in a great while, being deemed inconclusive. Maybe Bob did fake the prints? Bob's head was packed full of testimonials from his callers, many with the wildest tales, some crossing over into the paranormal, about portals, strange orbs of light, about aliens and other dimensions, for Chrissake.

Bob was trying to behave like a scientist, trying to be scientific, but he was out of his depth, caught in swift deep water. He didn't have the mental capability to be objective or truly scientific. For him science was a smorgasbord, where he could pick and choose those "facts" that supported his preconceived opinions, and walk by those that didn't. He had bought into the whole thing, with emotion and imagination, leading the way. There was no common sense in sight. And Stan knew something that Bob didn't: that Bob was trying to compare apples to Orangutans, not to other apples. Bob was trying to explain away one unfounded theory using another unfounded theory. And when not doing that, trying to compare a known factual thing, like all his dirt clod evidence, or the dubious castings of foot prints, to a mythical animal. Sure, even Stan had seen that one print in the sand during their hike, but *one* print? That was it? Again, the latex foot theory factored high in the equation. No matter how Bob wanted to cut it, no matter how he wanted to devise a rationale, to construct a reality around this delusion, it wasn't going to work, and Bob knew it, deep inside, that's why he was breaking down, and at this very moment, in crisis.

Stan wished Bob had chosen a better time to do it, and had done it with someone else, such as with a trained therapist. The "comfort of our campsite would have been a nice touch as well", Stan thought, "and not four friggin' miles up a mountain", but it was what it was, and Stan had to employ as much compassion as he could muster, not a quality that Stan had in abundance, as discussed, but he was doing his very best to be a friend.

He thought it highly ironic, that he had traveled all these many miles west to this remote place in order to deal with his own crisis, his breakdown of sorts, and now, here he was with Bob, needing to step up and help him with his. Maybe this is why he came here? Maybe, he thought, there were no such thing as coincidences? He seemed stuck on that question.

Right on cue, a rock about the size of an orange, landed ten feet from where Stan stood. This snapped him out of his contemplation, and he looked around to see where it had come from. Nobody in sight. They were on a gentle downslope, and not terribly near a hill or rock face that might've shed the rock. Odd. Bob was depressurizing by his boulder, and Stan was trying to assemble his thoughts, organize his plan of action for getting Bob off this mountain and getting him some professional help. And then another rock came flying in, about the same size, but this time a little closer. "This really is odd", Stan thought. He looked toward Bob and said, "Hey, Bob, you doin' okay? Did you notice these rocks, flying in?"

Bob, roused from his sad introspection, looked up and said, "What? Rocks?" just in time for a third rock, much larger, about the size of a honeydew melon, to come whistling in almost horizontally, landing next to Bob's feet.

It seemed to have come from a tree line thirty feet away. "Who the hell can chuck a rock that big, that far?" thought Stan.

Bob looked down, stunned, looked up at Stan, and said, "Get behind your boulder, *now!*"

Stan, thinking it some kind of a joke, hesitated, and as a result, got pelted in the back of the head by two small pebbles. "Yow! What the fuck?!" And dove behind his boulder, next to Bob's, about six feet away.

The two looked at one another, but it was Bob who knew what they were dealing with. Sasquatch had arrived, and he had brought some rocks for fun.

Bob took a quick leap for his knapsack that was on top of the rock, and pulled it down beside him. As

Stan had suspected, not included in the PB&J picnic layout had been his 44 Magnum. He pulled it out, checked that the chamber was full, switched off the safety, but all the while, kept it concealed, did not brandish it. Stan's eyes grew very large, realizing that Bob, in his decidedly unstable condition, might end up shooting some stupid teenage pranksters, who thought tossing rocks at them would be funny. It was still mid-afternoon, so lots of time to get down the mountain while it was still light out.

"How about we just take off now, you know, get away from these jokers?"

"You stay just where you are, don't show yourself" was Bob's response. Bob looked around to their sides and behind them, as if they might be surrounded.

The two men hunkered down behind their rocks and waited. Nothing happened. Stan realized that all of the birds had stopped chirping. All that could be heard was the wind in the trees, and the stream below. Stan and Bob looked at one another, cocked their heads to listen for anything else, anything at all, but there was nothing else to hear. Stan wondered if Bob's supernatural hearing had kicked in?

After ten minutes of this, Bob motioned for Stan to stay put, and stood up, very carefully, looking around for anyone, for anything, the gun in his hand but concealed behind him. The birds started to sing and chirp again. Bob motioned for Stan to stand up, and stuck his revolver back in his knapsack. Bob walked a few feet out in front of the boulder, scanned the tree line, both near and far, and then looked back at Stan, nodding and smiling, "Well buddy, you just had yourself, your first encounter".

As they made their way back down, trying to retrace their steps, the two men had lots to think about. For entirely different reasons, they both agreed to not camp out but to return to Bob's campsite. For Bob, he wanted to get to his podcast as soon as possible and report this. For Stan, he wanted to get the hell off the mountain and find relative safety from this unusual situation, probably the result of something seeming odd but actually normal, but he couldn't be positive about that, and admittedly, he was a little shook up.

For Bob, it was how he would describe it on his podcast, perhaps filling in a few details, to punch the narrative up. He wished he had stayed longer, hunting for tracks or other evidence, but his experience on the topic, most of it hearsay, told him that the Sasquatch was pitching those rocks at them because they wanted them to leave. He further knew to not show the gun, for it could likely provoke them. A gun such as that could, with good steady aim, make a sizable hole in a squatch, he knew, but would it kill it? And, from his study, he knew it likely not a lone squatch, but was with probably two or three others, most likely stationed behind them, or on their flanks, completely camouflaged.

Had he done something stupid, like present the gun, or fire it in the air to scare them off, it could have resulted in them being charged, their necks snapped or backs broken, and that would have been the end, their bodies never found. He brought the gun more as a deterrent to a bear attack, not so much for a squatch. He knew there had been hundreds of unsolved cases of lone hunters or hikers never having returned back from the deep woods. Was every instance due to a bear attack? Or someone losing their footing, and plummeting off a cliff? Or becoming lost? "Not too likely", Bob thought. He knew that the prudent thing was to pack up quickly, and leave, making it very obvious to anyone looking, they were doing so. He knew there were eyes on them, and there would most likely be, all the way down to his Beetle.

For Stan, while it had been disturbing, maybe even scary for a minute or two, it was far from convincing evidence of a Bigfoot. Not that he had an answer, but to immediately leap to Bigfoot was a bit much.

He thought that the rocks, which had been roundish in shape, had no doubt tumbled a long way from the vertical rock face, about a hundred feet away. It was not an unreasonable conclusion. There was a down-slope from the mountainside leading to where they had been, and a round-shaped rock, could have by chance, avoided hitting other rocks or trees, and ended up near them. Who knows how many had rolled and not reached them? Could have been a small rock slide. As to how they ended up flying in, not rolling in, was also explainable. Had they checked, there was likely a rut or berm in the ground that the rocks hit, propelling them into the air, and then landing near the two trailblazers.

There was a reasonable explanation for anything in this world, and it was not necessary to look beyond what was known and visible, for an answer. Not that Stan was void of belief in science, or the as yet undiscovered. He believed in the unknown but only if couched in known science, not a lot of pseudo-science gobbledygook.

He was a fan of the National Geographic magazine and documentaries, detailing all kinds of amazing actual facts about Earth's natural science, about human conditions, about deep space and other galaxies, geology and paleontology, about astrophysics (to the extent he could comprehend it) and what is to be found in the oceans. He liked facts. Science facts. Common sense facts. All these things were a friend to reasonable explanations of known things, or reasonable scientific theories about the great unknown. Of course, when science, which was ever evolving, pulled back a layer, and discovered something new, it would have to adjust. That was a given. But rocks landing near them, a pebble or two, meant it just *had* to be a Bigfoot? *Please.*

The long walk back had been done mostly in silence, with Bob thinking through his next podcast, and while keeping a wary eye on both sides of them, his gun at the ready, stuck in his pants, his jacket pulled down to conceal. Stan, with no such concerns, was glad that with every step downhill, he was one step closer to taking off his boots, grabbing a beer, and relaxing by the campfire. But he felt guilty about his plan to take off, and hadn't decided how to break it to Bob. He also felt torn, for it was obvious Bob needed to get some help, but was Stan up for that?

Before that day's excitement, Stan had planned on simply pulling out early one morning, having left a heartfelt thank you note and some cash to cover Bob's extra expense of having him visit. But now, maybe the situation had shifted? For one thing, was Bob stable enough to take care of himself, and not go off and do some crazy thing? Stan wished he could sneak the revolver away, but Bob watched it like a hawk. And what had become of his smaller black one? No great ideas struck Stan as he walked, so he figured, he would just improvise, for he was good at that.

The two men arrived at the campsite and were glad for it. Bob immediately scurried off to prep for a "special bonus podcast" and Stan concentrated on taking off his boots, rubbing his feet, and downing two beers. While Bob was otherwise detained, Stan went about making a fire, cooking dinner in a skillet, drinking a third beer, and presenting Bob with a steak, his version of Hasselback potatoes (delicious) and a dill pickle, the only green thing he could find in the fridge, all presented on a metal plate.

Bob barely looked at it, being busy firing up his equipment, and finishing his notes of the encounter. At first Stan wanted to hear what he had to say on air, wanted to hear the spin, but thought again, and walked over to the now roaring campfire, put up his feet, enjoyed the last of his potatoes, had a fourth beer, and zoned out.

Had Stan stuck around to listen, he could have enjoyed Bob's spirited recounting of their Sasquatch encounter. According to Bob, he had gotten a very brief glimpse of the big guy, standing just inside the tree line, about forty feet away. As they were walking down their trail, they had been followed by at least one of the creatures, perhaps two, on either side of them. He would talk of the common practice of being walked out of an area, being "paralleled" by the creatures, to make sure they were leaving.

Stan did not want to be an accomplice to Bob's nonsense, but at the same time, did not want to frustrate Bob's enterprise, for it was how he made money. Stan just stayed out of it.

In order to listen to the "Bigfoot Bob" podcast, you needed a link, which you needed to purchase by credit card, with a monthly fee of ten dollars. If it were true that Bob had close to three-thousand listeners, all paying ten bucks each a month, well, you can do the math. It was extremely doubtful that Bob was raking in thirty thousand dollars a month, let's just put it that way. Had he been, Stan thought, "he would have for sprung for a new Wrangler" Stan was enjoying the fire, having earned some R&R for what he had been through. Bob obviously needed some help, and Stan knew he was not the one to give it, for Bob needed the kind of help only a professional could provide, in a controlled setting, away from all this fairytale stimulus. Bob's drinking was no doubt a contributor to his problems, as he seemed to be self-medicating, for all the conspicuous textbook reasons.

And then it happened.

As Stan sat by the fire, his belly full and his feet toasty, there came the noise.

It wasn't actually a noise, like something crashing or a loud truck engine, but a howl. Unmistakably, a howl. It echoed through the canyon, bouncing off the rock face of the mountain. It seemed to come from a distance, perhaps a mile away? And it was loud. *Very* loud. It sounded like a combination of a gorilla howl and a truck's air horn, or perhaps an air-raid siren is a better description? It did not sound happy, or evoke warm cuddly feelings in Stan. It seemed far away because of the way it echoed, and Stan hoped that was true.

By Bob's standards, Stan might be considered a "city boy" but Stan had lived his whole life in a small town, adjacent to the country. He had done some traveling in the country wilds close by, done some camping, joined others hunting enough times, before giving it up, to be familiar with different kinds of animal howls, and he knew what a bear sounded like, what an elk sounded like. This was no bear. This was no elk. Other animals he was familiar with, due to his National Geographic docs, such as mountain lions, moose, gibbons, owls, rhinos, walruses, hippos, and wild boars. But this howl had not come from any of those, this much Stan knew for a dead fact. It was an organic sound, that is to say, not generated by a machine of some kind, for it had a vibrato to it, and went from a deep low pitch that was quieter, to a very loud higher pitch, nearly a woman's scream, and then at the very end, trailed off. Only something with a huge lung capacity could make such a noise, lasting well over thirty seconds, and to his knowledge, there were no Bull Crocodiles, or African Elephants, near Index.

As Stan flashed back to the rock-throwing, Bob bolted out of the trailer, "Hey! You hear that?".

Not without sarcasm, "Yeah, I heard it", said Stan.

Bob had his cell phone in hand, and was recording. The howl came again, and maybe it was Stan's imagination, but it seemed to be a little closer, which was not good news. But Bob was riveted, holding the phone up for the best recording quality. All the other sounds, save the sound of the creek, had gone silent.

For Stan, things were getting surreal, and fast. He stood up, looked at Bob for guidance, for reassurance, and only got back a wink and a big thumbs-up. Stan decided that the safest place to be was inside of something made out of metal. His truck keys were in his duffle, in the tent, which in his heightening sense of panic, was too far away. He headed for the trailer, giving a glance toward Bob, who looked back at him, beaming. Stan motioned to Bob that he was going to the trailer, and scurried up the steps, closing the door behind him.

Once inside, "Coward", he thought to himself. That's what he was, just a "little girl" which he immediately thought sexist, so he thought "little boy". He was going to leave his new best friend out there by himself, to face whatever kind of beast was making those blood-curdling howls? "Is that the way it was going to be?" he thought to himself.

He girded himself, took a deep breath, and opened the door. He peeked out, didn't see Bob anywhere, walked carefully down the steps, and in a loud whisper said, "Bob? Bob? You out there?" No answer. The howling had stopped. Oh Christ, were all the tall tales true? Something had nabbed his friend, carried him somewhere? His mind started to race, his heart thumping, and suddenly, Bob bounded out from the darkness into the light of the fire, jumping up and down like he had just won the Super Bowl or World Series. He was ecstatic.

"I got it! I got it!" he exclaimed. Somehow, Bob knew, or felt he knew, that whatever threat there had been, had now gone away. He played back the howling sound on his cell, with an enormous victory smile, he did a little jig, glancing at Stan, pointing to his phone, saying jubilantly "Ya see, this fucker is for real!" Stan felt like he had been transported to some parallel dimension where normal had been obliterated, and replaced by crazy.

Things were simply not the same after that. Bob had something that he could play over and over again on his podcast, and in fact, used it as the intro sound bite for all his future podcasts. As far as Stan could tell, it was a very real thing. Not that the rocks had not been real, but with enough contorting, Stan had devised an explanation for them. But the howl? Everything Stan tried to conjure up fell flat. The only thing that made any sense was that the howls had come from some kind of an animal, and certainly none that Stan had ever heard. He couldn't even imagine what kind of a machine or device could make such a sound. It would've had to be large, like a turbine engine from a 737. And even if there were such a thing, how did someone haul it up the mountain? Stan, now getting sucked into this Bigfoot vortex of Bob's, felt the need to get away from there, as quickly as possible. There was no helping Bob's condition, far as Stan could determine. And, to be fair, it appeared Bob had somewhat good circumstantial evidence supporting his goofball theories about a large unidentified hominid roaming the forests of the Pacific Northwest. So, was Bob batshit crazy or on target? He certainly had a host of personality disorders, and a drinking problem, but did that qualify him for being locked up, or dismissed as a lunatic? There was a time Stan would have thought so, but not now.

Stan had been shoved from committed skeptic to being on the fence. Stan was used to being indecisive about so many things, that it didn't turn out feeling nearly as bad as he would have guessed. But truth be told, this was lightyears away from anything Stan had expected to find when he began his escape from Tipp, and perhaps, it was all part of a huge design, meant to expose Stan to the wild varieties of life's meaning, and life's adventures, to offer him perspective and context? Was it divine intervention? Maybe it was meant to open him up to the idea of having endless fantastical thoughts, borne from fantastical events?

Maybe he should open up, accept it? Maybe it was meant to loosen him up, show him other worlds? He knew that the philosophical, theoretical, spiritual, and hypothetical worlds were not part of his makeup, another weak link perhaps, so he stopped thinking in those terms, and tried to concentrate on things more in his comfort zone, things more down to Earth, things more familiar, being the practical kind of person he was, and seek answers there? But he could not get those howls out of his head.

Stan, being the student and fan of the movies that he was, put perhaps an over-emphasis on the fact they had a creek next to the campsite. It for him was a poetic thing, something highly symbolic, and the centerpiece of so many movies he had seen over the years. It served as a metaphor, a thing that kept moving, that bled into a river, and a river that needed to be conquered or understood, something that brought a person face to face with their worst nightmares, their biggest regrets, challenges, and their greatest loves. He realized that his romantic side was being triggered by the thought of Sasquatch being real, and he was seducing himself into considering the nonsense to be possibly true. He could not allow that.

The rest of the night, there were no more howls splitting the otherwise calm night, no more things of nightmares, just peace and campsite normalcy, and the birds chirping contentedly.

When Bob had left the next morning, headed out once again to gather more evidence, he had no idea that when he got back, Stan would have left, and would have been gone for hours, perhaps by then, hundreds of miles away. He would read a kind note from his mixed-up friend, containing a promise to see him again sometime, and a wish for him to have all the luck in the world with his podcast and his quest. He would read a "p.s." stating that as soon as he got settled, he would subscribe to "Bigfoot Bob". Bob would at first be saddened, having wished for a better send off, but he knew that they both had difficulty with feelings, with expressing emotion, so maybe this was the best choice?

But it didn't play out this way, the way Stan had imagined it, had planned it. What did happen is that Bob had apparently left at his usual eight o'clock time, and headed up the trail with his knapsack. The moment he had left, Stan, already awake, jumped up, wrote a note, and left it on the steps of the trailer, weighted down by a rock. He started to knock down his tent, gather his things into his duffle, but the creek beckoned him for one more visit. He had a little time, and he could finish breaking camp in five minutes, afterwards.

He grabbed his fishing gear from the truck's bed, prepped his hook with three salmon eggs, attached the bobber, and walked to the sandy bank. He had only fished this spot once, when he first arrived, and from that point on, had explored for other fishing spots, that being a main part of the fun. But he was satisfied with this fishing hole choice, like bookends to his visit to Index, and to his unbalanced friend?

It was a beautiful postcard morning, with the resident birds singing and hopping about. The creek made its constant gurgling sound. He could hear a couple of squirrels engaged in their never-ending squabbling. He cast his line into the water, placing it in just the right spot, a wide pool on the far side, his bobber bouncing up and down to the current. His creel was sitting on the sand near him. He sat on a rock in the shade, and began to drift off, lost in his thoughts, as stream fishing can quietly encourage. He thought about Mandy, and if they could ever be friends, or at least friendly, or if he should make his way back to Tipp, which the more he thought about it, seemed an unlikely choice.

He had managed to break away, do something radical, and going back was not a realistic option. Maybe he had done some growing up, at his advanced age, and learned a thing or two about himself, about life in general? He sure hoped so. Also, he had been given a chance to think about someone else's problems, someone much more troubled than he was. He had become so bored, always thinking about himself. And then he turned his daydreaming to Hollywood and what he might find there? He was under no delusions about that.

He knew that showing up with no connections, with no leads, would place him among thousands of aspiring actors, trying to find a crack in the wall they could squeeze through. All he knew was that he had to give it a shot, give himself the opportunity to succeed, which sounded miserably like a bumper sticker slogan, but it was true. He had a fair amount of money, but he didn't want to fritter it away, so he figured he should get an affordable place to live, if that were possible, and some kind of a job, something compatible with his knowledge and experience, and something that would not interfere with his ambitions. Maybe a weekend job wearing an orange vest at Home Depot? Would it pay enough?

By now, a lot of auditions had gone virtual, which was to his advantage, but he'd have to pick up a decent laptop. Maybe he could get auditions by himself, starting with non-union jobs, or maybe he needed to join an acting workshop, get established, make new friends, network his way into getting an agent? If he caught any traction at all, it would mean being able to join the actor's unions, which would be fantastic. How long would he give it? Six months, a year, more? He had no clue, but decided to just wing it, cut himself a break.

His minutes spent at the creek was a worthwhile thing. He managed to pull in three good size trout: two Rainbow and a Brown. This time, he put them in his creel, wanting to leave them for Bob as a nice surprise. He'd walk a few steps one way, and then back, playing with the rod, whipping the line a bit, to reposition. He caught and hauled the trout in mechanically, buried in thought.

He fished some more, and felt, all things considered, he was on a good trajectory. He wished he had a solution for Bob, but Bob was cemented in, wasn't a kid anymore, and he was going to live his life the way he wanted to. After another short while of this reflection, he figured he should be getting on the road, but would give it another five minutes, for that one last lucky fourth strike, and besides which, he really loved being by the creek, it was so peaceful, he would miss it so much, it would make his heart ache. But he also knew he had better get moving pretty soon should Bob decide to come back extra early, and ruin his exit plan.

And then something peculiar happened.

He hadn't realized, that during his daydreaming, all the bird sounds had ceased. No more squirrel chatter either. It wasn't his hearing, for he could make out the gurgling creek just fine. The other thing he could now make out was the unmistakable sound of Bob on his far left, tromping through the shallow water toward him, inconsiderate and oblivious, and scaring all the fish away.

Stan thought, "Oh terrific, I'm busted, so now I have to stay here another night. This is so awkward. He's going to notice I've broken camp".

So here he came, back early from his walk-about as Stan had feared could happen, splashing along in the shallow water, almost as if he was doing it intentionally, to annoy Stan.

Stan was not going to give him the pleasure of getting angry, so he just kept his cool, acted like he was ignoring Bob, and kept looking ahead toward his bobber. But it became too much for Stan.

When Bob got just steps away, Stan motioned sharply for him to stop walking, and after another couple of steps, Bob stopped. But what would usually follow at this point would be Bob saying something loudly to him, no doubt something about another foot print or evidence left behind, such as a strand of hair, a broken branch, or one of his dirt clods, and loudly enough to be sure to scare off any remaining fish. Bob could be so terribly dense.

Stan, looking at his bobber going up and down, said to Bob acidly, "Hey, Bob, What's up? I'm trying to fish here, did you notice?". No reply.

Stan got a queasy feeling, running up his legs to his stomach, to his head. He felt nauseous. He got dizzy. He thought, "Oh shit, I'm having a heart attack" and faltered, dropping his pole to the sand, and looked toward Bob saying, "Hey, I don't feel so good, I think…" but he cut his sentence short when he couldn't make eye contact with Bob. He couldn't, because Bob wasn't there. Instead of Bob, there was a very large gorilla-human kind of a creature. About eight feet tall, maybe taller. Very broad shoulders, covered in four-inch-long chestnut-brown hair, with some gray hairs showing near the face and chest. The skin was grayish, and the face free of hair, with deep creases, looking nearly human with high cheekbones but with a very pronounced brow, and a flattened nose. Its mouth was very wide, and open just enough to breathe through, and panting rapidly. It had brown intelligent eyes, looking directly at Stan. It did not look pleased, and bared its large square teeth and two large sharp canines.

Stan, not more than five feet from this creature, looking up at it at, realized he was about to die. There was not a thing he could do about it. He wanted to scream, to bolt away in some futile attempt to escape, but he was frozen in place, couldn't make a sound, peeing in his pants, and terrified. Stan started weeping, shaking uncontrollably, and whatever nausea he had been experiencing had been replaced by his whole body feeling sickly numb and pointless. The creature remained still, giving Stan a menacing look, not advancing, not retreating, not growling or howling, just staring at Stan, pathetic little horror-stricken Stan from Tipp City, and then something undefinably weird happened. With tears streaming down his face, Stan started to smile, and his crying became a gentle laugh. He looked at the creature warmly, so glad that he had been able to see it, to experience it, and the fact his life was about to be snuffed out, was suddenly inconsequential. He was standing before an ancient species, an intelligent being, so incredibly powerful, that was not supposed to exist. He knew he wasn't hallucinating. Everything was too real, too actual. He could feel it in his chest, as if it were reaching inside of him. Stan was out of his mind delirious, starting to laugh uncontrollably, his initial terror replaced with a freakish and overwhelming sense of euphoria. It was as if he were looking up at a friendly god that had come to retrieve him. But he wasn't, unfortunately for him.

Suddenly, the creature starting talking loudly in gibberish, in a deep-toned rumbling voice, punctuated with growls and high-pitched tortured notes. Stan, his giddiness dissolving into an odd mix of terror and wonderment, spoke back to the creature, as if he had somehow made an inter-species connection. It was pretty corny: "I think they call you Tripleby. My name is Stan, I am human…"

The creature cocked his head to the side, as puzzled by Stan's language, as Stan was by his.

Stan thought, "Maybe it understands me?".

It raised its right hand in a blur, and with deadly force, swiped the left side of Stan's face, immediately drawing blood. Before Stan even registered that he had been hit, the return backhand swipe made contact with Stan's right side, just below his rib cage, shredding his shirt and making deep cuts, hurtling him back ten feet into shallow water, out cold. The creature advanced a step, took a look at Stan's lifeless body, looked around wary of being out in the open daylight, so exposed, stepped over him and grabbed his creel, ripping it apart, grabbing the three trout and eating them in large gulps. The creature must have weighed in at over eight-hundred pounds, had sinewy muscles, a slightly conical-shaped head, and long arms, the hands hanging well below its knees. It then inspected Stan's cap that had been blown off his head, sniffed it, and tore it to shreds. Turning back in Stan's direction, he grabbed the fiberglass fishing pole and snapped it in two places using just one hand, like it was a small twig. He glanced around, gave a loud snort, and walked across the stream, and up into the heavily wooded embankment in two seconds flat and disappeared as if never there.

Stan's body remained motionless, his blood swirling all around him in a sickly red mix with the icy water. He did not move. Everything was still, and then the first bird could be heard, and then another, and another.

At close to three, Bob plodded down the trail, made for the trailer, slipping off the knapsack with a moan, gave a quick glance around the campsite, and saw his Beetle, Stan's truck, everything seemed in order, but noticed Stan's tent, partially collapsed, and then something caught his peripheral. He glanced over at the creek, and saw a body lying in shallow water. It was Stan! Bob rushed over to him, coming to a sliding stop on his knees in the wet sand. Stan was laying in about three inches of water. Bob instantly noted the broken pole, the creel and hat. He quickly did a three-sixty, scanning for the perpetrator. He kept repeating "Oh shit, oh shit, hey buddy, oh shit". He gently lifted Stan's head up by the back of the neck, wanting to be careful of any broken bones, to look at the large claw marks on the left side of his face, still bleeding. On his right side, his shirt was torn open as if by very powerful claws, with a lot of blood loss coming from his side. Stan was pale and limp, his body ice cold, and either dead or near dead. Bob, staying calm as a paramedic, checked for vitals, found a heartbeat, and a faint pulse, and quickly examined Stan for signs of broken limbs, and detected none obvious. Bob looked around to see if the bear who attacked him was still lurking, about to make another charge. He pulled his 44 out of his belt, looked around, and then as a warning, aimed the gun up and pulled off a round, the thundering sound of the blast slapping against the rock walls half a mile away. He wanted the bear to know it would be a very poor decision to come back. Everything had gone silent again, but soon, they were alone with the chirping birds.

Bob picked Stan up, cradling him like a child, not sure if he was about to die, and managed with a rush of adrenaline, to carry him away from the river bank and place him on the picnic table. Stan, with a violent lurch and scream, exploded awake, lashing out with punches at his attacker. Bob restrained him, holding his arms down, telling him "It's okay, it's okay, it's gone, you're okay". Stan wriggled violently, trying to escape. It took Stan a good thirty seconds to realize he wasn't in the creek, that the attack was over, and that he was still alive. His breathing was shallow and he blinked rapidly. Bob recognized these symptoms, ran to the trailer and came back in a flash, armed with a bottle of Jack Daniels. Stan was in shock, and needed to calm the hell down. Stan took a couple of gulps. Bob went back to the trailer grabbed a blanket and draped it over Stan, who was starting to shiver. "Holy fuck man, holy fuck" is all Bob could come up with. Stan began to breathe normally, but now the pain from his wounds was coming on large, and he groaned loudly. Bob said, "Hey, we're gonna get you to the doc now, you hear? It's not a long drive, ten minutes if I fly. You're gonna be okay pal". Bob broke out his first aid kit and applied some disinfectant, some non-stick gauze, doing a crude patch up but it didn't do a lot of good, Stan was still losing blood.

Stan, grimacing and writhing from the fresh wounds, kept saying "Thanks Bob, thanks…".

Bob, satisfied that Stan was stable enough to transport, that he had to be stable enough, began to scramble, moving surprisingly fast, collecting another blanket, his keys, some cash, extra bullets, and then back to Stan. "Okay, ready to go?" he said to Stan.

Stan nodded.

It didn't matter if Stan was ready or not. Bob knew he was in shock, and getting worse, so he quickly helped Stan up on his feet, putting his arm around him, letting Stan put his weight against him. Bob walked Stan, who was limping badly, over to the Beetle. He got Stan in his seat, then ran around to the other side, whiskey bottle in hand, hopped in, cranked it up with a roar, and sped out of the campsite onto the dirt road, spitting dirt and gravel.

Bob floored it, a huge wall of dust rising behind the Beetle. Bob stared straight ahead, breathing hard. Stan was nearly passed out, shifting in his seat, groaning. After a couple of minutes, Bob asked, "So, you have frontal wounds, which means you saw the fucker who attacked you, right?"

Stan could only utter "Uh huh".

Bob pronounced, "I'm gonna go back, get that mother, I swear buddy, that fucker is toast". Stan passed out.

Not five minutes later, Bob turned into Doctor Mangal's driveway in Gold Bar. He had a home office, the entrance on the side of the house. Bob helped Stan hobble up the cement ramp leading to the door, helped him inside, eased him into one of the arm chairs lined up against the wall, walked to the little counter window, rang the bell, and waited. He looked back at his friend with worry, who came close to being killed, perhaps spared by having been knocked unconscious, or maybe because the attack had been done out in the open, and a car had gone by up on the road, and spooked the bear? Bob rang the bell a second time, cursing, just as Doc Alex, as he was known, came to the window, wiping his mouth with a napkin.

He didn't have to ask what was wrong, seeing Stan slumped in the chair, and obviously in bad shape. He dashed over to Stan, checked his vitals, asked Bob to help him get Stan into the exam room, where they gently laid him down on the stainless-steel exam table. The Doc went to work quickly, all the while asking Bob a battery of where, when, how, and what questions, and talking to Stan, getting him to respond to simple questions, keeping him awake, cutting his clothing off and pulling Bob's field bandages away, examining the wounds, flushing them with hydrogen peroxide, removing miniature flecks of sand, leaves and twigs, and gave Stan two shots of morphine ten minutes apart, the first having little to no effect. He checked Stan's right leg and knee, finding nothing broken or cut, just that the knee was badly sprained and scraped, from when he was knocked to the ground. It took about fifteen minutes for Stan's shots to kick in, and he was able to relax, to not be in intense pain, and as the morphine did its job, he became dreamy. Doc Alex began examining him a second time, checking for other cuts, bruising, swelling and for any broken or cracked ribs not noticed before.

All the while, the Doc was asking Bob questions about Stan. "Is he your friend? Where did this happen? Do you know of any medical conditions he may have? Any known allergies to medicines? Did you notify the police or park service", and so forth. Bob stood out of the way, in the corner, worried sick. "Stan got off very lucky, all things considered", said the Doc.

Stan's first coherent sentence was, "It was big, and I mean, BIG".

The Doc responded, "Yes, from the size of your wound on your side, it has large paws, unusually large, I would say. There are five distinct claw marks, a sure sign of a bear" and then launched into a dissertation about the stats on bear attacks in the county, the frequency, location, what can attract or provoke them, while Stan laid still, having been delivered to a soft fuzzy cloud. Sometimes the Doc would interrupt himself with a question for Stan, the tutorial also serving as a way to keep Stan engaged and awake. The doctor took a closer look at the claw marks and commented to Bob that while serious, and from powerful blows, the claw marks were not as defined, as deep, as with most bear attacks, as if the claws themselves were blunt, not sharp.

And then Stan, with a sudden recall of the incident, looked sharply at the Doc and said, "No, Doc! It wasn't a bear! It wasn't a bear, it was some kind of a big ape kinda thing, but with a person's face, kind of..." and drifted off in a cloud again.

The Doc nodded his head empathetically, and then turned to Bob who had now left the corner and moved to Stan's side.

"What's that you're saying bud?" said Bob.

Stan, coming around again, with urgency, slurring his words, said, "It's one of them Bob, one of your creatures, it just walked up to me, and then, then..." Stan was overcome with emotion, recounting his revelatory and terrifying experience, and went silent, withdrew inside of himself, reliving the encounter through the haze, terrified.

Bob gave the Doc a quick glance with an arch of his eyebrows, and then said to Stan, "Hey, sure, you saw yourself a Mister Big, but right now, let the Doc patch you up, don't be gettin' all stirred up, not a good idea".

Stan was now feeling the full effects of the morphine and didn't have any fight in him, and began to drift off.

The Doc ushered Bob away from the table and said to Bob quietly, "He doesn't have any signs of a concussion, or serious blunt force to the head, other than being swiped across the cheek pretty badly. He has two, maybe three, cracked ribs and of course deep lacerations and contusions on his side. Lucky it wasn't a stronger blow, we might be looking at something much more serious. Right now, he just needs some peace and quiet".

All Bob could do is nod his head, took a look at his buddy, and then said, "So, what now?".

The Doc replied, "I'll keep an eye on him for the next couple of hours, take some x-rays, make sure he's stable, and then you can take him home, I don't think we have to transport, no indication of internal bleeding. I think he'll be okay, but keep an eye on him for the next few days, he'll need some TLC, maybe a week or more. If he continues to show signs of trauma, beyond this immediate response, let me know, he might need some therapy", and then added, "Your friend is lucky, these bear attacks, as rare as they are, can turn out much worse, usually do".

Bob considered these words a moment, and then with a rueful grin, "He thinks he saw a squatch".

Returning the smile, the Doc replied, "Yes, I think he's been hanging around you too long".

It took close to three hours for the Doc to release Stan into Bob's care, and with the aid of some crutches, Stan, wrapped in the blanket, wearing only his boxers and boots, made his way down the ramp to the Beetle with Bob's help. It was dark, and the Doc's yellow bug light cast an eerie glow over the scene. Bob revved the engine to life and took them home. Once there, Bob kept the headlights on and helped Stan to the trailer, up the steps and to his single bed in the radio bedroom. Stan protested kicking his friend out of his own bed, but he was spent, and went to sleep the moment he hit the pillow.

Bob scooted out, hit the lights to his car, and went back in, nearly tripping on a rock that was on the steps, and kicked it to the ground, never noticing the note under it. He grabbed a cold one, sat at the table, deep in worried thought, downed the beer in three gulps, and pondered what Stan had said. "No fuckin' way" he said out loud to himself.

He stood up, pulled his 44 out of his belt, double-checked it for a full cylinder, took his Maglite off its clip on the wall, kicked the door open and stepped down into the pitch-black night boldly. He had learned that when in hostile territory, it was important to have a show of force, not be timid or indefinite. Animals can smell fear. He pointed the light down and around, scanning, as he walked the forty feet to the creek, and stood near the spot where Stan had been attacked. It was cold outside, and he had forgotten to put on his jacket, and shivered. He could hear a few birds chirping, the sound of the water pouring over and between the rocks.

He pointed the beam into the water, and all along the sandy bank. He could see where Stan had fallen, and could make out his own boot prints and skid marks when he had rushed over to Stan. He moved the light over to where he could see Stan's footprints, right at the edge of the water. This is what Bob wanted to see. They were about ten feet from where he found him out cold, which means that whatever hit him, hit him hard enough to send him flying through the air, not just knock him down.

Could he make out any tracks from the bear? He stepped closer, pointing the beam left and right, and could make out some of Stan's boot prints, and some depressions in about three inches of water, maybe bear prints, but they could have been made by most anything, and had had hours to become eroded and washed away. He looked for other clues, but found nothing other than Stan's splintered rod, creel and shredded hat. His fish line was still let out, with the red and white bobber bouncing up and down over a deep pool on the other side of the stream. He thought, "This is odd behavior for a bear, going after Stan's stuff like that…the creel may have had fish in it, or smelled like fish, so that makes sense, but how can a bear, with no opposable thumb, snap a fishing rod, and do it twice?" he pondered. "And even if somehow he could, why?"

Bob continued to study the evidence, trying to reconstruct what had happened, scanning the opposite side of the bank with his flashlight, pointing the beam up into the trees, upstream and downstream, all the while thinking: "The bear had to be motivated by something. It isn't in their nature to attack a person for no reason, especially a Black Bear, in broad daylight, in their own campground area, near a road". It made no sense.

In the grander scheme of things, everywhere around here was the bear's home, and being the only (officially) known apex predator in the entire region, it took a sense of ownership of that region, and offense at trespassers, but their campsite only represented a speck of square footage, located near a population center of humans, as compared to the vastness of the unexplored forest they were in the middle of. There was plentiful food for them in the mountains, so there was no need or desire to forage through human trash cans or tents for goodies. Black Bears were not known to attack people, and what few documented attacks there had been were connected to people carelessly leaving food out, or stumbling upon a mother and her cubs, or a hunter trekking deep into the forest, and startling one.

Brown Bears were the ones to be careful around, but in the lower fifty states, you had to almost try to bump into one, for most were extinct, such as the California Grizzly, nicknamed, "Golden Bear", Ursus arctos californicus, with the other surviving subspecies being in Alaska or Mexico. The only types of Brown Bear in the entire region were the Grizzly, Ursus arctos horribilis, or his close relative, the Stickeen, either one sometimes weighing in at an astounding nine-hundred pounds, standing nearly nine feet tall, and often mistaken for a squatch. The closest sightings were found in the far northeast part of the state, in the Selkirk Mountains, nowhere near Index.

The last reported sighting of any type of Brown Bear in the Cascade Mountains area, which includes Index, was in 1996, and are now both considered

State endangered species. It had to have been a Black Bear, in other words.

Bob's extensive Sasquatch research, his hundreds of testimonials he heard on his podcast, had supplied him with a solid, if not highly biased and quasi-scientific education, on the topic, which necessarily merged into discussions and research on bears, and their behavior. But something here didn't fit. He was missing an important piece of the puzzle. Bob knew he was not the "sharpest tool in the drawer", and knew that he was predisposed to believe that even the most dubious circumstantial evidence was further proof of Sasquatch's existence, but there was something very wonky about this.

He kept scanning with his light, the cold seeping into his bones through his flannel, and then, about twenty feet away, his eye caught something. He trained the beam on it, and walked to it. On the water's edge in the sand, he saw three very distinct foot prints, about sixteen inches long, and ten inches wide, two right's and one left, in a straight line about five feet apart. Foot prints, not boot prints, not hoof prints, not paw prints.

He knew that the squatch walked in such a way as to leave prints in a single line, not parallel lines. They didn't leave tracks like people, with a track of left prints parallel to a track of right prints. Neither did bears, for their left paws, and their right paws, both front and back, were also parallel track lines. Sometimes a bear print could be mistaken for another animal, even a squatch, but these were very distinct human or human-like prints, in the moist sand, no denying it. And the long stride of these prints, were consistent with what he knew. These strides were much longer than a human's or even the largest bear.

He went through his entire mental itemized checklist of things to look for, to consider. Bears could and did walk upright on occasion, but only for short stints. If it had been a bear, perhaps displaying its ferocity at Stan, walking on its hind legs only, it would not have left in-line prints, but parallel. And if showing such a display, it would have most definitely been accompanied by a roar of some kind, at least a grunt or two, and Stan would have heard it, and he would have seen it, standing out in the open, in the broad daylight a mere twenty feet away. He would have been startled, scared, would have taken a step back, maybe many steps back, or run to the safety of the trailer or his truck. But none of that happened.

There were prints of Stan, a cluster of them, as he walked a step or two to the right and left while fishing probably, and then two very distinct footprints where he had evidently turned and faced upstream, in the direction of what Bob could only conclude, was a Sasquatch.

The hairs on Bob's neck stood up. He could feel eyes on him. He was being watched. Bob pulled the 44 out of his pants, switched the safety off, and got a firm grip on the handle, ready for anything that might happen next. With his ears tuned to the tree line across the creek, he continued to inspect the scene.

There was no mistaking what Bob was looking at.

He stared at the prints, imagining how the creature had approached Stan, walking mostly in the shallow water, but had hit that little sand bar and left those prints. It was from the direction of a thick stand of bushes and saplings. If it had walked stealthily enough, which they do, Stan wouldn't have heard it, or seen its approach if he had been looking at the water, watching his bobber, thinking about all the damn things Stan always thought about. It would explain how it could have easily snuck up on him.

Drawing a straight line with his beam between the tracks and where Stan had been knocked down, the last few steps had been done in the shallow water, leaving no lasting impression in the sand, and maybe it had slowed its pace, not making much sound, or maybe Stan didn't hear it over the sound of the water pouring over the rocks nearby? Bob had reconstructed the scene, and said out loud, "Holy Kamoly".

ACT III

Bobsquatch

Chapter 14

Hubris can be a close cousin to stupidity, and Stan at times had a fair amount of both, but he figured rightly, he had nothing to lose.

It was hot and humid, the perspiration collecting on his back, in his armpits, on his forehead just moments after exiting his air-conditioned truck. By the time he limped up the stairs onto the front porch, he was already sticky wet. He knocked on the wood screen door. No response. He knocked again. Nothing. The front door was closed, but there were some lights on inside. It was a Sunday, in the afternoon, a car he didn't recognize was in the driveway. It was new, with paper plates. He knocked again, louder. He could hear approaching footsteps. She opened the door, holding her cell phone. It had been many months, but who's counting? To be exact, it had been four months, one week, three days, and roughly ten hours, more or less, since Stan had retrieved his belongings from the front lawn.

Mandy stood rock-still, and was annoyed, pleased, irritated, confused and speechless, as Stan, sporting a beard, stood on her porch with Bob behind him, who was also sticky wet, and whom she had only met once or twice before at the store. A hopeful look was on both their faces.

She spoke into the phone, in the even tone of a person in shock, "Uh, you are not gonna believe what the damn cat just dragged in. I gotta call you back" and hung up.

A week prior, Stan and Bob were in Index at the campsite, breaking camp. Bob had done most of the work, with Stan hobbling around doing what he could. They had secured all of Bob's radio equipment and possessions for the trip, and carefully wrapped all the plaster casts in padding, including the ones they had taken from the stream bank, documenting the attack. They had packed everything but the picnic table, had fixed the flat tires and running lights wiring on the trailer, had hitched it to Stan's truck, all the while discussing what they should do next. They concluded that Stan had had an actual encounter, no question about that, no alternate possible explanation existed, and that he had come nose to nose with a Sasquatch in a near-fatal meeting. They further concluded that the campsite location was no longer safe, and that they were in mortal danger.

As for the attack itself, they were short on answers. They didn't know what had motivated the enormous visitor, why he had come down the mountain so close to people, why he had smacked Stan around, if it had intended on killing him, if it was a happenstance meeting or targeted, how many were in his family group, and when he or they would pay another visit.

Bob had gone off-air for a week after the attack, and when he did go back on, he was convinced that the three-hour long "Violent Stream Incident, Episode

#588" would need to be the final episode of Bigfoot Bob broadcast from this undisclosed location in the Cascade Mountains. He had put Stan on the air and interviewed him thoroughly, and then took phone calls so the listeners could ask questions. It was by far the most popular show Bob ever did judging by the number of call-ins, but it was likely to have a very unpleasant sequel if they didn't bug out of there as fast as Stan's condition would permit. They were sitting ducks, forced to wait at least a week after the attack, before it was safe for Stan to travel. Doc Alex was convinced it had been a bear attack, but he didn't want to take any chances, so he refused to come up to the trailer for a follow-up house call, insisting the boys come down to see him, which they did, twice.

Stan lounged in the safety of the trailer in the radio- bedroom, with Bob at first bunking down in the back seat of Stan's truck, but finding it impossibly cramped and feeling vulnerable to attack, he made himself a nice sleeping pad on the floor of the kitchenette area. It was safer, adjacent to Stan, and also adjacent to the fridge, fully stocked with PBR's.

Everything had been quiet for a week, but then on two successive nights, they heard loud howling coming from a distance somewhere in the woods. It had that same air raid kind of a tenor to it. Very disquieting, but at least it sounded far away. But on the third night, it was especially terrifying, as they heard what sounded like two squatches, walking around the trailer again and again, for hours, talking in the same odd gibberish that Stan had heard from his attacker.

Some in the Bigfoot universe were not known for being politically correct, and they referred to this kind of talk as "Samurai talk" since it sounded quite a bit like dialogue from the iconic and epic 1954 movie by the monumental Akira Kurosawa, "Seven Samurai", starring the iconic Toshiro Mifune. ("Epic", "monumental", and "iconic" all in one sentence, not too shabby). In spite of how that reference may sound, it was not a racist slur, but a fairly accurate characterization of how their "language" sounded, if you did not understand Japanese and had to compare it to something. But a slur or not, it kept both men awake all night, scared to death, that at any moment, the visitors would rip the front door off and have them for dinner.

Bob kept his 44 next to him everywhere he went, and knew even though, according to Dirty Harry, it was "the most powerful handgun in the world", all it might do is injure a charging squatch, just before it separated Bob's head from his shoulders. Bob knew that a much more powerful weapon would be needed to actually down one of them, or that he would have to pull off the perfectly aimed shot in a terrifying two or three second window. He knew that the real purpose of his gun was to give him a sense of security by creating a buffer, something, that would make the attacker hesitate, and give them a chance to escape.

This was the kind of sweaty thinking Bob engaged in while listening to the two "ape men" do circles around the tin can he and Stan were holed up in. Stan was equally terrified, if not more so, suffering PTSD, and wishing he could get his hands on some more morphine. Their visitors went away at five in the morning, just before the first light in the sky. An hour later, Stan and Bob were on the road, eleven days after the attack in the creek.

It was no longer a question as to whether Stan needed more rehab time or not, and even though his side wound was still seeping, needing fresh bandages once a day, and that he could only walk very stiffly, carefully, what with two healing cracked ribs and a sprained right knee, they knew they had no choice. Stan took the lead with the truck and trailer, and Bob brought up the rear with his Beetle.

Only once they were over Steven's Pass and out of the dense forest, and past Leavenworth on Highway 97, heading eastward, did they feel safe. They grabbed some gas station burritos in Cashmere, filled up the tanks, and could finally relax and breathe.

After a few days of leisurely driving, and once near Tipp City, the two men strategized over milk shakes in West Milton, just east of Tipp. They rehearsed, over and over, what Stan should say to Mandy, and how he should say it. The "how" part was quite important, as they were both fairly positive that Mandy would not be overjoyed seeing him. The idea was to have Stan plead his case, do a major apology, and ask if they could possibly park the trailer at the rear of her driveway, and that Stan would sleep in there with Bob. They just needed a place to put the trailer, preferably somewhere discreet, off the street, so the fine citizens of Tipp wouldn't see Stan, and get out the tar and feathers.

When the moment came, standing there on the porch, it took a large amount of pleading that sounded a lot more like begging, to convince Mandy to allow it, but allow it, she did. They did not utter one word to her about the encounter with Stan, still showing obvious evidence of his injuries, and told her that he had fallen down a hill, and hit some rocks. Upon hearing that, she gasped, and her impulse had been to immediately start comforting him, but she resisted, and just couldn't go there another time. She told them that whenever she was not home, they could come inside to use the bathroom, but only the bathroom, no watching TV, no kitchen privileges, no access to the fridge, and could only do so when she was not home. They could run an extension cord from the house to the trailer for power as well, but they were "absolutely, definitely, positively" not to step foot inside when she was home, "especially Stan". They thanked her for her generosity and understanding, and quickly got off the porch before she changed her mind.

Once they unpacked the trailer and vehicles, stashing much of the stuff out of sight under plastic tarps between the trailer and the fence, they settled in for the night, and went about making their plans.

Early the next morning, Stan drove by the store, and it was still vacant, with a "For Lease" sign in a window, being offered by Regal Rentals, the name of

Riptick's outfit. Being careful not to be recognized, he hobbled up the stairs to the deck wearing a hoody, and walked to the glass door, and wondered if Riptick had bothered to change the locks, reached into his pocket, feeling for the keys still on his key ring. He looked through the dirty glass, and it appeared Mateo had done a good job emptying the place of all the merchandise and fixtures. It was swept clean as if there had never been a hardware store inside. He considered again about tempting the lock, but then thought the better of it, and went back to his truck. "If only the town's collective memory could be swept as clean". The broken window was still covered with the sheet of plywood.

Stan then called Mateo, and they met discreetly a few minutes later behind the Chinese restaurant. Mateo was delighted to have Stan suddenly appear, and being the inquisitive cub reporter he was, wanted to know all about Stan's time in the Northwest, how he got injured, if he had ever met up with Bob, if he was planning on opening another hardware store in town, and so forth. Stan was less than transparent about all of it, and told him the story about falling down an embankment.

Mateo got handed a large check which pleased him immensely, and Stan still had a goodly amount of cash on him, and a very nice nest egg in the local bank.

Stan swore Mateo to silence, since he still worked for the city's main bullhorn, and wanted to keep his presence in town a secret for as long as possible.

Returning to the trailer, he and Bob started to work out the final details of their plan, which they had discussed on and off in only the vaguest of terms, the entire time they had traveled eastward to Tipp. After two hours of throwing ideas back and forth, one playing devil's advocate to the other, they reached their final decision: they were going to start up their own podcast. This involved a lot of moving parts. Stan was better on the detail stuff, but Bob was surprisingly resourceful, and very good at thinking outside of the box.

Mateo was to be their front man, with all money and documents laundered through him while Stan and Bob would remain invisible. Bob was all too aware that Stan's Achille's Heal was his urge to always "go big" and did not seem satisfied with a plan that was designed to "go small". "Where was the fun in that?", Stan liked to say.

Bob had to openly resist and redirect this self-destructive trait, steering Stan away from the outlandish, and toward the reasonable.

"You want the plan to work, right? You want people to like you, not keep hating you, right?" Bob would repeatedly say to him.

They spent many more sessions and long hours at the table in the trailer, strategizing, and glad they were not being stalked by Mister Big and his brother.

They coached Mateo for two hours before sending him in to see Jana Alabaster, an independent local real estate agent. He parroted everything they had told him: He told her about inheriting a "trunk full of money" from his uncle, how he had "always dreamed of opening up a store", arranged for a walk through of a storefront space for lease in Old Town on Main Street, negotiated for a month-to-month lease for the first year, then if all went well, a four year lease following that, signed the papers, paid the first, last, and security with a paper-banded stack of fresh hundreds, and Mateo improvising "that Mateo's Arts and Crafts would be something she would not regret".

Main Street in the Old Town district was chosen for a few reasons, not the least of which is that all the ground floor units backed up to an alley, and came with a basement.

The plan was coming together except for one large piece, which was Bob. Bob had numerous impediments to his ability to behave in a rational or thoughtful way for usually more than a few days at a time. He always succumbed to his beer fueled rants, his myriad insecurities, paranoia, and vitriol about the outside world. The fact he had allowed Stan to penetrate his defensive wall is significant, but it did not change Bob's basic behavior any.

Stan had arrived on Bob's doorstep as a broken and lost person, seeking refuge. He had not gone there to challenge Bob, or argue with him, or in the beginning, to question his absurd theories about an ape-man. Of course, all doubts about that had been washed away with Stan's encounter, but it did not alter Bob's core personality or practices one iota. It seemed that as long as Bob was given an assignment, a task to be accomplished, was called into action in some way, such as bringing Stan under his protective wing, focusing on his hunt for evidence, dedicating his Tuesday and Friday nights to Bigfoot Bob, helping give aid to Stan when he had been attacked, or road tripping to Ohio, he was much more level and balanced. The moment the undertaking of the day or week had been accomplished, it triggered something in his head, flicked off a switch, which instructed him that it was now time to go unleashed.

This is when his beer consumption and rants were at their worst. At his best, he was fuzzy and always a little confused, except when in an immediate crisis or under direct threat, but those situations were few and far between. This is a thumbnail description of Stan's partner, so it goes to reason, that the odds against any plan forged with him had little chance of succeeding in the long run. Bob was too much of a wild card. Looking ahead, always the planner and improviser, Stan figured that once the podcast equipment was all set up, he could pretty much run the show himself, although that was not his wish. He wanted Bob to be by his side, so they could banter, and bring some life to the show.

It had been a couple of days since Mateo had secured the storefront on Main Street, and it was now time for Stan and Bob to move forward with the second phase of the plan, and move into the basement. On the scheduled morning, Mateo was standing in the driveway shivering in the cold, ready to help them lug all the radio equipment over. But there was a hiccup. Bob had gotten an early start with his beer consumption, putting down a six-pack for breakfast, and was on a diatribe about Bigfoot names, stomping back and forth inside the trailer. Stan had tried to placate Bob, settle him down, knowing that Mateo was about to show up. The morning's tirade was regarding the term "Bigfoot". Stan had not wanted to challenge his thinking, just get along, and get the day started. When Stan had first used that term long ago it had rankled Bob and apparently, he held onto that and felt a lecture was in order.

Bob was pacing back and forth in the trailer, becoming louder with each beer, furious about the term, blanking that he had chosen it for the name of his podcast. Stan remembered the day when he had used the forbidden name, how Bob had reacted, and how he had said that he chose that name for his show because it "liberated' better with "Bob" and that he was attempting to reach a wide audience, to his thousands of listeners, and appeal to "the mass market" and other tropes.

Back then, Stan didn't know what he knew now, that Bob was lying about his listenership. He had come upon Bob's journal book in the trailer, that told the whole story. It was during Stan's convalescence in the trailer, sometimes left alone for hours while Bob ventured out. Stan was curious about all of Bob's evidence, and now giving it vastly more respect, as he examined his wounds in the mirror.

He had been examining the foot print castings, the baggies of scat, the hair samples, the clippings and photos taped up everywhere, and drawers-full of field notes Bob had scribbled while out on his many recon missions.

The journal was shoved to the back of one of the drawers. It contained Bob's list of subscribers, comprising one-hundred and twenty-four names, and included their email addresses and phone numbers. One-hundred and twenty-four, not three-thousand. Furthermore, Bob had put a little check mark next to those who were the paying customers, depositing money via auto-pay into his bank account each month. That number was twenty-seven. So, the assertion by Bob that he had this rather large following, many of them paying listeners, and by implication that he was raking in many thousands of dollars a month, morphed into a number closer to three-hundred dollars, not even quite that much. Stan's suspicions were confirmed.

Also, there were indications that his podcast was open for anyone to hear, not just selected listeners, so perhaps his show did have a wide and far reach, but the money was small. Stan never had understood how Bob could somehow restrict people from listening in from a radio signal available to anyone, but then, Stan knew next to nothing about how all of this worked. Regardless, it had not come as a surprise to Stan, for he knew Bob to be the king of embellishment.

But there was another realization as well. As Stan looked through all the field notes, and all the other materials and samples, it occurred to him that Bob had been as astonished as he had been about the attack, and about the actual existence of the creature.

It had validated Bob's endeavor. Up until then all of it had been nothing more than a mountain of speculation, based on layers of circumstantial evidence, blended with unsubstantiated testimony. Although Bob had yet to see one of them in person, he had gotten close to it when the attack happened. With the evidence surrounding it, it was undeniable. For the first time, Bob came to realize that this creature actually existed, that it was no longer a theory, but instead of giving him the relief of validation, it seemed to make him more manic.

But on this morning, camped in Mandy's driveway, Bob's voice was booming in the confines of the trailer while Mateo stood outside, waiting. Each step Bob took gave a tremor to the rig, while grasping a freshly-opened beer, downing it between thoughts, then grabbing another. Stan sat in the relative safety of the back of the booth, the table serving as a protective three-foot spacer between his wild man friend talking about the Wildman:

"You wanna talk Himalaya's? You got the Yeti. How 'bout the Almasti from Indonesia, the Orang Pendek from China, the Yeren in North America? These ain't fuckin' monsters, these are actual fuckin' ape-men, all over the damn world! British Columbia for Chrissakes? The Ba-oosh. Know what that means? Means 'ape monkey imitates man'? You hearin' this? There's a shit load more. There's the Buk-was. How 'bout the Dsonoqua? They's the female squatch. Ever hear that? The natives up there, in the British Columbia place, near the ocean, the Kwakiutl, the

Tsimshian, they make those face carvings, ya know? You seen 'em, right? Whaddya think they're doin', just makin' that shit up? It goes back hundreds and hundreds of years, maybe shit, thousands, I dunno, but you know what I'm sayin'?" He continued, "How 'bout the Warm Springs tribe? They got a million stories 'bout them. Go ask 'em, go ahead! They fuckin' kidnap their women, you know that? And we ain't in some exclusive evolution club, ya know that, right? Us people, we're just part of the whole big thing. Yeah, just part of it. Us people, we think we're so damn special and distinct, well guess what? You got the Dmanisi Hominin, the Turkana Boy, African Homo Erectus, Peking Man, Tautavel Man, Java Man, Homo Hobilis Homo Rudolfensis, and that's just some of them. Some died out not all that long ago, ya know that? What makes us so damn special, to think there ain't more varieties out there, walkin' around right now?" Stan was amazed at Bob's knowledge, and how lucid he could be, especially when rip roaring dead ass drunk.

With his last pronouncement about everyone's human relatives, Bob staggered, leaned his back against a tall kitchen cabinet, and slid down like he was made of pudding, all the way to the floor, and passed out. He had not topped his previous record of sixteen beers, but had come close. Stan slid out of the booth, went out the door, and walked over to Mateo, who was waiting patiently, and had heard Bob's roars.

"I'm sorry Mateo, but it looks like we'll have to reschedule, I hope this didn't put you out"

"Nah, I'll fine. Is he going to be, okay?"

"Oh yeah, he gets like this sometimes, not to worry" but Stan was very worried.

"Harriet wants me to go in and refile all the back copies of the paper, so this'll give me some time for it. Let me know when you need me again. And Bob? He's a good guy, doesn't mean any harm", and with that, walked off down the sidewalk to his car, unflustered.

Stan took a walk around the block to do some thinking. He was wearing his simple but effective disguise; a Baseball cap, sunglasses, and his beard that he grew to disguise the scar on his cheek. He looked almost unrecognizable. As he walked, he concluded that he didn't entirely need Bob on a constant basis to confer with about every detail of the plan, and for that matter, hardly needed to confer with him at all about it. Except for setting up the radio equipment, and of course being his on-air partner when the time came, Bob's contribution wasn't that important anymore. Stan stopped, leaning against a big tree next to the street, and pondered. He had at one point, discussed with Bob the idea of going to an entirely different town in Ohio, or some other state, where they could enter as strangers, make their mark, but both men had been born in Tipp, raised there, and had roots, however withered they had now become. Tipp had tugged at them, had wanted them back, was their feeling.

The next day, things were very different. Stan, Bob and Mateo packed up the radio equipment and all of Bob's specimens, and driven over to the alley behind the new shop. They carried it down to the basement, set it up, and had a celebratory pizza from the parlor around the block. Just a day earlier, Bob had been a puddle on the floor of the trailer, and today he was friendly and upbeat. He was his usual fuzzy self, but no trace of yesterday's drunken rant. Stan was grateful for that, but held no illusions about Bob's future behavior. This had become a routine with him, and through habit, he never did this on his former broadcast days of Tuesday and Friday. The red flag days for Bob tended to be Wednesday, Thursday and Sunday. Saturdays were up for grabs. Stan put a line through those days in his mind's calendar, assuming Bob would not be present and accounted for. He also wondered if he should record any of Bob's rants? It could make for a good podcast one day.

As the days went on, at the front of the store on street level, Mateo made busy setting up his arts and crafts store, which was more or less a ruse. If he could generate enough sales just to pay for expenses, that would be great, for Stan anticipated making lots of money with this podcast.

The plan was not without its obstacles. For example, there was an antiquated city ordinance still on the books that outlawed any form of broadcast from a building in the historic district, except one. There had been a radio station there in the 1930's, WTIP, and the owners saw to it, with friends at city hall and at the state capitol, that only their station could broadcast from the district, which was of course back then, not "old" town at all, but the "current" and only downtown district in Tipp. They had had a storefront with big plate glass windows, and they would do news broadcasts, with particular attention paid to the effects of the Great Depression, the politics of the day, and do live radio dramas and comedy shows. Everything was viewable from the sidewalk through the windows. It was a huge hit, with people huddled on the sidewalk looking in. This is when radio was the only thing going but then with the advent of television, and it taking over in the 1950's, the station folded up.

In so doing, the ordinance was made obsolete, and forgotten about, never reversed or modified.

Both of the conspirator's knew that if they went legit, it would result in a year or two of paperwork, variances, approvals, permits and fees, inspections and perhaps worst of all, total public exposure. The public condemnation of Stan having dared to return combined with the general public's disbelief of Sasquatch, would mean they would be out of business before ever getting a chance.

Faced with all this, Stan and Bob decided to move forward, and bootleg a live radio podcast show.

As for the location, beyond the advantage of being able to operate covertly in a basement off an alley, they felt there was an old-world prestige in having a storefront there, and because it was the oldest part of town, free of any form of big box stores or shopping malls, all of which were to be found on the west side of town. The foot traffic was low, customers few and far between, leaving many storefronts vacant for months. For that reason, the rental prices were driven down to affordable levels. As for broadcasting and prying eyes, Bob assured Stan that they could successfully bootleg the signal, and not be a bother to the city's regulators, already over-taxed with paper work, or hassle the FCC with such a small concern.

Stan had quite a bit of money left from the blowout sale at his general store, and had calculated that their new podcast show, Sasquatch Encounters with Stan and Bob, would attract swift and wide attention. Bigfoot enthusiasts were growing exponentially and they would be charging a monthly fee for their show, plus developing a full line of licensed merchandise. Stan's favorite idea being a plastic bobble-head of Bob. The set-up costs were ghastly, but once in production, they cost pennies on the dollar. The plastic figurine of Bob, with an exaggeratedly large torso, lots of body hair and a big white beard, would sell huge. He was going to call it "Bobsquatch".

The dicey but manageable part of the plan was that it was to be literally, an underground operation, their location kept a secret. It would be the podcast equivalent of a speakeasy. They would enter and exit from the steps leading up to the alleyway. They would only broadcast at night, making their comings and goings more difficult to notice. They would never mention where they were broadcasting from, only to say "the Midwest", and that was as detailed as they would get. Unless they said or did something in town or on the air to provoke the curious, their whereabouts could be kept secret for a long time, indefinitely Stan figured. Mateo would operate his store up top, doing conventional retail for the public with paid employees, who would not be told of the existence of the basement operation, or of the basement itself. There was a door in the back of the storeroom, leading to the basement, but it was always kept locked, and the door masked with boxes and empty shelf units. Mateo would hold down his reporting job at the paper, allowing him to pursue his dream of working for the Cincinnati Herald one day. He would also keep an eye on Trowner, to make sure she hadn't gotten wind of the podcast's location.

Stan knew this had all the makings of a Frank Capra or Howard Hawk's 1940's screwball comedy, but figured, what's the worst that could happen?

He could, however, imagine one scenario that would be bad, very bad: if the locals found out about it too soon, squelching their chance for success, or if the crazies in the greater Bigfoot community, ever found out their location and started gathering there. And then there was the small matter of Mandy.

Before things had gotten messy, his relationship with Mandy had been pretty good, graded on a curve. True, she had become increasingly frustrated with him because he wouldn't commit to her, as he had not cared to talk about marriage, which understandably, made her sad-angry, but they had gotten along very well in the beginning, years ago, and were a good match in all or most of the other departments, he felt. The "future is marriage" department had never done well. As to things having gotten messy, that was on him, and he was all too aware that his Scalopini scheme, his grandest prank ever, had not only blown up in his face but had been the final blow for him and Mandy. It was "at the end of your pattern of reckless behavior" as she put it once.

He couldn't blame her for being furious, for wanting him out of her life. As for having children? It had always been a very attractive but abstract concept to him. He loved the idea of having a couple of kids, the idea of having kids to play with, teach things to, go places with, but he was gun shy on the entire topic, due to his own upbringing, and was fearful he might have welled up inside of him similar, malfunctioning parental tendencies, some kind of twisted-up DNA, that would condemn his kids to a youth filled with being dismissed, not adored.

On top of all this, there was a singular driving problem, namely that he still was desperately in love with Mandy, and wanted more than anything, to be back with her again.

He had to prove himself. His hope was that this latest move was verging on being, to the most part, legitimate, and she might respect that. He was torn between being totally candid with Mandy, or wanting to keep it quiet for the time being. He wanted the podcast to become a huge hit, and then he would reveal it to Mandy. It wouldn't be a success overnight, he knew that. It might take a few weeks to catch on strong. Success first, truth second. But wasn't this what he had done before? Was he repeating the same pattern of deception? Could he ever be trusted?

While these thoughts and questions rumbled through his mind, he also knew that anybody with half a brain and some skills, could detect where their broadcast was emanating from, but he could not control that, and did not know how to jam incoming signals, if that were even possible, so that was the one big wild card. Bob had said something to him about their IP (Internet Protocol) address being protected by the encrypted VPN (Virtual Private Network) he had set up. Paul, with all of his tech savvy, would have come in very handy right about now. But what tech nerd who would even go to the bother of figuring out where they were housed? Who would be motivated to do so? Stan, considering his track record, didn't want to know the answer to that.

As for the legal aspects, beyond the piddling issue of the old ordinance, they did not want to draw attention to themselves from the FCC, in terms of legality of content, beyond the issue of the legality of their very existence. Stan had done some homework and so long as they were not defaming someone, not promoting anarchy or illegal behavior, and being careful about not infringing on someone's copyright protections, such as using someone else's intellectual property, they were good to go. They could talk about someone's book, for instance, all day long, but could only read a very small passage from it. Follow these rules and a simple format call-in talk show was in the clear. People could call in, tell them their story, and they in turn could comment on that story, and that was it. But the one big rule he could not get around, could not cleverly ignore, was the Mandy Rule. He realized he simply had to be up front with her if he had any notion of one day, earning her back. He had to tell her all about this idea, before their first episode.

It was a risky proposition. He could try knocking on her door one day after work, or while she was in the back tending to her vegetable garden. He could just lay it on the line. But it was entirely possible she simply had enough Stan Time, and did not want to hear one more word out of his mouth, describing yet another idea or plan. Maybe she was over it? Maybe her reaction would be volcanic, and would order them off her property, and who knows how many people she would tell? The whole thing could implode before it even started. Stan wanted to be open and honest with her, but did not want to destroy their chances of getting the podcast up on its feet. It was about trust, and whether he could trust her, and whether she could trust him. She had given up on him months ago, but maybe he had a chance? It was all so confusing.

His head was awash with such thoughts as he toiled away with Bob in the basement, getting the place all set up. He knew he could probably count on Bob to help him two or three days a week, while the rest of his week would be taken over by his drunken jags. Bob had to be the one to set up the equipment, for Stan hadn't a clue. He knew how to plug a cord into an outlet, that was about it.

At one point, Bob started looking around the room everywhere, his concern building, looking in boxes, behind shelf units and in drawers. He went round and round the room searching for something, with increasing alarm, and finally, standing in the middle of the room, looked at Stan with panicky eyes and said, "Where's the Shure?"

Stan, as with many of Bob's disconnected questions, replied, "What?"

Bob brushed the question aside, and dove into a pile of empty boxes he had gone through twice before. "The Shure man, the fuckin' Shure is fuckin' missing! How you gonna do a fuckin' podcast without the fuckin' Shure?".

He had gone from normal Bob to madman Bob in the space of fifteen seconds. Stan tried to slow him down, get him to breathe, and from what he could tell, he hadn't had a single beer that day.

"Bob, Bob, slow down a sec, help me out here. Look at me. I will help. What are we looking for?"

Bob wheeled around, giving Stan a crazed stare, "The mic, you fuckin' comb-overed, uneducated, emotionally imbalanced, fuckin' narcissistic bullshit fuckin' artist, the fuckin' mic!"

"The glove box, Bob. It's in the glove box. We put the mic there so it would be safe, not get lost. I was supposed to know the brand name? And what do you mean, comb-overed?"

Bob looked at Stan, the gears in his head disengaged and whirring, the panic button turned off, the red face and sweat receding, his breathing becoming less rapid, and said "Oh yeah, that's right, I remember" and went for the door to retrieve the mic from the truck.

Stan snuck a peek in the mirror, and then studied Bob as he went, taking an assessment of his partner's description of him. Here was Bob, he thought, a guy that seemed to have cotton balls stuffed in his head half the time, who just made the most concise and unambiguous description of his faults he had ever heard. He even topped Mandy. He took some exception at "uneducated", for he felt he was reasonably well-informed, and he decided at that moment he would start pushing his hair to the side instead of forward, but beyond that, the concise review had been pretty spot-on.

Still, of larger and more immediate concern, was his partner's mental state. However nuts, he had thought Bob to be, he was obviously much more nuts than he had fully realized. But "nuts" was not a pejorative Stan liked to throw around carelessly, for he had been described that way, numerous times by numerous people. Granted, those people were his detractors, members of the local lynch mob that had less than kind things to say about him, but that did not mean there was not some truth to it. It was a touchy subject.

Bob came back down the stairs, his Shure mic in hand, stopped on the last step, and gave Stan a look. "I think that squatch followed me back to camp one day. And maybe later, that's why he was there, why he came at you".

"What? You're saying what?" said Stan, caught totally off guard.

Bob, his head bowed in shame, had evidently decided that this moment was when he needed, when he had to, confess. Obviously, it had been weighing on him.

"Why would he follow you? You were miles up the trail, why follow you?"

Bob, his head still bowed, said in a low voice, "You remember how I came down the trail one day, told you I had found something?"

"No, not really, you said that pretty much every time you came back" replied Stan.

"No, no, this time was different, you don't remember I guess".

A long pause followed, and Stan stood still, not wanting to break the moment.

"But then I got all caught up helping you make that God-awful dinner of yours, what was it, green beans and rice, and that fucking garlic salt in a frying pan? Think you used enough of it? Damn, that was nasty. You eat that kinda crap all the time?"

No shared laughter this time, just a long pause.

Stan said, "Nope, guess I don't remember you telling me something, why?"

Bob's words came hesitatingly. "Well, I took what looked like a crude path off the main foot trail, 'bout four miles up, and followed it through some pretty heavy brush, some brambles, and there were branches laid across the path, like put there on purpose, to keep people out or to catch up a deer or somethin', so I kept going, and pretty soon, I came on what looked to be a nest".

"A nest?" said Stan.

"Yeah, like there was a bunch of fresh snapped branches with leaves and pine needles on 'em, fresh broke, and laying down all inter-twined, like woven or somethin'. And it was large, maybe four, five-foot across. No way in hell nature made that. Looked exactly like what gorillas do, they make a bed".

This sent chills up Stan's spine, and he was glad he was not back at the campsite.

"Yeah, a bed all right", said Bob.

"That's something", said Stan.

"Yeah, something for dead sure, and it stunk too. Smelled like they say they do sometimes. Wet dog mixed with fecal mixed with rotten trash. Awful. Only kinda gorilla that stinks, sometimes, is the Silverback, not the female or kids. They emit that they say, to warn others, or when they get hostile or territorial sometimes, not always, just sometimes...". Bob continued, "What I think is that I came upon it, startled it, woke him up, you know, they're usually nocturnal, and he ran off someplace, close by, and watched me as I checked out his bed. He may not have liked that too much, you know?"

Stan looked at his friend, still standing on the step, looking ashamed. "So, what you're saying is, if you hadn't come upon the nest, he wouldn't have followed you down to the camp, and ended up attacking me, is that right?" said Stan.

"Yeah, that 'bout sums it up", said Bob.

Stan reassured his friend that his theory was silly, that the squatch was defending his territory that day down by the stream, didn't like him catching what he considered to be his fish, didn't like how they had set up camp in this remote spot, too far from town, and simply wanted them gone. It had nothing to do with a nest. Stan said all this to Bob, which made Bob feel better. Stan knew that Bob was probably correct, however.

Stan could now add this latest entry to his nightmare menu, as he had been troubled by an increase in them lately, and needed new material.

It was odd too, because right after the attack, he fully expected to have nightmares, but didn't. He had been prescribed some pain pills by Doc Alex, mostly to aid in sleep, and had stopped taking them early on, hating the idea of getting hooked, as so many had in Tipp. The Doc said they would help him to sleep deeply, and might help with not having any nightmares. It was true, for he stopped having them.

For years, he had always had nightmares, way before his attack, but then, after the attack, they had vanished for a while, which seemed weird, but he figured the pills had a lot to do with that. But now, here they were again, very anxious ones. The pills probably did do their job but he was unwilling to take them on a regular basis. The nightmares were mostly about being out of time, out of chances, such as a flood with water rising, or running away from something on a road, dangling from a cliff, avoiding getting hit by a car. None of them were about the attack, not a single image of the squatch. He knew they were more likely a result of anxiety about his deception with Mandy, and whether the podcast would succeed or fail.

Stan knew that dreams were supposedly metaphors for what was going on in the "real world" and to help him figure things out, to work out problems. He had gotten to the point where he didn't want to go to sleep, knowing he would have another. He had considered going to see a therapist about it, but he would most certainly blow his cover once the therapist, or someone else in the office, mentioned having seen him to someone else and it would be a wild fire. He soon realized that his best therapy for now, was to stay busy, stay focused on the job at hand, which was to set up the podcast station. The nightmares, he reasoned, would run their course and finally go away, once his life settled down.

And busy he was. He had to spend some of his funds to get additional equipment, or to acquire updated versions of Bob's tired equipment, and coach Mateo out extensively with creating the store upstairs, but found he needed to help Mateo out less and less, since he was a very capable and smart young guy, and retail is more instinct than science. So, Stan's days were mostly spent doing the finishing touches. It was coming together nicely. But Bob's confession was very disturbing, if true.

Anticipating a strong positive response, Stan had invested in logo-ware, from t-shirts to coffee mugs, and creating a catchy promo poster. He had even ordered a gross of the Bobsquatch bobble heads that were due in any day.

There were dozens of online blogs and sites he reached out to that were part of the Sasquatch Universe. It was almost limitless. So many thousands of people were members of various Sasquatch groups around the country, people who commented on blogs, people who called into podcasts or listened to them intently. He infiltrated many sites using pseudonyms, posing as just another believer, but then letting it slip out that he had heard about a new podcast about to start, and in other cases, being upfront about it. All of this with an aim to let people know about the roll-out of the Stan and Bob podcast.

When they had cleared the trailer's radio-bedroom of all the equipment and cabinets, they were able to turn it into a bedroom-bedroom. Bob found a gently used recliner at the local Goodwill, and they set it up opposite the bed. Bob took the recliner, Stan the bed. It was not the most comfortable of accommodations, or private, but it served the temporary purpose that was needed. Stan was reasonably sure he would end up over at Mandy's again and Bob could have his trailer to himself. Stan would make low profile visits to the local market and gas station, always with his disguise, driving his generic white truck which was not recognizable as being his, as it was the most common color, and he had made a point of not putting any personalized stickers on it.

During all of this time, his mind would wander, and it had increasingly occurred to him that his ongoing nightmares were tied into his unresolved issues with Mandy. He had to resolve the conflict, one way or the other, and do it by way of open honesty and with no more tricks, no more concealment. He had done pretty much all he could do to get the podcast ready for launch, and it would be what it would be. He knew that he would have to get around to the nerve racking task of talking to Mandy next. He had a plan.

The plan was to have no plan at all. His whole life had been about making plans, so this time, he would purposely not make one, and just go over to her place one afternoon, on a weekend day, when she was not worn out from her stressful job, politely knock on the door, maybe bring some flowers, he wasn't sure about that part, it might be a bit much, but in any case, knock on the door and be the picture of contrite. Contrite was a very important element to this non-plan-plan, as it would demonstrate to her that he was serious, humbled, extremely remorseful for his past behavior, and ready to make a commitment to her. He did not expect a miracle. He knew that there was a lot of residual anger and disappointment in her toward him, because of him, and a fair amount of hurt as well, so he would take it very slow, very cautiously, and she would see and appreciate that too. He didn't want to invade her space, but wait to be invited into it. Even though their past difficulties had not been all his fault, he would adopt the attitude that they had been. It seemed a good tactic, and one from his heart, and if not entirely from his heart, then it had a very good chance of appearing that it was. He was ready.

He waited until the next Saturday morning, asking Bob to go to the storefront basement to work on the foot print castings inventory and display, for it needed doing and he didn't want Bob anywhere in the vicinity, in case Mandy took his visit well, invited him in for some coffee, and then it evolved quickly into make-up love making in the kitchen or living room, both of them quickly stripped down as far as it required, buttons and zippers open, panting, legs, fingers, mouths, tasting, breathing, heaving, gasping, moaning, should they not make it upstairs. He didn't want to count on that but he figured there was at least half a chance the "new Stan" would score big points.

He had imagined all the possible reactions she might have to his visit, from all out rejection, throwing clay pots or books at him, all the way to complete acceptance and impassioned sex. There were many points on the scale in between those two, and he wanted to be ready for anything, so he could in an instant, calibrate her reaction, and counter-react in the best possible way.

He gave himself one last look in the mirror, looking bright-eyed with hair combed, beard trimmed, and smelling of a new cologne with notes of leather and tobacco he had bought himself at Macy's for the occasion. He walked down the trailer steps, down the driveway toward the street so he could knock on the front door, hung a right at the low picket fence, and headed to the front gate. It wasn't until that moment he saw it. How long had it been there he wondered? Was it put there just this morning? "Could it have been here for days and I just now noticed it?" he thought to himself. He didn't think it possible he could have overlooked such a thing. But there it was, a sign planted in the ground next to the gate, standing nearly six feet tall, with the unmistakable white and blue logo. It read:

"Coldwell Banker Realty, Tipp City, Barbara Simmons, certified agent" and below that, "FOR SALE".

There seemed to be a force field around it, and Stan couldn't take another step closer. He stared at it, his mind spinning for a few seconds or five minutes, he wasn't sure which, and then turned, his blood pressure peaking, his face flush, went back up the driveway headed to the trailer, recoiling, feeling sick, his heart racing, regretting the new cologne, but then hit the brakes, and decided to seek Mandy out, who was likely to be in the back yard, gardening. She was.

"Just like that? Just like *that*, Stan?" She stood up from her gardening. "You spent eight years avoiding anything serious with me, and then you wigged out, did some crazy thing with your store, didn't breathe a word of it to me, became the biggest jackass in town, and you're saying to me, that it is *my* fault, that I have decided to sell my place and move, just like *that*?"

Her answer to his less than contrite question was so complete and puncture proof, he didn't have much of a comeback, other than to say lamely, "But Mandy, I was going to tell you how things are different, what we're up to, what all the secrecy is about, I've been so busy I didn't have the time, but now...", and she cut him off.

"That's it, Stan. That's it" she said. She gathered up her garden tools into a bucket, pulled off her gloves, and walked toward the back porch, while Stan stood, speechless, stunned.

She was definitely pissed. "I am done. D, O, N, done. You have been here for weeks, for *weeks*, and have I heard a single word from you as to what you guys are up to? No, not a *single* word.... You could have included me, ya know?"

She paused a quick moment, collecting herself, calming down, and continued, "Looks like my place will go into escrow on Monday, and I have two good back-ups if that falls through. I have a new job in Cleveland at the Clinic, a much better job. I have signed the papers for a new little place in Shaker Heights, and if you want to come visit me sometime, that would be okay with me, I'm not trying to be enemies, I am an open book, always have been, but if you come, check with me in advance, get a hotel room, and we can attempt to be friends, but for now, we can get on with our lives, and I am not going around, even one more time, on your fucking carousel, this is it".

With that, she turned, went up the three steps to the porch, to the back door, slamming it behind her, and inside. Stan knew his non-plan-plan had not gone as well as he had hoped.

There wasn't a damn thing he could do or say. She was right. All Stan could do is stare at the door.

Mandy popped her head out the doorway, giving Stan a fleeting last hope, and said, "And, oh yeah, you guys gotta be out of here by next weekend", and went back inside.

Stan stood, his whole body numb, having not the slightest sense of what to do next.

Mandy came out for an encore. She came down the steps, and right up to him, with a kind expression, gently touched his left cheek, her fingertips through the beard, going over his scar. "You know, you could have told me about what happened, about the Bigfoot or whatever attack…" she said.

Stan, caught completely off guard, muttered, "How'd you know about that?"

She pulled her hand back and her face got hard again. "Bob told me after I grilled him".

"Well Bob, he's the honest type…"

You think it was a Bigfoot huh? Couldn't possibly have been a bear? No chance of that? Your memory not playing tricks on you? Like that's never happened before?"

"I didn't want to worry you, told you I fell, that's all".

Getting agitated again, she said, "No, that's not it, Stan. Since when have you really worried about me? You were worried about yourself, about how I might take it, how that would impact you, worried I wouldn't believe you, it's always been about you Stan".

Stan's eyes grew wide, not accustomed to such direct talk, especially when it was so accurate, and on the heels of Bob's description. "It really was one of them, I swear..."

Not believing a word of it, she said, "Sure it was". Then, with a concerned look on her face, "You be careful Stan, I worry about you..." and with that, made her final ascent of the back porch steps, and went inside.

In the fourteen minutes it took Stan to get into his truck, drive to the Main Street location, park in the alley, go down the stairs into the basement, he was in a complete daze, was on some kind of auto-pilot. It's amazing he didn't go through a red light or crash into another car. When he got to the basement, it was quiet. No Bob. He figured Bob was out, doing his usual carousing in one of his favorite bars around town. Stan sat in a swivel chair in front of the radio table and swiveled himself to the right, then to the left, then right, left, right, and so on, for a long time. It was mid-afternoon, and he could hear the sound of footsteps from above, in Mateo's newly opened store. At first, they were the sounds of footsteps walking casually, back and forth, as if window shopping for just the right Play-Doh or watercolor set, but then the footsteps became much faster, louder, as if people were scurrying about. Stan pulled himself out of the chair, and plodded up the stairs to the store's storage room door. He opened it, and maneuvered around the stack of big cardboard boxes, and he could hear people talking excitedly, but he couldn't quite make it out. He walked a few steps, and opened the back door of the store itself.

Mateo saw him, and instantly ran over to him. "It's Bob, he's on the roof! He's going to jump!"

"Of course, Bob is on the roof. Why shouldn't he be?" Stan thought to himself sarcastically. "Mandy is selling her house, leaving town, leaving me, and Bob is on the roof, gonna jump off. Everything seems normal" he further thought. But did he say it out loud? He did. Mateo stared at him with moon eyes.

There were two customers in the place, all shook up about Bob, wondering out loud if he was about to jump or if they should call the fire department, the police?

Suddenly snapping out of it, Stan said, "No! No! don't do that, no police. I can handle it". He did an about-face, ran back down the stairs to the basement, then up the back stairs to the alley. He had remembered a metal ladder bolted into the outside brick wall, that led to a platform, and then made its way to the roof. He climbed up, muttering to himself

"Bob's gone too far this time, he's going to jump?", and peeked over the edge.

There was Bob, grasping his long aluminum pole with the antenna on top, and it was swaying back and forth, with Bob holding on for dear life. "Hey, Bob, what the hell?"

"Hey, buddy-o, I could use some help here", said Bob.

Stan rushed over, helped Bob steady the pole, and then braced it as Bob tried many times to bolt it with his socket wrench, into the foundation anchors he had installed in the brick roof surround. It wasn't an easy job for two, let alone one, and they struggled and cursed their way through it for ten minutes, until it was good and solid. "I'll hook up the coax later", said Bob.

Both men stood up, catching their breath and admiring their work. Stan said, "I thought you were going to wait for me to help?"

"Yeah, I know, but I thought I could get it done myself. I put it up on the trailer by myself".

Bob started gathering his tools, putting them in his canvas bag, and then it occurred to Stan to ask, "How come you're here?"

Bob, as nonchalantly as he could, simply said, "I'm puttin' up the antenna".

"Yes, I know that, but what are you doing here, today, it's Sunday?" said Stan.

"Just gettin done what needs to get done, is all".

By now, Bob had finished gathering up his tools, and took a couple of steps toward the ladder.

Stan, still puzzled, said, "This is Sunday, you're here, working, not bar-hopping".

Bob stopped, his back to Stan, and said "I don't drink no more. I stopped. I got work to do", and proceeded to the ladder, and went down.

Stan, having a hard time processing this, followed him down the ladder and once inside the basement, peppered him with questions. "What do you mean you just quit? You can't, just quit, it doesn't work that way" making perfect sense to himself.

Bob shot him a look and said, "I can do anything I want, what the hell do you know about it?"

Stan poked and prodded, but Bob was resolute with his simple formula for putting down the beer.

Apparently, Bob had made a clear-headed decision, and had simply decided that his drinking days were getting in the way of him doing his best work, and he wanted to "shine at this new opportunity", and was "grateful to Stan for all he was doing" for him, and he "didn't miss beer one little bit".

Stan, not being well versed about alcoholics or alcoholism, had assumed that Bob was afflicted with the disease, and Stan, equipped with a lot of misinformation gleaned from magazine articles and movie plots, had planned on talking to him about it, but just like with Mandy, had put it off. The only person that Stan was reasonably sure to be an alcoholic was Carl Lethrow, the used car lot owner, who by most afternoons, was looped. It did not affect his negotiating skills though, as he was still able to squeeze every last nickel out of a sale, as he had done with Stan's purchase of his truck. From what Stan had heard, Carl made the occasional vow to quit, attended meetings, and did well for a month or two, but then predictably, slid back into cheap vodka. He had gotten a lot of moral support, had burnt through a few sponsors, had tried hypnotherapy, Yoga, jogging, meditation, and joined a local church, but nothing could combat his horrible addiction.

The point was, for most, being afflicted and trying to get away from it was a huge production, and not just something you could drop like a hot rock. As for Bob, Stan had always figured he needed to join a local program, like Carl Lethrow did, such as Alcoholics Anonymous, the obvious choice, and get his life straight, like magic. Stan had gone as far as looking up where and when there were meetings, and to his surprise, for such a small town, there were many. Some catered to all men, others to all women, one open to everyone, with an open Saturday night meeting at the Kiwanis, some meetings for newcomers, and smaller intimate groups for seasoned veterans, but the point was, there was lots of opportunity should Bob wish to avail himself to one or more of them. But apparently, Bob had not been so inclined.

Stan had figured he was another Carl, and there was nothing to be done about it, sadly. But now, Bob is telling him that he simply quit, and it sounded like Bob was on the level about it. Stan thought to himself, "How is it I am so wrong about reading people? How can I be that far off?" Seeing that Bob was unambiguous on the topic, and had already moved on, had no apparent need for going to meetings or commiserating with similarly stricken people, Stan figured, he ought to move on as well, and stop harping on it. Perhaps that same attitude should be adopted when it came to Mandy, he thought? Time to move on.

And then his old demon companion started to slither back into his mind. If he had been that far off in reading Mandy and Bob, how is it he thinks he's got his own act together? Was Mandy, right? Had he reverse-engineered the attack to be a Bigfoot and not a bear in his memory? Was it the by-product of PTSD? Was his recollection completely scrambled, due to shock?"

He thought back. He had managed to stay busy, to stay distracted, by driving all the way to the Northwest woods, to camp out for months, not to mention being attacked by a Sasquatch that he knew did not exist, and perhaps due to Bob's carelessness. And now, here he was back in Tipp, staying incognito, setting up a basement for a podcast about the big creature, and during all of this, was able to shove his fiendish companion way back in the catacombs, but there were so many triggers for Stan, so many unresolved threats, borne of so many unresolved fears. Was his memory tricking him into an elaborate fiction? Was he in the process of pulling his biggest scam yet, but on himself? He was dueling with two creatures, one very real from what he could recall, made of flesh and bone and standing eight feet tall or taller, and the other, made of vapors, but just as real, having taken up residence in his mind for decades. So many spider webs and trap doors. Obviously, the sudden news about Mandy had thrown him down, scrambled his brain. Hadn't there been many clues, some as big as a building, that he had chosen to not look at? Was this all for real or just him hoaxing himself?

As for Bob, he was relieved that he may not have to keep compensating for Bob's wild ways, to keep being his emotional support, which is comical if looked at from the outside in, for Bob looked at Stan the same way, knowing that Stan needed emotional support. They were an un-likely pair living together in a house of mirrors.

As for thinking about Mandy, he could not devise of a way to escape all the clattering noise in his head. He felt so low, he figured he had little to lose or risk, by exposing himself to the judgment of the town's citizens. Maybe their anger toward him had simmered these last months, and he would at worst, suffer various insults or sarcastic remarks once he outed himself, but that was okay, he felt he deserved it. He decided he would venture out in broad daylight, without his disguise. He shaved the beard off, took off the shades, removed the hat. But where to? He figured, why not Billy's? That was a hub for most of his friends, so why not give that a shot?

He drove over and parked about half a block away from the diner, walked up the sidewalk past some folks who didn't seem to recognize him, and walked in. Lou Anne was hustling as usual, and the place was busy, being just before their five o'clock dinner specials. He swung open the glass door carefully, being on the lookout for a plate being hurled his way, and sat down as if the stool were a pressure sensitive bomb. He opened the menu, which he had memorized years ago, but it served as a good prop. He pretended to read about the two specials, the buttermilk fried chicken and the taco meatloaf, both with steamed vegetables. The usual ambient sound of the place was familiar. The din of people discussing their lives, children, businesses, politics and upcoming plans, was in full gear.

Something seemed off to Stan. What was missing? An unfamiliar waitress whizzed by, said blankly, "Coffee?" He nodded, and she placed a coffee mug in front of him, poured it almost full, and continued down the line without so much as a comment or steely glare. Something was definitely off. He poured some milk in his coffee from the stainless server, tore open a packet of brown sugar, stirred up the brew, and took a sip. All of this was done slowly, carefully, being ready for the first assault. He figured someone would be daring enough to be the first to tell him what a low life he was, or about having the nerve to show up here after what he did, or maybe Lou Anne would suggest he try the Denny's a few blocks away? But none of that happened. In fact, nothing happened at all.

The waitress took his order, as uninterested in him as humanly possible, and zipped off. Lou Anne was busy working a section of booths. He looked her way and once or twice, she looked his, but with no recognition, no smile or glare, as if he were a door or refrigerator. His bowl of "Billy's Homemade Vegetable Soup" arrived shortly thereafter, piping hot. He took a spoonful, thinking that surely now, somebody would have a nasty remark to make.

Then, out of the blue, the elderly Irene Ling and her forty-something diminutive daughter, Donna, approached, and stood next to Stan. Donna leaned in close to Stan and whispered to him.

"Far as I'm concerned, you're an asshole no-count bum, but I never did like your store anyway, you were always out of everything"

Stan looked up, nodding his head, "Sorry".

"My mom has been battling dementia, not that you give a flying shit, but she thinks you're not the owner of your rat ass store, she thinks that nice man Gary is, she has it all ass backwards, so she just wanted to say hello. She feels sorry for you. What a joke".

"Oh, all right, that's nice…"

Donna ushered her mom closer to Stan, and she said, with a sweet smile, and in a delicate voice, "Hello Stanley, I just wanted to say hello, and let you know how sorry I am that the owner, that older man, Gary, is a fucking horse's ass, screwing you over like that, taking such horrible advantage of you, I'm so sorry you got tricked by that low life fucking scumbag".

Stan nodded at her, with a polite smile, "Thank you for your kind words". Having such language come out of the mouth of such a sweet looking old woman, not to mention the daughter, was startling, but Stan was discovering that there should be no more surprises, and that everything civil or friendly was now off the table.

Mrs. Ling was one of the only two Chinese people in the town, her husband Richard, having passed away years ago. Ignorantly, years back, many people assumed that she and her husband owned the Hong Kong Chinese Restaurant, but that was never the case.

A very nice Honduran couple opened the restaurant, having arrived in town about eighteen years ago, with only the clothes on their backs and a box of gold coins, cleverly smuggled away from the in-humane gangs of cartel cut-throats now controlling much of their homeland.

Mrs. Ling's husband had been a successful attorney, and she was a talented portrait artist, having done numerous commissions in the Dayton area for years, before she started drifting into her own netherworld. Stan was grateful for the mis-directed sympathy, as he would accept any he could at this point. As for the mix-up in identities, it explained why Gary kept receiving burning death stares from Mrs. Long every time he encountered her in town. He never would figure that out.

As for the rest of the inhabitants of the diner, there was nothing coming from them. He had not made even the slightest wrinkle in time or space with them, other than occupying a stool at the counter. After the Ling's exited, he was so creeped out, that after only three more spoonsful of the undeniably delicious soup, and feeling invisible, he slapped down a twenty, and fled meekly into the approaching darkness of early evening to his home in the driveway. He slept like a rock.

The next morning, a clear bright Sunday with six days to go before Mandy's deadline for them to leave, he was awakened by the annoying beep-beep-beep of a truck backing up. He looked around, saw that Bob was already gone, or had not even come back to the trailer last night, and peeked through the curtain. There was a box truck positioned in front of the house, with large but faded block lettering, stating, "Williams and Sons Moving" and below that, in smaller script lettering, "We'll Move You In, We'll Move You Out". There were three youngish guys, two of them African Americans, and a third who appeared to be East Indian. They seemed very efficient, pulling out the ramp from the rear of the truck and commencing to carry out various packed boxes and household objects from Mandy's place, walking them up the ramp to the inside of the truck.

Stan threw on some clothes and walked over to the action, down the driveway past the empty space where Bob always parked his Beetle, and gave lots of berth to Mandy's new car. Stan, not wanting to appear needy or sad, and not wanting to be the cause of a confrontation with Mandy, approached the scene guardedly. He overheard them discussing how they would be coming back for "the big stuff" on Thursday. She wasn't kidding around. He never did see Mandy appear, just the guys going back and forth. After a few minutes, Stan grew tired and discouraged by the show, hopped in his truck and took off. Mandy, peeking through the kitchen window, relieved he had finally gone, ventured out, giving the guys a hand.

Stan felt disembodied without a store to run. He drove by the still-vacant space, slowing down to look at the front deck and windows, naked except for Riptick's "For Lease" sign. The front window had been fixed and the place detail cleaned, walls painted with a fresh coat of off-white, and ready for the next hopeful. He couldn't help but think about how it used to be, and how things would have been, if he hadn't started out on the promotion which spiraled downward into complete chaos and banishment.

But now here he was, back in town with a story to tell (not that anyone would believe it) and a whole new chapter in his life about to unfold, to reveal itself to him. He was hopeful about the podcast enterprise with Bob, thinking it a sound business move, but how could he possibly know if it was or not? His old friend, self-doubt, had crept back into his mind, making him wonder if it hadn't been a bear attack instead?

He knew that if the podcast were to succeed, the hook would be the telling of his experience, but how many times, how many ways, could he tell it before it became boring or subject to scrutiny? The long-range success, or failure, of the podcast, and its ability to generate a decent income for the two, would be entirely dependent on who called in, with whatever story they had to tell, and how well they could interview that person, long after his own story was forgotten.

He figured that there would be far more people trying to get on the podcast, than would end up on it, so he could pick and choose, seeking out the best stories and storytellers. But was the premise of the podcast true? He wasn't altogether sure about that anymore, and made the mental adjustment that it was a job, a form of showbiz, something he could earn a living at, and that it was all about entertainment, performance, and his acting chops.

Once done with his self-examination, feeling like an orphan standing in front of his vacant former store, he drove around town, decided to stop at the local market, and test the reception he got there. It was no different than the diner, it turned out. Some people recognized him, some people didn't. Those that did, gave him a quick non-committal glance and continued deciding on which cereal or shampoo to throw into their cart. No one looked at him directly, or spoke to him whatsoever, and just went about their business, as if he were a total stranger, new to town. He recognized people who he knew, knew him, at a hundred feet distant. Not one of them gave him any more recognition than a shopping cart or bulk stack of tomato soup. He had become an animated inanimate object, a walking talking mannequin, or like with the diner, simply invisible, a non-entity. This was something that transcended persona non grata. At least with that, there is recognition, rejection, emotion, but with this, it was the big nothing.

Maybe their experience with him a few short months ago had been upstaged by more current events concerning the town? Maybe there had been a huge and tragic fire at the hotel, or the police had violently busted up a KKK rally, or the city council race was heating up with accusations of illicit sex or graft? Whatever it might be, it was totally eclipsing the town's desire, or perhaps even its ability, to include him into their existence. It was downright existential.

Stan was weary of memory lane, and went to the basement where Bob was busy toiling away, putting the finishing touches on setting up all the equipment. He had tagged each cord, each jack, each outlet, each port, with a color-coded label, making it easy to re-hook something should it become un-hooked. "See anything interesting out there" said Bob, as he was bent around the backside of a receiver unit.

Stan didn't want to get into it, and said, "Nah, just drove around, laid low. You been here all night?"

"Yeah, pretty much", said Bob. "Went out for a bite but came back, wanted to finish up, slept over there, not bad" pointing at a cot with bedding in the corner. Bob stood up, rubbing his stiff back, and proclaimed, "Well bud, we can light her up any old time you want, she's ready to go".

Stan thanked Bob profusely for all his hard work and they popped open two ice cold ginger ales, to celebrate.

Bob said he needed a shower, and left Stan alone with his thoughts in the basement. Stan walked around the equipment, admiring the professional workmanship Bob had performed, ran his finger over the dials and switches, remembering what Bob had taught him. Sat in one of the two swivel chairs and adjusted his Shure to his mouth level, making sure the spit guard was cinched down in place. He leaned over and checked Bob's set up as well. He looked around the room, admiring the display of footprint castings in a neat row on a shelf, and Bob's exhibits of excrement, now neatly contained in clear acrylic boxes and labeled. There were posters on the wall depicting Sasquatch, one or two of them coming close to what Stan thought he had encountered. There were some comedic posters as well ("Bigfoot doesn't believe in you either") but they didn't go into that too much, most of the comedy posters available being too low brow or simply not funny. They had Bob's topo maps, and had added more. There was a large shelf unit crammed with Bob's reference books, and then another shelf holding their podcast show's inventory of merchandise, with a large flat work table next to it, with shipping materials. The place was about as ready to launch as conceivable, nothing stop-ping him now except for high anxiety, another term for stage fright.

    Stan knew all about that, having suffered it for years, and then finally, having been taught by way of acting, a near-cure for it. The cure was simple, so simple, it had never occurred to Stan. It was simply about acceptance of the fear, rather than the denial of it. If he accepted the fear into him, did not try to reject it or ignore it, he could then turn that fear into energy.

He learned that stage fright could be turned into something his character was feeling, such as being nervous or anxious, hyper or happy, or angry, and to "use it". Denying fear only made an actor more fearful, more self-conscious, more stressed, and pushed out of character, out of the moment, out of the here and now. Stan vowed to himself he would apply that same thinking to his life. Breathe in the fear, make it your friend, use it toward something positive rather than trying to pretend it didn't exist. It was a big step for Stan. He had turned over a new leaf.

This was no play, but there was a possibly vast audience out there, waiting, tapping its feet, fluttering their programs, waiting for the house lights to go down, the stage lights to go up. All Stan had to do is flick a switch. Of course, the initial audience would probably consist of just a handful of people, such as the ones he had contacted online, on blogs and websites, but that was okay, all he had to do was send out the word, wait a day, or only a part of one, and then open up with episode #1. He could be up and sailing by this time tomorrow night if he pushed it. The night after if he wanted to give himself some wiggle room.

He took a final survey of the room. Everything was in place. He hit the lights, and went up the stairs to the alley, and drove home to the trailer. On the way there, he thought about where they were going to stash the trailer, and he figured he would try the alley just behind the store front, and if that didn't pan out, approach Carl and see if they could park it in the back of the car lot, behind his small office, which was nothing more than a trailer that Carl had acquired years ago from a construction site.

He arrived at Mandy's place, the lights were all turned off, and he pulled in next to the Beetle. Mandy's new car was gone. Maybe she had already made her move to Shaker Heights and her reborn life? It was getting chilly, Stan pulled up the collar on his jacket, and walked over to the front of the house and stood, remembering all the times he had there with her, both wonderful and some not so wonderful. But now it was just a place made of wood, plaster, siding, and nails, no longer a living thing that contained their years and lives together.

He knew, because someone long ago had told him so, that you weren't supposed to go through life with regrets, and that feeling guilty was a wasted emotion, but he did have regrets, and he did feel guilty. Maybe he'd venture up to see her one day, but it didn't seem like a very good idea. "Let the past stay in the past" he told himself as he turned and walked to the trailer.

Once inside, he took off his jacket, opened the fridge, poured some orange juice in a glass, peeked into the bedroom and saw Bob in his recliner, asleep. It was all pretty normal, except for one minor detail that forced Stan to throw a second glance at Bob: He was dead.

Stan could tell that Bob was lifeless from the twenty feet that separated them. He put down his juice glass on the kitchen counter very quietly, as if the sound of it might wake Bob from his sleep. He slowly walked into the bedroom-bedroom, close to the recliner, knowing that Bob was not in the throes of a heart attack or choking, as it was obvious, he was at permanent rest, and had been for at least a few minutes. Bob's expression was eerily untroubled, his eyes closed, his hands folded on his lap. His hair was still damp from a shower, and he had slipped on his pajama bottoms and a Stan and Bob Sasquatch t-shirt (an intimidating portrait of an angry Bigfoot with the caption below, "You wanna a piece of me?") The vignette laid out before Stan was so very incongruous. And Bob was so very still. It would have been laugh out loud funny in any other circumstance. Stan glanced at his watch. He had seen Bob at the basement location about an hour ago, so it couldn't have been too long since he passed. He neatened the blanket that Bob had pulled over his legs, and took a long hard look at his larger-than-life friend.

He couldn't help but chuckle fondly, thinking of the Bobsquatch bobble head. Stan thought for a moment about their podcast, and how this would alter things, perhaps threaten things, but he didn't care anymore. All the fight had been taken out of him. But mostly, he thought tender thoughts of Bob, but then, his mind seized on a horrible idea: had Bob committed suicide?

Stan looked around the room for evidence, such as an empty bottle of pills, or liquid poison. Bob's body was intact, so he hadn't put his 44 to his head. It didn't seem like something intentional, but he wanted to be sure. As one last check, Stan scanned the room for a note left behind, somewhere out in the open. There was nothing out in the open, so he started searching drawers. They were all empty of their plaster casts and tools, and two had been refilled with Bob's boxers and socks.

Stan went to the other side of the small room and checked his drawers as well. Pretty much the same results. Everything was so quiet and Stan was so very alone. Should he call someone? Mateo? Then he noticed an envelope up on a high shelf. He walked over to it and stretched to reach it, brought it down, and written on the outside was a date. Three days ago. He opened it, and inside was a small silver utility key and a single sheet of yellow legal paper. Written on the paper was "to Stan the Man" in Bob's scrawl.

Stan, grateful that Bob had never called him that out loud, started to read the sole paragraph: "Hey Bud, I haven't been feeling all that great, always tired, can't get enough air, and figured the beer had something to do with it, so quit. If you find this it means I dropped dead someplace or it means I'm a stupid ass for writing this - ha! If I am gone up to see the crazy guy in the sky then here is a key - top small cabinet in kitchen - good luck - take it all, all the stuff is yours, your pal, Robert. P.S. Look out for Mr. Big". There was so much to unpack in this letter, so many things to read between the lines, that Stan was overcome. He crumpled down on the floor, unable to stand, felt sick, and wept loudly, like a little kid, for a long time.

It seemed an hour had gone by, and Stan was completely drained, his throat soar from yelling and dry heaves. He stumbled to his feet, went to the sink and splashed water on his face, dried it on a dish towel, and looked along the top line of cabinets. There it was, way over in the corner, a small cabinet door with a lock. Stan stood on a box to reach it, unlocked it, and inside was an old Converse shoebox. "That's funny, Bob never wore sneakers", Stan thought to himself. He lifted it down carefully, and placed it on the table. Removing the lid, he discovered Bob's time capsule. There were small toys and other things, all worn and used, but lovingly saved, probably from when he was a kid: Tonka and Matchbox metal cars, a Duncan yo-yo, three comic books, "Batman", "Superman" and "Donald Duck", some random coins, a horseshoe magnet, some aged snapshots of presumably him and his parents at what looked like a lakeside resort, and saving the worst for last, a yellowed newspaper clipping, torn from a page:

"Husband and Wife Killed in Tragic Accident" and below that, "Only Child Left Orphaned".

Only the first three paragraphs of the old article were there, telling the story of his parent's sudden death on the night after Halloween in 1962. The gist of it was that his parents, Bill and Marcie Johnson, had just left a movie house near home, having seen "Whatever Happened to Baby Jane?", and while driving home, swerved to avoid hitting a donkey that had jumped its fence and was standing in the middle of the dark road. Their car went flying off the hill, landed hard on its side, and rolled down an embankment many times, killing them both instantly. It had been a freak accident by any standard, and had thrown the young ten-year old Bob into the world of foster care.

"Holy shit" said Stan out loud. On top of the clipping it said, "Gary Dispatch". "So, he grew up in Indiana, or maybe somebody took him in, here in Tipp?" Stan speculated. Stan, assisted by his fingers, counted back the years. 1962 was sixty-one years ago, so maybe Bob was older than he looked? The article said he was ten years old, so that means he was born in 1952, which makes him seventy right now.

Stan was bursting with curiosity to know more, but knew it was all fairly pointless, and knew it didn't really matter in the end, whether he spent six months or six years in Gary after the parent's death, before arriving in Tipp, assuming he even did move here when he was a kid. It just didn't matter, he told himself, but he knew it did. Their young lives had both been stung by the loss of a parent, two parents in Bob's case. Stan looked around the trailer, and knew that life had just given him a swift rude kick in the butt, but for a change, his thoughts were more about Bob than himself.

Stan knew he had to take action, and called the police, who showed up within a couple of hours, accompanied by the fire department, and then the coroner's wagon from Dayton. They all did their usual inspections, asked Stan all the usual questions, and carried Bob out on a gurney, zippered up in a bag. It was a hell of a thing to see.

Stan felt hollowed out, unable to say more than four words without choking back tears to whomever had a question for him. There was no foul play evident, and Stan had been careful to stash Bob's 44 under the seat of his truck wrapped in a towel before the entourage arrived, just in case it was unregistered or needed to be taken away as "evidence". He stashed the knapsack as well. He was given a number to call for final arrangements, from a weirdly upbeat young woman who was driving the coroner's wagon. He called the number and quickly made cremation and internment arrangements, having no clue what Bob's desires would have been, but guessing he would have been satisfied with his middle of the road choice.

Stan, not knowing if he would be the only one in attendance at Bob's service, set a date six days hence, and went about trying to find Walter and Allen. Even if no one else came, those two and he would make for a good and respectful threesome. Something told him to let old things lay, and he didn't try to inform Dave or Gary. Everyone at Stan's had thought Bob an eccentric, the source of many jokes behind his back, but Dave and Gary seemed to actually dislike Bob, which always bothered Stan, for he had always known that underneath all that grime, and gravelly personality, there was a good person in there.

Stan pulled out some cash from his account and covered all the necessary expenses. He was not planning on a reception of any kind, just a graveside service. Word of mouth only. Short and simple.

The day came, a Thursday, raining in sheets, at exactly eleven in the morning, at the Maple Hill Cemetery, with no less than sixty people in attendance, including Allen and Walter, plus Dave and Gary. With Stan, that made for five of them all wearing long sleeve dress shirts and ties at the same place, at the same time. Stan was the only one not wearing a rain jacket, but even so, it was historic. Perhaps it would be the only time in all of recorded history, such a thing would ever happen. Stan placed the small box, containing a plastic bag with Bob's ashes, onto a small table next to his gravesite, that was protected by a pop-up. Everyone stood in the rain, umbrellas in hand. Bob was not to be put near anyone he knew, for he had no family burial sites of record.

Stan had tried to contact the city hall in Gary, to discover where the Johnson's, Bob's birth parents, were buried, but that led nowhere. The death and burial records from that era had been tossed, as they had been completely destroyed by black mold due to the flooding of the basement at the old city hall. Bob's last name was a given name, after having been adopted by the Kaminsky's and to make matters even murkier, the Kaminsky's had no records in Gary, or in Tipp, so it was anybody's guess where they had lived with Bob after adopting him, or now currently lived, assuming they were still around, or as he supposed, where they might be buried.

Everyone that Bob knew, as far as anyone could tell, was either still alive, but whereabouts unknown, or gone, and whereabouts unknown.

So, with that, he was to be placed in his own small location, next to a mature Chestnut tree.

Stan, declining an umbrella, and bracing from the wind and rain, was shocked by the large turnout. He knew most of the people, and as they gathered around to listen to Stan's brief homily, they behaved as if he was invisible, excepting the foursome of Allen, Walter, Dave and Gary. It was not about him, Stan reminded himself, but about dear Bob, gone too soon, and apparently, a friend to many more than Stan would have ever imagined. Maybe it was all those wood carvings? Stan noticed Mateo standing about fifty feet away, partially hidden by a tree, looking on, but not wanting to be part of the ceremony. He seemed to be overwrought.

Stan chose a passage made popular by how inclusive and warm it was. The last thing he or Bob would have wanted was fire and brimstone or something that sounded like a recruitment. The rain had by now soaked clear through Stan's suit jacket to his skin, and he shivered. He unfolded a piece of paper and read aloud: "My father's house has many rooms, if that were not so, would I have told you that I am going there to prepare a place for you? And if I go and prepare a place for you, I will come back and take you to be with me, that you also may be where I am" (John 14-1-6). Stan looked up from his paper, scanned the crowed, all shivering from the cold, and went on, this time with a Chinook prayer from the Pacific Northwest, where Bob had felt so at home: "May all I say and all I think, be in harmony with thee, God within me, God beyond me, maker of the trees". And that was that.

To the one, all but the foursome, treated Stan the same way as before, as if he was invisible, no one making eye contact, and that the sound of his voice was apparently disembodied, perhaps coming from a speaker mounted up in the tree? "Even now, even today, this is the treatment I get?" he griped silently to himself.

Stan, drenched to the skin, folded up his now soggy sheet of paper, cradled the box of ashes, got on his knees and lowered it into the small grave. He shoveled the dirt turned to mud into the small hole with the help of Walter and Allen, while some watched and others walked away quietly. Once that was done, Gary, followed by Allen and Walter, and then Dave, came up to Stan, shook his hand, said a brief condolence, and made for shelter. The bitter cold rain saw to it that this would not be the time or place for reviewing the past, making amends, or plans to get together soon. Maybe it had served as a convenient excuse as to why none of that occurred?

After that was done, Stan walked to his truck, sat in it for a while, watching the last of the people walking to their cars through the windshield flowing with water, fired up the engine and headed to the trailer. He arrived, went inside, soaking wet, peeled his suit jacket off, held it outside the door to shake it off which was futile, closed the door, put some water on to boil, sat at the half round booth, his elbows on the table, his hands covering his face, the rain pelting the metal roof, and said "Now what in the hell am I supposed to do?"

Stan felt very uncomfortable with the idea of bunking down in the trailer's bedroom, so he went to the closest motel. He got a simple room with a queen size bed that felt like a sheet of plywood under his back. He couldn't sleep but when the rain finally stopped around two in the morning, he was able to drift off with Ancient Aliens on the flatscreen, that featured interviews with people who claimed they had been abducted by aliens. No wonder he had nightmares.

Seven o'clock came soon, and he awoke, groggy and disoriented, had just a few seconds of blissful memory loss, and then all the recent events came flooding in, like shards of glass. He hadn't bothered undressing the night before, and left the room, craving breakfast.

The diner had become not the most welcoming place, so he opted for getting a McDonald's "Big Breakfast" at the drive-thru window, but hung a U-turn when he spotted a lunch truck by a construction site. He stopped, got in line with the hard hats, ordered a breakfast burrito with extra hot sauce. He went to his truck and wolfed it down. It was sloppy and disorganized, onions and potatoes and bits of egg spilling out onto his pants. In all his years in Tipp, he had never once, done this. He had always gone to the diner, or fast-food places. He had always been conventional. The servings were always so neat. The food so mild, verging on tasteless. It was just a food truck, just a burrito, but he thought, maybe this *means* something. He finished up, thinking about what he was going to do next? Could he simply continue on with the Stan and Bob show, without the "Bob", go solo, would that be acceptable to him or to Bob, wherever he might be now, perhaps observing Stan's next steps?

At first, all the radio equipment and how to operate it, had looked very daunting to Stan, impossible to learn, but once Bob had coached him, taught him how to troubleshoot, and had labeled everything, it seemed fairly easy and intuitive. Eating the last of his burrito, he knew what it is he had to do. He had to leave. But he had no idea as to where to go. Stan didn't let that detail get in his way, as he drove to the basement, and commenced to pack up everything.

To prepare for his departure to a location unknown, he had much to do. It took the remainder of that day and all the next full day to unplug all the equipment, pull the displays off their shelves, gather the "Stan and Bob" merchandise and shipping materials, and pack the more fragile items into boxes, cushioned with crumpled up pages from the illustrious local newspaper. He then carried the items up the steps to the awaiting RV, and packed everything into the back room. The furniture pieces that he could tackle on his own, he took, the others, he left behind. He ventured to the roof and carefully unbolted the antenna and let it down gently by rope to the alley below, strapping it to the roof of the RV. He would take breaks, taking a look at the maps of the Northwest, Bob had taped to the wall. Bob had identified certain "hot spots" with a red marker. Those included Index, but also included many other locations in Washington, such as Snoqualmie Pass, the Olympic Peninsula, Mount Hood and Rainier, and then Bend and the Crater Lake area in Oregon, and many other spots, such as along the northern California coast, from Carmel northward, and in the Coastal Redwood forests, and inland locations such as Mount Shasta, Willow Creek, Hoops, Bluff Creek and Happy Camp, and so many more he had circled in the three-state chain. On another map, Bob had made numerous circles on Vancouver Island, and up the Canadian coast into Alaska. Thanks to Bob's tutorials, Stan knew there were other known locations throughout the country, some not far away from where he stood, but Stan felt the Northwest beckoning him, and he knew that he needed to land somewhere there. Perhaps it was Bob influencing him telepathically from the Great Unknown, he half-joked to himself, but Stan's internal compass was pointing that way, regardless of the reason, and he knew to not question it.

Stan spent the end of the day looking more closely at the various marked locations, while enjoying Bob's remaining PBR's as a tribute. Some of the locations were marked with stars, or check marks, drawn next to them. He could have chosen any one of these to establish a base camp, but with each inspection, he would eliminate one or two, winnowing the list from thirty to twenty to ten to the final three, but perhaps it was all an act? Maybe he had to go through this exercise to satisfy some need to reassure himself he was being thorough and reasonable, but inside, he knew from the beginning where he had to go. Something about Index attracted him, which made no sense, as there was one hairy and enormous reason it shouldn't have. He reasoned, that maybe it was because he was familiar with it, wouldn't have to get acquainted with another new town? Or maybe it had something to do with facing his fear, and overcoming it? The moment he thought that, he knew that was the core reason. Everything else was secondary.

He had been through so much shit in his life, much of it self-inflicted, some of it not, that he had gotten to a point of thinking that nothing really mattered anymore, and that putting himself in harm's way, whether it be from a squatch or a bear, was of no concern. What could be the worst thing that could happen? He could get killed, that's all. So what? He had spent so much of his life being careful, thinking things through to the last detail, and invariably making a complete mess of things, that being careless, not thinking this through, felt liberating. For him, it wasn't illogical or reckless, it was invigorating. He felt it was his destiny.

Two days later, he was eastward bound on highway 80, passing Gothenburg, Nebraska, headed to Index, his stereo cranked up, blasting music from

Israel Kamakawiwo'ole. Stan had never listened to Hawaiian-style music before, had never even considered it, but now, strangely, listening to the silken and affecting voice of the over-sized and deceased singer, gave Stan a connection to something new and emotional. There was no explaining it. Maybe Stan was now connected to the Universe, or maybe he had finally managed to lose the last of his remaining marbles. He sang to the music loudly as he sped down the highway to an uncertain and perhaps risky future.

ACT IV

Ground Zero

Chapter 15

He had barely slept, fueled by coffee, Rockstars and adrenalin. He had given Bob's souped-up Beetle to an incredulous Mateo, thanked him for all his help, and encouraged him to get away from Trowner. He also arranged with him for a similar close-out plan for the arts and crafts store, leaving an extra month's rent for Alabaster.

The one day and ten hours of predicted non-stop driving time to Index he accomplished in one day and eleven hours, thanks to little sleep and excessive speeding, arriving at ten on a Sunday night. He pulled over on the side of the road just outside of town, and slept until late morning on Monday. He had emptied the trailer's fridge of all food, so he walked into town and made for the bar and grill. He was anxious to see Hailey, even if it didn't turn out romantically. She was his one friend in town.

Early fall was starting to come on, and the day was cool but clear. Hailey greeted him at the counter, poured him some coffee, and had remembered his name. She noticed the faint limp, and the scar on his face, but diplomatically, did not mention any of it. He ate some toast and jam with his coffee, told Hailey he'd see her later, once he set up camp, rushed back to the truck and trailer by way of the general store to pick up some basics, and aimed for the old campsite. He wasn't altogether sure whose property it was on, if it was on National Forest land or private, but it hadn't ever been an issue for Bob, so he figured, it was okay to return.

He came upon it, and negotiated the trailer into the dead center of the site, the closest bush or tree no closer than fifteen feet away. He got out of the cab, and looked long and hard at the sandy creek bank where he had been nearly killed. For the first time since he left Tipp, the sense memory of the attack came back to him, and it was frightening, making him wonder why in the hell he was standing here, inviting trouble, but he was also drawn to it, fascinated, almost in disbelief that he was standing there. He stayed motionless, listening to the familiar gurgle of the water over the rocks, heard the birds singing, and with the 44 sitting comfortably on the dash, just a step or two away from his reach.

Bob had taken him out for a little target practice once, up far in the foothills away from everybody, so he could get a feel for this canon. If you weren't ready for it, it would tear your arm off, and make you deaf for ten minutes, but now he knew his way around the weapon, and felt confident that if he needed to squeeze the trigger, he could do it and come close enough to disabling his target, to be effective.

He was not there to wage war or cause harm, but had come in peace, to live and let live. Stan knew, even from his limited education, that the very idea of Sasquatch, should be treated with the utmost regard, even if, after all is said and done, the damn thing doesn't even exist. So, the idea was, give it the same respect as a bear, except in theory, these imposing creatures can think and reason much like people.

Bob once said to him, "Some people want to think of them as a cuddly, 'Harry and the Henderson's' creature. They're not, oh my fuck, they are not".

As for Stan's experience? He had lots of time to think on this while driving westward and he concluded, that he was not in denial, and had not been a victim of his own imagination and altered memory. He knew that what had mauled him was a very pissed off and large hominid. Stan had reached his verdict somewhere between Kellogg and Coeur d'Alene. And he was going to return to the same campsite. He knew he had to stake his claim.

For as many self-appointed experts as there were, there were as many theories as to the origin and behavior of these creatures. Most believers of Sasquatch thought this species to be potentially quite dangerous, and that people should not put themselves in harm's way, intentionally or unwittingly. It was a big gamble to get too close.

However, some believers felt that as with any society of animals, there are those who are more aggressive to outsiders than others, but that the overall personality of this species was not violent, and did not mean harm to people, especially if not provoked in some way.

There were so many credible stories, and some were ancient, coming from the First Nation people. There were stories about Native children or women being taken away by "hairy beasts" and so much of that had to do with proximity and encroachment, and perhaps superstition?

There were stories about people hiking alone, deep into unmapped forests, and never being seen again.

There were other stories about dog owners having been killed by their dogs while on a hike deep in the woods, and all of these stories, even the most credible of them, were incomplete, and left many questions.

There were accounts of people leaving treats near their cabins, for years, with nothing bad happening. Some thought that treats left out would encourage a sense of bonding and trust, that it would demonstrate peaceful intent, be a nice and neighborly thing to do. There were even stories about people having treats left out for them, in the form of pine cones, decorative rocks, leaves, and berries.

Some people come upon them miles deep into the woods, other people have encounters just steps from a well-traveled road, or busy campground.

For every position on this topic, there is a counter-position. But all these tales deliver someone to the same place: nobody really knows.

Some felt the only way to conclusively prove the existence was to bag one and have it necropsied (autopsied). Stan had agreed with Bob, that killing one would not lead to anything but more killings, as people would want to bag and tag other varieties of the species in other regions, or simply be the second, or tenth, or fiftieth to have killed one. There was too much money and notoriety to be made. Regardless of how many were killed, the skeptics would never be satisfied. Nowadays, truthful fact was an interpretive medium.

In short, nobody really knew anything at all, and a corpse on a table would not move the needle one way or the other in the short term, for it was all just smoke and mirrors, it seemed.

But he had to be honest and objective with himself, and not get too caught up with a favorite theory, pushing aside the rest, for it could turn out very badly if he didn't keep an open mind. It was better to look at the big picture, and allow all possibilities to co-exist.

He also realized, that it was very likely Bob did in some way provoke them by messing around with one of their nests. Perhaps the alpha male in the group took exception?

Also, it is possible that when this provocation caused the creature to come down to the foothills a day or two later, to where the campsite was, and saw Stan fishing, taking fish that were his as far as he was concerned, sticking them in the creel, he snapped.

Parked there at the campsite, he was admittedly scared, but knew he would not go down without a fight if it came to that. Taking a look around every few seconds, the 44 always nearby, he performed the long and involved process of setting up camp, getting his equipment set up in the trailer, following all of Bob's color-coding, mounting the antenna to the side of the trailer, tying his hammock between the two trees, and fixing up the campfire ring for later use, starting that night. He had bought some solar-powered security lights that would be triggered should someone, or something, come within twenty feet of the front, rear, or sides of the trailer. He didn't have time that day to go fishing anyplace, so he had bought some fresh trout at the general store after his toast and coffee. He took the trout, and laid it on a rock on the far side of the creek. He then took three Snickers bars and three apples, and lined them up on a log that was on a sandbank in the middle of the creek. He would do this repeatedly. He figured, he needed to make some peace offerings, should his visitor or his family, still be around.

Would this be a horrible strategic error? He didn't really know, one way or the other, but figured he had come this far, and at last, had to face his fear. That all sounded rather melodramatic to the usually placid and indecisive Stan, but he knew in his gut he was right.

He spent his first night in the trailer after enjoying a campfire. It was un-eventful, and there were no nightmares. He went back to the bar and grill the next day near lunchtime, got a cup of coffee from Hailey, even though he had already had two cups at the trailer. He lingered through two refills, checking and re-checking that she did not have any hardware on her fourth finger, left hand. She rushed here and there, taking and delivering orders. Every now and then she'd come to his end of the counter, and do something busily, and he hoped she was playacting, waiting for him to say something. Finally, he got up the nerve.

"I'm here doing a little research on, you know, the big guy, and I'm starting up a podcast too, I mean, that's why I'm here".

Hailey, amused at his somewhat awkward opening, said, "You don't say?" She wiped the Bunnomatic coffeemaker on the counter behind her, to a brilliant shine, as he spoke to her back.

"Don't know which side of the topic you're on, but just in case you're curious as to why I'm, you know...here".

Hailey looked over her shoulder at him while putting the finishing touches on the machine and replied, "I definitely lean toward believing, but I don't know, maybe it's that I just want to believe, but don't really? Seems pretty far-fetched".

Stan nodded, knowing that most people anywhere feel this way, who could blame them?

"Be nice if somebody could take a photo that was in focus" she said, and then jetted down to the far other end of the counter.

He lingered, not knowing if that was going to be the extent of their conversation.

She came back, stood in front of him, and said, "Lots of folks around here are dug in deep on the topic, almost like a religion, and others think those people are batshit crazy" and then leaning down to him close, "but you don't come across as batshit crazy, are you?"

Stan, leaning in to her, said, "Some people have said as much, but no, I don't think so".

Hailey, noticing a new customer, moved down to the other end of the counter to take an order. She clipped the order on the order wheel, yelled out, "Burn one with wax, side fries", and returned to Stan's end of the counter, this time making herself busy refilling Heinz Ketchup bottles.

Stan could not take his eyes off of her. She appeared to be in her late thirties, a brunette with a hint of cinnamon, very pretty but not too pretty, penetrating and intelligent hazel eyes, a quick smile, and a great bod as far as Stan could determine, trying out his x-ray vision through her frumpy waitress outfit. He thought to himself, "How can someone this nice, be single?"

But he decided to not let that question slow him down, for whatever the reason was, he was sitting there now, in front of her, and this might be his only shot. He decided to go all in, with no plan.

While she was carefully topping off the last bottle with a funnel, he said, "I have a bunch of plaster casts at my place, you know, tracks, foot prints, in case you'd ever like to see them?"

She wheeled around and said cheerfully, "Are you kidding? Of course, I would. Then you can come over to my place, see mine!" He wasn't sure if she was kidding or not, but either way, he didn't care.

Things moved quickly. The next day she rolled up in her old Dodge truck, and they wasted no time examining his plaster casts, and then divulging the retrospectives of their lives, their loves and joys, a cook's tour of his radio room, and then on another day, a tour of her small guest house next to the fire station.

What followed were corny jokes, long daytime hikes on well-traveled trails, moonlit nights around the fire, and they held one another tight. Their love for one another, or something very much like it, grew quickly. As for Stan, he fell head over heels, and it seemed, she had been waiting for him, or if not him, someone extraordinarily similar to him. Stan thought, coincidence? He hadn't a clue, but what he did know is that he may have been a screw-up all these years, but he had finally wised up, and was not afraid of being hurt. He was going to dive in.

One night, the fire crackling under the stars at the campsite, their bellies full of spaghetti with veggie meatballs, Stan's 44 at the ready, Hailey asked, "If this creature showed himself to you, attacked you, right over there, why have you decided to camp at this very same spot again? There are other spots, closer to town, you know".

Stan considered the question for a moment, and then "They are intelligent, have families to protect, and while I'm not one hundred percent, I'm pretty sure that he will not do an encore unless I give him a reason to do one. I'm going to do everything I can think of, to show them I'm not here to cause trouble, or take anything away from them".

As he talked, it was obvious to Hailey that Stan was fully convinced his attacker had not been a bear, but she was not as sure. "The mind can do funny things after a trauma", she thought to herself. "The mind can reimagine an event, make all kinds of stuff up".

He had gotten an education from Bob and had taken on a born-again zealotry on the topic. Barely taking a breath, he went on to say, "These creatures can reason, they plan, react, and have smarts. They make choices, so perhaps the alpha male made his choice, which was unfortunate for me, seeing me stick the fish in my creel, already being pissed off about his nest getting discovered? These creatures can plan, it's not all improvised…Sorry, I guess I went on too long"

"Yeah, you did" was her reply, laughing. She added, "So, your treats, they take them?"

Stan, looking over into the darkness toward the stream, rubbed his chin, "I dunno. Somebody takes them, but that could be anybody. Raccoons, deer, birds, maybe even a bear, who knows? I've put them out a few times, same treats, same log, and they're gone by morning."

She nodded, saying "So you think you're safe here, that we're safe here, right?"

Stan replied, "Yeah, safe, and besides which, I don't fish this creek anymore, not here in this location" with an unsure laugh.

She stared at him, thinking, "Geez, maybe he is batshit".

Five nights later it was showtime in the trailer's radio-bedroom. Episode #1 was about to go on the air. The table was laden with equipment that was switched on and triple-checked. Stan had his headphones on, and everyone he had contacts with had been notified. Hailey was seated next to him. Stan, with a nervous glance toward her, flicked the "On Air" switch, gave another glance to Hailey, leaned into the Shure, and launched into his show.

The first few minutes centered around his introduction, complete with a short piece of Bob's recording of the air raid siren howls they had heard, and then all about his encounters, and the attack at the creek. He left out no details, and filled in the parts he didn't know about, with things Bob and Doc Alex had told him. He tried very hard to not embellish, wanting the story to be recounted in a straightforward way, so it could speak for itself. He knew it was going to be very good showbiz, for whatever small group of listeners were out there.

Later that night, and on successive shows, when people called in, his story was accepted at face value. A few challenged him, that was to be expected, but all his answers were so credible and plainly expressed, that people by and large accepted his story in full. There was a credibility to his words, to his manner, that had never seemed to exist with his acting, which had always been about just that, acting, not being. But now, it appeared he had found a comfort zone, and an audience.

For the first show, it turned out that he had many more people listening in than he had guessed there would be, and his switch-board was lit up. His format was to do the intro, tell a brief version of his story, take a few calls no more than five minutes each, do an interview with a pre-scheduled guest who he had emailed back and forth with beforehand, and then take a few more calls before doing the wrap-up. The first show would last almost three hours he figured, and subsequent shows closer to just two, but he was still working out the kinks, basing most of the structure on what Bob had done with his.

With Hailey seated next to him, he started his first "interview call", and spoke in a calm, reassuring voice.

"Hi Jake. Welcome to Squatch Ground Zero."

The voice of "Jake" came thru on the speaker mounted on the wall of the radio-bedroom, and into Stan and Hailey's headphones.

Jake sounded young, perhaps around college age, nervous, and un-rehearsed. "Sure Stan, thanks for taking my call…"

"Hey, my pleasure…so if you could, tell us something about your encounter…"

"Okay, this was about two months ago, and I was you know, camping with my girlfriend, just to the southeast of Crater Lake, next to Sand Creek, in Oregon, you know?"

"Yeah, I'm familiar with the area…"

"You could see Mount Scott, over just a little ways, and we had gotten into the area the night before, pretty late, and set up our camp quick, it was a small unimproved camping area, BLM land I think, not sure, and we sacked out. I have to tell you about that too, what happened. Anyway, the next morning, we went for a walk and nobody else was around, and it was a nice morning, not wet, nice and sunny, and after about two miles along the trail, we came around a bend, and I looked up, and I saw what I thought for sure was a bear, standing on his hind feet, and we stopped, but then, after we came to a stop, I looked at it for a few seconds, saw its face, its arms, we knew this was not a bear".

"How close was it to you do you think?"

"Maybe fifty feet off the trail, and I pointed it out to my girlfriend when I first spotted it, and we both saw it, standing sorta half way behind a tree, looking at us, scared the shit out of us, we just froze, this was the just the first morning we were there, and you know, there's a lot of pumice in the dirt, on the ground, for miles around the lake, you know?"

"Yes, I know about that", said Stan.

Jake continued, "Yeah, so I tried to take a photo but that was a joke, it was gone in a second, just moved back into the trees so fast, and then we waited there for a long time, we were afraid to move, to go further on the trail or to even go back, my girlfriend pulled out her bear spray, I don't have a gun, and we didn't know what to do. Finally, we decided to go back and we noticed there were some prints in the dirt, big prints, right across the trail where we had just been, I don't think they were there when we walked on it the first time, and I took some shots of those, and they came out real good, the dirt is so fine, you know?"

Stan jumped in, "Please send some photos, I'd love to see them, but Jake, first, let's go back, before that, you wrote that you two had heard some howling the night before, that shook you guys up...?"

"Oh God yeah." said Jake, "Woke us the hell up. We didn't know what it was, like nothing I ever heard before, and I've been camping all my life, this was very weird, and loud".

"Okay, wow, that does sound very frightening" said Stan. "Did it sound anything like this?" Stan replayed part of the recording that Bob had made of the howls. The sound was haunting, no matter how many times Stan played it.

Jake exclaimed, "Yeah, a lot like that, very loud"

"So, even though you heard those sounds, you decided to take a walk the next morning?"

"Well, yeah, we didn't connect the sounds to anything that we might see on a short hike, in the daytime, we weren't thinking that way"

"Okay, so Jake, tell me, have you ever gone back to that spot again?"

"No way man, I'm never going there again, not ever. In fact, now, I only hang out in the woods, go hiking, in the day time and I always bring friends, I just won't go out there with just two of us anymore"

Stan reacted, "Yeah, that makes sense, but I'm sorry it has ruined your camping days, and hiking."

Jake said, "No, we still go camping, but we like going to a regular campground now, where there are some other people around, we still have a good time, and we take hikes in the daytime, at least three or four of us at a time, but it pisses me off too".

Stan replied, "Yeah, I get that. So, Jake, going back to the beginning, when you saw the creature, did you get a pretty good look at it?"

"Not all that good, saw a little, but not much, it was hiding half way behind a tree and the sunlight was behind it, real bright, hard to look at directly".

"Once you've seen one, it changes the way you look at the world, doesn't it?"

"Oh yeah, it's opened up a whole new thing".

"Would you like to see one again?"

"I dunno", and with a laugh, "maybe if it was on the edge of a lake and I was on a motor boat about two hundred feet away, but not up close like that again, once was plenty".

"Okay, gotcha, I don't blame you one bit. Being out in the woods unprotected like that, changes the way you think, right? But I was wondering if you could make out any details at all, on its face? In other words, did he look more like an animal, like a gorilla, or some type of an ape, or more human? Just tell us how it all began, you know, take your time, don't leave out any details, from the beginning, walk us into it…".

The red lights on the call-in board were all lit up and on hold, blinking. It was going to be a good night.

The animated conversation between Stan and Jake continued for many more minutes, while outside, the night sky was cloudless, the air crisp, the moon waning, and the stars happily showing themselves. It was quiet and still, excepting the creek, that flowed around the small round rocks, and spilled into the deep pools.

In the middle of the creek on a sand bar, there was a mother, a father, and two children, concealed almost completely by the darkness.

If at that moment, you had been standing in the doorway of the trailer, and looking in that direction, you could have made out their faint, dark silhouettes. The mother and younger child were seated next to one another, on a fallen tree that was laying across the sand bank. Behind them you would have seen the father and the older child standing. They were like statues, all looking at the trailer in total silence, as if intently watching a movie. The family had been there a good long while. They stared with curiosity at the windows, glowing with light, and heard the sounds of voices coming from inside.

And then the mother, almost imperceptibly, moved her hand over to above the younger child's waiting and open palm, and placed a Snickers bar into it. The child, excited by the tasty treat, put the whole bar into his mouth all at once, and ate it, wrapper and all.

The End

About the Author

Born and raised in SoCal, a lifelong actor and lover of the outdoors. Married with three smart and creative kids. Has written on and off over the years. Comes from a long line of noteworthy sculptors.

Credits and References

Front Cover: courtesy of Sean Hurts
Back Cover: photo by Brian Pietro
Author's Portrait: photo by Kristen Pietro

Excerpt from "Islands in the Stream" by Ernest Hemingway

"Sasquatch, Legend Meets Science", a Forge Book, by Jeff Meldrum, professor of anatomy and anthropology, Idaho State University.

"Sasquatch Chronicles" podcast, hosted by Wes Germer

Trout fishing specialist: George Appel

Storyline assistance: Emilio Estevez

Technical and editorial assistance: Stephen Scarpitta

Made in the USA
Middletown, DE
19 May 2023

30786215R00225